Titles by Olivia Blacke

THE RECORD SHOP MYSTERIES

Rhythm and Clues
A Fatal Groove
Vinyl Resting Place

Praise for *A New Lease on Death*

"This novel is by turns funny and tingly scary, with a bit of gumshoe work thrown in." —*New York Journal of Books*

"A mystery that keeps much yet to be explored and leaves you wanting more from these characters and their journeys."
—*Manhattan Book Review*

"A lot of twists and turns . . . I highly recommend *A New Lease on Death* for readers who enjoy paranormal novels, as well as a detective duo with vastly conflicting but complementing personalities."
—*Aunt Agatha's*

"A fun, supernatural mystery."
—*Red Carpet Crash*

"Droll, a touch maudlin, and featuring two outstanding characters."
—*firstCLUE*

"Witty, fun, and propulsive, *A New Lease on Death* was an absolute delight." —Amanda Jayatissa

"Absolutely addictive." —Lyn Liao Butler

"Smart. Quirky. Suspenseful. Everything you could want in a whodunit." —Darcie Wilde

"My new favorite sleuthing odd couple . . . This delightfully dark mystery is well-crafted with humor and heart."
—Celeste Connally

Olivia Blacke's Mysteries Are:

"Colorful [and] winning." —*The New York Times Book Review*

"Charming." —Elle Cosimano

"Fantastic." —Mia P. Manansala

"Terrific." —*Mystery Scene*

"Full of twists and turns." —*First for Women*

"Completely absorbing." —*firstCLUE*

A NEW LEASE on DEATH

A Ruby and Cordelia Mystery

Olivia Blacke

MINOTAUR
BOOKS
NEW YORK

This is a work of fiction. All of the characters, organizations, and events portrayed in this novel are either products of the author's imagination or are used fictitiously.

Published in the United States by Minotaur Books, an imprint of St. Martin's Publishing Group

EU Representative: Macmillan Publishers Ireland Ltd, 1st Floor, The Liffey Trust Centre, 117–126 Sheriff Street Upper, Dublin 1, DO1 YC43

A NEW LEASE ON DEATH. Copyright © 2024 by Olivia Blacke. All rights reserved. Printed in the United States of America. For information, address St. Martin's Publishing Group, 120 Broadway, New York, NY 10271.

www.minotaurbooks.com

Designed by Jen Edwards

The Library of Congress has cataloged the hardcover edition as follows:

Names: Blacke, Olivia, author.
Title: A new lease on death / Olivia Blacke.
Description: First edition. | New York : Minotaur Books, 2024.
Identifiers: LCCN 2024016438 | ISBN 9781250336675
   (hardcover) | ISBN 9781250336682 (ebook)
Subjects: LCGFT: Paranormal fiction. | Novels.
Classification: LCC PS3602.L325293 N49 2024 | DDC
   813/.6—dc23/eng/20240415
LC record available at https://lccn.loc.gov/2024016438

ISBN 978-1-250-33669-9 (trade paperback)

The publisher of this book does not authorize the use or reproduction of any part of this book in any manner for the purpose of training artificial intelligence technologies or systems. The publisher of this book expressly reserves this book from the Text and Data Mining exception in accordance with Article 4(3) of the European Union Digital Single Market Directive 2019/790.

Our books may be purchased in bulk for specialty retail/wholesale, literacy, corporate/premium, educational, and subscription box use. Please contact MacmillanSpecialMarkets@macmillan.com.

First Minotaur Books Trade Paperback Edition: 2025

10 9 8 7 6 5 4 3 2 1

For Mama C,
who would have pretended
to be embarrassed to have a
book dedicated to her

CHAPTER ONE

CORDELIA

I didn't know how long I sat cross-legged in the snow, waiting for the dead man crumpled on the ground in front of my building to wake up. Might have been five minutes. Might have been five hours.

As I watched, pellets of snow accumulated on his flannel-pajama-clad legs and fuzzy-sock-covered feet. The dead man wasn't dressed for the weather, that much was certain. Boston in the winter was harsh and unforgiving, but he hadn't died from exposure. If I had to guess the cause of death, I'd wager it had something to do with the bullet hole in the center of his forehead.

I guess someone could have shot him then walked off with his coat and boots. This wasn't exactly a crime-free block, as evidenced by the body collapsed on the cold, hard sidewalk in front of me. His sleeves were pushed up to his elbows and he had a bruise on one of his bare wrists. Judging by the phone still clutched in his other hand—the latest model—robbery hadn't been the killer's primary motive. That phone cost a month's rent in this neighborhood.

It was either very, very late, or very, very early, depending on how I looked at it. Despite the weather—which was nasty, even by Boston standards—eventually someone would pass by, maybe walking their dog before work or hurrying for the bus. They would notice the snow-dusted pile of clothes that with each passing flurry looked less and less like a human body. Someone would eventually call the cops, but the dead man was already beyond help.

A few cars had passed while I sat vigil. Drivers struggled through as-yet-unplowed streets in near-whiteout conditions without so much as a glance in our direction. Not that I blamed them. In weather like this, they'd need all their attention on the road. The street was steep, and if they slowed too much, they'd never be able to crest the slippery hill. Besides, in this neighborhood? At night? If I didn't live here, I wouldn't stop, either.

Distracted by patterns forming in the swirling snow as it drifted lazily to the ground, I almost missed it when the dead man sat up.

"Easy, buddy," I told him, but I doubted that would be much help. The next few minutes were going to be rough for him.

"I know you," he said, blinking at me in confusion. It wasn't yet daybreak. The streetlights—the few that were working—reflected off the low, heavy clouds and the thick layer of snow coating every surface, bathing the street in a bluish light. Despite my advice to take it slow, the dead man pushed himself to his feet. He swayed for a moment, struggling to regain his equilibrium, which couldn't have been easy, not in his condition.

I got to my feet as well, keeping a fair distance between us as he tried to process what was going on. Now that he was upright, the snow fell away from him as though it had never been there. He wore an oversized Boston Bruins hoodie. Out of habit, he flipped the hood over his head, yanked his sleeves down, and shoved his hands into the front pocket, slouching as he did so. The sweatshirt wasn't nearly warm enough to protect him from the bitter cold, but whether or not he realized it yet, he was beyond caring about such things.

"You're not the pizza delivery guy," he said. He gave me a long assessing look, the kind that made me feel like I was on display at a market. "Wait a second. I *do* know you. You're that girl," he said.

"Cordelia," I told him. I made no move to shake his hand. "Cordelia Graves, 4G."

"Jake Macintyre," he replied automatically. "4H. You live across the hall."

"Yeah," I agreed. He'd been my neighbor for going on two years. He was a nice guy. When the building manager told me he couldn't fix my leaky sink until Monday, I asked Jake if he could loan me a wrench or something. Instead, he came over and fixed the leak himself, and then insisted on helping me rehang a sagging curtain rod.

Jake was a slightly below average height white man with a full head of dark hair and the beginnings of a beer paunch concealed under his hoodie. He ordered a lot of pizza, and sometimes let the empty boxes pile up in the hall over the weekend. Occasionally, I would hear him shouting at his TV when hockey was on, but like many Bostonians, he was more likely to watch the game down at the corner bar than alone in his apartment. He had loud friends over all the time, but he didn't stomp around when he came home late after a pitcher (or three) of beer, so while he wasn't the best neighbor I'd ever had, he was far from the worst.

"Wait a sec. I remember now. You're dead," he stated, sounding bewildered.

I nodded. "Yup."

Best I could figure, I'd died a few months ago, sometime around Christmas. Those first couple of days after my death were a confusing jumble, but I had a distinct memory of Jake and a couple of other neighbors standing in the hall, watching the paramedics wheel my body out of my apartment. "I am. Dead, that is. And we need to talk."

"Bobby put you up to this, didn't he?" Jake asked. "Or was it Ryan? Maybe Markie? Nah, it wouldn't be Markie. He's not speaking to me right now."

I wouldn't know if this phenomenon was unique to Boston, because I've never really lived anywhere else, but it seemed like half the men I met ended their name with a "y" or an "ie."

"Markie's the cute one, right?" I asked. I held my hand up several inches above the height of my own head. I was no slouch myself, a few inches taller than Jake, but Markie—if he was the guy I was thinking of—had to duck to get through doorways, especially those made in the eighteen hundreds when the population was significantly shorter. Come to think of it, I wasn't so sure Markie was actually cute so much as he was tall. In a city where we spent half the year so bundled up I wouldn't recognize my own mother if I passed her on the street, I suppose looks didn't matter all that much.

Granted, I hadn't seen my mother in decades. I probably wouldn't recognize her unless she walked up to me and introduced herself, but that was neither here nor there.

"You're thinking of Scotty," he corrected me. "Markie's the one with—" He stopped himself mid-sentence. "You *are* her, right? The dead girl?"

"Yup, that's me," I confirmed again, even though he was only partially correct. I was in my forties, hardly what I'd call a girl. The dead part, well, that was spot-on.

"And you're *dead* dead. Not fake-your-death-to-get-out-of-child-support dead?"

"As a doornail," I said. I wondered what kind of person would ever consider faking their death to avoid paying child support. "About that—"

He cut me off. "You're kinda cute for being dead."

I know, I should have been offended. Because feminism and empowerment and all that. Don't get me wrong. I was a feminist. I was one hundred percent one of those kooks who thought women were whole-ass people in their own right and deserved to be treated as such. Wacky, right? I didn't love having my cuteness judged by someone I barely knew, as if somehow their opinion of my appearance mattered. Jake's comment, while not entirely PC, didn't bother me—much. Not when I hadn't had a two-sided conversation with another soul in months and was craving any meaningful human interaction.

"Well?" he asked when I didn't respond. "Care to explain how you're dead but you're not dead?"

"Wish I could," I said. I hardly understood it myself, and I'd had some time to get used to it. He'd helped me when he didn't have to, and now it was my turn to return the favor by helping ease his transition into the afterlife. Jake was in for a shock. It was unavoidable, but maybe I could soften the blow. "Jake? Aren't you cold?"

"Nah," he said. He stomped his feet out of habit. Then, he noticed that he was standing in ankle-deep snow, his feet clad only in fuzzy socks, but he wasn't freezing. His feet should have been blocks of ice, but they weren't even damp. "What the heck?" He stomped his feet again. "That ain't right."

"You're gonna want to brace yourself," I tried to warn him. But now that he was looking down, he finally noticed the corpse at his feet.

The dead body crumpled on the sidewalk was wearing Jake's

flannel pjs. Jake's fuzzy socks. Jake's Bruins hoodie. He was holding Jake's phone. His eyes were wide open and staring up at us. His exposed skin was starting to turn the bluish-gray color of freezer-burnt meat. And there was a bullet hole in the middle of his forehead.

Jake touched his own ghostly forehead, where the bullet hole was, and said, "Shit."

"Yup," I agreed.

I didn't know how to comfort him. I didn't even know if he wanted comfort. From what I knew about Jake, he was a man's man. The kind who thought therapy was for wimps and emergency room stiches were a badge of honor. I'd be willing to bet a shiny new MacBook that he'd never exfoliated, and he wasn't about to start now. If he wanted comfort, he'd reach for a beer.

"Holy shit," he said again, poking his finger up to the second knuckle into the hole in his head.

I felt obligated to help him, one dead person to another. Besides, he was the only ghost I'd met in all my weeks of searching, and that kinda made us kindred spirits . . . with an emphasis on *spirits*. "Here's the deal," I said. "You're dead."

Was I a brilliant conversationalist or what? Although, to be fair, I was out of practice.

"Seriously?" he asked. "That's the best you can do?"

"It's complicated." I shrugged. Yes, I knew I didn't have physical shoulders to shrug anymore, but after a lifetime of shrugging and blinking and clearing my throat, I hadn't quite gotten the hang of doing nothing yet. "Well, maybe not complicated, exactly. More like confusing. Look, there's no manual or anything. I don't know all the rules. I've just been kinda making it up as I go along."

I was blowing it. I hadn't spoken to anyone since I'd died, at least not to anyone who had heard me. I finally had a chance to remedy that, and all I could do was ramble.

"Dead," he repeated, thoughtfully. He started to nudge his dead body with his fuzzy-socked foot, but caught himself at the last minute. "What would happen if I touched him?" He thought about it, then corrected himself. "Me? It? Whatever."

"Don't know," I admitted. "I don't make a habit of going around poking dead bodies. But it's probably not a good idea."

He hesitated, his foot hovering slightly off the ground, just an inch away from his own dead leg. If he took a minute to think about it, he'd probably realize that he was off-balance. He'd wobble, even though gravity didn't work on incorporeal beings. Ghosts—or whatever I was, whatever *we* were—had all sorts of limits I was still discovering, but were outside the laws of normal physics.

I shook my head, as if I could change my train of thought as easily as erasing an Etch A Sketch. I'd never been much into the physical sciences. I'd never given a fig about thermodynamics or entropy or any of that stuff back when I was alive, and if I stopped to try to figure it out now, everything got a little blurry around the edges.

Take this particular moment, for instance. I was standing on the sidewalk in front of a dilapidated apartment building in Boston because I *believed* I was standing on the sidewalk in front of a dilapidated apartment building in Boston. If I stopped believing that, even for a split second, then I would sink into the pavement like it was quicksand. I'd tried a little too hard to wrap my head around the physics of my situation one time from the comfort of my fourth-floor apartment, and ended up sinking through the floor only to end up buried to my neck in the concrete pad of the basement before I could stop myself. "Don't stop believing," I muttered.

"Huh?" Jake asked.

"Never mind," I told him, as if I hadn't just spaced out. I did that on occasion back when I was still alive, but it happened more often lately. My mind would wander off on a tangent, and the next thing I knew, hours had passed, or days. Once I was daydreaming about a tropical retreat and woke up on a beach in Bimini. Which didn't suck, but that would have been counterproductive right now. "Let's get out of here," I said.

"And go where?" he asked.

"I don't know," I admitted. "Inside. Out of this storm." *Away from the dead body*, I added mentally. Yes, I was dead. But that didn't mean that standing over a dead man with a bullet hole in his forehead didn't creep me out, especially when I'd known him before he was a corpse.

An ear-splitting siren bleep cut through the night, announcing the arrival of a blue-and-white Boston police car. In the apartments around us, curtains and roll-up shades twitched as bleary-eyed people peered out of ice-frosted windows to see what all the commotion was about.

"You think he's here for me?" Jake asked as the patrol car slid toward the curb. Its wheels spun helplessly in the drifted snow.

"Nah, they probably got called out for the other dead body," I replied.

It said something that Jake's first instinct was to look around to see if I was joking or not. Seriously though, it wasn't the worst neighborhood in the world. It wasn't even the worst neighborhood in Boston. It was cheap and the garbage trucks came by more or less on the regular. There was a decent bar on one corner that's neither clean nor well lit, but the beer was cold and who really cared if your shoes stuck to the floor? It was a dive bar, not a hospital.

There was a small market catty-corner to the bar. I heard a

rumor that it was a front for something nefarious, and the prices they charged for fresh vegetables were downright criminal. But, they were open 24/7 for those late night SpaghettiOs cravings, so I'd been a loyal customer.

The cop hadn't gotten out of the cruiser yet. He appeared to be talking to someone through his walkie-talkie. Was he calling for backup? Or was he stalling, buying himself one more precious minute in the comfort of his heated car before facing the brutal cold outside?

I knew from experience how traumatic it was to watch strangers poke and prod at your dead body before carting it away. Jake didn't need to witness it happen to him. I tugged on Jake's sleeve. "Come on. Let's go."

Jake stared down at my hand, watching the sleeve of his hoodie move as if by magic. Earlier, he'd been able to put his hood up without even thinking about it, but now, when he touched his own sleeve, his hand passed through it. "Teach me how you did that," he said. "Please?" He tried to cover my hand with his free hand, but it went right through me. Misfiring neurons that didn't exist any longer set my hand on fire, and I jerked away from him.

I could touch objects in the physical world if I really, really wanted to, but it came with a price. A completely inanimate object like a sheet of paper? No problem. But something with a little juice in it, like a remote control, would fry my circuits for hours, not to mention what it did to the remote. And touching a human being? Forget about it. Jake's hoodie sleeve was fair game, but touching his bare skin freaking hurt.

"Make you a deal," I told him, shaking my hand as if it were asleep and I was trying to jump-start circulation. I knew my hand wasn't there anymore. I had no skin, no fingers, no nerves. There's no reason that something that didn't exist should hurt this much, but it did. "Come inside with me, and I'll teach you what little I know."

Without waiting to see if he was following, I headed up the steps toward the front door of the building. Could I have hurled myself Kool-Aid Man–style at the brick wall and gotten the same result? Probably. But in my mind, I still believed that people were supposed to walk through doors, not walls, and so that's what I did.

I slipped through the door with only a slight tingle. If I concentrated, I could feel every grain of sand that was melted into the smooth glass. But after monotonous weeks of having nothing better to do but experiment with passing through solid objects, I finally had someone to talk to who could actually hear me and talk back, and that had my entire attention.

It didn't take my eyes any time to adjust to the dimly lit lobby. Dark, light, it made no difference to me anymore. Just like I no longer felt the cold, I no longer needed light to see. Pretty convenient, if you asked me.

I heard a loud crash behind me. I whirled to see Jake plastered against the door. His features were smushed against the glass, cartoon-style. "Open up," he called. He pressed his hands on the door. His voice should have been muffled, but it was as clear as if we were standing in the same room.

"Come on inside," I urged. "Forget about the door. The door isn't real." I held out my hand.

He pushed his hands against the glass, but remained stubbornly solid on the other side.

"Oh, for crying out loud," I muttered. With my body still inside the lobby, I poked my head through the glass. Was I showing off? Maybe. Just a little. "There is no door, Jake. It doesn't exist. Just walk right through it."

"I can't," he said.

"I believe in you," I said. I pulled my head back through, so I was standing wholly on the other side of the door. I crooked a finger at him. "Come on. You can do it."

Jake closed his eyes, screwed his face up with concentration, and stepped through the door.

My earliest memories after my death were jumbled, with huge gaps missing, but I remembered the first time I got up the nerve to walk through a closed door. It was terrifying. Halfway through, I had a sudden fear that I would get stuck, so of course, I did. Mind over matter goes out the window when you're not made of matter anymore. It took Jake minutes to master what had taken me days.

"Great job!" I told him. "I knew you could do it."

Jake looked down at his hands. "I . . . did it." He sounded like he didn't believe he'd made it. He glanced back at the door, then at his hands again. "I just walked through a friggin' door. How'd I do that?"

"Like I said, you're dead," I reminded him gently. I was trying to be patient with him. Being dead was confusing. And frightening. And horribly lonely. And I wasn't just talking about the first few hours. But my initial transition would have been a lot easier if someone had helped me the way I was determined to help Jake. He'd have someone to show him the ropes, and I'd finally have someone to keep me company. It was a win-win.

"It's going to be okay," I assured him. And it would be. Because now we had each other.

"I'm dead," he repeated. It was finally sinking in. "You're dead. We can walk through closed doors." He lifted his hand in front of his eyes and stared at it. "We're ghosts." He shook his head. "No. That can't be true. I don't believe in ghosts."

"Jake! Don't even *think*—" I started, but it was too late. His hand shimmered and began to fade. Just like when I had worried about gravity and the earth beneath my feet quit being solid, Jake couldn't exist as a ghost if he didn't believe in ghosts. His body convulsed, exploded into static, and disappeared.

In a flash, Jake was gone, and I was all alone again.

CHAPTER TWO

CORDELIA

Fourth-floor walk-ups should be illegal.

Back when I was alive, grocery days were the absolute bane of my existence. They were worse than a visit to the dentist and the gyno combined. Should I try to carry everything up in one giant, heavy load? Or should I make multiple trips up and down the stairs, panting for breath and crossing my fingers that whatever I left in the lobby didn't grow legs and walk away before I got back for it?

Yes, my building had an elevator, but the last time it worked, Cyndi Lauper had a number one song on the charts. And even if it was in perfect order, I'd never take another elevator again. Electronics were no longer my friend. I'm sure there was some kind of logical reason that a decent theologian or physicist could explain, but all I knew was if I got too close to electricity, things went kablooey, which was sad, considering that while I was alive, I worked at a high-tech software design company. I'd only been dead a short time, and I already missed the Internet.

As I trudged up the four flights of stairs to my apartment, the light bulbs flickered in the claustrophobic stairwell. I could only imagine how much worse it would be if I ever attempted to take the elevator, if it wasn't already on the fritz. At best, it would get stuck between floors. At worst, it would short out half the power relays in Boston. It wouldn't bother me any, but my fellow Bostonians might complain, especially those who relied on electricity to not freeze to death during the long, frigid Massachusetts winter. I wasn't desperate enough for company to wish that on my beloved city. Not yet, anyway.

Besides, I didn't much mind the stairs anymore. It's not like I was huffing and puffing as I struggled to lug groceries to the fourth floor these days. I'd been experimenting with other less conventional means of transportation. Since I'd discovered entirely by accident that simply by questioning the existence of the floor, I could drop several stories in an instant, I thought it would be fun doing it in reverse. The only problem was, it didn't work.

Theoretically, if I could imagine myself weightless, I would be weightless. I could float up the four flights of stairs. I could zip up a chimney like Old Saint Nick. In practice, every time I tried to levitate, nothing happened. Maybe I didn't believe it enough. Or, maybe I needed a bit of pixie dust to jump-start the process. Too bad I was all out of pixies.

I didn't even have a Jake anymore.

As I slipped effortlessly through my apartment door, I felt a stab of guilt. Could I have saved Jake-the-ghost if I'd done something different? How could I have possibly warned him without triggering the very event that zapped him? If I'd still had lungs, I would have sighed. Telling someone not to think about something was a waste of energy.

Maybe that's why I hadn't encountered any other dead people.

Nobody believed in ghosts anymore. If they did, Boston would be lousy with them. Granted, I hadn't searched every inch of the city yet, but I'd covered a few hundred square blocks. I hadn't found a single one, but I still went out every night, looking for other ghosts. It wasn't as if I had anything better to do.

My own apartment was dark, so I walked to the window and flung open the heavy blackout curtains. The apartment faced a small strip of lawn that separated my building from the one directly behind us. The view left something to be desired, but for a short time every day, there was natural light, and I wasn't about to miss it.

Back when I was alive, I developed a bit of a, well, I guess I could call it an obsession with houseplants. I collected them like some people collected Pop! bobble head dolls. Every plant had a name, a backstory, and a complicated care routine. If it didn't sound so pathetic, I'd say that they were my best friends. Now, much like me, most of them had withered away and died. Only Eunice remained.

Eunice was a hearty large-leafed philodendron. The thought of anything happening to her absolutely killed me—metaphorically, at least. She didn't need a lot of light, or else she would be a goner already. But she needed as much as she could get, especially in the long, dark Boston winter, and the very least I could do for her now was open the curtains and let her try to get a glimpse of the sunrise.

"It's a little early for this, don't you think?" Ruby Young, my sorta kinda roommate, asked as she entered the room. Ruby was everything I wasn't. Petite. Perky. Alive.

Sometimes I pretended her constant chatter was aimed at me. It made me feel less alone. Not that I got much alone time since she moved into my apartment. Okay, sure, technically I guess my lease expired when my physical body did, but as far as I was concerned, this apartment was still mine, as was all of the furniture, the dishware, and Eunice the philodendron.

After my death, the building manager advertised my apartment as "fully furnished," and twenty-year-old first-time-living-on-her-own Ruby jumped at it. She'd taken one look at my wardrobe and declared it cheugy—whatever that meant—and shoved most of my clothes into the nearest donation box. Now my closet was filled with colorful T-shirts with nonsensical sayings like "Taco to the Hand" over a cartoon image of a taco, thrift store denim, and her vintage Doc Marten boots. She reheated fast-food leftovers in my grandmother's Pyrex pie pan and ate them with my mismatched silverware.

She shuffled across the living room floor wrapped in an old fuzzy pink robe. It went down to her shins even though it had barely reached my knees. She had rainbow-colored furry slippers shaped like unicorns on her feet. The robe used to be mine. The slippers were all Ruby.

Her straight, dark hair was pulled back in a ponytail, as it was most days. Her eyebrows were jet black and lush without being messy, the kind I'd envied back when I was alive. "Seriously, I'm not dressed yet," she said as she jerked the curtains closed. She was generally more cheerful than this, but she hadn't had her coffee yet. She talked to herself incessantly, which, after a while, almost felt like we were having a conversation, one-sided as it was. "What if someone is looking in?"

Ruby was rarely ever home, which was a definite plus, but when she was here, she bopped around listening to music or podcasts on her phone. I'd never seen her pick up a book, and she hadn't once turned on the television I paid the delivery folks extra to mount on the wall. Honestly, the only thing more humiliating than having a roommate in my forties was living with someone who couldn't name a single Pearl Jam song. Well, that and the fact that she *murdered* most of my plants.

My apartment—*our* apartment?—was cozy, which was just another way of saying it was tiny. Technically, it was a one bedroom, but when the door to the bedroom was open, it blocked the bathroom, and when it was closed, I froze, so soon after I moved in, I took the door off its hinges and stored it in my locker in the basement. The living room was just barely big enough for a loveseat, a coffee table, a bookshelf, and a floor lamp. The kitchen doubled as a dining room if I pulled a stool up to the counter, and the bathroom had lime green tile and a single tiny window that opened to a tiny sliver of air between it and the solid brick wall of the building next door.

Not that I wanted to think about the bathroom. My dead corpse had laid scrunched up in the bathtub for almost a week before the EMTs arrived. If I ever stepped inside that bathroom again, it would be too soon.

As soon as Ruby disappeared into the bathroom, I reopened the curtains. Seriously, Eunice wasn't the only one around here that could do with a little sunlight. Vitamin D did everyone good, even me.

A burbling sound caught my attention and I drifted into the kitchen. The last time this room had gotten a facelift, Jimmy Carter was president. There were only enough cabinets to hold a few essential dishes, a box of cereal, and a jar of peanut butter. The cabinet doors had gone missing long before I moved in. The countertops might have once been yellow, but now were so spotted with stains they were closer to muddy brown. The overhead light flickered and blew as I entered the room, reminding me to maintain a respectful distance from the brewing coffee pot.

Me and electricity didn't mix, and it would be a shame if my proximity blew up the coffee pot. The only thing that Ruby and I seemed to have in common was our love of coffee. She brewed a pot first thing in the morning and continued to drink it right up until bedtime. No wonder she was so perky. I couldn't smell the coffee anymore, but I could remember what it was supposed to smell like while it brewed, and that was enough most days.

"Almost ready, my darling," Ruby said to the coffee pot in a singsong voice as she breezed into my kitchen.

I plastered myself against the wall, careful to not get too close to the appliances while staying out of Ruby's path. The sensation of a living walking through me was about as pleasant as getting hit by a train.

She stopped in the middle of the kitchen and frowned up at the dark light. "Again?" she asked. She flicked the light switch off and back on. Nothing happened. I could have told her that. She pulled out her cell phone and texted the building manager. He spent so much time in my apartment changing light bulbs, he was probably starting to suspect that Ruby had a thing for him. Ruby begged him to call a real electrician to get to the heart of the problem, but she'd be better off with a priest.

Not that I wanted to be exorcised. I just knew that as long as I lived here—and I had zero intention of ever leaving—Ruby was going to experience occasional electrical issues. I hoped that eventually she'd wise up and invest in a step ladder and light bulbs in bulk, but for now, she seemed content to notify the building manager and wait for him to take care of it.

"Ahh, coffee, have I told you today how much I love you?" she asked the machine. While it finished brewing, she put away dishes that had been drying overnight in the rack over the sink. Ruby got down my largest mug and sat it next to the coffee maker. As always, her phone was already in her hand. She started scrolling. "And what's on the agenda for today?" she asked.

The way she talked to herself all the time was *almost* endearing. If I was being completely honest, Ruby wasn't the worst roomie in the world. She didn't have any pets and she picked up after herself. "Ooh! I'd almost forgotten I have a job interview this morning! Better shake a leg."

I was tempted to peek over her shoulder to get a glimpse at her phone, but I didn't want to fry its delicate circuits. Besides, I had a good idea that whatever job interview she had lined up would be a disaster. Ruby was smart and full of energy, but she continuously applied for positions that she was either seriously overqualified or woefully underqualified for. As a result, she hadn't gotten a single call back yet.

It was almost like she didn't want to get a job, which made no sense. She had bills to pay. Most importantly, rent was due soon. Ruby was growing on me as a roommate, and if she got evicted, what would happen to Eunice? I couldn't risk having the next occupant kill my last remaining plant.

Knowing that she couldn't afford to get turned down for yet another job, I headed for the bedroom to check out what she planned to wear. Sure enough, she had a pair of jeans with threadbare knees and a T-shirt featuring a cartoon sloth with the caption "Just Lazing" on it folded on the edge of the bed. I had nothing against sloths, but it wasn't exactly the impression you'd want to give a potential employer. Maybe she'd get lucky and never have to take off her coat and scarf so the interviewer wouldn't see what she was wearing, but instead of counting on that, I dug through her closet.

"You really shouldn't have tossed out my clothes," I muttered to myself as I riffled through everything she owned. "I had some really nice pieces. I mean, would it kill you to wear a skirt on occasion?" Okay, maybe skirts weren't the best idea in the dead of winter, but it beat showing up to a job interview in jeans that were falling apart at the seams.

At the very back of her closet, wadded up and shoved onto the shelf above the hangers, I found a cowl-necked sweater. It was an unfortunate shade of green, but it didn't have any cartoons or silly sayings on it, so it would have to do. The only pair of pants she owned that wasn't blue jeans was a pair of gray corduroys that didn't completely clash with the sweater. I carried the sweater and cords to the bed and laid them out neatly on top of the covers. Then I returned the jeans and tee to the closet. I was tempted to toss them out the window, but I knew how much she liked that sloth T-shirt, and I'm not a monster.

The first dozen or so times I tried to move something, my hand went right through it, just like Jake's hand had passed through his hoodie when he consciously tried to touch his sleeve. After a lot of patience and practice, I eventually got the hang of it. All I had to do was believe I could move something, and I could. Now, I could carry pretty much anything I could have lifted back when I was alive. I couldn't hoist a pickup truck over my head or anything cool like that, and trying to do too much left me exhausted until I had a chance to recharge, but folding a T-shirt and shoving it back into a drawer was no problem.

Ruby returned to her bedroom, both hands wrapped around the mug of steaming coffee to warm her hands. I hadn't noticed it, being dead and all, but it was likely frigid in the apartment. The building was old and drafty. It cost an awful lot to keep the heat on high enough to make a noticeable difference, and walking around in a big robe was cheaper than running space heaters. The more

I thought about it, the prouder I was of the interview outfit I'd selected for her. It was way too cold for her to be running around town in ripped jeans and a tee.

She stopped short at the foot of the bed. "Where did these come from?" She scooped up the outfit I'd laid out and tossed it in the dirty clothes hamper. She turned slowly, surveying the room. When she spoke, her voice came out in a squeak. "Cordelia? Cordelia Graves?"

When I died, it was like I'd fallen through the cracks of the universe. I could see and hear everyone around me, but they couldn't see or hear me. I was alone. I was unnoticed. I was invisible. Then Jake came along, but I totally screwed that up. I thought he was my last chance to interact with another soul, but now this interloper, this annoying trespasser in my apartment, acknowledged my existence even as I was starting to give up all hope of ever mattering again.

"You can see me?" I asked. "And you know my name?"

Ruby cocked her head to one side. "Come on, Cordelia, I know you're here. Show yourself."

CHAPTER THREE
RUBY

Ever since I could remember, I've wanted to believe in ghosts. And not just ghosts. All sorts of paranormal creatures my mom used to call claptrap. Sasquatch? Real. I mean, I've seen the videos! Chupacabra? Nessie? Champ? Skunk apes? Why not? UFOs? The government practically admitted they exist. But ghosts? That's the dream.

The moment I first stepped foot in this apartment, I just knew it was haunted. There was this odd sensation in the place that's hard to describe. The first time I flew in an airplane, I didn't notice the change in air pressure because it built up gradually. Then I yawned and the pressure popped. That's the closest I could come to explaining how the air inside the apartment felt. Not threatening. Not scary. Just off. Different. It pops.

Then there's the fact that the rent was dirt cheap. It was a steal, even in this neighborhood. The apartment came fully furnished, and not with just a lumpy sofa and a saggy mattress left over from the last tenant. There were socks in the drawer, matched and folded, arranged in neat rows. Lush green plants covered every surface. Seriously, what kind of person moves out and leaves that many plants behind?

Of course, I googled this place before signing the lease. It wasn't hard to find info about the recent tragedy. Cordelia Graves, the last resident, dead at forty-three of apparent suicide in her—soon to be my—Boston apartment. She'd OD'd on pain killers and booze in the bathtub. No family members were listed in the article I'd read. I guess there were worse ways to go, surrounded by all these pretty plants.

I tried my hardest to keep the plants alive. I did, but I only ever managed to make things worse. Too much water. Too little water. Too much light. Too little light. One by one, they went in the trash. All of them but one stubborn philodendron were gone now. If there really was a ghost in this apartment, she probably hated me.

I hadn't told anyone that my apartment was haunted. People already thought I was a flake. Whatever. Personally, I preferred "eccentric" but apparently, I wasn't old enough or rich enough to be called eccentric. For now, I was just weird. It's okay for weird people to believe in ghosts, but if they tell people there's a ghost living with them, then they're not weird. They're not eccentric. They're crazy. And not the socks-on-hands, aren't-they-fun-at-parties kind of crazy, but the seriously-we're-worried-about-you-Ruby crazy.

It's not like I had proof or anything. Sure, things weren't always precisely where I remembered leaving them, but I've been called scatterbrained a time or three. Light bulbs randomly burned out—which honestly could just be that the cheapo landlord bought cheapo bulbs. I heard strange noises sometimes, but the walls were thin and my neighbors were loud.

The curtains opened by themselves when I wasn't looking, like they'd done this morning, but I supposed there could be a logical explanation for that. Maybe there was a nearby underground train track, or when trucks passed by outside, it rattled the foundation and the heavy curtains slid open on their own. I mean, nothing in this building was square or level. It *could* happen.

But this was different. Even if I wanted to, I couldn't ignore that ugly green sweater and those itchy corduroy pants lying out on my bed. As if I'd ever wear that sweater. The only reason I even had that puke green sweater was because before I moved here, my ex, Jerky McJerkface, borrowed my car and when I got it back, that sweater, along with a skanky bra and a tube of lipstick, was wadded up under the passenger seat. Two years of being madly in love and thinking we had a future together, and this was all I had to show for it. I kept the sweater as a reminder of why my ex was, and always would be, my ex. I wouldn't wear that sweater any more than I would wear her nasty lipstick.

Here it was, actual proof positive that I wasn't alone in this apartment. It was about time that me and Cordelia Graves were formally introduced. And if I was wrong, and I was talking to thin air? Well, no one would ever know, now would they? "Where did these come from?" I asked, hoping for a response, any response.

When there was none, I shook my head. Was I imagining things? It wasn't possible that I'd laid *that* sweater out by accident and then forgotten. Sure, I did things on autopilot sometimes—who didn't?—but that wasn't something I would do. Then again, a spontaneous four-hundred-mile move to a city I'd never even visited, without a job or a single friend, just so I could "start over" didn't seem much like something I would do either, and I'd done exactly that.

I tossed the outfit in the dirty clothes hamper so I didn't have to look at that sweater anymore, then I took a good hard look around my room. Nothing else was out of place. There were no unexplained shadows or strange movements out of the corner of my eye. But I knew down to the tattered soles of my favorite unicorn slippers that I wasn't alone.

"Cordelia? Cordelia Graves?" My voice sounded high-pitched and squeaky like it always did when I got overexcited. Which, according to my mom, was pretty much all the time. But could you blame me? This was by far the single most coolest thing that had ever happened to me, and I'd once found a megalodon tooth on a Maryland beach. "Come on, I know you're there. Show yourself."

My request was met with total silence. Nothing. Nada. Not even the flutter of curtains. I looked around, hoping I could catch a glimpse of the apartment's former occupant. Was she happy I knew she was there? Scared? Upset? There was nothing to see, nothing to hear.

When I looked down, the green sweater was back, laid out neatly on the bed. I could barely contain myself. There really *was* a ghost in my apartment. It wasn't just my overactive imagination.

I still wasn't putting on that sweater.

"Wow. Okay, you really *are* here. But I'm not gonna wear that, no matter how hard you try." I held it up. "See what that color does to my skin? And it's at least a size too small." I balled up the sweater and shoved it under my bed with my foot.

"My boyfriend, Jerkface, cheated on me," I confessed out loud. I didn't know why I admitted that. I hadn't told anyone why we broke up, not even my mom or my sisters. I was too embarrassed. Everyone had warned me that Jeffrey was bad news, and I didn't want to admit that I'd gotten duped. I knew I was far too trusting, but he'd seemed so sincere. A ghost wouldn't judge my bad decisions, would she? Not like my sisters or cousins would. "That was her sweater. The girl he was cheating on me with. Now you see why I can't wear it."

I reached into the closet and gathered up the clothes I wanted to wear today. "I'm gonna be late for my interview." I hugged the T-shirt and jeans to my chest. "You don't, you know, watch me change, do you?" I asked. I didn't know why the idea of having a ghost in my apartment was amazing until I thought of her seeing me undressed, but I was suddenly self-conscious. "I would really appreciate it if you didn't."

Still clutching the clothes, I scurried off to the bathroom and slammed the door behind me. Ironically, the bathroom was the only place in the apartment I ever felt completely alone. I would have thought that if anything, this would be the *most* haunted room in the place, not the least. I knew the previous tenant had killed herself from the info I found online, but it wasn't until I chatted up some neighbors—Jake, the old guy across the hall who apparently lived on pizza and beer, and Milly, the busybody in the unit next to him—that I found out Cordelia had intentionally OD'd in my bathtub.

I didn't know which was sadder, the fact that Cordelia died alone in the tub in this lime green bathroom or the fact that no one noticed she was missing until she'd been dead for a week. Milly and Jake both even asked to see where she died. As if I didn't know better than to invite strangers into my apartment.

They wouldn't have seen anything interesting. I got rid of most of her personal effects, donating her old-fashioned clothes to charity. I bought all-new sheets—there was just something icky about sleeping on a dead woman's sheets—and towels, and lugged her collection of empty liquor bottles down to the recycling bins. I didn't know why she'd kept them, but that woman had more empty bottles of Jack Daniel's than she did houseplants. She killed the bottles. I killed the plants. I guess that about made us even.

Dressed now, I glanced at the clock on my phone. I was going to be late for my interview. I was dragging my feet on purpose. The interview was at a call center. It wasn't the worst job I'd applied for. It wouldn't even be the worst job I'd ever had before. At least it was an in-bound call center, so I didn't have to call anyone and have them curse me out before hanging up on me.

Thank goodness for cell phone spam filters and Millennials who never answered their phones because in a few years, cold calls might finally become obsolete. Until then, the robocallers would keep trying to get in touch with me about my car's expiring warranty. Joke's on them. I didn't even *have* a car. Not anymore.

I didn't have time to enjoy the rest of my coffee, but there was no way I was leaving home without it. I riffled through the kitchen cabinets in the dark, grabbed a travel thermos, and dumped the rest of my mug into it, topping it off with what was left in the pot. I preferred my coffee sweet and light, but since I couldn't exactly afford sugar and cream right now, I'd take what I could get. Thermos capped, I unplugged the coffee maker before pulling the filter out. How many days had I reused this filter and beans? Two? Maybe three? Considering the murky light brown color of the coffee in the pot and the fact that the filter all but disintegrated when I touched it, it might have been more.

It was times like this I missed home the most. It wasn't just that there was always fresh coffee, but there was always someone to drink it with. Between my mom, my sisters, all the nearby aunts and uncles, and a neighborhood where everyone knew everyone, I was never alone. I didn't appreciate that until after I'd moved away.

Although I was tempted to try to stretch one more day out of the coffee grounds, I knew I had to let it go. I opened the trash can to dump the filter, and there, on top of the trash, was the puke green sweater I'd kicked under my bed. I chuckled to myself. Living in a haunted apartment apparently had its upsides. "Thanks, Cordelia," I said out loud to my ghostly roomie as I dumped the coffee grounds. "I knew you'd understand."

CHAPTER FOUR

RUBY

I was unprepared for the unholy blast of freezing air that hit me when I opened the lobby door downstairs. It was March, for Pete's sake. There should be crocuses blooming in the planters separating the street from the sidewalk and hints of spring in the air, not well over a foot of fresh snow on the ground and more of it still coming down.

But it wasn't just the frigid air and drifts of snow on the unshoveled walk that surprised me. After living in Boston for six weeks, I was used to that. What I wasn't expecting was three cop cars, an ambulance, and a white van parked in front of the building. Police officers huddled around one of the cars. The one in plain clothes with his badge displayed on a chain around his neck glanced my way. "Active crime scene," he told me tersely. "Back inside."

"I have a job interview," I told him.

He tilted his head and studied me. "What's the job?"

"Call center," I said, as if that was any of his business.

"Reschedule," he said.

"I really, really need this job," I answered. Did I want it? No. Did I want to eat? Yes.

He huffed. The puff of warm air hung suspended in front of him. "Fine. Name and apartment number?"

"Ruby Young. 4G."

He wrote that down in his notebook. "Okay, Ruby Young from 4G, you got any ID on you?" I dug my license out of my bag and handed it to him. "Maryland?" He asked. "You realize we're in Massachusetts, right?"

"I just moved," I explained. "Haven't gotten around to getting a new license yet." I tried to look past him to see what all the commotion was about, but all I could see was where dozens of boots had trampled down the fresh snow, turning it to gray slush, and a lumpy blanket on the ground that seemed to be the center of attention. "What happened?" I asked.

He glanced over his shoulder. "4G you said? You know a Jacob Macintyre?"

"Jake from across the hall? What did he do?" Jake was a decent guy. Loud, but friendly. He was a little rough around the edges, but I had a hard time picturing him getting involved in something that would warrant such a big police presence. I strained to see around the officer, but he moved to block my view.

"He's dead," he said.

"He's *dead*?" I repeated. I felt numb, and it wasn't just from the cold seeping into my boots. I couldn't wrap my head around it. I'd seen him just the other day. Some of my mail had ended up in his mailbox, and he stopped by to drop it off for me. And now he was dead? It didn't seem right. It didn't seem fair.

"You okay?" the cop asked. "You're shivering."

My wardrobe had been sufficient for Maryland, where it got

bitterly cold on occasion but never stayed that way for long, but it wasn't cutting it here. If I was going to tough out the Boston winters, I needed to invest in better clothes. But to do that, I needed a job. I was already late for my interview. That wouldn't make a great first impression.

The wind kicked up, snatching the blanket that had been covering the lump on the sidewalk, revealing a frozen body clutching a cell phone. I caught a glimpse of pajama pants, a hooded sweatshirt, and fuzzy socks before one of the cops snagged the blanket and tucked it back into place around the body. *Jake's* body. I shuddered.

"What happened?" I asked.

"Looks like a mugging gone bad. You seen any sketchy suspects hanging around lately?"

I dragged my attention back to the cop. Answering him seemed more desirable than thinking about the dead body on the sidewalk a few feet away from me. "In this neighborhood?" I asked. It wasn't like I lived on Skid Row—that was a solid three, maybe four, blocks away. This was affordable housing that attracted young families, older singles, a few ruffians, and me. Okay, maybe more than a few unscrupulous types to be honest, enough to keep the tourists away and the rents affordable.

The officer continued to hold his pen above his notebook while he stared down at me, seemingly impervious to the snow falling all around us. "What can you tell me about Jake?" he asked.

"Huh?" Between the cold and the knowledge that there was a dead man, a man I'd known, right on the other side of him, it was hard to concentrate on the cop's questions.

"You know him well?"

"Not really," I admitted. "Hardly at all." A gust of wind blew a swirl of snow pellets into my face. It stung, and I dipped my head to protect myself. I could feel my lips chapping and my nose starting to run. I needed to get out of this weather, and the bus stop was still two whole blocks away. "We're neighbors. We bump into each other sometimes. Are you sure he's dead?"

The cop nodded.

I let that sink in. It wasn't like I'd never known anyone who'd died before, but it was all so unexpected. I hadn't woken up this morning expecting to find a ghost in my apartment and a dead man outside on the sidewalk. It was overwhelming, so much so that I momentarily forgot I had to be somewhere. My phone buzzed, reminding me that my job interview was supposed to start in a few minutes. "I'm sorry, but can I go now? Please? I'm really late."

"Where are you parked?" the officer asked. He glanced down the street and I saw what he was seeing, a line of cars waiting to be shoveled out, disguised as identical lumps of snow lined up against the curb.

In the distance, I heard the distinctive sound of snowplows working their way around the neighboring streets. The *beep, beep, beep* as they backed up. The scrape of the plow over the pavement. The wet swoosh as they dumped their loads. A growl of a diesel motor revving, and then more beeps as they reversed to do it all over again until the street was passable. They hadn't gotten to my street yet. With all of the emergency vehicles blocking the road, they might not be able to for a while. Good thing I took the bus.

"I'll be fine," I said, instead of answering his question directly. The cop didn't need to know that I'd sold my car, figuring I could get a few months of rent for it to tide me over until I found a job. My stomach grumbled and I thought of my empty refrigerator upstairs. Maybe I should have held out longer and tried to get more money instead of selling it to the place with the catchy jingle.

I was tempted to call home and ask for help. I didn't need

much, just enough to last a few more weeks at most. But I didn't because I knew Mom would send me money even though she couldn't afford to do it, and because the whole point of moving to Boston was to prove to myself that I could make it on my own. And I would. Somehow.

"Be careful, Ruby Young in 4G," he said. He handed me his business card before returning to the huddle of officers in the street.

I glanced down at the name on his card. "Sure thing, Detective Mann," I called out.

"Good." He nodded. "You never know what's out there."

. . .

I waited twenty minutes for a bus that never came. There was no way I was going to make my interview now. Maybe the bus broke down, or the weather was causing delays, but I couldn't wait there any longer. Even though the bus stop offered some shelter, I had to get up and move around before I ended up frozen to death and shelved next to Jake in the morgue.

If I went back to my apartment so soon after leaving, the cops might think I was acting suspicious. The attention I'd received from Detective Mann was enough interaction with the police to last a lifetime, so without a formal destination in mind, I headed toward the main drag. As I walked, I glanced up at the windows surrounding me and wondered if every apartment I passed was haunted like mine. In a city as old as Boston, I had to assume that every building was at least a *little* haunted.

People died all the time. In the last few months, two people had died that lived in the same building. On the same floor, even. Across-the-hall neighbors. I shivered, and not just from the frigid temperature.

By all accounts, Cordelia Graves had killed herself. No one seemed to know her well, but judging from the contents of her apartment, all she ever did was read books and drink booze. Don't get me wrong, I'm not one to judge anyone's lifestyle choices, but as far as I could tell, she didn't have any family or friends, at least none who cared enough to come by and claim her belongings.

I assumed she, unlike myself at the moment, had a job that she went to every day. Judging by her boring, corporate wardrobe, it was a boring, corporate job. Considering the neighborhood we lived in, it couldn't have paid much.

Come to think of it, I had no idea what Jake did for work, either, unless eating a ton of pizza was a job. I always saw him hurrying to meet the pizza man at the front door. Delivery folks usually decided that climbing four flights of stairs was too much work for a measly tip. Jake had friends over a lot. I'd know when he had company because the walls were thin and his friends were boisterous. I assumed that he, unlike Cordelia, had someone to mourn his death.

I stopped at a corner. Rather than take my hands out of my warm pockets, I jabbed at the crosswalk light with my elbow. Traffic was as heavy as ever. Boston rarely took snow days, and it was still rush hour. I wasn't sure where I was heading. I'd already missed my interview. I should email them and explain, but my cheap phone plan was out of data.

My stomach grumbled, but I couldn't afford to have breakfast out—or in for that matter. My cupboards were bare. I really needed that job. Well, maybe not *that* job, but *a* job would be nice.

As I waited for the light, I unscrewed the lid of my thermos and took a sip of the coffee. It was tepid now. I'd drank most of it waiting for the bus and now I really needed to pee. Across the street was a convenience store, a dry cleaner, and a local branch of the library. The light changed, and I hurried through the crosswalk.

Inside, the library was warm and welcoming. I knocked the snow off my shoes and stood in the entrance for a minute soaking up comfort from air that wasn't actively trying to hurt me. When I could feel my fingers again, I made a beeline for the public restroom. Once the important things were taken care of, I headed for the stacks.

Cordelia had left behind an impressive collection of books. She had sci-fi, romance, YA, fantasy, women's fiction (or, as I called it, fiction). But she didn't have any true crime, which was what I mostly read. I kept meaning to donate her books to a local shelter, but the thought of carting her collection down four flights of stairs kept pushing the project to "maybe next weekend." I wound my way around the aisles, glancing up at the genre signs until I found the true crime section.

I ran my finger along the spines, seeing familiar authors and beloved titles. I'd read most of these already. Some people thought true crime was dark and depressing, but I found it comforting. I liked how in the end, the bad guy almost always got his comeuppance. I mostly read e-books or listened to audiobooks on my phone that I'd check out from the library and download using their Wi-Fi. Thinking of their free Internet connection, I left the true crime books behind as I made my way to the computer lab.

After signing in at the nearest open computer, I composed an email to my interviewer explaining why I'd missed the appointment, but ended up deleting it. Only a desperate company would hire someone who flaked on an interview, and I didn't want to work at a place like that. I wanted to work someplace cheery. Someplace fun. Preferably someplace with benefits and a living wage and coworkers who slipped out early on Fridays.

The warmth of the library was a welcome change from my freezing apartment. Apparently, I wasn't the only one who'd had the idea of coming in from the cold, because around me, the other computer stations were filling up.

I opened a new tab on my browser and typed "Cordelia Graves, Boston" into the search engine. The first result was from LinkedIn. I clicked on it, and was prompted to log in. Seriously? Who even used LinkedIn? Cordelia, that's who. I signed up for an account, knowing I'd probably regret that the minute the spam started pouring in, but was able to open her profile.

The Cordelia Graves in the profile picture was a white woman with long red hair and sad blue eyes. She was posed against a green tiled wall with a hanging plant over her shoulder. I recognized that wall. It was the same lime green tile that was in the bathroom in our apartment. I recognized the plant, too. Despite my best efforts, it was the first of many I'd killed. I felt a pang of guilt at the memory, but at least I was now certain I'd found the right Cordelia.

I scrolled down her profile. The latest job listed was at TrendCelerate, which, according to the ad banner, was hiring. Cordelia had worked in their Boston headquarters. I had not expected that. What was someone with a decent job at a tech company doing living in a flophouse like our building? I mean, it wasn't a literal flophouse, but there had been a dead body outside when I left this morning, so it wasn't exactly the Downtown Ritz.

Before TrendCelerate, she'd worked for a string of other companies with names that all sounded like random word generator soup. CloudIndus. SoftWaverly. VisionCycle. I scrolled through her experience, with titles ranging from office manager to receptionist. My own résumé was only a single page long, but the background was lilac and my name was in a pretty, scrolly font. What I lacked in experience, I more than made up for in spunk.

I entered "Jacob Macintyre" into the LinkedIn search bar. Lots of hits came up, but none were a match to Jake across the hall. I had better luck on Facebook, where he apparently spent his days posting silly memes and commenting on an inordinate amount of fishing videos. According to his About, he was single, worked at a local warehouse, was an avid bowler, and rooted for the Boston Bruins. He had a couple hundred friends, but there weren't any In Memoriam messages, so the word of his recent passing hadn't gotten around yet.

I checked the news sites next. I wasn't expecting to find anything about this morning's incident so soon, but what I did find sent a chill down my spine. "Boston Death Ruled a Suicide" by Penny Fisher. I skimmed the article since I'd already read it before. It was the same one I'd found when I was researching the neighborhood before I signed the lease. Apparently, suicides of low-profile office assistants in sketchy Boston neighborhoods didn't warrant a lot of media coverage, so there was only the one article.

One sentence jumped out at me. "Neighbor Jacob Macintyre claims to have seen a well-dressed man carrying a laptop bag leaving Graves's apartment late on the last night anyone saw her alive, but there were no signs of foul play . . ."

The computer screen glitched. Twenty new apps launched simultaneously and a commercial began playing loudly. There was a loud pop and smoke began to pour out of the top of the monitor.

I jumped up and took a step back. The images on the display warped even as the smell of melting plastic hit my nose. The library patrons on either side of me noticed. One rushed over and unplugged the monitor. The other hurried off, either to get a librarian or to escape the noxious fumes.

"Stand back," an authoritative woman's voice said. A Black woman with a fire extinguisher braced in her arms strode up to the computer I'd been using. As she hit a button, chemicals spewed out one end, coating the monitor in foam.

For a moment, I thought I caught a glimpse of a silhouette of a tall woman with long hair in the swirling mist that hung in the air. I blinked and the image was gone. A day ago, I might have dismissed the apparition as a trick of my admittedly active imagination, but now that I knew for certain that ghosts were real, I wondered if I'd just caught a glimpse of one. Were there ghosts in the library, too? What were the odds?

"Did anyone else see that?"

"I think everyone saw your monitor burst into flames, yes," the stern librarian said, bringing my attention back to her. "Care to explain what happened here?"

Everyone looked at me. I held my hands out to indicate my innocence. "No clue. One minute I'm surfing news sites, and the next, well, whoosh."

"Whoosh," the woman repeated, pursing her lips. She put down the fire extinguisher and checked the monitor to make sure it had stopped smoking. She noticed my coffee thermos. "Is this yours? There's no eating or drinking in the library."

"It, uh, I wasn't . . ." I stammered.

"Never mind." She raised her voice, something I'd never heard anyone do in a library. "Sorry folks, the computer lab is closed for the day. You'll have to come back tomorrow." There were audible groans from the other patrons as they packed up. She waved her arms at them like one might do when herding actual geese, and they slowly made their way to the door. "You," she said, turning to me.

"Me?" I asked meekly. I glanced over my shoulder, wondering if the librarian might have also seen the ghostly shape of the woman in the aftermath of the fire extinguisher's spray. If so, maybe she was talking to her, not me. But there was no one behind me, at least not that I saw now.

"Are you okay?"

I nodded, a little too rapidly. "Yup. Fine and dandy."

"In that case, move it along. And don't let me catch you with food or drink in my library ever again."

I snatched up the thermos in question and quickly covered it up with my coat. Out of sight, out of mind, right? "Yes, ma'am," I said. I retreated to the back of the library, where the biographies were kept, and rested a hand on a shelf to steady myself as I caught my breath.

Ever since I'd come to Boston, I'd been plagued by weird electrical problems. Brand-new light bulbs burned out. My earbuds shocked me when I put them in. The door buzzer went off at all hours of the night, even when there was no one downstairs. I couldn't be sure if the old wiring and cheap appliances or the ghost of Cordelia Graves was to blame, but this was different. That monitor looked new, and I was blocks away from my haunted apartment.

Beside me, one of the books twitched on the shelf. It quivered, then slid off the shelf onto the floor, landing spine-up with the pages open on the carpet. I picked up the book and glanced at the cover. I didn't recognize the title or the author. I smoothed down the pages and placed it back on the shelf. The book next to it fell onto the floor with a loud thud.

"Shh!" someone hissed nearby.

"Sorry," I said, which earned me another shush. In a whisper, I asked, "Cordelia?" I didn't know if Cordelia could venture this far away from our apartment, but the presence in the library felt the same as the one at home. In response, more books thudded to the ground.

The librarian who'd extinguished the fire appeared at the end of the row. She brushed past me, picking up books even as more titles rocked off the shelves and hit the floor. Unable to help myself, I laughed. It was all just too ridiculous not to. "I've had about enough of you, little lady. Out. Now." All of this was said in the hushed tone of a professional librarian but with the authoritative bite of a woman didn't take any nonsense from anyone. "Scram."

I scurried for the exit. At the end of the row, I glanced back to see books continue to leap off the shelf. As the exasperated librarian struggled to collect them, her arms already full, another book flew off the shelf and landed with a thud. "Cordelia, stop it," I hissed.

"Are you still here?" the librarian asked. "Are you trying to get banned?"

"No ma'am," I said, and hurried out of the library. The cold air smacked into me as I opened the front door, but at least it wasn't snowing at the moment. I wiggled back into my coat. "Cordelia? Is that you?" I asked, not expecting a response. On the curb in front of me, the plastic door of a free newspaper dispenser clanged open, spilling newspapers out onto the sidewalk.

An accident? Maybe. It was a blustery day.

A newspaper swirled up and plastered itself to my face. I peeled it off and glanced at the headline: "Boston Murder Rate on the Rise." "No kidding," I muttered to myself, thinking of the dead body outside my apartment. I folded the newspaper and shoved it back in the dispenser, but it was too late for the other papers. The ones that weren't blowing all over their neighborhood were already damp from the snow. They stared up at me with the same word repeating over and over in the headline.

"MURDER"
"MURDER"
"MURDER"

I snatched at another newspaper as it blew past, the headline practically screaming at me. "Wait a sec. Murder? What murder? That cop said Jake was killed in a mugging."

Another paper smacked me in the face. "Sheesh, I can take a hint," I said, as I tore it off my face and wadded it into a ball. "You think Jake was murdered." I looked down at the crumpled paper in my hand. The wind died down, and the remaining newspapers drifted to the slushy sidewalk.

I couldn't stop thinking about seeing the body lying on the sidewalk in the snow. Poor Jake. Plus, something was off about the scene. Jake was holding a phone, wasn't he? Why would a mugger kill him and leave the phone?

Call it an overdeveloped sense of fair play or one too many true crime podcasts, but I was struck by the idea that if the cops dismissed Jake's death as a random mugging gone wrong, the killer was going to get away with it. If he was free to roam the streets of my neighborhood, who would he kill next? Maybe he had a thing for short, spunky brunettes, like me. "Just so I understand, you, Cordelia Graves, formerly of apartment 4G, want me to solve a murder?"

CHAPTER FIVE

CORDELIA

The thing with the monitor? That was an accident. I swear.

One minute I was straining to look over Ruby's shoulder, trying to read the article about me on the screen, and the next thing I know, I got the shock of my life. Literally. Or, at least, the shock of my afterlife.

Before I died, I spent most of my day on a computer. Now I couldn't get close to a monitor without it blowing to smithereens—and the resulting jolt hitting me like the business end of a cattle prod. Don't tell me the universe doesn't have a sense of humor.

But it wasn't the monitor fire that had my mind racing now. It was the article. I didn't remember my death, which was probably a kindness. Every time I thought too hard about it, it was like trying to focus on the last snippets of a dream as they fluttered away. I didn't remember killing myself, but to be completely honest, I *had* struggled with suicidal thoughts, on and off, for my entire life. The holidays were especially hard, precisely because I didn't have anyone to share them with. There had been someone special, for a while, but even before we called it quits, he'd never been in my home.

My place might have been in a crappy neighborhood. The building might have smelled like stale corn chips. But surrounded by my plants (before Ruby killed most of them), secondhand knitted blankets, and my books, I could relax. Growing up, we moved so often—sometimes with no warning, leaving everything we had behind—that I never had a place to call home. Even on the rare occasions when we did have a stable roof over our heads, I never had my own room. I rarely even had my own bed. But this tiny apartment was all mine.

I didn't invite people over, not because I was embarrassed, but so I would never have to share my space again—at least, not until Ruby came along. Could I have afforded to move somewhere nicer? Probably. But this was my home and I didn't like visitors, unless you counted my brother, and he wasn't exactly in a position to come by lately. Even when I was dating, we always went over to his place instead of mine.

The newspaper article quoted Jake as seeing a man leaving my apartment around the time of my suicide. Either Jake was mistaken, or someone had invaded my sanctuary. Someone who wasn't supposed to be there. Jake mentioned my mysterious visitor to a reporter and then turned up dead himself a few months later. If that wasn't suspicious, I didn't know what was.

How could I warn Ruby that she might be in danger, too? Since she was the only person in the whole world that even realized I still existed, she was by default the closest thing I had to a friend. And as her friend, I had to protect her. I'd failed Jake miserably, but I wasn't going to fail Ruby. I needed to scare her away before anything bad happened to her, but how? She actually thought that having her very own ghost was cool, which meant I had to put a lid on my friendly Casper routine and get down to business.

Usually, trying to move too much was exhausting, but after the monitor surge, I felt supercharged, like I could do anything. I thought a few books flying off some shelves would send the message to back off, but instead, she thought it was funny. Seriously, what was wrong with this girl? I had to up my game. The newspaper was a stroke of luck. As soon as I saw that headline, I knew it was exactly what I needed to get through to Ruby. I mean, who could miss the threat in a headline like that?

Ruby freaking Young, that's who.

"Help you solve a murder?" I screamed in frustration, even though she couldn't hear me. "You think *I* want *you* to help me solve a murder? Are you an idiot? What on this green earth makes you think that either of us can solve a murder? You can't even get a job, and I don't actually exist!"

If I wasn't already dead, I would have needed a stiff drink. No, that wasn't entirely true. Dead or not, I *did* need a stiff drink, but there was nothing to be done about that.

Ruby chatted incessantly all the way home, seemingly unaffected by the cold. I've never seen anyone in such a good mood about a murder. Even when we reached the building, she was unfazed by the crime scene tape fluttering around the sidewalk and the police cars still parked on the street. It made no sense. I was a ghost, and I thought dead bodies were icky. It was like she had no survival instinct at all. Not that I could talk.

As we climbed the stairs to the fourth floor, I found myself wishing, as I often did, for an elevator, but not for the normal reasons. If I could cause a fire by getting too close to a monitor, just imagine what I could do with an elevator. I could burn down the whole building. Ruby would have no choice but to move someplace safer.

Then where would I go? There was nothing keeping me here, not physically at least. But it was still my home. Still my sanctuary, even if I had to share it with this chipper chatterbox with the common sense of a chipmunk. And it was the home of Eunice the philodendron. Maybe I couldn't rescue Ruby, but I could rescue Eunice. The thought of startling a neighbor or two when they saw a large potted plant floating down the hallway seemingly on its own was almost enough to cheer me up. But I knew that the second she hit the frigid temperature outside, she'd be deader than, well, me.

"You've got no idea how lucky you are," I told Ruby as we approached our apartment. "That philodendron is about the only thing keeping both of us from being homeless right now." Not that I would burn down the building, not really. But in any event, the elevator was a dead end, just like our hallway.

The A and B apartments were closest to the stairs, alternating letters across the hall until we reached the end. Having a corner apartment had its perks. I had a tiny window in my bathroom. It didn't have a view, but in the summer, I could almost catch a cross breeze. I only had to worry about having loud neighbors on one side. But on the downside, with two walls separated from the cold weather outside by nothing but a layer of bricks, it was a bear to heat in the winter.

If anyone was coming or going from the end of the hall, they had to be coming from Jake's apartment or my own. If Jake said he saw a man coming out of my apartment, there was little chance he was mistaken, even though I never got visitors.

It also made it easy to tell if anything was amiss, like if Jake's door was standing wide open—like it was now. A uniformed police officer was stationed outside his apartment, glaring at Ruby as we approached. "Nothing to see here, missy," he said as we got closer. "Turn around and go back home."

"I *am* home." She pointed at our door. "That one's mine."

The officer spoke into a handset clipped to his shoulder. He clicked the button and was met with a loud squeal of feedback. That was probably my fault. I took a step back. The officer turned his head to yell into the apartment. "Detective, a minute?"

Detective Mann, the same cop who'd questioned Ruby earlier, appeared in the door. He was white, average height, and wore a dark gray suit under a navy blue peacoat. His loafers were stained with salt from the winter sidewalks. His hair was receding, and combed meticulously as if to make it look like he had a lot more of it than he did. He wasn't fooling anyone.

He studied Ruby for a second. He ignored me, of course. He had no idea I was there. "Ruby Young," he said. He glanced at the plaque next to our door. "4G." He gave her a terse nod. "How was your job interview?"

"Didn't get it," she said, straining to see around him.

He shifted to block her view. "That's too bad."

They faced off for a second more before Ruby slumped her shoulders and said, "Guess I ought to be getting inside now."

"You do that," Mann said, his expression and tone of voice never changing.

Ruby turned to unlock our door, but I hesitated in the hall. The cops couldn't very well keep me out, now could they? As soon as I heard our door close behind me, I slipped past Detective Mann, right into Jake's apartment.

Jake's apartment was a mirror copy of mine—right down to the same worn carpet and dingy paint on the walls. The bedroom was to the left and the kitchen to the right, the opposite of my layout. Like me, he'd removed the bedroom door but he'd replaced his with a genuine-looking 1970s-era beaded curtain.

His living room furniture consisted of a large sectional that barely fit in the cramped room, but provided plenty of seating for his constant flow of visitors. He had an oversized television and a coffee table buried under old magazines. A rickety stand against the wall held a stack of videogame consoles plugged into the back of his TV by a tangled nest of wires.

There was an empty pizza box next to the sink, along with several coffee mugs that could use a deep scrubbing with a flame thrower. A movement caught my eye. For a second, I thought Jake had a cat, but then the largest roach I'd ever seen scuttled across the floor. Gross.

I glanced out the window. Unlike my unit, Jake's apartment was south facing, so it overlooked the street. The curtains were open. Even on a brutally cold day, warm sunshine flooded his living room. I bet his heating bill was half the size of mine.

Driven by curiosity, I continued exploring. The bedroom was dominated by a large bed with a headboard. The bed was unmade, the dark blue silk sheets slipping off the corners. I felt the urge to straighten them, but resisted for the sake of the cops poking around. No reason to draw any attention to myself.

Jake's closet was filled with faded blue jeans hanging on sagging hangers, T-shirts, two bright orange safety vests, a shapeless suit, and an extensive collection of Bruins jerseys. A voice in the back of my head corrected myself. I'd dated a hockey player for a hot second back in high school, and he'd gleefully schooled me that they weren't *jerseys*. Technically, they were *sweaters*. Whatever. They'd always be jerseys in my mind.

I glanced into the bathroom. It wasn't as bad as I expected.

Judging from the state of the kitchen, I had expected a colony of science experiments to be growing in the tub, but it was relatively clean. I guess even a bachelor had to scrub their bathroom on occasion if he wanted to entice women to sleep over.

The detective walked past me, holding his phone horizontally in his hand and talking directly into the microphone. I pressed myself against the wall, staying as far away from his phone as possible without sinking into the plaster. "I think we're about done here," he said into his phone.

The voice on the other end came through in fragments, with loud pops of air in between the few words I could make out. To hell with the drywall. I backed up farther. Only my head poked into the room. The reception didn't improve much. "Get . . . station . . . weather . . . worse . . . neighborhood . . . sap . . . expect? Wrap . . . day."

I filled in the blanks. "Get back to the station before the weather gets any worse. The poor dead sap lives in that neighborhood, what can you expect? Wrap it up and call it a day."

"You heard Sarge," Detective Mann said to the room at large. "We're done here." Guess he was used to lousy cell phone reception.

One of the uniformed police officers, a tall Hispanic woman in her late twenties if I had to guess, walked over to him holding several clear plastic bags. One held a toothbrush, and the other, a wallet. She also had a white box about the length of a shoebox tucked under her arm. "Wallet was by the front door in a bowl, next to the keys. Vic wasn't planning on going far. Got a DNA sample if we need one." She held up the bag with the toothbrush. Then she gestured at the box. "Found a gun sealed in a plastic bag and taped inside the toilet tank."

Well, that was a surprise. I wasn't shocked that Jake would

own a gun—they weren't illegal or uncommon—but why would he conceal it in the toilet tank? Then again, I hadn't thought to check in there, so maybe it was a decent hiding place.

"Leave the wallet and keys where you found them, but the toothbrush and gun come with us. Poor bugger has a gun but doesn't take it with him, gets mugged, and gets shot in the face. Guess it wasn't his day." The detective glanced at the wallet. "Mugger probably got frustrated he didn't have any money on him, popped him, and took off," he concluded with a note of finality in his voice. "Keep an eye out, maybe check the shelters, see if anyone's got any useful information, but I doubt we'll catch the guy."

"You're not gonna find a witness in a shelter," I said, as he ushered his team out and closed the door behind them. I wasn't sure what time the shelters closed for the night, but when I left the building around midnight, there hadn't been a corpse outside on the sidewalk, and when I got back right before sunrise, there was. Most of the unhoused population in the neighborhood that was willing, and able, to go to a shelter would have been tucked in ahead of the storm, long before Jake was killed. Those who weren't wouldn't go volunteering any information to the police.

And then there was the matter of Jake being dressed for a night in. What was he doing out in the storm in his pjs and socks? Who was he meeting? Why was his wallet upstairs? And if he was mugged, why did he still have his phone? I had a lot of questions, but the detective had all the answers he needed. I guess deaths in my neighborhood weren't worth more than a cursory investigation and a few flippant comments about the victim's lifestyle.

I glided through the closed door and glanced back at it, expecting something, anything to indicate that someone who lived here had just lost their life. Police tape. Fingerprint powder. Maybe one of those big stickers across the doorjamb marking this as an active crime scene. There was nothing. As far as the authorities were concerned, the case was already closed. Unless the killer walked into the station with a signed confession, he would walk free.

As much as I hated to admit it, Ruby might have had a point. Someone needed to solve Jake's murder. The cops didn't care. But no matter how eager Ruby was to play Nancy Drew, letting her do so would be irresponsible.

That left only me. I couldn't scare her away from the building, but there were other ways of keeping her safe. If I got Jake's killer off the streets, then there would be no more threat to my annoying-but-growing-on-me roomie. It was dangerous, but I was already dead. I couldn't get more dead. Plus, solving Jake's death wouldn't bring him back, but it might make us even.

CHAPTER SIX

CORDELIA

"Come on, Cordelia, talk to me. Do something, anything!"

I could hear Ruby talking to herself as I slid through the door to our apartment. It took me a second to realize that she wasn't actually talking to herself. She was talking to *me*. Only, I wasn't in the room.

She had no way of knowing when I was and wasn't with her. Up until now, that hadn't been an issue, because I hadn't realized that she knew I existed. Now that she was aware of me, I guess she assumed I was like one of those faithful little purse dogs that never left their owner's side. But, I wasn't a dog, and Ruby didn't own me. She was my roommate, and even roommates needed a little alone time now and then.

I cleared my throat to announce my presence. Then I remembered that she couldn't hear me. Or see me. Or even smell me, for that matter. We needed a way to communicate that wasn't just Ruby holding one-sided conversations in an empty room.

Ruby sat on the loveseat with her legs tucked up under her and one of the throw pillows on her lap. That didn't look comfortable, but I was more than twice her age—or at least I would have been if I'd still been alive. The last time I'd sat like that, my knees hadn't forgiven me for a week. But now it was different. A few months ago, I could have sneezed and thrown my back out. Now, I couldn't sneeze. But I could sit any way I wanted, for as long as I wanted, without it hurting. I guess there were *some* perks to being dead.

"Seriously, Cordelia," Ruby said, sounding exasperated. I didn't blame her. The situation was trying on my side of the relationship, too. "Would it kill you to give me some kind of a sign?" She gasped and pressed her hands to her mouth. "Sorry, I didn't mean that. It was insensitive. Can you ever forgive me?"

"Of course I forgive you, silly," I said, even though she couldn't hear me. Sure, Ruby was a lot. As in *a lot* a lot. She was so chipper that sometimes it made my teeth ache. But she was also kindhearted. And it was hard to feel lonely when she was around. "Dead is dead, and there's no harm in pointing it out."

Although, to be fair, I wasn't actually so sure that was true. If Jake hadn't realized that he was a ghost before I could convince him to believe in ghosts, maybe he'd still be here. Which was totally my fault. If I'd managed to ease Jake's transition better, he'd still be around to ask who killed him.

Then again, I had absolutely no memory of my actual death or the hours leading up to it. I assumed it was my brain's way of sheltering me. Personally, I was glad I couldn't remember what had driven me over the edge from my everyday baseline depression to finally giving in and washing down a bottle of pills with Jack Daniel's. Ironically, I even failed at that because I was still here, at least in a limited capacity.

Why would it have been any different for Jake? When he woke up, he didn't even realize that he was dead, much less know how he got that way. Getting shot in the face had to be traumatic. Not remembering the who, what, how, and why of it was a kindness. Asking him to go through that, even if it would help us catch his killer, would have been cruel.

"I'm right here," I said to Ruby. I considered reaching out to pat her knee, but restrained myself. Touch a living? No thank you. I shuddered at the memory of the time I'd done it by accident. It was a little like doing a belly flop onto a concrete pad from a thousand feet up. It wasn't something I wanted to ever experience again.

There was an old afghan draped over the back of the loveseat that looked like it had been lovingly crocheted by someone named Maude or Gertrude. I'd bought it at a thrift shop because it was the perfect combination of cozy and practical. It was warm and soft and smelled very faintly of old people. I reached for it, intending to tuck it around Ruby's shoulders, but my hand passed right through it.

Huh. That was weird. Shifting a blanket should have been easy. I tried again. Nothing happened. It had been like this in the early days before I learned how to move things in the physical world. Maybe I wasn't concentrating hard enough? I put all my willpower into it, and still, nothing. Great. Just when I needed it, I'd lost my mojo. I felt darkness creeping over me. I closed my eyes to gather my thoughts, and when I opened them, everything was different.

Ruby was no longer sitting on the loveseat beside me. I could hear the shower running. How much time had passed? I had no idea. I couldn't say that I'd slept since I died, not exactly, but there were voids when I went... somewhere else, usually after I'd exerted myself too much. Sometimes during these gaps in time, I had vivid dreams, flashbacks of a life squandered. I guessed even ghosts needed to top off the tanks on occasion, and between finding Jake's body and trashing a public library, it *had* been a draining day.

Ruby probably thought I'd abandoned her. I wished there was some way to communicate with her besides opening and closing the curtains and tossing poor, defenseless library books around. Over the water running in the shower, I could hear her singing at the top of her lungs, and had a flash of inspiration.

As much as I wanted to, I couldn't avoid the bathroom where I'd died forever. I slipped through the closed door. Steam hung in the air as Ruby continued belting out a song I only vaguely recognized. We had very different tastes in music. The steam wasn't because she ran the shower too hot. I knew from experience that what came out of the old water heater was lukewarm at best, but compared to the cold air in the bathroom, it might as well have been one of those hot springs in Japan that attracted the macaque monkeys.

The mirror was fogged over. Bingo! Using my finger, I carefully traced out the words, "I'm here."

I didn't have long to wait before Ruby turned off the shower and stepped out. She wrapped a towel around herself quickly, shivering as she rubbed her long hair in a second towel, shifting from one bare foot to the other. Finally, she glanced at the mirror and stifled a yelp.

"Sorry, didn't mean to startle you," I said. It didn't matter that she couldn't hear me. Speaking aloud was a habit I'd yet to break.

She stared at the mirror. "Glad you're back, Cordelia." She put her hands on her hips. "But I thought we agreed to respect each other's privacy," she said. The motion caused her towel to slip, and she hastily reached for the top of it and twisted the ends together in a tight grip. She studied the mirror a little more. "In lore? What's that supposed to mean? Do you want me to research something for you? Maybe something about ghost lore?"

"In lore?" I asked. "Where'd you get that?" I looked at the

mirror. The words I'd scrawled in the condensation had dripped a little, but not enough to obscure them that much. "It clearly says 'I'm here.' Can't you read?"

As if answering me, Ruby said defensively, "No one uses cursive anymore." She tilted her head and studied my admittedly sloppy handwriting as if it were a form of ancient cuneiform. "I have no idea what that says."

"I'd heard that your generation doesn't use cursive, but I thought that was a myth," I admitted. How could that possibly be? I traced a giant question mark in the rapidly clearing surface of the mirror.

"If it's not on the standardized test, they don't teach it in school," she said matter-of-factly. "Besides, who needs it? It's not like I can send a text in cursive." She made a shooing motion. "Now give me a minute. Alone. Please?"

I made a point of opening the door to leave the bathroom, and then closed it behind me. I could have just as easily walked through the closed door, but I wanted to make a show of leaving to give her some privacy. Back in the living room, I touched the old afghan. It moved easily. I guess I really had just needed a recharge after all the energy I'd exerted at the library. That was a relief. It was hard enough being invisible and silent. If I lost the ability to affect the material world completely, I might as well fade away.

As Ruby finished up in the bathroom, I searched the apartment. There wasn't a single notebook or pen anywhere. Sure, I got it. When I was alive, I was more likely to use the notes app on my phone or email myself a reminder rather than scribbling something on a Post-it, but I still wrote things down on occasion. Ruby apparently didn't. I couldn't touch a keyboard, and she couldn't read my handwriting. We really were the original odd couple, weren't we?

Ruby came out of the bathroom dressed but barefoot. She hurried to her bedroom, where she had to dig through her laundry hamper to find a pair of thick socks. "Time for laundry," I told her.

"Time to do laundry," she echoed.

It figured. Even when we *were* communicating, she didn't know it.

As if to prove my point, she stopped, a pair of mismatched socks dangling from her hands, and looked at the wall. She was looking in the opposite direction from where I sat in the middle of her bed, surrounded by her fluffy pillows. "How are we going to solve a murder together if we can't talk to each other?" she asked.

We really were in sync about some things, whether she realized it or not. But not about this. I didn't want to put her in danger, and I had my doubts that someone who couldn't even manage to keep on top of their laundry could unravel the complexities of a murder plot and catch a killer.

I felt bad about letting Jake down and wanted to redeem myself. I wanted to protect Ruby from a killer running free in our neighborhood. I wanted something to distract me from the crushing loneliness and boredom that was my afterlife. What was *her* excuse?

"Oh! I've got it!" Ruby exclaimed. I trailed behind her as she wandered back into the small living room, tossed the throw pillows onto the other cushion, and plopped down on the loveseat. "I'll get a Ouija board. Then we can have conversations like normal roomies."

"That's the absolute dumbest idea I've ever heard," I told her. "Do you know how long it would take to spell out every single word?" I thought about how I'd been drained of energy earlier. "I'd have to take a nap between paragraphs. If you really want to chat, just buy a notebook. How is it you don't have a single piece of paper in the whole apartment?"

As if the universe was listening, there was the faint sound of footsteps in the hallway and then the whisper of a piece of paper being slid under the door. Ruby didn't notice. I walked over to the door, bent, and picked up the flyer for Caparelli's, a local pizza joint. I recognized their logo from the countless pizzas Jake had ordered over the years. I wondered how they'd react when they found out their best customer was dead. They'd probably go out of business.

I carried the flyer over to Ruby and dropped it on her lap. She looked startled as the paper drifted gently to rest. "It's called paper," I said. "Now, all we need is a pen. You do know what a pen is, don't you?" It was meant as a joke, but in this day and age, I couldn't be certain.

"You want me to order pizza?" Ruby said, shaking the paper. "What, are you like hungry? Sorry, but money's a little tight right now." She got up and rummaged through the cabinets. She came up with a packet of ramen noodles and a jar of peanut butter. She put the dried noodles back, grabbed a spoon, and dug into the peanut butter. She leaned against the counter as she ate a spoonful, and then held one out for me. "Want some?" When I didn't take the spoon, or the offered peanut butter, she licked the spoon. "More for me, then."

I was glad to see Ruby eating something, but if she didn't get a job soon, she'd have to resort to eating ketchup packets for dinner. That was something I could help her with, and it might even distract her from this foolish notion that she should get involved with Jake's murder. I couldn't scour the job postings online, not without blowing up the computer, but I knew people in this town, didn't

I? I couldn't call them up and ask for a favor, but there had to be something I could do.

Ruby put down the spoonful of peanut butter, opened the refrigerator, and pulled out a carton of milk. She shook it. It was empty. "It's times like this I miss living with my sisters," she confessed. "Now, when I'm out of milk, there's no one else to blame it on." She tossed the empty milk carton and poured herself a glass of water from a filtered pitcher in the refrigerator instead.

The refrigerator, like the rest of the apartment, was pretty much exactly as I'd left it, which meant it was past time to change that filter. My plain yellow mustard was still in the door. Personally, I wouldn't eat a strange dead woman's mustard, but beggars and choosers and all that jazz. There were several magnets I'd left on the fridge. There was a poison control magnet, an emergency maintenance magnet, and a magnet advertising a Thai take-out place that had gone out of business a year ago. But the one that caught my eye was blue and red and shaped like a gear, with the TrendCelerate logo printed in bold white letters in the center and the phone number and website printed in black.

I started to peel the magnet off the fridge. Thankfully, the refrigerator was an old model and my proximity didn't seem to interfere with its operation. If it was a smart refrigerator, the kind that displayed a picture of the contents while the door was closed or kept an inventory and texted you when you were low on milk, I'd probably blow it up being this close, but this unit didn't even have an icemaker.

If I could hand Ruby the magnet, maybe she would get the hint and call them. TrendCelerate didn't have a lot of turnover. Most of the developers had been there for ages. But I remember seeing a banner on LinkedIn—before the library computer self-destructed—that said they were hiring. With any luck, they'd had a hard time finding someone as organized as I was who was willing to commute into a physical office when everyone else worked from home these days. If the office manager position was open, Ruby would be a great fit.

She genuinely liked people, was meticulous, and wouldn't have to worry about a dress code since TrendCelerate didn't have one. Her weird little T-shirts would fit right in with the nerd squad, as I affectionately thought of the techies who made up most of the company. The front desk job didn't pay a lot, but it sure paid more than nothing.

It took a couple of tries to figure out how to get my metaphysical fingernails between the refrigerator door and the magnet. I was concentrating so hard on that task that I almost missed the obvious.

I remember the first time I bought a magnetic poetry kit. I used it to leave funny notes on my friends' lockers at school. Of course, the notes almost always got mixed up and were twisted into the dirtiest sentences high schoolers could think of, much to the chagrin of the faculty. I'd bought more kits over the years, mixing sets and losing words as time passed. Ruby fiddled around with it on occasion. The current poem was a bit abstract for my taste:

> **birthday** is *FOR* fiddle AND WINE
> *ENJOY* **warm** MOON *IN* **high** seas
> ALONE A **peach-y** *BEAR* nears

"You have got to be kidding," I muttered to myself, which was redundant. Everything I said—up until now at least—was to myself. I stared at the random words as a grin spread across my face. Of course. The answer was right in front of me all along.

I could have sorted through the jumbled pile of words, and later, I would take the time to organize them somehow to make them easier, but for now, I had what I needed. I slid one word away from the rest, pushing it slowly to a blank space on the refrigerator.

HIGH

Behind me, I heard Ruby let out a soft gasp. "High?" she said, reading the word I'd isolated. "Oh, you mean *hi*. Well, 'high' back to you, ghost of Cordelia Graves."

I almost collapsed in relief. It might be clunky, but we finally had a way to communicate.

CHAPTER SEVEN

RUBY

I couldn't believe my eyes. My very own ghost was sending me messages with old refrigerator magnets. I'd meant to toss those out ages ago. I mean, sure, they were popular back in the nineteen somethings, but so was David Hasselhoff. Some vintage things defied explanation.

The poetry magnets were dingy with years of kitchen grease and fingerprints. They were all slightly different colors, sizes, and fonts, as if someone had combined words from a dozen different sets. One day, as I was waiting for coffee to brew, I started peeling them off the fridge. And I do mean peeling—they were stuck. Eww. Anyway, I was about to throw them in the garbage when I accidentally made my first poem:

THE sky IS **lined** *WITH* WORDS
even *IF* **I** LOVED forever
YOU WERE **never**
enough *PROMISES*

Okay, I admit it. I'm no poet. But those strange, random lines hit me like the lyrics to a favorite song that felt like they were written just for me. I got it now, why every refrigerator in America at one time or another was plastered with these silly magnets. They're fun. And, apparently, they're a great way to communicate with dead people.

I had so many questions. "How many ghosts are in here right now?" I asked, thinking back to the scene in the library. I had a hunch that had been Cordelia throwing books around the stacks and pelting me with newspapers, but as far as I knew, the library—and my apartment—was wall-to-wall ghosts.

The magnets moved.

ALONE

That made me feel marginally better. If I'd been addressing a whole roomful of ghosts as "Cordelia," that would have been pretty embarrassing. "You are Cordelia Graves, right?"

y

"Why? I guess I just want to know what to call you. I mean, I assume you're Cordelia because the last person who lived here . . ." My voice trailed off.

The magnet moved. The "**y**" was replaced with a "**yes**."

"Ah, I get it." I had to stop being so literal. Sure, I was basically texting with a dead person, minus the emojis, but I needed to remember that she was old, like in her forties old. I kinda wished the magnet set included emojis, at least the poop emoji. I never got tired of that one. I could live without the eggplant, though. I was letting myself get distracted. "Okay, so there's only one ghost in here right now and it's you, Cordelia." The magnet didn't move. "How many ghosts are there in the building? I bet there are lots."

ALONE

"Not even Jake from across the hall?" I asked. I didn't know how any of this worked, but I guess I'd assumed anyone who died would stick around as a ghost.

The single word stayed where it was.

"Well, that sucks. Don't you ever get lonely?"

you

noise

I had to giggle at that one. "No kidding. My mom says I never shut up. You'd like her, my mom."

WATER

I stared at that one for a moment. "You're thirsty?" Then I realized that more magnets were moving, shuffling as she searched for another word.

WATER planet

Now I was stumped. "Hold your roll. You're not... from a different planet, are you?" I was already excited that my apartment came with its very own ghost, but an alien ghost? I mean, there's cool, and then there is alien-ghost-from-another-planet cool.

The word "planet" disappeared, replaced with "**FLOWER**."

"Ohh! You want me to water the *plant*." There were only so

many words to choose from, and Cordelia was doing the best she could with what she had to work with. This was going to take some getting used to.

I ran some water from the sink into a clean mug and brought it over to the big, leafy plant. I touched the soil. It was dry. "Sorry, plant," I told it. Obviously, I wasn't the best plant caretaker in the world. After I moved in, I'd spent a few hours in the library identifying all the different houseplants and what I was supposed to do with them, but I'd still managed to kill most of them. I'd read that they like it when you talk to them, and so I tried to chat up the last remaining plant as often as possible. "You must be thirsty. I'll try to remember to water you more often."

"Wait a second." I turned to where I presumed Cordelia was. "You can move things. I've seen you do it." Although, more often than not, I saw things appear where they hadn't been before rather than watching them float through the air. I wondered why that was. Maybe I couldn't see something when Cordelia was touching it? Or maybe she moved too fast for me to keep up? "Why didn't you water your plants instead of watching idly as they died of thirst?"

As I sat the mug down on the windowsill, something glided under it, which kinda ruined my theory of not seeing objects that Cordelia was holding. "Come on, Cordelia, you can't be serious. It's a windowsill, one that could use a little TLC at that, not a fine antique table. I don't think I need a coaster." The mug slid to one side and I realized that it wasn't sitting on a coaster. It was sitting on another magnet.

I picked it up. The magnet was shaped like a gear and was about the size of the palm of my hand. "TrendCelerate," I said, reading the name in the center. Then I remembered what I'd read on Cordelia's LinkedIn page. "You worked there, didn't you?" I studied it. The graphic was bold, with good use of primary colors. It was eye-catching, but I didn't understand what my ghostly roomie was trying to tell me. "What about it?"

There was no answer, not like I expected one. Then I remembered the refrigerator and turned toward it in time to see words shifting and moving as I walked into the kitchen. "Don't get me wrong, this is the bee's knees, but unless I drag this fridge with me everywhere I go, our conversations are going to be limited."

need HAVE MOON-y

"Yes," I agreed. "I need money. Which means I need a job." I looked down at the magnet in my hand. "What do they even do?" I read the tagline on the magnet. "'*Developing the future of transformation.*' That tells me nothing. Less than nothing." I flipped over the magnet as if there might be a clue on the back. There was only the dark gray magnet backing. "I don't think I'm exactly qualified to develop the future of transformation," I said.

ask from DRESS

I stared at the words. They made no sense to me. I shook my head. "What's that supposed to mean? You gotta give me more to work with here."

CALL
copy
DATE
LETTER

"Not any clearer," I muttered. "Wait a second. Answer calls? Make copies? Keep calendars? Sort mail? Not *from dress*. You mean *front desk*, don't you?"

y

Now we were getting somewhere. I'd had lots of jobs. I worked at the drive-thru window at a national fast-food chain, and got fired for chatting with the customers too much. I did check-out at a grocery store and got let go for ringing up organic produce as iceberg lettuce once too often. I answered the phones at my uncle's muffler shop one summer while I was in high school and—minus the smell of oil and grease that never fully washed out of my hair—I liked it. Then my cousin moved back home and wanted her old job back.

"I can answer phones," I said. "And make copies and file stuff." The job did sound perfect for me, but if it was so great, why was there an opening? For that matter, how would Cordelia know there was an opening? "You don't, like, go to your old job every day, do you?" I asked. I stopped short of telling her that was cringe. "I mean, I've heard of places that work you to death, but you're free now."

The magnets didn't move. I didn't know whether to interpret that as an admission that she *did* in fact still haunt her old job or if she didn't. Either way, a front desk job at a swanky tech company downtown with an indecipherable mission statement sounded a bit out of my reach. "I'm qualified to answer phones and stuff, don't get me wrong, but don't places like that normally want references? I guess they can call my uncle, but I worked for him years ago, and he's my uncle. He's not exactly an unbiased referral."

WE

Then the magnet swung around until it was upside down.

3M

It took me a second to figure out what she meant. "Me? You want me to use you as a reference? How would that conversation go? 'Hi, yeah, I'm calling about a job. How did I hear about you? The ghost in my apartment gave me your number.... Hello? Hello?'" I shook my head.

I heard a muffled voice, and for a split second, I thought Cordelia was answering me. Yes, I knew how crazy that sounded but stranger things had happened. Stranger things were *currently* happening, right here in my apartment. Then I realized that the voices were coming from the hall. I slapped the TrendCelerate magnet back on the fridge. "Hold on," I said. "Be right back."

Out in the hall, the neighbor who lived across from me and one door down, Milly the busybody, was arguing with a man I didn't recognize. Milly had been one of the people who'd been so eager to gossip about Cordelia when I first moved in. She had tried to talk her way into my apartment several times to, in her words, "get a better look at where that poor girl died." And now, here she was again, right after the death of another resident, standing at his front door. Either she was a ghoul, or my neighbor was a serial killer.

She didn't look like a serial killer, but then again, no one looked like a serial killer. Or everyone did. I guess that's kind of the whole point. Other than having two neighbors die within a few months of each other, there was nothing suspicious about her, so if she was a serial killer, her disguise was working.

Milly was a tiny woman, white with brassy red hair despite being in her mid to late seventies. She reminded me of a Shar-Pei whose wrinkles had wrinkles, and she wore a yellow velour track suit today. She was inches away from a man several feet taller than she was, and was poking a finger into his chest. "And I'm telling you, you got no business being here," she said in a manner that made me think it wasn't her first time saying it.

"Listen here, lady, I got as much right as anyone," he replied with a slight slur in his speech. His eyes were bloodshot and he had a thick Boston accent, the kind that when I'd heard it in movies before moving here, I assumed was an exaggeration. It wasn't. He added *r* sounds to words that didn't have an *r* in them, and dropped the *r* in words that did. He had short, dark hair that stood up with the help of shiny gel and wore a gold saint medal on a chain around his neck. Despite the freezing cold outside, he wore an orange sleeveless puffer vest instead of an actual coat.

"What's going on?" I asked.

Milly turned to me. "Caught this hoodlum trying to break into Jake's apartment," she said.

Gotta love it. Here we were, in the not-nicest neighborhood, and when a little old woman hears someone trying to break into a locked door, does she call the cops? Does she grab a baseball bat? Nope. She charges in, tiny and unarmed, to confront them.

The irony wasn't lost on me that I wasn't much bigger than Milly, was equally empty-handed, and had also charged out here without thinking. But there was safety in numbers, I told myself, and I wasn't alone. I had my very own ghost by my side. Besides, if we made enough of a racket, maybe one of the other neighbors on this floor would have the good sense to dial 9–1–1 and let the professionals sort things out.

"Why were you breaking in?" I asked, drawing myself up to

my full height, not that I would have been intimidating even on stilts.

To his defense, he didn't pretend that he hadn't been caught in the act. "I'm not breaking in. It's my cousin's apartment." He turned away from Milly and held out his hand. When he spoke, I could smell sour beer on his breath. "Jake said the chick across the hall was cute. He's not wrong." He waited a beat. "I'm Bobby. And what's your name, cutie?"

I ignored his question and let his hand hang in the air. He was twenty years older than me and wore a wedding band. Eww. "Jake's not home."

Eventually taking the hint that I wasn't going to shake his hand, he dropped his arm by his side. "No shit Jake's not home. He's dead. Dead men don't come home, not as a rule."

I shrugged. Yesterday, I might have agreed with him. Today, not so much.

"Dead or not, you don't get to go snooping around his apartment," Milly said, crossing her arms over her chest.

"Who said anything about snooping?" Bobby asked. "I came to get some of my cousin's things for Aunt Jackie."

"Like what?" Milly asked.

"Like an outfit? For the funeral?" Bobby's answers sounded like questions.

"We'll just see about that," Milly said, turning and disappearing into her apartment. She threw the deadbolt with a loud thud.

Our apartment was advertised as having state-of-the-art security, which was no more than an old-fashioned buzzer system on the front door that constantly glitched, interior doors that locked automatically when they closed—whether you wanted them to or not—and a deadbolt. I'd found out about the automatic locking doors the day I moved in. I'd run downstairs for the final load of my stuff—I didn't have much, which was why finding a fully furnished apartment had seemed like such a bargain at the time—and the door locked behind me. I had to call the building manager, and he charged me to come unlock the door even though he lived on the second floor and all it cost him was walking up two flights of stairs. Soon afterward, I realized that my lock didn't engage if the door wasn't deliberately pulled completely shut, but by then I'd learned my lesson to always take my key with me when I left my apartment, just in case.

"You think she's calling the cops?" Bobby asked, sagging against the wall and looking like he was going to cry, pass out, or both.

"Either that, or the super," I said. With Milly, it was hard to tell. If she believed Bobby's story about being Jake's cousin, and she got the building manager to unlock the door, she'd have a chance to poke around the dead man's apartment. If she thought Bobby was lying, she might call the police, but there was only a fifty-fifty chance they'd bother showing up for something like this. "You really Jake's cousin?" I asked.

"Yup." He pulled out his wallet, flipped it open, and shoved it at me.

"'Robert Macintyre,'" I read off his license. "Doesn't prove anything. That's a common enough last name."

"It's Bobby," he corrected me. "Not Robert."

"Mercer Street. Where's that?" I asked before handing it back.

"Southie," he said.

South Boston, much like my own neighborhood, was working class. In the summer, it would smell of hot dogs grilling. Kids would play ball in the street. In the winter, the uneven sidewalks were shoveled free of snow by the homeowners and local business owners long before the city came by with plows.

"Sorry about your cousin," I said.

"Thanks." He glanced back at Jake's door. "Any chance you got a key?"

I shook my head. "We weren't that close. Doesn't your family have a spare somewhere?"

He shrugged and blinked hard. "Maybe. Probably. I ransacked Aunt Jackie's junk drawer." He pulled a handful of loose keys out of the pocket of his sleeveless coat. "None of them are labeled. And none of them fit."

Call me a sucker if you will, but if one of my cousins had just died a sudden and violent death, I would be a wreck. Bobby looked like he was barely holding it together. "A little help?" I whispered, hoping Cordelia was nearby.

"What was that?" he asked, tilting his head and studying me with glassy green eyes.

"I asked if you could use a little help," I repeated.

"Gee, duh. Isn't that what I just asked for?" He straightened and glared at the door. He rattled the knob, then kicked the bottom of the door for good measure. It swung open.

CHAPTER EIGHT
CORDELIA

"'A little help,' she says," I muttered to myself. How on earth was I supposed to help Ruby break into Jake's apartment? It wasn't like she and drunko cousin over there could walk through the door.

Wait one second. They couldn't. But I could.

I slipped through the door and glanced around. It looked exactly the same as when the police left. Jake's keys were still in the bowl next to the door, along with ticket stubs, a handful of coins, an ID badge on a lanyard, his wallet, and a half-empty packet of gum. I picked up the keys and headed back into the hall, but halfway through, I stuck fast. My body could pass through the door, but my hand holding the keys could not. Bummer.

I stepped back through the door and dropped the useless keys back into the bowl. The deadbolt was already open—the police hadn't bothered with it—so all I needed was to disengage the automatic lock. The door handle rattled from the other side. The cousin, I presumed, or maybe Ruby, was trying to open it. I twisted the knob and the door flew open.

"How . . . ?" Bobby asked, stepping into the apartment. He shook his head.

"Old building," Ruby explained, following him inside.

He accepted her explanation without questioning it further and headed straight for the refrigerator. Like mine, it was covered in magnets. But unlike mine, each magnet pinned a take-out flyer to the door. There were layers of menus and coupons so thick that I was surprised the magnets didn't slide off.

He opened the refrigerator, pulled out a beer, popped the top, and took a deep swig. Then he raised his arm as if making a toast to an invisible friend. "To Jakey. Gone too soon." I was tempted to return the toast, but refrained. Bobby looked in rough enough shape already without having to see a beer fly through the air on its own.

Ruby followed Bobby around the small apartment. "Where did you guys grow up?" she asked.

"Southie," he said, pulling the silverware organizer out of the drawer and inspecting it before putting it back.

"What was Jake like as a kid?"

"Same as ever. You know, life of the party." Bobby was checking the cabinets now, opening and closing pots with lids on them before restacking them the way he'd found them.

"I actually didn't know that," Ruby said. She wasn't being completely honest. She'd lived across the hall from him long enough to know that he had friends over constantly. But I had to admit, she was good at getting Bobby to talk. "We weren't close. Did he have a lot of friends?"

"Tons. Everyone loved Jake." Bobby moved into the living room. He shuffled through the stack of grease-stained paper plates and old magazines on the low coffee table. "He was a good dude."

"Yup," Ruby agreed.

I'd never had a problem with Jake. He wasn't the quietest

neighbor I'd ever had, but he wasn't the loudest, either. He was always helpful. I'd asked to borrow a screwdriver to fix a loose leg on my coffee table once, and he insisted on fixing it for me. He even sanded down the other leg that was always a hair too long. And he didn't ask for anything in return.

He was different with Ruby. More attentive. He showed up a couple of times, knocking on her door at odd hours to invite her over for pizza or beer. He asked if she wanted to meet him at the bar on the corner, and even once dropped by with extra hockey tickets. He never made any overtures like that to me. Guess I wasn't his type.

Then again, I was in my forties, rarely bothered with makeup, and would never fit into a size ten. Ruby was young. Perky. Cute. Petite. Guys liked that. Not that I was complaining. Jake wasn't my type, either. I had a thing for nerdy businessmen in suit jackets who drove Beemers and collected vintage comic books. What could I say? I knew what I liked. Or at least what I used to like.

"Where did Jake work?" Ruby asked, continuing to pepper Bobby with questions.

He chugged the rest of the beer and dropped the empty on the coffee table. "Warehouse out by the shipyard," he replied. That didn't narrow it down by much. There were dozens of warehouses, maybe more, down by the shipyard. He bent over, checking under the enormous sectional.

"How's the pay out there?" she asked. I knew Ruby needed work. Soon. With Jake gone, they were likely hiring, but I had doubts that Ruby would have what it took to fill his shoes. She had moxie in spades, but was lacking in upper-body strength and had to stretch to reach the top cabinet in our kitchen. I couldn't picture her working in a warehouse, at least not for long.

"Enough to keep Jake's bookie in business, if you know what

I mean," Bobby said as he flipped through a lopsided stack of the sports sections pulled out of newspapers.

"Did Jake gamble a lot?" Ruby asked.

"Define 'a lot,'" Bobby replied. He felt around the cushions of the sectional like he was looking for lost change. Not finding whatever he was looking for in the couch, he tried to peer behind the TV. Like mine, it was mounted flush to the wall with little space to hide anything behind it.

"Whatcha looking for?" she asked. "I doubt his suits are in the cushions. They're probably in his closet."

"Maybe he's looking for the gun," I said aloud. "It was stashed in the toilet tank."

I wondered about the gun. What was Jake doing with it? If he needed a gun for protection, wouldn't he keep it someplace more convenient than the toilet? If he was into something nefarious, there would be more signs around his apartment. Drugs. Drug paraphernalia. Cash. The cops hadn't found anything like that. Then again, from what I'd seen, their search hadn't been quite as thorough as Bobby's.

So far, Bobby seemed as harmless as his cousin, but if he knew about the gun, he could know more about whatever shady stuff Jake was into that might have gotten him killed.

"Nothing," he said.

"If I knew what we were looking for, I could help," Ruby offered.

"He knows something, Ruby," I said, for all the good it would do. It wasn't like she could hear me. "Keep asking questions."

"His watch, okay?" Bobby said.

"His watch?" I asked.

"His watch?" Ruby echoed.

"I'm looking for his watch. It's a family heirloom. It was our great-grandfather's. Jake wore it all the time, but it wasn't in his personal effects."

"And you thought it might be in the silverware drawer or under the living room couch?" Ruby asked.

"You never know with Jake," he said, as if that explained it. "Have you seen it?"

"I wouldn't know," Ruby said.

"It's old. Silver face with a leather band. There's an engraved message from Pops on the back," Bobby said, describing the watch.

Ruby shrugged. "I never noticed any watch."

The beaded curtain rattled as Bobby moved into the bedroom and started searching through the nightstand. He pulled out a box of condoms and dumped them on the mussed silk sheets on the bed. There were only three condoms left in the box, and no watch.

"Did Jake have a girlfriend?" Ruby asked.

"He had lots of girls," he answered, nodding at the nearly empty box of condoms. "And lots of friends. Don't know that any of them stuck around long enough to qualify as a girlfriend."

"But he had lots of friends, though?" Ruby asked. I was proud of her. She was asking all the right questions. It wasn't her fault that Jake's cousin didn't have any useful answers. "Need help calling them? You know, to invite them to the funeral? We could make a list."

Bobby squatted on the floor so he could see under the bed. I crouched next to him. There was a phone plugged into a charger that had slipped between the nightstand and the mattress. I scooted away before my presence could scramble its circuits. He looked up at Ruby. "You ask a lot of questions."

"I'm a talker," she said.

"Understatement of the century," I added.

"We've got it covered."

"Got what covered?" Ruby asked, sounding innocent.

"The service. The friends. All of it. Look, lady—"

"Ruby," she interrupted him.

"Look, *Ruby*, I appreciate your help and all, but I'm good here. Why don't you run along?"

She bobbed her head. "Sure, sure. But how about I fetch you another beer first?" Without waiting for him to agree, she stepped into the kitchen and pulled another beer out of the fridge. She handed it to Bobby, who was now rummaging through the closet. I had to admit, she was a natural at this snooping business. "That suit's nice," she said, pointing to the only one hanging in the closet.

"Nah," Bobby said. He flipped through hangers with one hand and chugged his beer with the other. "Jake wouldn't be caught dead in that monkey suit." The irony of that statement went over his head. He pulled out two Boston Bruins hockey sweaters. "Orr or Pasta?"

"Umm, Orr?" Ruby said.

"Good call." He tossed the Orr sweater onto the bed and hung the other one back up. I didn't know much about hockey, but even I had heard of Bobby Orr, who had retired just before I was born. "It's a classic."

"You're going to bury your cousin in a hockey jersey?" Ruby asked.

"Sweater," he corrected her. "And, yeah. It's what Jake would have wanted."

Personally, I didn't think Jake would have wanted to be shot in the forehead and left out in the snow for hours. He wouldn't have wanted to be dead at all. But would he want to be buried in a vintage Boston Bruins sweater? Yeah, that tracked.

"And are you going to bury him with his great-granddad's watch, too?" Ruby asked.

"Hell no. That watch is mine, now."

Geez, priorities.

"It must be worth a lot," Ruby said.

I'd had some less-than-charitable thoughts about Ruby since she moved in. She killed my houseplants. She talked incessantly. She killed my houseplants. She was just so damn cheery all the time, even when she had no reason to be. And, oh yeah, she murdered my houseplants. But as far as investigation partners went? She kinda rocked. Although, she'd probably say she "slayed" or something. Honestly, I never felt old until Ruby moved in. I didn't understand her half the time, and she didn't understand me at all. Some team we were turning out to be.

"What's worth a lot?" Bobby asked. He'd moved into the bathroom and was going through the medicine cabinet. I hadn't understood why Jake had hidden his gun in the toilet tank, but other than setting his beer down on top of the tank while he checked the rest of the bathroom, Bobby hadn't taken any notice of the toilet itself, so maybe it was smarter than I'd thought.

"The watch," Ruby said. "The watch that you're looking for?"

"The watch has sentimental value. To the family."

"Because it was your great-grandfather's."

"Yup," he confirmed. "He brought it over with him from Ireland. Only thing he had worth more than two pennies, and he managed to keep hold of it. I'm not gonna be the one to let the family down by losing it."

Technically, if it was missing, hadn't Jake lost the watch? Not that I had a voice in this conversation. Literally.

"Tell me more about this girlfriend," Ruby prompted.

"I already said, there was no girlfriend," Bobby said.

Ruby gestured at the box of tampons stored under the sink.

"Yeah, one hundred percent. Because most bachelors keep feminine hygiene products just in case."

In my experience, some guys did. But guys like that didn't stay single for long, and Jake was a dyed-in-the-wool bachelor. I had trouble picturing him as the kind of man who kept Band-Aids in his medicine cabinet, much less feminine hygiene products.

Bobby shrugged. "I mean, I guess he *had* a girlfriend, but I think they broke up."

Well, wasn't that interesting? I'd learned more about Jake today than I had during the years we were neighbors. I now knew he had a gun hidden in his apartment, wore a family heirloom watch that was currently missing, and had recently broken up with his girlfriend. None of it explained why he was murdered, but it was a start.

"What's her name?" Ruby asked.

"Whose name?" he asked. He upended the box of tampons on the floor. Either he was easily distracted, or he'd had enough beers for the day.

"Your cousin's girlfriend?" Ruby prompted.

"Why would I know that?" He sounded defensive.

"You knew *my* name," Ruby pointed out.

"No, I knew that Jake said some cute chick moved in across the hall after the redhead killed herself." Bobby sat down on the bathroom floor. "It's not here."

"I'm sure it will turn up," Ruby assured him.

"Yeah. Maybe. Hey, can I see your phone?" he held out his hand. Ruby handed it to him. He punched a few buttons. "You've got my number now. Call me if the watch shows up. Or, you know, if you need a friend or something. In the meantime, I kinda need to be alone. Grab me another beer on your way out?"

"Um, sure thing," Ruby said, taking her phone back. I couldn't imagine her calling Bobby anytime soon, at least not because she was lonely. She headed to the kitchen, but instead of reaching inside the fridge, she poured a glass of water from the tap and took it to him. "Maybe try this instead," she said, handing him the glass. "We'll let ourselves out."

"We?" Bobby asked, studying her quizzically. "I told you, I'm staying here for a bit."

"We, as in the royal we, of course," she said, forcing a laugh. "What else could I possibly mean? It's not like there's a ghost in here with us or anything." She backed toward the door. "Wouldn't that be silly? Ha ha. No such thing as ghosts, no sirree."

"Weird chick," Bobby muttered as Ruby opened the door and stepped into the hall. "Cute, but weird."

CHAPTER NINE

RUBY

There was a knock on my front door.

I glanced over my shoulder, wondering if I was hearing things. I couldn't remember the last time anyone had knocked on my door. Food and package delivery drivers never made it past the downstairs lobby, which probably had something to do with the fact that I lived on the fourth floor and there was an "out of order" sign on the elevator. Even if I had been expecting a delivery—and I wasn't—no one had buzzed in from downstairs.

There was another knock.

I approached the door quietly, so I could pretend to not be home if it was someone I didn't want to talk to, like a big scary dude or the building manager. I wasn't behind on my rent, not really. I was still within the grace period. Kind of. But the person at the door was a stranger, and unintimidating. I opened the door.

A Black woman stood in the hall. She was maybe a decade older than me, if that, and five or six inches taller than I was. However, she was wearing heels, so maybe we were closer in height than

I first assumed. I didn't know what kind of person wore heels in Boston in the winter. Someone with a car and good parking spot karma, I guessed.

"Hello?" I asked.

"Hi!" she said, and walked right past me, straight into my living room. She took the time to get a good look. Was it my imagination, or did she stiffen when her gaze reached the bathroom? I must have been mistaken, because she finished her brief visual inspection of my apartment before proclaiming brightly, "Charming place you got here."

"Um, thanks?" I said, still standing in the open doorway. I had to twist around to address her. "I don't remember inviting you in."

"I don't mind," she said. She had a pretty smile, but there was something disingenuous about it, as if she practiced it in the mirror every morning to make sure it was perfect. She didn't strike me as the kind of woman who ever got lipstick on her teeth. Or someone who waited for invitations, apparently.

"Who are you?" I asked. Other than the fact that she'd walked right into my apartment and made herself at home, there was nothing threatening about her. If anything, it felt like she was an old friend even though we'd hardly exchanged a dozen words. I felt oddly at ease with her.

"Penny. Penny Fisher. And you're Ruby?"

"No, I mean who *are* you? And what do you want?"

"Oh! I'm so sorry." She touched her breastbone and looked aghast, but I got the impression she was more worried that I had no idea who she was than the fact that she'd all but broken into my apartment. "I'm a reporter. For the *Herald*? I called earlier and left a message. I assumed you were expecting me." She glanced around again before sitting on the loveseat.

"I didn't get any message," I said. Then again, my phone was nearly out of minutes and I wasn't in the habit of wasting them on checking voicemail when no one I knew would ever leave a voicemail, not even my mom. If Mom wanted to talk, she'd text me, like any normal person would.

"My bad," she said, grinning again. "Let's start over from the beginning, shall we?" She pulled her phone out of her bag, launched a recording app, and balanced it on her knee. "I'm Penny Fisher, from the *Herald*. I'm doing a story about your neighbor, Jacob Macintyre. Do you mind if I record this conversation?"

"Jake's dead," I said, the words coming out of my mouth before I could stop myself. I glanced down at her phone. Even when I wasn't talking, the recording line was going haywire. Remembering the effect Cordelia'd had on the library's computer, I wondered if that was her interference.

"Thus, the story," she said brightly. "Would you be more comfortable if you sat down?" She patted the loveseat cushion next to her. "Don't be shy, Ruby. It is Ruby, right?"

I nodded and took the seat that she indicated, pulling the throw pillow onto my lap. "Ruby Young."

"Nice to meet you, Ruby Young." She sat back and studied my living area. I had a good idea what she was seeing—a twenty-year-old woman living in a much older woman's space. There should be posters on the walls, not built-in bookcases filled with newish paperbacks. I should have water-stained rings on the coffee table and maybe a beer bong, not marble coasters and the December *Vanity Fair*. In print.

Sometimes it was hard to remember that Cordelia was only in her forties. Her style was hand-me-down chic. I wouldn't have been surprised if her grandma decorated this apartment.

The reporter focused on the large green plant in the corner, the one Cordelia had to remind me to water. "That's a very nice plant. What is it?"

"Not sure." I'd looked up all the plants when I first moved in, trying to figure out how to care for them, but I'd long since forgotten what this one was called.

"Well, it's very nice, whatever kind it is. Now, how about you start with how long you've lived here and how well you knew Jake Macintyre."

I shrugged. "Six weeks, give or take, and I didn't, not really."

"Six weeks? Really, is that all?" She looked around again, this time really taking in every detail as if she might be asked to describe it later. "You're very settled for having just moved in. I swear, I moved in with my girlfriend six months ago, and half my stuff is still in boxes. Drives her up the wall."

"The apartment came fully furnished," I said. I didn't know why I felt the need to explain anything to her. There was just something about her that made me feel comfortable, like I could tell her anything. Which, come to think of it, was probably the point. She wouldn't be a very good reporter otherwise. "Move-in ready."

"That's convenient. And you say you didn't know Jake?" she asked.

"Not really, no."

She sat forward in her chair. "I met him once. Not too long ago," she confided in me. "He was, well, he was a lot, wasn't he?"

I shrugged again. "Like I said—"

"You didn't know him that well. Gotcha," she finished for me. "He was one of those guys that was larger than life, you know? Makes an impression on people. I bet he was a loud neighbor, right? Always having people over. The life of the party."

"Yeah, I guess. He had people over sometimes. They weren't

that loud." I heard him through the walls when he had friends or dates over, and I could hear his TV when he didn't have company. But it didn't bother me much. I grew up in a house with two boisterous sisters—one older and one younger. Plus, we always seemed to have a friend or cousin staying with us. I didn't know what to do with myself when it was quiet.

"You know he's dead, obviously, but do you know how it happened?"

"Shouldn't you be talking to the police about that?" I asked, suddenly nervous. What did she think I could tell her that the cops didn't already know?

She flapped a dismissive hand at me and settled back against the cushions. "Of course, I already did. I just wanted to hear what *you* thought."

I certainly wasn't about to tell her that the ghost of the former occupant of this apartment and I had been poking our noses into places we didn't belong, like a dead man's apartment. I doubt that was the kind of story Penny Fisher was sniffing around for. Besides, if Cordelia had wanted to make her presence known, she would have done so by now. On the contrary, it felt like the apartment was holding its breath.

"I don't really have an opinion, to be honest," I said, then immediately regretted it. Any time someone said "to be honest," they usually were hiding something, much in the way that anyone who said "trust me" was usually the last person you should trust.

"And you don't think it's weird?" she asked, letting the question hang in the air.

Fine. I'd bite. "What's weird?" I asked.

"Two people, living on the same floor of the same apartment building, dying just months apart? Under suspicious circumstances? You wouldn't call that a little odd?"

"What do you mean?" I asked. Jake's death was certainly disturbing. A man I knew, a neighbor, killed right outside my apartment building made me justifiably nervous. I wanted the killer caught before he hurt anyone else—especially if that someone else turned out to be me—and the police weren't being very proactive. I didn't expect around-the-clock surveillance or anything, but a cursory inspection of the victim's apartment and a shrug of the shoulders didn't seem sufficient, either.

But suspicious? A mugging in this neighborhood didn't actually qualify as suspicious. Assuming, of course, that the cops were right and Jake died from a mugging gone wrong. But why would a mugger not take his phone? There was enough doubt that I was willing to go along with Cordelia to snoop around his apartment when his cousin Bobby showed up, especially after that trick with the newspapers about the Boston murder rate earlier.

"You don't know, do you?" Penny said. She leaned forward again, as if letting me in on a big secret. "The woman who lived here before you killed herself around Christmas."

"Oh, she did?" I asked meekly, as if I hadn't researched the suspiciously furnished apartment before I signed the lease. As if my neighbors hadn't delighted in telling me all about it. As if I hadn't been having a full-on conversation with the ghost of Cordelia Graves this very afternoon.

Even if Jake's death didn't quite sit well with me, the circumstances around Cordelia's death were completely different. Her accidental-on-purpose overdose was tragic, of course, but was an open-and-shut case. A chronically depressed woman committing suicide near Christmas wasn't suspicious. It was a statistic.

"The holidays can be hard," I murmured. Not that I would know. I hadn't been alone for a major holiday even once in my life. President's Day didn't count. I was already counting down the days until Memorial Day, so I would have an excuse to take the long train ride back home to Baltimore, even if it was just for a few days.

Yes, moving to Boston was all my idea. No one had made me do it. Sure, it had been a little rash. And maybe not *quite* thought out but still, it was all mine. I needed a fresh start, far away from my cheating ex, Jerky McJerkface. I trusted my willpower about as much as I trusted my taste in men, which was zero. I'd seen what happened when my cousin took back her worthless boyfriend time after time. Now, she was single and raising two kids alone while living with her parents, but it was just a matter of time before she gave him another chance and the cycle started all over again.

I wasn't going to fall into that trap, which was exactly why Boston was the perfect place to start over. It was far enough away that I wouldn't be tempted to go home every weekend, but if I wanted to go for a visit, I could. I needed to prove to everyone—especially myself—that I could stand on my own two feet. Even if those two feet were still freezing no matter how many layers of socks I wore.

"I heard someone saw a man leaving this apartment near the time of Cordelia's death. A well-dressed man carrying a bag. Ring any bells?"

"That was before my time," I told her. I'd been so distracted by memories of home, and why I'd left, that I hadn't been paying much attention to the reporter. But that particular phrase did sound familiar. I remember reading it at the library, before the monitor went kaput. "Wait a second. You're the one that wrote that article," I said. "The article about Cordelia's suicide."

"I did," Penny said, straightening. "I thought you didn't know about the former tenant? So how did you know her name and that I wrote an article about her death?"

"I, um . . ." I tried to remember what I'd said. That was the problem with lying. It made it hard to keep my story straight. "I guess it must have slipped my mind?" I said meekly, but it came out more like a question.

"It must have," she agreed cheerfully, as if people moved into apartments all the time without ever thinking twice about the previous occupant killing herself in the bathroom every single time they brushed their teeth. Or, maybe I was the weirdo for doing my research. "Apparently, Miss Graves didn't have company over often. Hardly ever, in fact."

"Is that so?" I asked. I didn't know why that tidbit surprised me. What did I know about Cordelia, other than she had horrific taste in clothes, drank too much, and wanted me to help her solve a murder? I knew nothing about her friends, family, or social life.

"She'd lived in this building for several years, and the first time anyone saw a man coming or going from her apartment was right about the time she died. Curious."

"Is it?" Why didn't Cordelia have many visitors? I didn't have people over much, either, but I was new to the city. I didn't know anyone here. What was her excuse?

If Cordelia never had anyone over, there had to be a reason. Did she not have any friends? And if so, was she happy that I was here now, with her? Or, did she not invite anyone into her space on purpose? In that case, she must really hate my intrusion.

Not that I was intruding. This was my apartment now. If anything, Cordelia was the intruder. I'm sure she saw it that way, too. As if.

"I'd say it's strange." She shrugged. "But what do I know? What's more curious to me, is when I was asking around, only one person saw this supposed visitor."

"And?" I asked. Trying to follow this conversation was making my head hurt.

"It was Jake Macintyre." She let that sink in. "And now he's dead, too."

I had to admit that was weird. Whoever was seen leaving Cordelia's apartment—my apartment—that night might have been the last person to see her alive. Maybe he knew something about her state of mind. Maybe he even knew why she had killed herself. That would be good information to have, seeing as Cordelia didn't leave a note and I didn't feel right asking her directly. I'd love to track him down and ask him all these questions, but the only person who knew what he looked like was Jake, and Jake wouldn't be talking to anyone anymore.

Maybe Milly had seen the man, too. If anyone saw anything out of the ordinary, normally it would have been the neighborhood busybody.

Penny got up and pulled a business card out of her purse. "It was awful nice chatting with you, Ruby Young." It sounded weird, the way she kept repeating my name. Then again, I'd heard that repeating a name as often as possible when you first met someone was a good trick to help remember people's names.

I had to glance at the business card to remember Penny's last name, so maybe there was something to that. "Nice to meet you too, Penny Fisher."

"If you hear or see anything odd, you will give me a call, won't you?" she asked, but it was more of a command than a question. Penny Fisher was good at her job.

"Of course," I promised.

"Excellent. I'll see myself out," she said. Then she left.

I studied the card in my hand. "Call her if I see anything odd," I repeated with a chuckle. The card was yanked out of my hands and ripped in half. The two pieces fluttered to the floor. "I don't suppose that counts as odd?" I said as I scooped up the pieces and shoved them into my pocket.

Cordelia didn't want me contacting Penny Fisher. Why not? The article she had written about her had been flattering, so there was no reason to dislike her. But who knew what was going on in Cordelia's head? It might come in handy to have a reporter in my contacts, just in case I ever needed one.

CHAPTER TEN

CORDELIA

For most people, the best part of being dead would be not ever having to go to work again.

Not me, though. I used to love my job at TrendCelerate. I was an office manager, and I was good at it. It felt satisfying to be the one responsible for everything being organized and in its place, especially when my personal life was a complete mess. Work me didn't have bad days. Work me was never lonely. Work me was confident, outgoing, friendly. Work me had a grip. The fact that I was, entirely by my own choice, back in the office months after my death was actually exciting.

"I can't do this," Ruby whispered under her breath.

"Yes, you can," I assured her. I knew she couldn't hear me but it was nice to have someone to talk to, even when our conversations were decidedly one way.

"Ruby Young?" The door to one of the offices opened and Sally Madison stuck her head out. Sally was TrendCelerate's HR rep. She was a pretty Black woman who was a few years younger than me. Most of the people in the office dressed like Ruby. "Professional attire" at a software development company normally meant clean-*ish* blue jeans paired with a polo shirt with the company logo embroidered on it. But Sally, like me, was more traditional.

I'd never been comfortable in casual wear at the office. Since I was behind the front desk, I was usually dressed in a skirt or slacks, paired with a nice blouse or sweater, unlike my coworkers, who often worked from home and, even when they were in the office, sometimes came in wearing sweats and ratty T-shirts. Sally took the dress code to the next level. Today she was in a navy blue pinstriped knee-length pencil skirt with a matching tailored blazer. Under the blazer, she had on a bright red silk blouse with a giant bow at the neckline. She wore shiny black high-heeled shoes that I knew from experience she would swap for snow boots before going outside.

"That's me," Ruby said, announcing herself as she jumped up from one of the guest chairs, as if she wasn't the only person in the lobby, at least the only one that Sally could see. There was no one behind the reception desk, which was the reason they were hiring.

I had absolute faith in Ruby that she would nail the job interview. Her personality would be a better fit at a hip, young company like TrendCelerate than mine had ever been. As long as she walked into Sally's office with confidence and was unapologetically herself, she'd get the job. If I was in there with her, I'd just be a distraction. Besides, I was feeling oddly nostalgic about being back here, and I wasn't sure I was up for listening to Sally talk about how it was a great place to work.

After I died, I began to wander farther and farther from my apartment, testing my limits and exploring nearby buildings that I'd never had an excuse to visit before. I even spent a few days wandering around the government offices, but that was even more boring than going through strangers' apartments.

As much as I'd liked working here while I was alive, the one place I'd steadfastly avoided after my death was TrendCelerate. But now that I was here, I figured I might as well take a look around. In stark comparison to the high-rises in downtown Boston, TrendCelerate was housed on the second floor of a three-story brick building on a mixed-use block. The first floor was a shoe store. The building was sandwiched between a dry cleaner and an apartment building with a fusion take-out restaurant on the ground floor.

The space was ringed with individual offices for the management staff. They had large windows that overlooked a tiny park and a busy street. The cubicles in the bullpen in the middle of the space didn't have windows, a view, or any natural light at all. No wonder so many employees preferred to work from home.

I wandered through the cubicles. I didn't know what I'd been expecting. Surely TrendCelerate wouldn't erect a shrine to me in the office or anything, but I'd hoped there would be something to mark the years I'd spent there. A plaque would have been nice, or a photo. Instead, it was the same old nameplates clipped to the same old cubicle walls.

When I'd worked there, I'd kept an overgrown pothos plant on my desk. Now it was on someone else's desk, next to a monitor and docking station with no laptop attached to it. The desk belonged to Melissa, one of the coders. A Mason jar of colorful pens sat next to her stapler, and a sweatshirt hung from the back of her ergonomic chair.

Melissa and I had been office friendly. We'd say hi when we passed each other in the kitchen on the way to the coffee maker, and she'd occasionally drop candy off on my desk for the whole office to share. We went to lunch together once or twice, but I'd never seen her outside of work or TrendCelerate events. I was surprised, and touched, that she was the one who'd ended up adopting my pothos, but it was clear that she was neglecting it.

A pothos didn't require a lot of attention, but like every other living thing, it needed water and light. If she'd brought it into the break room or even balanced it on the wall of her cubicle, it would have gotten at least a little light, but even worse, I could tell that no one was watering it.

I remembered Ruby's suggestion from earlier that I could just as easily water a neglected plant as I could ask her to do it. I felt bad that I hadn't thought of that myself sooner. I couldn't go back and save my other plants, but this one still stood a chance. I glanced around. Out of the twenty or so cubicles in the bullpen area, only three were occupied today. I could hear rapid clickity-clack keyboard strokes coming from two of them and a muffled conversation from the third. The nearest manager's door was closed.

No one was looking in this direction. There was a reusable steel bottle next to the keyboard. I lifted it. It felt at least half-full. I unscrewed the cap and sloshed the liquid around. I took a sniff to make sure it was just water in the bottle and not stale coffee or something, but I couldn't smell anything. Not that I should have expected to.

I could see as well now as I could when I'd been alive. Better, even. I could see in near darkness and could make out a license plate a block away. My hearing had improved, too. If I concentrated, I could hear every word of the conversation taking place in low tones in the cubicle on the other side of the office. One of the software testers, Seth, was on the phone making reservations at a fancy restaurant and kept his voice low to prevent anyone else in the office from overhearing, but to me, his words were as clear as if he were addressing me directly.

That was as far as my enhanced senses went. If I tried, I could pick up solid objects instead of my hand sliding right through them, but I couldn't tell if they were scalding hot, freezing cold, or anywhere in between. I'd tried drinking a beer. It had gone right through me. Literally. I couldn't taste a thing. Nor could I smell anything.

I'd tried to wrap my head around it and failed miserably. I didn't have taste buds. I didn't have nostrils. I didn't have skin. It made sense that I couldn't taste, smell, or feel anything. But on the converse, I couldn't explain how I had no eyes or ears but could see and hear better than I ever could when I was alive. Not that anything made sense anymore, but that made even less sense than the rest of it.

Maybe if I believed I could smell, I would be able to. I concentrated hard. I remembered what steel water bottles smelled like. They had a slightly tangy metallic scent that never fully went away no matter what liquid you put in them. The outside coating always smelled faintly of plastic.

Remembering what water was supposed to smell like was more difficult. Some people thought that water smelled like nothing at all, but then how could they explain the damp scent in the air before a good rain? I could remember how it tasted when an ice cube melted on my tongue, or the first swig of water out of a public faucet on a hot summer day in the park. Holding this memory of water in my head, I took another deep sniff of the bottle and instantly regretted it as the scent of pure alcohol hit me like a physical slap. I didn't know what was more shocking, that it worked or that the contents of the bottle smelled like nail polish remover.

I dropped the bottle. It bounced off the desk with a loud metallic clang. It toppled to one side and rolled, smacking into the armrest of the chair and skittering across the floor, leaving a trail of liquid, until it rolled to a halt under a man's shoe.

The man leaned down to pick up the bottle and it was as if the rest of the world faded away. Adam Rees was COO and cofounder of TrendCelerate. He was a tall, lanky, sharply dressed man who paired a suit jacket with blue jeans and rarely wore a tie. He wore silver-rimmed glasses and got a haircut once a week on his lunch break, so he always looked perfectly coiffed. He was married to Karin Rees, a Massachusetts senator with presidential ambitions. And up until a few days before my death, I thought he was the love of my life.

Sure, it was cliché. The office manager and one of the company founders, a married man. But the heart wanted what the heart wanted.

Becoming a ghost had a pesky side effect of blowing up any electronics I came into contact with, which was a good excuse for steering clear of an office where even the water cooler was connected to the internet. But if I was being honest with myself, which was something I avoided at all costs, I might admit that Adam was the real reason I hadn't been back to visit TrendCelerate after my death. I wasn't ready to see him again. Being in a secret on-again, off-again relationship with him for years had prepared me for standing right next to him without being able to touch him, but this was different. I could never touch him again, and my heart ached with that knowledge.

I knew the emotionally mature thing to do was to wish him happiness and peace, but it would have been nice to see some outward sign that he missed me as much as I missed him. Instead, he looked as perfect as ever, without so much as a hair out of place. Adam took a sniff of the now nearly empty water bottle. His face crinkled in disgust. "Whose is this?" he bellowed, his voice carrying easily around the nearly empty room. He often got invited to speak at tech symposiums, and knew how to command an audience's attention. "Anyone?"

Three heads popped over the cubicles like a nature documentary about meercats. I recognized them all. Seth, who'd wrapped up his phone call, was the youngest of the lot. He was a scrawny white man in his early twenties with bright carrot-orange hair that had been shaved on the sides and left curly on top. He used to loop me in for beta testing of new software, and I enjoyed finding things all the highly trained testers missed. I didn't know if that was a testimony to my thoroughness or evidence of the laziness of the other testers. Some of the programmers resented when I pointed out their bugs, but I was proud to be making our product better.

Marc was in the cubicle next to him. A Hispanic man in his late thirties, he was responsible for database administration. A year or so ago, Marc and his wife had twin daughters. About the same time, he started working from the office almost daily because it was, he claimed, the only place he could get any peace and quiet. He came in earlier than everyone else and left at noon so his wife could work from home in the morning and go into her office in the afternoon. The arrangement seemed to work for them, but sometimes he'd walk around the office like a zombie from lack of sleep.

The third employee was Blair, the bane of my work existence. Or, at least, he had been, back when I was alive. Blair could have been a walking advertisement for Nautica. White. Blond. Tan. Tall, but not too tall. He was on the crew team at college and liked to talk at length about his daddy's sailboat. He thought he was god's gift to women. Women thought otherwise.

Blair, like Melissa, was a coder. He was horrendously bad at it.

But his daddy, the one with the sailboat, had gone to college with one of the company's founders. They were in the same fraternity together. I knew this because Blair liked to brag about that fact, like it was some kind of achievement. "What's this all about?" he asked in a bored voice.

If it seemed like there were an inordinate number of men in the TrendCelerate office, that was because there were. Two of the three founders were male. The majority of the staff were also male. Myself, the CEO, Melissa, and Sally in HR were the exceptions. Presuming that Ruby got the job, she'd be another exception. But, if the bottle of liquor—cheap vodka judging by the rubbing alcohol smell of it—on Melissa's desk was any indication, she might not be employed here too much longer.

Adam shook the bottle. "Whose is this?" he repeated.

"It's not mine," Blair said. He picked up the plastic bottle off his desk and shook it. "I can't stand those reusable bottles. They taste like spit."

"Blair, I've already told you, we're trying to reduce single-use bottles in the office," Adam said with a sigh. "If you don't like the metal ones, we've got reusable plastic bottles in the break room."

"Yeah, but who's gonna clean them? It's not like Cordelia's around anymore to take care of the kitchen." I growled at him. Cleaning the kitchen had never been one of my official duties, but someone had to pick up after the slobs—like Blair—in the office, and that task usually fell to me.

Adam stiffened. I knew there were a million things he wanted to say in response, because he'd said them all to me in private. It was one of the many things we agreed on. Blair was an entitled ass. But even as a cofounder, Adam didn't have the power to fire him. "Seth? Marc?"

Marc shook his head and held up a coffee mug. "You know me." After the twins were born, Marc had started mainlining coffee. His daughters were his whole world, but I worried that if he didn't get a good night's sleep soon, he'd collapse.

Seth just shrugged. "Not mine, boss. What's the big deal, anyway?"

"None of you want to claim this bottle?" Adam said, instead of answering the question. "Care to explain what it was doing rolling across the floor?" All three employees looked at him as if expecting a punchline. "Bottles don't drop themselves," he said. "It had to be one of you."

"Adam?" Sally asked. She'd come out of her office with Ruby in tow. Ruby's head swiveled over the block of cubicles. To anyone else, it probably looked like she was checking out the office, but I knew she was looking for me. Which was ridiculous. I certainly couldn't give her a sign that I was here, not while Adam was already curious about the bottle.

Although, in fairness, he was mostly concerned about the alcoholic contents of the bottle. In my experience, people were quick to dismiss little things like bottles moving on their own as tricks of their imagination.

"Do I need to start bringing a Breathalyzer to work?" Adam asked, glaring at the three men. I thought his reaction was a little over-the-top, considering how many times he and I had gotten wasted together in his locked office during working hours.

"What's this all about?" Sally asked. Adam handed her the bottle. She took a sniff. Her nose wrinkled. She put the bottle down on a nearby desk. "We'll address this later. First, I want to introduce you to our office manager applicant, Ruby Young."

"Pleased to meet you, Ruby," Adam said with a polite nod in

her direction before returning his attention to the three other employees. "I'll deal with you guys later."

"I know you!" Ruby blurted out.

I froze. Had she seen something in my—I guess I should get used to calling it *our*—apartment that gave our secret relationship away? I couldn't imagine what it was. There were no pictures of him, and we didn't exchange long, handwritten love letters or anything that would get us caught. We'd always been so careful, but now Ruby was going to blow it.

"You do?" Adam asked. He didn't sound suspicious, but then again, he had no way of knowing that Ruby and I were roommates. I doubted he would ever put two and two together. He'd never come over, not even once, while I was living there. He shouldn't even know my address. And, unless he read her application, he wouldn't know her address, either.

"I saw your TED Talk," Ruby said.

I could have fainted with relief, if I could have still fainted.

Adam grinned. Ruby had inadvertently stumbled into his good graces. There were three things Adam liked to talk about more than anything: vintage comics, TED Talks, and himself. She'd managed to walk right into a twofer. "Which one?"

Ruby looked panicked for a minute. "Um, I think it was about how electronics affect our sleep patterns?"

"Ah yes." I could tell he was loving this. He was practically glowing with pride. "The one about REM cycles. That was a good one." He straightened his shoulders. "Ruby, let me give you the grand tour."

I watched them walk away, trying to not be jealous that Ruby was getting Adam's attention. The tour would be short. An office for each of the three cofounders. Offices for HR and accounting. A break room. A front desk with a supply closet for extra pens and toner for the printer. The cubicles. A video-enabled conference room. Bathrooms out in the hall. TrendCelerate wasn't large.

I turned back to Melissa's cubicle. I hadn't meant to get her in any trouble. Not like it was my fault she was stashing twenty ounces of vodka at her desk, concealed in a reusable water bottle. I was glad I'd thought to check it before pouring it out onto the pothos plant, though. Ruby had killed enough of my plants already. I didn't want to add to the death count.

"Thanks for the tour," I heard Ruby say. She, Adam, and Sally were standing by the front desk. "You'll call me?"

Adam glanced at Sally, who nodded. "Let's give it a shot," he said. "You can start Monday."

"Wow, sure, that sounds perfect!"

I was happy for her. She needed a job, and this would suit her. TrendCelerate was a decent place to work. Not counting Blair, everyone was pretty cool.

As much as I was happy for Ruby, I was a little sad for myself. I didn't mind spending time at TrendCelerate. I didn't mind seeing my old coworkers, even Blair. I just wasn't sure that I was ready to face Adam every day and have to watch him living his life without me.

CHAPTER ELEVEN
RUBY

"I got the job!" I shrieked as soon as the door closed behind me. "Did you see that, Cordelia? I got it! I can't believe that worked!"

I liked to think she was as happy as I was that I was going to work for her old company. Then again, she might be frustrated that it was going to take time away from the other task she'd given me. "I know what you're thinking," I said as I took the stairs down two at a time. "Jake's killer is still out there, and the trail's growing cold. But if I can't pay the heating bill this month, the case isn't the only thing going cold."

At the bottom of the stairs was a heavy door. I pushed it open and was greeted by a blast of arctic air. I'd been so nervous about the interview and so stoked to have aced it that for a moment I'd forgotten that I might as well be living on the freaking North Pole. Or was it *in* the North Pole? Did it even matter?

Despite the frigid air, the sun was shining. The sidewalks were mostly clear of snow. And I had a job. It was a very good day.

"Let's go celebrate," I said. It sounded good in theory, but I barely had enough money for the bus ride home. My apartment was close enough to TrendCelerate that I could walk if I wanted to, but it was cold. Three miles might as well be three thousand miles on a day like today.

"And oh my gosh. You did not warn me. That Adam Rees is a certified hottie. I don't normally go for guys with glasses, but he was a total zaddy. Yeah, I know, I know, I saw his wedding ring. But a girl can look." I was so happy I could have skipped to the bus stop. Then I decided that I really would skip if I wanted to. I was an adult. No one would stop me.

I skipped for a couple of steps before realizing that even if no one else was around to see me, Cordelia could. Or at least, I thought she could. I assumed she was with me, but I could never be certain. There were times that I could almost imagine her standing right next to me and other times when the room felt empty. Like in the HR lady's office. I was trying to pay attention to her spiel. Really, I was. But while she was explaining how a 401(k) worked, I was distracted trying to figure out if Cordelia was there or not.

"We should put a bell on you, Cordelia," I said. "That way, I'd always know where you are." Then again, everyone else would, too. I'd have an awfully hard time explaining why there was a bell sound following me around wherever I went. Assuming, of course, that Cordelia was always following me.

I thought she was. I mean, it's not like she had a life. "No offense," I said out loud, as if she could read my thoughts. Then again, who said she couldn't? Who knew what she could and couldn't do? I reached my bus stop and had stopped to check the schedule when someone collided with me.

"Pardon," a snooty voice said.

I half turned to see the woman who'd run into me. She was on her phone, presumably calling someone to come rescue her from this part of town. I assumed she was lost. Her designer purse was worth more than my old car, but what I really envied was her full-length down-filled puffer coat. I would need something like that if I was going to survive another Boston winter, but even a knock-off generic was out of my budget right now.

"Don't just stand there. Apologize," she demanded. Her words were crisp and refined. Definitely not from this neighborhood.

"You expect me to apologize because you bumped into me?" I asked, only mildly annoyed. I wished she was the first woman in an overpriced coat with a snooty attitude I'd ever encountered in my life. It wasn't just that they thought that the world revolved around them, it was that they were right about it. And when someone had the nerve to disabuse them of that notion, they got flustered.

"If you hadn't stopped in the middle of the sidewalk, I wouldn't have nearly tripped over you," she said.

I shrugged, not that she could see it. In the absence of my own puffer jacket, I'd wrapped up in a fluffy scarf, a hoodie, and my thickest jacket instead. I had so many layers on, I looked like the Stay-Puft Marshmallow Man. I was still so cold I could barely feel my face, and my attempt to shrug caused, at best, a shift of my whole torso.

And then I wondered if the Stay-Puft Marshmallow Man was offensive to ghosts. I'd never stopped to consider it before, but I'd never had my own ghost at my side before. I would have to be careful about what I said, lest I inadvertently hurt Cordelia's feelings.

"Well?" she said again, tapping her foot impatiently.

"I'm sorry you were so distracted that you walked right into me," I told her. My mom had raised me to respect my elders, and this woman certainly qualified, but I didn't see why I should kowtow to another person just because she was used to getting everything she wanted.

"I'll be," she said with a huff. "Kids these days."

As she whirled and began to stomp away, her designer handbag opened and her wallet clutch flew through the air and landed at my feet. "Cordelia, you're terrible," I whispered. Then louder, I said, "Ma'am, I think you dropped something."

She stopped and turned her head toward me as I scooped up the wallet off the sidewalk. I sighed when I recognized the logo. I couldn't afford brand-name peanut butter and here she was walking around with a wallet worth more than anything I owned. For a second, I regretted saying anything. I could have kept the wallet and she'd never be the wiser, but it wasn't the right thing to do.

"I knew it!" she said, scuttling toward me. "You stopped short on purpose to pick my pocket. I'll be." She reached for the wallet.

I hugged it to my chest. "How can I know this is even yours?" I asked. It was a silly question and we both knew it. The wallet and purse were a matched set, which made me cringe. Did she had a different five-hundred-dollar-plus wallet to go with each of her five-thousand-dollar-plus purses? Probably. Oof.

"Of course it's mine, wretch. You said yourself that I dropped it."

I opened the wallet.

"What on earth do you think you're doing? Get your grubby hands off my wallet," she protested.

I held the wallet up so I could compare the pinch-faced white woman on the driver's license to the pinch-faced white woman in front of me. They matched.

"Happy?" she asked.

"Not quite. Name?"

"Agnes Astor." She snatched at her wallet. I let her take it. There was never any doubt that it was hers, but it felt good to question her entitlement, even if it was for just a minute. At least now she'd have a story to tell at whatever high society event she was going to this weekend.

"Have a fine day, Agnes Astor," I said.

She sniffed haughtily. A black Lincoln Town Car pulled up to the curb, blocking the bus stop. The city bus driver coming in behind it laid on his horn. The Lincoln's driver hopped out, hurried around the car, and held the rear passenger door open. The bus inched up on him, releasing a hiss of air as it pumped its breaks. "Ms. Astor," the driver said, nodding at the woman.

"Good day," she said to me and walked unhurriedly to the car. Once she was settled, the driver pulled into traffic without waiting for an opening, causing another flurry of honking horns.

The bus lumbered into the bus stop. I held my breath as I swiped my card, hoping I had enough on it to cover the fare. I did. I took a seat. "There's got to be a better way to do this," I told Cordelia, picking up the one-sided conversation we'd been having before being bumped into by Agnes Astor. "Don't get me wrong. The magnets are cool and all but they aren't the most practical method of communication."

The man seated next to me got up and moved across the aisle.

I realized too late that having a conversation with myself on a crowded bus might not be the smartest play. I pointed at my ear and shrugged at the man. God bless the inventor of Bluetooth earbuds. These days, it was nearly impossible to tell who was on the phone, who was having a psychotic break, and who was talking to their friendly neighborhood ghost. "Hey, I gotta go," I said, pretending to wrap up a call. "I'll call you back when I'm off the bus."

When we reached our stop, I hopped off. "See? That's what

I was talking about." I resumed the conversation with Cordelia. The man who'd been seated next to me earlier was staring at me through the window as I walked away.

I noticed an empty water bottle at my feet and tossed it into the nearest recycling can as I continued. "I can't just go around talking to myself. They'll lock me up. We've got to come up with a way to—"

Without warning, the sidewalk dropped out from underneath my feet. I lurched toward the nearest solid object and wrapped my arms around a light pole. For a second, I thought it was an earthquake. Did Boston even have earthquakes? Then I noticed that everyone else around me was going about their business like nothing was wrong.

"Whoa. I gotta sit down." I slurred my words. I let go of the light pole and staggered toward the closest building. I let myself slide down the side of the wall until I was crouched on the cold sidewalk.

A woman leaned over me, her face mere inches from mine. "You okay?"

I waved a dismissive hand at her. "I'm fine, I'm fine," I said, my voice coming out as weak as I felt.

A man glowered at me as he passed. "Sheesh. Get yourself together. It's not even noon."

The world continued to spin wildly. I took a deep breath. And then, as quickly as the vertigo came, it was gone.

I waited a moment, just in case another wave hit. When nothing happened, I slowly got to my feet. I rolled my head from side to side and flexed my fingers, but I couldn't shake off the dull ache in the back of my skull.

I was a good girl. I recycled. I respected my elders. I didn't cheat. I didn't steal. I didn't even curse. Much. But even good girls did bad things on occasion. For me, it was last January. The night I found out my boyfriend was cheating on me, I let a few of my friends take me to a house party in Baltimore, the kind of party that good girls didn't go to.

I drank shots of Jägermeister. Goldschläger. 151 rum. The night got fuzzy after that. I vaguely remember staggering back to my friend's car. I didn't remember them pulling over because I was going to be sick, but they teased me mercilessly about it afterward. I'll never forget the hangover I had the next day.

If I didn't know better, I'd think that a second ago, I'd been drunk. Not just drunk, wasted. Blitzed. Three sheets to the wind. Which was impossible, because, especially after that house party, I didn't drink.

But Cordelia did. I lost track of how many empty liquor bottles I'd lugged down to the recycle bin when I first moved in. It had taken me several trips, up and down four flights of stairs, to get rid of them all.

"Did you just roofie me?" I asked Cordelia. Okay, maybe "roofie" wasn't the right word. But what was I supposed to call it when a ghost got me insta-drunk with no warning? Whammy? Bewitch? And why had she done it?

"Lady, I don't know who you're talking to, but you need to get a move on," a man's voice said.

I turned to see an impatient-looking man scowling at me. He wasn't much taller than I was, maybe five six on a good day. He was wide, though, built like a rock wall. His shoulders strained against motorcycle leathers. "You hear me? Get."

"Sorry, I just..." My voice trailed off as I noticed the shop behind him. It had a large glass storefront. I could barely see inside for all the brightly colored signs in the windows. "We buy gold!" "Cash today!" "Buy / Sell Jewelry!" "Need a loan?" "Best selection!" As if I needed any more hints about the nature of the business, a neon sign proclaiming "Lizard Pawn" blinked in the window. As I watched, the sign glowed brightly for a moment before erupting in a shower of sparks.

The man turned to see what I was staring at. "That damn light. And I just had it fixed." It popped and went dark. "Damn it all." He pulled a phone out of his pocket, scrawled though his contacts, and dialed. "Hey. It's Lizard. I thought you said you fixed that sign . . ."

As he argued, loudly, with the man on the other end of the phone, I edged past him to peer into the window. I'd seen lights blow out like that constantly since moving to Boston. It was Cordelia. It had to be. It didn't take a genius to figure out what she wanted. First, the whammy that stopped me in my tracks and now a literal sign beckoning me inside?

I opened the door.

Lizard moved his phone away from his mouth. "I thought I told you to scram."

"I'm just browsing," I said, and stepped into the pawn shop.

Inside there were even more signs plastered to every available surface. "Sale!" "Limited time only!" "Half off!" Every shelf promised a special deal. I wandered past rows of bicycles, snow blowers, guitars. None of it interested me. I ignored the display of laptops and sports memorabilia. The back wall was covered in cell phones locked behind glass. There were more glass cases by the cash register filled with jewelry.

Lizard followed me inside. He watched me like a hawk while he finished his phone call, like at any minute I was going to break through a glass case, grab a handful of gold, and make a run for it. He hung up as I studied the case full of watches. "You looking for a watch?" he asked.

"Actually, I am. A specific one. It would have come in within the last few days."

"What does it look like?"

"I don't know," I admitted. Bobby, Jake's cousin, had said that the missing watch was a family heirloom, but that wasn't very helpful. I guess maybe I'd seen Jake wear it before, but I'd never paid any attention to it. "One sec."

I pulled out my phone and texted Bobby. "This is Ruby, Jake's neighbor. Send me a pix of Jake's watch?"

Without knowing if Bobby was going to text me back in five seconds, five hours, or not at all, I put my phone back in my pocket where I would hear it when he replied. "It would have come in recently," I told Lizard again. "It was old. I think maybe it had a leather band?"

He folded his thick arms over his barrel chest. "Haven't got any watches lately."

"None?" I asked him. I found that hard to believe. Pawn shops bought and sold stock constantly. "Not a single watch?"

"That's what I said. Lady, I don't know what your deal is, but you're scaring off the customers."

I looked around the empty store. "What customers?"

"Exactly," he said. "Get going. And I don't want to see you back in here again unless you got something to pawn or sell."

"Yeah. Okay. Sure." I checked my phone. There was nothing from Bobby. "Have a great day!"

Lizard grunted.

I let myself out. "Well, that was a waste of time," I said as I headed for home. The effects of whatever had happened earlier dissipated without a trace, for which I was grateful. I didn't want to deal with a hangover on top of embarrassing myself in front of the pawn shop for all to see. "There's got to be a better way to find

Jake's watch than checking every pawn shop in town." I paused. "There is, isn't there?"

I took out my phone and searched for nearby pawn shops. I was expecting dozens of results. I was wrong. There were dozens of *pages* of results. "You've got to be kidding." I turned my phone to face away from me. I had no idea where Cordelia was. I couldn't see her, but she could see me and if she had to walk around me to see the screen, so be it. "That's a lot of pawn shops."

I continued, "And don't forget, I start work next week. Now that I've got a job, I can't be running around all day visiting every pawn shop in Boston." Then it hit me. I wouldn't have to. If I had any downtime at work, or after work, I could call around. I'd start with the closest shops and work my way outward. I might not be able to find Jake's missing watch at a pawn shop, but it was worth a few phone calls at least.

As I neared my apartment, I approached the bar on the corner, O'Grady's. On the weekends, music and smokers poured out of its doors. This time of the day, it was deserted. I could actually walk past it without enduring any catcalls. Only, it wasn't completely empty, or the door wouldn't have opened as I approached.

I made sure to walk wide of the door so I wouldn't bump into whoever was coming outside, but no one did. "Hey, make up your mind," a gruff voice called from inside the darkened bar. "In or out. You're lettin' all the heat out."

My first thought was that the wind must have blown the door open. As was usual for this time of year, it was cold and blustery. Since no one else was near the door, I decided to close it. Only, when I tried to push it shut, nothing happened. The door was some heavy solid wood, oak maybe. The inside was covered in black acoustical panels, presumably to keep the neighbors from complaining about the late-night noise.

As I tugged on the door, trying to get it to close, I realized that maybe Cordelia wanted me to go inside. "I'm starting to think you're a bad influence," I said aloud. "Sure, you helped me get a job, but you also dragged me into a murder investigation. And after the drunken whammy you dropped on me in front of the pawn shop, now you're encouraging me to go to a bar in the middle of the morning? Are you trying to turn me into a day drinker?"

"In or out," the bartender repeated.

I went inside. It was nicer inside the bar than I'd expected, but then again, I didn't hang out in a lot of seedy neighborhood bars, so I didn't have much to compare it to. There was a bar along one wall with the requisite selection of liquor bottles lined up on shelves. The windows had been bricked over from the outside, but on the inside, there were fake stained-glass windows inserted into where the original windows had once been. They were backlit, forming an illusion of sunlight filtering in through the colorful glass.

I spotted a pool table near the door and two more in the back. A few booths lined one wall and long family-style tables took up most of the floor. Dropkick Murphys, or one of the dozen or so of other popular Boston Irish rock bands—they all sounded the same to me—was playing over the speakers. Television screens were mounted over the bar. They were tuned to sitcom reruns, but the sound was all muted.

Since it was before noon, I was the only customer. I took a seat at the bar.

The bartender came over and stood in front of me. "How old are you?" he asked in a gruff voice.

"Old enough to order a glass of water," I replied.

"We don't serve minors in here," he said, crossing his arms over his chest. He was a big man and he didn't look happy to see me.

"Not even for lunch?" I asked him. I half stood on my stool to reach a stack of paper menus on the far side of the bar, then sat back to study it. "What's good?" I asked.

He barked out a laugh. "Nothing here."

"Okay then, what's not terrible?"

He lifted one eyebrow. "I'd recommend literally anywhere else."

I sighed. He was probably right. I didn't have the money to blow on an overpriced microwave dinner at a dive bar, and even if I wanted an alcoholic drink, there was no way this man would serve me without checking my ID, which would confirm I was underaged. So why did Cordelia drag me in here? I reached into my pocket, where I had a few crumpled bills, my ID, and my bus pass. Except when I pulled out my hand, I was holding three crisp hundred-dollar bills.

The bartender clocked the bills at the same time as I did. "The beer-battered fish and chips ain't bad," he said, quickly changing his tune.

My stomach rumbled at the thought. "Yes, please. I'll take that. And a Coke maybe?"

"Coming right up," he said, reaching for a clean glass.

I looked down at the bills. "Let me guess," I whispered under my breath. "A generous contribution to the neighborhood charity fund from our dear friend, Agnes Astor?" I swear I heard a laugh. I was starting to think that I was just scratching the surface of the benefits of having a pet ghost.

CHAPTER TWELVE
RUBY

The bartender returned with my fish and chips. The fish had freezer burn and the fries were oversalted, but I wasn't complaining. As I dunked a crispy fry into the ketchup, I felt a stab of guilt. I hadn't been the one to steal the money from Agnes, and she certainly wasn't going to miss it. That's not what I felt guilty about. I would happily consider her donation an apology for her rudeness.

What was eating me was whether or not I was using Cordelia. I mean, sure, she was dead. She was beyond caring about such things, I assumed. Or was I wrong?

I'd always thought it would be cool to meet a ghost, but now that I had, I wondered if there was more I should be doing for her. Did she need my help to cross over, or whatever it was called? Did I have a responsibility to help her? Sure, I was going to call around pawn shops looking for Jake's missing watch, to assist with her murder investigation, but that hardly felt like enough.

"You okay?" the bartender asked. He leaned his elbows on the bar while I ate. "You seem lost in thought."

"I guess that's because I am," I admitted. I knew that bartenders were supposed to be easy to talk to, a kind of therapist even, but it wasn't like I could spill my guts to him, especially when he'd barely given me the time of day before I inadvertently flashed a handful of bills. How would that sound? *I moved into a haunted apartment, but the ghost is real nice. She got me a job and now I'm helping her solve a murder.*

Dear god, they're gonna lock me up in a rubber room.

"Don't know if you noticed, but I ain't got a lot of customers in here this time of day. You'd be doing me a favor if you tell me what's on your mind. Think of it as keeping me entertained."

"I'm afraid I'm not that entertaining," I said.

"Somehow, I doubt that. Refill?" Without waiting for my response, he took my soda and topped it off. "What gives?"

I glanced around at the dozen taps on the bar and the TV screens mounted overhead. The walls were decorated with photos of the Red Sox and a framed, signed Boston Bruins sweater. If Jake's cousin Bobby was right about Jake wanting to be buried in one of his hockey sweaters, then he was a die-hard fan. This was exactly the kind of place Jake would have loved, and was just steps from our apartment building. Surely, he was a regular. "You know Jake Macintyre?" I asked.

The bartender nodded. "He might have come in here a time or two. What's your name?"

"Ruby Young," I said, offering my hand to shake.

He wiped his hand off on a towel. "Sean. Sean O'Grady."

"Nice to meetcha, Sean O'Grady," I said, shaking his hand. I didn't know what Cordelia was trying to get out of me coming here, but I wouldn't know if I never asked. "Jake was in here a lot, wasn't he?"

"A fair amount," Sean confirmed.

"Was he ever in here with a friend?" I asked.

"Jake had lots of friends," the bartender hedged.

"Any female friends?" I asked. His cousin said that Jake didn't have a girlfriend, but maybe the bartender might know something that Bobby didn't.

"Jake had lots of female friends," he confirmed.

I grimaced. That was almost the same thing as his cousin Bobby had said, and it was no help at all. "Anyone special?"

He grinned. "Aren't they all?"

"You wouldn't happen to have a surveillance system that might have caught him with one of these female friends, would you?" I hadn't seen any cameras, but it didn't hurt to ask.

"In this dump? Are you kidding?"

I pointed at the television screens over the bar. "Jake ever come in here to watch the game?"

Sean nodded.

I thought about what Bobby had said about Jake keeping his bookie in business. "Did you ever know him to put money down on the games?"

"Now and then." He topped off my soda again. "He was the worst kind of idiot."

"How so?"

"He bet with his heart. Do I want to see the Bruins hoist the Cup? Hell yes. Do I think they're gonna make it this year?" He shook his head. "Not unless they fix their power play. Do you know we haven't had a PPG all month?"

It was my turn to shake my head. I didn't even know what a PPG was. "Did he watch the game alone? Or with friends?"

He glanced over at the other customers in the bar. They'd come in while I was waiting for my fish and chips. Sean had poured them a pitcher of beer without being asked and they'd taken it straight to one of the pool tables in the back. "He hung out with that lot a bit."

"Thanks." I finished up my last piece of fried fish and pushed the plate away from me. I picked up my soda and carried it over to the pool table. "Hiya," I said to the players.

There were three men at the table. Two of them had red hair, one with a short beard and one without, both with similar features. The other was tall and skinny. The taller one was bent over, lining up a shot. One of the redheads poured the last of the beer into his glass, then handed the empty pitcher to the third man. "Your turn," he said.

"It's always my turn," he grumbled as he took the pitcher to the bar.

As soon as he was gone, the bearded redhead turned his attention to me. "What's your name, sweetheart?"

"Ruby," I said. Did men think we liked that? Calling someone you didn't know "sweetheart" wasn't friendly or cute. It was creepy. Especially when the woman in question was half their age.

"That's a beautiful name, Ruby. You looking for a turn at my stick?"

The other redhead returned with a full pitcher of beer. As he passed, he smacked the bearded man in the back of the head. "Don't be an ass, Ryan." He looked at me. "Liam." He pointed to the tall man, who was lining up his next shot. "Scotty."

"I didn't mean anything by it," Ryan said. "Ruby didn't mind, did you, Ruby?"

I didn't know how he did it, but he managed to make my own name sound crude. "I'm not much of a pool player," I said, hoping he'd let it drop.

"Then have a drink with us." Liam poured a beer into a clean glass he'd brought over and held it out to me.

I shook my head. "No thanks." I held up my soda. "I'm good."

Behind me, I heard the bartender grunt. It made me feel better knowing he was watching me like a hawk. Sure, he was more concerned about losing his liquor license over serving an underaged patron than whether or not a bunch of dudes made me feel uncomfortable, but it was nice nevertheless.

"You don't play pool or drink beer. Then what are you doing here, Ruby?" Ryan asked.

I was starting to wonder the same thing myself. "You guys know Jake Macintyre?"

"What about him?" the man playing pool, Scotty, said. He straightened and I realized he wasn't just sort of tall, he was awkwardly, uncomfortably tall. At my height, pretty much all the men around me were tall in my mind, but Scotty was the kind of tall that hit his head on doorways and low-hanging ceiling fans.

"So, you do know him?" I asked again.

"Used to," Scotty said. He shot again. The black eight ball went into one of the pockets. There was a pair of twenty-dollar bills on the table. He picked up one of the bills and made a show of tucking it into his wallet. "He's dead. Who's next?"

"I've lost enough money already," Ryan said. "It's Liam's turn."

Liam shook his head. "Do I look like an idiot?" He looked at me. "Maybe Ruby can take him on."

"I already told you, I don't play pool." I'd only been here for a few minutes and I was already talking in circles. "What about Jake?"

"It's like Scotty said. He's dead," Liam said.

I let out a huff of frustration. Even conversations with Cordelia weren't this exasperating. "Yes, I know that." I was about to identify myself as Jake's across-the-hall neighbor but then decided I didn't want these three knowing where I lived.

"Shot during a mugging. This neighborhood's going to hell, I tell you," Scotty muttered as he racked up the balls again. "Come on, Liam. I'll spot you a ball and let you break."

"Fine. Whatever. But I'm tapped out so you're gonna have to spot me a twenty, too."

Scotty rolled his eyes. "Get it from your brother."

"I'm good for it," Liam argued. Scotty and Ryan cracked up at that. "Fine. Whatever, assholes." He dug through his wallet and pulled out a few crumpled bills, a five and a few ones. He laid them on the table. "That's as good as I've got."

Scotty grunted. He removed the rack from the table and hung it on its space on the wall. "Your turn." While Liam broke, Scotty turned his attention to me. "I don't remember ever seeing you in here before."

I had to crane my neck to talk to him. "You know Jake's cousin?"

"Which one? He's got like a dozen."

I hadn't considered that. Bobby heard his cousin was dead, and the first thing he did was show up to claim Jake's watch. Odd. Then again, if there were a dozen other cousins all with an eye on the family heirloom, it made sense that the first-come-first-served rule was in effect.

I recognized the phenomenon. Back home, we called it a Baltimore Will and Testament. When my great aunt died, everyone in the extended family descended on her house like locusts, stuffing their pockets with anything that wasn't nailed down. Family, am I right?

"Bobby," I said. Thinking about him, I checked my phone. He hadn't texted me back about the watch. What was taking him so long? "He said Jake had a girlfriend, but he couldn't remember her name," I fibbed.

Scotty exchanged a glance with Ryan. At the table, Liam shouldered him out of the way. "My turn." He lined up his shot.

"Jake didn't have a girlfriend," Ryan said.

"Oh."

"Jake had girlfriends. Plural. Lots of 'em."

"Oh," I repeated again. Everyone seemed to love Jake, but I was starting to have second thoughts about him.

When I caught my boyfriend cheating on me, I'd had plenty of choice words to say to him. If I was being completely honest, if he fell off the face of the earth, I wouldn't shed a tear, but I never considered being the one to push him over the edge. I wondered if Jake's girlfriends had hotter blood than I did. Not that I would blame them. Cheating boyfriends got what they deserved. "Any of them got names?"

"All of them got names." Ryan cocked his head. "Why do you want to know so bad?"

"Like I said, his cousin, Bobby, was planning the wake and—" That approach hadn't worked with Bobby, but I was hoping one of these guys would fall for it.

Instead, Scotty cut me off. "Bad idea, Ruby." He leaned against his pool cue. "Let me guess. You're planning to invite all of his side pieces to the funeral? Might as well toss lit bottle rockets into the firecracker factory."

I shook my head. "No, I just want to talk to them."

"Which one?"

"Any of them. All of them."

"Sorry, Ruby. Can't help you there." Scotty turned his attention back to the pool table.

"Yeah okay. Thanks anyway." I went back to the bar and settled my tab. The bartender checked the crisp hundred-dollar bill two different ways before accepting it. Not that I blamed him. I didn't exactly look like someone who carried around hundred-dollar bills, and as Scotty had so helpfully pointed out, this neighborhood was going to hell. I tucked away my change and headed for the front door.

Liam caught up to me. "Patty," he said.

"Excuse me?"

"His most recent girlfriend. Her name was Patty."

"Patty what?" I asked.

He shrugged. "All I know is Jake called her Patty. Pretty. Young. Petite. Dark hair. Kinda looked like you. Can I walk you home? This block's not safe for a girl walking alone."

"Thanks, but I'm good. My Uber's almost here," I lied.

Once the door was closed firmly behind me, I crossed the street and headed for my building. The greasy fish and chips were good, but the rest of it? A total waste of my time. What was I supposed to do, go door-to-door hoping to find one specific girl named Patty in all of Boston? There were probably three Pattys in my building alone.

There was an annoyed-looking pizza deliveryman standing outside of my building, looking up at the windows. I'd seen him around before, but this was the first time I'd eaten a big enough lunch that I wasn't tempted to swipe one of his pizzas. "Gail in 3C?" he asked hopefully.

"Nope. Ruby. Sorry." I keyed open the front door and held it open for him.

He followed me inside the lobby, but stopped short of the stairs. "You're not coming?" I asked him.

"Ain't nobody in this building tip good enough to get me to climb all those stairs." He stomped his feet to get the blood circulating. "Cold out there. Least they can do is buzz me in. Here." He thrust a flyer for Caparelli's Pizza at me. "Next time you order, tell them Arlo said to give you twenty percent off."

"Cool. Thanks," I said, pocketing the flyer even though I had a stack of identical ones upstairs. I started up the stairs, passing a woman hurrying down from the third floor. 3C, I presumed. I hoped she had a good tip ready.

When I got to my apartment, I glanced around, looking for a decent hiding spot. Even after lunch, I had two hundred and eighty dollars left over from the Agnes Fund. That was a lot of money for me, and I didn't feel comfortable carrying it around. The problem was, I didn't feel comfortable leaving it out in the open, either.

The silverware drawer slid open.

"Good thinking," I said.

I pulled out the flimsy plastic tray that held cheap, mismatched silverware, and found out that I wasn't the first person to try to hide something in here. There was a pair of white envelopes already in there, one on either side so the tray was even. I sat the tray and my cash aside.

The first envelope had a ten-digit number written on it in blue ink. A phone number maybe? I didn't recognize the area code. I was tempted to call it and find out who it belonged to, but I decided to open the envelope first.

Inside was cash. A *lot* of cash. I slid it out and counted it. There were ten crisp hundred-dollar bills. For the first time since moving in, I said a silent thanks for having a lazy landlord. If he'd taken any effort at all to clean up after Cordelia died, he would have found—and pocketed—a cool grand.

"This is yours, right?" I asked the air. I glanced over at the refrigerator.

y

"Thought it might be," I said. I tucked the money back in the first envelope and dropped it back into the drawer.

The second envelope held a folded piece of paper. To be completely honest, I was disappointed. I was hoping for more cash. I unfolded it. Written on it was a series of nonsensical letters and numbers, broken up with random punctuation. All but the last grouping in the series was crossed out.

7x#dBLj!FXr9

"What's that supposed to mean?" I asked, studying the paper. "I mean, it's a password, obviously, but a password to what?" I glanced at the other envelope. What if that wasn't a phone number? It could be an account number. A bank account, probably. But for which bank? "You're just full of surprises, aren't you?" I asked.

After adding two hundred and forty dollars to the stash, I put the envelopes back where I'd found them. I tucked the remaining bills into my wallet. "This has been quite a day," I told Cordelia. I wondered why she'd stolen money out of that nasty Agnes woman's wallet if she had this much tucked away in her apartment. Then again, she might never have thought to show me her hiding place if I didn't have money to hide.

"Were you some kind of criminal?" I asked. The drawer slammed closed. "I'll take that as a no." I poured myself a glass of water from the refrigerator. Cordelia had a decent job. So why did she live in this dump? And why squirrel away a thousand dollars in the silverware drawer if she had a bank account?

I looked around at the apartment. I'd gotten rid of a lot of Cordelia's things when I moved in. Things I didn't think I'd ever use, like her old clothes. Things I didn't want to use, like her sheets. But for the most part, my apartment—*her* apartment—was almost exactly how she'd left it. What else was hidden in here?

CHAPTER THIRTEEN
CORDELIA

Ruby was wrecking my apartment, and there was nothing I could do about it.

"Stop!" I yelled. She opened the zipper on one of the loveseat cushions, and chunks of orange foam exploded all over her. I'd been meaning to replace them. The loveseat was lumpy and uncomfortable with years of use. I'd tried to take the covers off the cushions once to wash them and discovered, like Ruby was now finding out, that they'd been stuffed with foam with no inner liner. It had been a pain to shove the foam back inside and keep it compressed long enough to close the zipper. I didn't envy the clean-up chore ahead of her.

Ruby pawed through the foam, tossing it on the floor when she was done.

"What are you looking for?" I asked. She didn't hear me. "That's the only cash I have in the apartment. I swear it." I crossed my hand over my heart. And I meant it, too. That was the only *cash* hidden in the apartment. Anything else I might have stashed was none of her business. Besides, what was the world coming to when a girl couldn't even trust an honest ghost anymore?

"Come on, Ruby, listen to me," I pleaded, knowing she wouldn't. Couldn't.

But it didn't have to be this way. She'd heard me before. She might not realize it, but she saw me. She heard me. She talked to me. Not *at* me, *to* me. I needed her to do it again.

Spending the morning at TrendCelerate had been bittersweet. I didn't like that Melissa was drinking on the job. I mean, sure, I'd been known to throw one back now and then, but never on the clock—at least not alone. Happy hour with Adam behind locked doors and office parties didn't count.

TrendCelerate had the most epic holiday parties, right before a two-week paid holiday break. Maybe they'd invite Ruby to the next one.

The last one I'd been to was last Christmas, although they called it the Holiday Celebration. Didn't matter much to me, either way. Christmas had bad memories for me. I was just as happy celebrating generic winter holidays instead.

I'd bought a new dress for the occasion. We rented out a meeting room at one of the swanky hotels downtown. The decorations were silver snowflakes. The drinks were free and flowing.

My dress was purple and extremely flattering, if I did say so myself. I'd never been skinny, and the older I got, the more things sagged in places they hadn't sagged before. But this dress fit me just right. I looked good that night. Better than good. Great, even.

And Adam noticed.

He'd brought his wife to the party, of course. He had to. It was expected. Karin wore something black and silky that made her look like the perfect polished politician she was. Her hair was just right. Her makeup was just right. Even her jewelry was just right. But her husband wasn't watching her all night. He was too busy watching me.

Karin was so wrapped up in herself that she never noticed anything around her that wasn't the press or her own reflection. She didn't even notice when her husband snuck off halfway through the party to have a quickie with me. Then again, this thing we had, whatever it was with me and Adam, had been on and off for four? five? years right under her nose and she'd never caught on. She was either the least observant person in the world or she simply didn't care. My money was on the latter.

From what I could tell, they lived totally separate lives. He was well-known in the cutthroat field of software development, and he was invited to speak at tech conferences all over the world. She split her time between Boston and D.C., and when she wasn't meeting with lobbyists and fellow politicians, she was holding televised town halls and doing the morning talk show circuit. Weeks passed without them ever being in the same room, but as luck would have it, she just had to be home for Christmas.

The party wound down and he'd followed her upstairs, leaving me alone at the open bar. Not smart. I'd already had a few drinks, and there was no stopping now, even if I wanted to. And I didn't want to. I knew I had no claim on Adam. Karin was his wife. But still, it hurt. And the drinks dulled the pain.

I found myself sitting alone at a table under a spinning snowflake, drawing circles in the pools of condensation left by my mostly empty drink when a man, a stranger, sat down across from me. "What's your poison?" he asked.

"Jack and Coke," I said.

He chuckled. "I guessed wrong." He passed me a wine glass filled nearly to the brim.

I emptied my own glass before taking a sip from the one he

handed me. I wasn't normally a wine drinker, but I could see them packing up the bar. I didn't have much of a choice.

"I'm Eddie," he said.

"Cordelia," I replied. I hadn't seen Eddie around before. He was young, too young for me. Cute. A little blurry, but that might have been the Jack's fault. "Who'd you come with, Eddie?"

"Come with?" He looked around. "Oh, I don't work here."

I chuckled. "I know that. I think I would have noticed you around the office. Party crasher?"

"Hotel guest," he admitted. "Couldn't sleep. Saw the place was emptying out and decided to help myself." He winked at me, as if he already knew that me going up to his room tonight was a done deal. He wasn't wrong. "Glad I did, too."

He was wearing a blazer over a T-shirt. Not exactly typical corporate holiday party attire. "You should have shown up sooner. There were these little puff pastries." I gestured at the now-empty banquet table set up near the makeshift bar. "They were delicious."

He nodded. "I'll have to take your word on that, Cordelia. Cordelia. Cordelia!"

I realized that Ruby was calling my name. I must have drifted off again. It wasn't like sleep, not really. One minute I was in the here and now, and the next, I wasn't. Sometimes, when I blinked out, I was a little kid growing up in the outskirts of Boston, in the middle of a snowball fight with my baby brother. Sometimes I was a teenager, hitchhiking to the mall. And sometimes, it was just a few months ago and I was in a gorgeous purple dress about to stumble upstairs with a stranger named Eddie I'd met at a holiday party.

"Geez, Cordelia, would it kill you to say something?" Ruby clapped her hands over her mouth. Her eyes grew wide with concern. "I didn't mean that." Her voice was muffled under her hands.

Around her, the apartment was in shambles. While I'd been—I didn't know what to call it, elsewhere?—she'd been busy tearing the place apart.

"I'm not going to help you clean this up," I told her. I picked up one of the empty pillowcases and tossed it at her.

Watching the pillowcase drift through the air gave me some satisfaction. When she decided to turn my apartment inside out, I hadn't even been able to lift a finger to stop her. I must have been exhausted by the encounter at the pawn shop, but now, after I had a chance to recharge, I felt invigorated and ready to go.

Wait a second.

The pawn shop.

I looked down at my hands. They looked the same as they had when I was alive. Pale. Dry. My fingernails were short and my nail polish was chipped. If I'd known I would become a ghost, I would have painted my nails before I offed myself. Now I was doomed to spend the rest of eternity in dire need of a manicure and some hand lotion.

My hands were solid enough, from my point of view. They were as solid as they'd always been. But as far as Ruby was concerned, my hands, along with the rest of me, were invisible. Except for that brief moment in front of the pawn shop when I wasn't.

Walking back from her triumphant interview at TrendCelerate, Ruby's normally perky personality was downright jubilant. I was decidedly less so. Seeing Adam had brought up all sorts of emotions that I didn't want to feel. It wasn't like I expected him to be moping around wearing a black veil, but it would have been nice to see some sign that he missed me, even a little bit.

I was thinking about how much it sucked to be dead when we passed a man on the street wearing a Bruins knitted cap, which made me think of Jake. That's when I realized we were in front of Lizard Pawn. Not far from my apartment, the pawn shop was pretty much always open. I didn't know how late it was open during the Nor'easter earlier in the week, but after someone robbed Jake, as they were leaving the block, that would have been the first pawn shop they would have come across. If I'd just killed someone and all I got out of it was a crappy old watch, especially with a big storm bearing down on the city, I would have wanted to get rid of the evidence pretty damn quick.

But how was I supposed to convey all this information to Ruby? It wasn't like she was carrying around a magnetic poetry kit. I tried to get her attention. I knocked over a planter. She ignored it. I found an empty water bottle in the gutter and rolled it at her feet. She picked it up and tossed it in a nearby recycling bin like the good person that she was.

I was desperate. She was about to walk right past the pawn shop. I was standing in front of her, waving my arms like an idiot and calling her name, hoping she'd notice me when instead, she walked right through me. And it hurt.

I'd brushed people before, and I thought that was bad, but that was nothing compared to having a living pass all the way through me. It was like walking across broken glass barefoot. Only the glass was electrified. On fire. Covered in ants.

Right about the time the pain started to subside, I noticed Ruby was crumpled up on the sidewalk. I ran over to her in a panic, not knowing what to do or how to apologize. I hadn't meant to hurt her, and I couldn't help a living. I leaned over and studied her face. She had a thousand-yard stare. "Shit," I muttered. "I broke her."

I didn't know what I was thinking. Flapping my arms and hoping she'd stop? What if I'd done real damage? What if she never recovered?

Then she blinked.

"You okay?" I asked.

She shooed me away. "I'm fine. I'm fine."

"Thank goodness," I said, taking a step back and giving her room to breathe. "Damn, Ruby, I'm so sorry. I don't know what I was thinking. I wasn't—" My jaw dropped. "What did you say?" I knelt in front of her. "You can see me? You can hear me?"

I waited for her to respond. "I know you saw me. You shooed me off. You said you were fine." Her eyes were coming back into focus. We were drawing attention. A couple of passersby chuckled or made rude comments, without stopping to see if she was okay or not. Even Lizard came out of the pawn shop, but instead of checking on her, he told her to scram.

"If you can see me, do something. Anything. Wiggle your foot," I said. I stared at Ruby's boot, willing it to wiggle. Nothing happened. "For Pete's sake, do something," I yelled in frustration, clapping my hands in front of her face. She didn't flinch. Instead, she got up, looking unsteady, and started back for the apartment.

"No!" I yelled. "Come on, Ruby, listen up! It's a pawn shop! Don't you know what that means? They might have Jake's watch! The killer could have been here. Someone could have seen him, talked to him!"

It was no use. She didn't notice me. But she did notice when the neon sign in the pawn shop window blew out, which I guess was the next best thing. Funny thing was, I was nowhere near the light when it malfunctioned, so for once it wasn't my fault. It was about time I had some decent luck.

She didn't find the watch at Lizard Pawn. Which, yeah, okay, it was a long shot. But at least the seed was planted now. She was thinking about the watch. She figured out that finding it might lead us to the killer. She was even coming up with a plan. Which, sure, calling around wasn't nearly as good as walking in and asking questions in person. It's all too easy to blow someone off over the phone. But it was a start. It was the closest thing we had to a lead.

Maybe I was wrong about Ruby. Maybe she *would* make a good investigator. And to be perfectly honest, I needed her. I couldn't find Jake's killer on my own.

One minute, it really felt like we were getting somewhere. And now, she was tearing my apartment up. Not that she would find anything. There were some secrets that I got to take to the grave.

CHAPTER FOURTEEN
RUBY

By Sunday morning, Jake's cousin still hadn't texted me back, which was rude. He's the one who asked for my help. It would be hard enough to find the missing watch even if I knew what it looked like. But that was okay, because I had other leads to follow.

Since I already had my phone out to check my lack of messages, I opened the notes app and started a new note.

1. Missing watch—heirloom? Worth $$$?
2. Girlfriend(s)—Patty? Who else?
3. Work—sketchy warehouse? Mob ties?
4. Gambling debts?

Until Bobby texted me a picture that I could show around at local pawn shops, the watch was a dead end. The girlfriend angle was promising, but I didn't have enough to go on yet. Next up was the warehouse. The problem was *which* warehouse?

If Jake worked at a snack food distribution center, I doubt he was killed over his packing of salt and vinegar chips. But some warehouses, I presumed, were less legitimate. What if he worked for the mob or something? That would be highly relevant.

And also, not something I wanted to stick my nose into.

It was one thing to wonder what my across-the-hall neighbor was into that got him killed. It was another kettle of fish to go poking around mob business, even if it was at a friendly ghost's behest. Our window to figure out what happened to him was closing. It was only a matter of time before Jake's family cleared out his apartment, taking any potential clues with them.

"Hey, Cordelia? Can you get me back into Jake's apartment?"

In response, the door to my apartment swung open. From my vantage point, I could see that Jake's door across the hall was ajar.

"You're the best," I told her.

Sure, if I thought too long or too hard about it, living with a ghost had a major creep factor, just knowing that she could be watching at any time and I wouldn't even know it. But growing up in a big household, I never had a room to myself. I was used to the lack of privacy. If anything, I enjoyed knowing I wasn't alone. It was like having a friend around I just didn't happen to see much.

Plus, she'd found me a job. She'd picked a rich lady's wallet for me and then shared the location of where she kept her stash of cash. She even—for what it was worth—tried to get me to dress like an adult. Which I grudgingly added to the plus column. Not that I was giving up my T-shirt collection anytime soon.

Today's tee had the caption "I've got an axolotl of love" with a cartoon axolotl on it, on a peach background. To be completely honest, I wasn't entirely sure what an axolotl was, but it was super cute. Plus, my little sister had given it to me on my last birthday, so when I wore it I didn't feel so far away from home. I missed her so much, but every time we Facetimed, I ended up even more homesick after we disconnected than I was before we talked, which wasn't helping strengthen my resolve to prove my independence.

As soon as I stepped out of my apartment, the door to 4F popped open and Milly stepped into the hall. Today, she was wearing a lavender velour tracksuit that made her look even more frail and washed-out than usual. "Ruby!" she said, as if surprised to see me.

Milly wasn't wearing a coat. She wasn't carrying a purse. She didn't have a basket of laundry on her hip. She didn't have a dog to walk or a grocery bag slung over her arm. She obviously wasn't planning on going anywhere, which meant she'd been waiting patiently at the peephole for something, anything, interesting to happen in the hallway. Which was ridiculous. Nothing interesting *ever* happened out here. Okay, sure, a few days ago, the hallway was crawling with police after our neighbor was killed. And a few months before that, the paramedics were here for Cordelia. But other than that, nothing happened.

The weird thing was, with as much time as she spent observing the comings and goings on our floor, why hadn't Milly been the one to notice a suspicious stranger leaving Cordelia's apartment around the time of her death? And why wasn't she the one who reported that she hadn't seen Cordelia around for a few days after her death? Surely, her mail had to be piling up, not to mention the advertisements and flyers collecting under her door. Cordelia's death had gone unnoticed by everyone. I wasn't sure who'd finally called in a welfare check, but it hadn't been the nosy busybody across the hall. It was a horrible way to die, only compounded by the fact that no one missed her when she was gone.

Then the hair on the back of my neck tingled. Maybe I was looking at this all wrong. Maybe Jake's killer was closer to home than I realized. A *lot* closer. Like right-next-door-to-him closer. It wasn't the first time that the thought had crossed my mind, but it was silly. Wasn't it? Even if Milly had been a killer back in the day, she would have retired a long time ago. Right?

"Hi, Milly," I said, unable to keep a grin off my face at the thought of there being some kind of AARP-sponsored retired serial killers Facebook group. I bet their get-togethers were a hoot.

"Going somewhere?" she asked.

I realized that my earlier assessment of her went for me as well. I wasn't dressed for going outside. I didn't even have my cell phone. My mind raced as I tried to think of a good excuse. I could say that I was going down to the basement to check on my laundry or had to pick up a delivery in the lobby, but the second I came back empty-handed, I was busted. So I lied. "I thought I heard something."

She narrowed her eyes at me. "Huh? Did you now?"

I was careful. I didn't look toward Jake's apartment. If I did, she might notice that his door was open a crack. She might call the cops and report it. Or worse, she might insist on investigating herself.

"Did you hear anything?" I asked her. I flapped my hand in her direction. "I mean, you're out here, too. You must have heard something." Had she been waiting at her door like I'd assumed, spying on her neighbors? Had she heard Jake's door open? Or was she waiting for someone? "Or maybe, I heard you?"

"Hrumph," she said. She had to know I was calling her bluff, but she wasn't giving anything away.

Two could play at this game. "Okay, then," I said, retreating back to my door. "Have a nice day, Milly." I closed the door.

Now what? How was I supposed to sneak around Jake's apartment if it was guarded by Milly? If only I could make myself disappear.

I laughed. Too bad Milly couldn't see me now, laughing to myself. It would really blow her mind if she saw what happened next. "I can't make myself invisible," I said aloud, to my seemingly empty apartment. "But as luck would have it, I don't have to. Cordelia, can I ask another favor?" I didn't wait for a reply. "I need something with the name of Jake's employer on it. A paystub, maybe?"

Then again, who got paystubs anymore? Everything was electronic, and I didn't have access to Jake's online bank records. I wondered who did. His mom, maybe? I assumed she was his next of kin. He didn't have a spouse or kids, at least none that I, or presumably his merry-go-round of girlfriends, knew about. He had a couple of cousins and more than a few rowdy friends. I wondered if the guys I'd met at the bar—Ryan, Liam, and Scotty—had ever sat across the hall drinking beer and watching the Bruins.

Cordelia might know. She'd lived here longer. Maybe "lived" wasn't the right verb tense. She was still here. I might not be able to prove it scientifically, but I wasn't imagining things.

Almost as if I'd spoken my fear that all of this was just a delusion out loud, something slid under my door. I bent to pick it up. It was a laminated photo ID on a lanyard. The ID featured Jake's face and name on the front. There was a bar code below it. The lanyard was bright orange, and I recognized the logo instantly. Just to be sure, I flipped the badge over, and there was the address of a local distribution warehouse.

"Thanks, Cordelia," I said, holding up the badge. "You up for a field trip?"

I put on my scarf, coat, hat, and boots before I left my apartment. I waved in the direction of Milly's peephole as I passed, hoping she was watching. I wondered what she did all day. Did she have any friends? Any hobbies? Any murderous secrets?

Could I have been living across the hall from a cold-blooded killer—retired or otherwise—this whole time?

The bus was pulling away from the stop as I approached and I cursed. Silently. To myself. Yes, I was a grown woman, but my mother would not hesitate to wash my mouth out with soap if she heard me say what I was thinking right now. Sure, she was four hundred miles away, but I had no doubt she would find out if I said it aloud, so I kept it to myself.

Fortunately, the driver saw me running toward the bus and stopped to wait. I climbed aboard, out of breath, thanked the driver for waiting, and tapped my CharlieCard on the reader before finding a seat in the middle of the bus. Morning rush hour was over, and there were only a few other riders beside myself. As soon as I sat, one of them moved to the empty spot next to me.

"How you doin'?" he asked.

Instead of answering, I looked around the bus. Most of the seats were open. It was bad enough being squished in next to a stranger on a crowded bus, but being squished in next to a stranger when the bus was almost empty? No thank you.

"You deaf? I asked you how you doin'."

The woman in front of me got up and found another seat closer to the door. The man seated across the aisle turned up the volume on his headphones before returning his attention to the crossword in his lap. I didn't know if they were deliberately ignoring the uncomfortable situation or if they were too absorbed in their own distractions to notice. Either way, I knew I couldn't count on either of them to intervene. I had to stand up for myself.

"Excuse me," I said. My voice came out higher than normal. I hated it. It was bad enough that I looked like a teenager without sounding like a little kid when I was nervous.

"Oh, so she does talk," he said. He was half-turned in his seat, blocking access to the aisle as he leaned closer to me. I flattened myself against the window. "What's your name, sweetheart?"

"I'm not your sweetheart," I mumbled.

"What?" he asked. He used this as an excuse to move even closer to me. "I didn't quite catch that. Don't be shy."

"Excuse me, can you scoot over?" I asked. My voice sounded as desperate as I felt. "You're sitting too close."

He laughed, and I felt his hot breath on my face. "These buses are always too crowded, amiright?" He wiggled closer, pressing his leg against mine. "Where you headed?"

I squirmed in my seat.

"I asked you a question," he said, raising his voice.

"Please move," I said. I stood up. He was still blocking me in. I shuffled toward the aisle, trying to squeeze past him.

He grabbed my wrist.

"Get your hands off me!" I shouted. The man seated across the aisle slid over to the window seat without so much as glance in our direction. I jerked my arm away from my seatmate, but his grip tightened.

"Not until you ask nicely," he growled.

Then he let go and tumbled sideways out of the seat. He landed in the aisle with a thud. Cordelia's doing, I supposed. Chalk it up to another plus to having a friendly ghost on Team Ruby. Or was that Team Cordelia? Team Corby, maybe? Or Rudelia?

The man snarled at me as he got to his feet, making me realize that I had more pressing matters to worry about. "All you had to do was say 'Please,' bitch."

I scrambled out of my seat and bared my teeth at him. Knowing I had my own private guard dog at my side, for the first time in my life, I didn't feel completely powerless. "Please, *bitch*," I said as calmly as I could muster, glad that my mom wasn't around to hear me. "And all *you* had to do was move." I sounded more confident than I felt as I turned toward the front of the bus, focused on the seats closer to the driver.

Despite my confident reply, I trembled as I headed up the aisle. I was five foot four. He was a foot taller and easily had a hundred pounds on me. I got squeamish if I had to squash a spider. He looked like he ate spiders for breakfast.

Everyone else on the bus continued to ignore us. I didn't blame them for not wanting to get involved, not really, but if I ever saw a man harassing someone half their size, I'd like to think that I'd at least try to help instead of pretending nothing was happening.

He grabbed the back of my scarf. It tightened around my neck as he yanked it. "You need to take a seat until you learn how to behave in polite company," he said, jerking me back toward the seat I'd just vacated.

The pressure on my neck increased and then, just as suddenly, was gone. I whipped around in time to see him fly backward down the aisle and slam into the floor of the bus. The bus swerved and lurched to the curb.

"What's this, then?" the driver demanded, getting out of his seat to face us.

I held up my hands in a show of innocence. They were shaking. "I didn't touch him."

"Bullshit," the man growled. He was back on his feet and stalking toward me again. "Someone needs to teach her a lesson."

"You," the driver said, pointing at him, "off my bus." He pulled a lever, and the side door opened with a hiss. "Now."

"Whatever. It's my stop anyway," he said. "I'll be seeing you," he told me with a menacing grin. Then he stomped off the bus.

The driver looked at me. I could imagine what he was seeing.

I was tiny, and I was quivering. It took all my willpower to hold back tears. "I don't want no trouble from you."

"Me? What did I do?" I protested. "I'm the victim here."

"Uh-huh," he grunted.

I guess I would have been more credible if the guy hadn't gotten tossed across the bus in full view of several reluctant witnesses, but despite how it might have looked from their point of view, I hadn't laid a finger on him. Even if I had, I shouldn't get in trouble for defending myself against a bully. Maybe next time he'd think twice before he picked on someone.

The driver settled himself back behind the wheel and merged into traffic.

Still trembling, I traded in my seat for one closer to the front. "Thanks, Cordelia," I said under my breath. I wondered what I would have done without her. Then again, if it wasn't for Cordelia convincing me to look into Jake's death, I wouldn't have been on the bus in the first place.

To calm myself down, I studied the map posted across from me and counted the stops to our destination. Normally, I would use the app to plan my route, but I was out of data for the month. Although I suddenly realized that I didn't have to be. With the cash that had literally dropped into my bag yesterday and the promise of a paycheck on the horizon, both thanks to Cordelia, I could afford to reload my cell phone.

Three stops later, I'd almost composed myself when it was time to switch over to another bus line. The driver glared at me as I disembarked. The man who'd been so absorbed in his crossword puzzle earlier filmed me on his phone as the bus pulled away. I wondered if he'd secretly been recording when Cordelia threw that man down the aisle. That would be difficult to explain if he decided to post it online later.

Then again, between deep fakes and AI, no one would believe it even if they saw it on video. Fully grown men simply did not fly backward on public transit.

"You gotta be more careful," I whispered as I huddled in the shelter of the bus stop waiting for my next connection. There were two other people waiting with me. One was an older woman whose nose was buried in a paperback novel. The other was a teenager too intent on a game he was playing on his phone to pay any attention to me.

Here I was, cautioning Cordelia to be careful while I was muttering to myself. That was rich. I dug the earbuds out of my purse and popped them in. I could at least pretend to be talking on the phone instead of to my invisible friend.

"Don't get me wrong," I continued, now that the earbuds were in place. "I'm really, *really* grateful you intervened. I just don't want anything to happen to you."

There was a gust of wind. A few feet away from me, the heavy garbage can tipped over and rolled toward the curb, scattering trash in its wake.

I grinned. "I get it, Cordelia. You're untouchable."

CHAPTER FIFTEEN
CORDELIA

I might be untouchable, but Ruby wasn't.

The jerk on the bus was proof of that. I'd stood by as idle and helpless as the other passengers when he started harassing her. The only difference was they didn't want to help. I wanted to, I just didn't know how. But when he grabbed her, I acted out of pure instinct.

Thinking about how close Ruby had come to getting hurt, I shivered, but not from the cold. I should be freezing, but the temperature didn't affect me anymore. I didn't need gloves. I didn't need a coat, or a hat, or scarves, or any of the proper Boston winter protection. I was wearing nothing but a ribbed tank top and pair of Adam's fleece pants, and was perfectly comfortable.

"Where are you going, babe?" Adam asked as I sat up in bed and pulled on his pants. It wasn't a conscious decision, I told myself, but I always seemed to find an excuse to wear his clothes, especially his T-shirts. I liked the way they smelled. This time, it just so happened that his pants were the closest, balled up on the floor next to his king-size bed, next to my blouse. I had no idea where my own pants were, or the rest of my clothes. Scattered about his condo, no doubt.

And I was in no hurry to find them. His wife was out of town, and we had the place to ourselves all week. I had Adam all to myself.

"Coffee," I replied. I slipped on my shirt before padding barefoot into his enormous kitchen. If this was my apartment, I would have needed more layers, but it was warm in his uptown condo. Adam Rees didn't worry about whether or not he could afford his heating bills.

Adam grabbed his glasses from his bedside table and put them on. He got out of bed and followed me, wearing only boxers. "Let me help," he offered.

"I think I can make coffee," I said. I'd been here often enough to know where everything was. A few minutes later, I could smell the beans brewing, and could hear the occasional sizzle as a drop missed the lid and rolled down the pot onto the warming plate.

"Honey, come back to bed," Adam said.

He came up behind me and wrapped his arms around me, toying with the stretchy elastic waistband around my waist. I was wearing his favorite fleece pants, the gray ones that were softened from countless washes. The same pants I would eventually die in. "You're gonna have to give those pants back eventually, you know. I think my wife would notice if they went missing."

"Oh, please. Karin wouldn't notice if you walked around in a chicken suit."

Sad, but true.

Karin was ambitious. She was never at home. Instead, she was always out schmoozing. Other than going home once for clean clothes and to water my plants, I'd spent most of that week at his place. Adam's Egyptian cotton sheets were nicer than mine. Adam's *everythings* were nicer than mine. Although, none of this was really Adam's. Even his buy-in of TrendCelerate had come out of his wife's checking account. She came from a long line of rich assholes.

As far as I could tell, she mostly kept Adam around because, like her many designer purses, he looked nice on her arm at parties. For Karin, Adam was an accessory. For me, he was my everything. It wasn't fair. She didn't deserve him. He belonged with me.

Adam laughed. "You're probably right." He brushed the hair away from my neck and nibbled on the lobe of my ear. "But enough about her."

"You're the one who brought her up," I pointed out.

"Don't be like that, Cordelia," he said.

I hadn't set out to get involved with a married man. We barely interacted at work. It was a small company, but he was one of the owners and I was the receptionist. We might never have shared more than a few mediocre cups of coffee in the break room if we hadn't bumped into each other at the midnight screening of a superhero movie. From that moment on, it was like one of those romance novels I liked so much where we were destined to be together.

Adam said all the right things, of course. His marriage had been over for a long time, he said. They were just staying together to avoid any scandals, he said. He couldn't leave her in the middle of the campaign, he said. Which was nonsense, and I knew it. Politicians got divorced all the time these days. Whatever their situation, there was no getting around it. He was well and truly married. I was the other woman. I was the homewrecker.

I hated it.

Things were good right now. They always were, when we were together. Until they weren't. We'd get into an argument, usually about Karin. Sometimes about my drinking. Occasionally, about something that had happened at work.

He'd accuse me of being needy. I'd accuse him of being whipped. We'd break up. Each time, I promised myself that it was the absolute last time. That we were over. That we were done. Then he'd text me a funny joke or a dumb meme, and the next thing I knew, we were both naked. It was a vicious circle, one that I desperately needed to . . .

I jerked back to the present and realized that I was standing in the middle of a trash can that was lying on its side in the middle of the street. Cars were swerving around it. Which was probably for the best. It wasn't like they could kill me, not when I was already dead, but I shuddered to think what it would feel like to collide with a living at forty miles per hour.

I looked around, but Ruby was nowhere to be found. I must have zoned out for a while. It wasn't surprising. I'd exerted a *lot* of energy tossing that dirtbag around the city bus. And the trash can? That was supposed to be funny, a demonstration that I didn't have anything to worry about. But it had sapped away the last of my strength, proving exactly how vulnerable I really was.

Sometimes I wondered what would happen if I pushed myself too far. If I spent myself out. Would there be a time that I couldn't recharge and respawn like a video game character? Would it be game over and I wouldn't even realize it until it was too late?

And these dreams, or flashbacks, or whatever they were, why did I always have to relive low points in my short but sordid life? Why couldn't I have a nice flashback of watching a marathon of *The Bachelor*? Or I could be sitting on the balcony of a cruise ship drinking a mai tai with just a hint of sunburn on the bridge of my nose. What I wouldn't give to curl up in a comfortable chair and reread a favorite book. If I had to get stuck in a rerun with Adam, was it too much to ask to at least get stuck in a spicy scene instead of a shameful one?

Seeing him again made me feel the shame all over. Were the flashbacks the price I had to pay for being a bad person in life? Adam might not be the biggest regret in my life, but our sleazy relationship was certainly in the top ten. Hah. And here I was, calling it a relationship. Still trying to justify it. "Call it what it is, Cordy," I muttered to myself. "It was an affair. A stupid affair."

Even the word made me feel dirty. Or, maybe, it was because I was—literally—up to my ankles in garbage.

Another bus pulled up to the bus stop. I glanced at the number. It was the route that Ruby had been waiting for, but how long ago was that? Had she left fifteen minutes ago? Or a week ago? It wasn't like I could tap a stranger on the shoulder and ask them what day it was.

I got on the bus. It was a good thing that ghosts didn't have to pay to ride, because I'd left my CharlieCard in my purse, which was who knows where now. It was nowhere to be found when Ruby moved in. I supposed my no-good slumlord building manager had helped himself to it. Probably justified stealing it as a tip.

In the end, he made out like a bandit. Sure, he'd had to pay to get the bathtub I died in cleaned by a professional, but then he stuck Ruby with the rest of the cleanup. I knew for a fact that my bank account had more than enough to cover several months' worth of rent, which was set up for autopay. I wondered how that worked. Once I was dead, did my account get frozen or did rent checks keep going out? Unless the building manager called my bank to stop the charges—and that slimy bastard would never turn down free money—he might keep cashing my checks like I was still living there.

Which, technically, I was.

As the bus lurched forward, I worried about Ruby. I knew she was a grown-up, on paper at least. She could take care of herself. Probably. Maybe she could have handled that jerk on the bus without my intervention, but there was no reason why she should have to.

I chewed on my fingernails as the bus navigated the crowded Boston streets. It was a horrible habit. But what was a ghost to do? It wasn't like they could get any worse, not anymore.

I wish I knew how long I'd been out. Did Ruby go to the warehouse district all alone hours ago or was she on the bus a few blocks in front of me? She'd put on a brave face, but she'd been shaken by that jerk. I didn't blame her. I would have been, too. Maybe she'd changed her mind and went home. But I didn't think she would have. Ruby wasn't a quitter.

It was one of the things I liked about her. I could overlook that she was loud and obnoxiously cheerful. I'd even forgiven her for killing my plants, especially since half of that blame apparently fell on me. If I was being honest, Ruby was my closest friend these days. Who was I kidding? She was my only friend. But I couldn't protect her if I didn't know where she was.

I closed my eyes and let my mind drift, but instead of getting lost in old, sordid memories, I focused on the present. I reminded myself that the only reason I was on this bus was because I believed I was on this bus. All I needed to do was believe that I was with Ruby, wherever she was, and, in theory at least, I would be by her side, ready to protect her if need be.

A tiny voice in the back of my head told me that it didn't work that way. That it was impossible. The laws of physics and yadda yadda yadda. I told the tiny voice to shut the hell up.

When I opened my eyes, I was in an unfamiliar cafeteria. The overhead lights were too bright, too harsh. They dangled from long metal chains, suspended from a ceiling that soared at least another story above me. The floor was scuffed by thousands of feet that had trodden over the industrial surface throughout the years.

Scattered throughout were long white tables—the kind that got dragged out for backyard barbeques or bake sales—and colorful plastic chairs. Everyone sitting at a table was wearing a safety vest. Some wore hairnets. I spotted a few hardhats resting next to cafeteria trays. The man closest to me was wearing a back brace. Seated across from him was Ruby.

If I'd still been alive, I would have sighed in relief.

Did she know I was back? Did she even realize I'd been gone? How did that work for her? If she assumed that she had an attack ghost and/or guardian angel with her at all times, was she more reckless than usual? I had to find a better way to communicate with her so I could warn her that I wasn't always around, but for the time being, I would settle with letting her know that I was here now.

There were no refrigerator magnets in sight, and I wasn't about to risk phasing out from exertion after walking through her, but luckily, there were plenty of easier solutions lying around. Literally. The man sitting at the table across from her was shoveling in food at such a breakneck speed, I was worried he would choke. He took a huge bite of his sandwich, and while he was still chewing it, chatted away.

At his elbow was a thin napkin, along with a fork. There was a spoon, too, but it rested in a bowl of soup that I could only presume was hot. Ignoring the spoon, I reached for the fork, and set it to spinning.

Ruby looked at it in surprise, then glanced around as if expecting to see me standing over her shoulder. The man noticed the fork. "That's weird," he said. He waved his hand over the spinning fork, as if checking for invisible wires. The fork slowed as it lost momentum. "You saw that, right?"

Ruby had the good sense to look confused. "Saw what?"

The man poked the fork. It moved a lackluster quarter turn. "I, uh, never mind." His eyes were bloodshot with dark bags under them like he hadn't slept well recently.

"You were telling me about Jake?" Ruby prodded.

"Yeah. Man, I still can't believe he's gone." He looked down at the last bite of sandwich left on his plate. He picked it up and shoved it into his mouth, then followed it by upending the energy drink in front of him into his mouth. He barely swallowed before adding, "He was one of the good ones, you know?"

Ruby nodded solemnly. "Everyone loved him."

"Well, not everyone," he said. And then he cleared his throat and looked guilty. "Not to speak ill of the dead or nothing. I mean, Jakey would give you the shirt off his back in a heartbeat. Wouldn't even think twice."

"Of course," Ruby said. "But for some people, that's not enough."

"Tell me about it. Jakey was a giver. A real good dude."

Ruby nodded. "Yup. You said that already. But some folks didn't like him? Like who? His bookie?"

He laughed. "You've got to be kidding me. His bookie *loved* him. Used to joke that Jakey was sending his kid to college."

"There's got to be someone he didn't get along with," Ruby pressed.

"Well, there's Markie, of course. You know about that."

"He had a beef with Markie?" Ruby asked, leaning closer.

"I mean, after that thing with Patty, of course there was some tension. I wouldn't really call it a beef."

"Patty?" Ruby sat up straight. "Jake's girlfriend, Patty? Was Markie jealous?"

I was proud of Ruby. She was good at questioning people and getting them to give up information without even realizing it. I just wish I had a way to tell her about the gun the cops found in his apartment so she could ask his friends about it. I mean, the ex-girlfriend angle was great and all, but if we knew the reason Jake had a gun hidden in his toilet tank, we'd be a lot closer to figuring out who killed him.

"Jealous of his own sister?" He snorted. "Not hardly. Plus, Patty and Jakey broke up. That's the whole... Wait a sec. You said you were friends with Jakey. So how come you didn't know about Patty?"

Ruby crossed her arms. "I musta forgot, that's all."

"Yeah, okay." The man stood. "Look, I gotta get back." He reached for his tray.

"Don't worry about that," Ruby said. "I've got this. But, hey, if you see Markie, send him my way, will ya?"

"I don't know when his break is," he said. "He's a picker. I'm a packer."

"That's okay, I can wait," she assured him.

He got up and hurried away.

Ruby gathered his trash onto his tray, then looked around to make sure no one was watching her. "Cordelia?" she hissed. "Where have you been?"

Aha. She *did* notice that I'd phased out earlier. I wondered how. I reached over and swirled the spoon in what was left of the soup.

"Yeah, good to have you back." Ruby carried the tray over to a station where she sorted out the garbage, silverware, recyclables, and various dishes into their designated spots. "You gotta tell me before you disappear like that," she whispered.

"I wish I could," I told her.

"Seriously, we've got to come up with a system," she said.

"A system for what?" a man asked.

Ruby dropped the tray. It clattered loudly on the floor. The man who'd interrupted our one-sided conversation bent over, picked it up, and set it on a stack of similar trays. "Sorry, didn't mean to startle you."

"Don't apologize. I'm just jumpy today," she said with a lackluster grin.

I'd be jumpy, too, if I'd just been attacked by some goon on public transit.

"You're Ruby, right? Jake's friend?"

She nodded. "How'd you know?"

"You're the only one in here not wearing a vest."

I scanned the room. He was right. Everyone else, except the cafeteria workers, had a bright orange safety vest on.

"Plus"—he shrugged—"Jake had a type."

"Oh?" Ruby asked.

The man jerked his head toward the nearest table, then started walking. She followed at his heels. "Don't mean to be rude, but breaks are pretty strict around here. You know how it is."

She nodded, as if she did know how it was. Just wait until she got started at TrendCelerate. She'd get an hour-long break for lunch, and if things were slow, she could leave at four. She'd have a nice, comfy chair with arch support and one of those blue-light screens over her monitor to protect her from eye strain. When she got bored, maybe the developers would ask her to beta test software, and that was always fun.

If Ruby played her cards right, it would be the cushiest job she could ever hope for. Judging from the bags under this man's eyes, which were almost identical to the last man she'd spoken to, they didn't have it quite so cushy here. I had no idea what the pay was here compared to TrendCelerate, but at TrendCelerate the snacks in the break room were free.

"And you are . . . ?" she asked.

He sat. This time, she took the chair next to him. He unpacked his lunch onto the table. He had a meatball sub, a baggie of chips, a banana, and an energy shot. He unwrapped the sub and took an enormous bite. "Markie," he said, his mouth full.

Ruby's eyes got big. "You're Patty's brother."

"Yup." He chewed. "She's heartbroken over this."

"Yeah, I'm sure she would be. But, I was under the impression that they weren't together anymore?"

"Not together anymore?" He barked a laugh then tore another bite out of his sandwich. This time, he finished chewing before continuing. "You mean that son of a bitch cheated on my baby sister. Just like he cheats on 'em all."

He ripped open the bag of chips. It was a generic clear plastic baggie, not a factory packaged bag they sold in vending machines. He shook half the bag into his mouth. "You're lucky."

"I am?" Ruby asked.

"He's dead. Can't cheat on you. Assuming he hasn't already."

"Oh no, we weren't dating. We were just friends."

"Uh-huh. Sure." He swallowed the rest of his chips. Either he was in training for a speed-eating contest, or he wasn't kidding about short lunch breaks. "You guys weren't dating. Good one."

"Seriously," Ruby said.

"Whatever you say," Markie replied. "How come you're here then?"

"I just wanted to talk to his friends."

"We weren't friends, lady."

"Oh? I heard you were," she said.

"Used to be. We were like brothers. Then he cheated on Patty. And now, he's roadkill." His eyes got big, and for a second, I thought he was about to choke on his meal. Ruby must have thought the same thing, because she started to rise in her chair. He waved her off. "I didn't mean it like that."

Markie pulled a chain out from under his shirt. It had an oblong silver medallion on it. He kissed the medallion, then tucked the necklace back under his collar. "I'm not saying Jake didn't get what he deserved, but Jake didn't deserve that."

Ruby blinked, as if trying to untangle the contradiction of that statement.

I was having a hard time understanding what he was getting at, too. Even if he did play fast and loose with women's hearts, Jake didn't deserve to be shot in the head and left on the sidewalk like a bag of garbage. Just because he didn't believe in ghosts, Jake didn't deserve to lose his shot at an afterlife because I was a lousy mentor. And Jake *certainly* didn't deserve to have his killer go unpunished.

Markie sighed. "Alls I'm saying is Jake got what was coming to him."

"Where were you the night of the storm?" Ruby blurted out.

He let out another barking laugh. "That's a good one. Look here, you don't know me so I'm gonna let that one pass, but trust me, sweetheart, if I wanted to get rid of Jake, ain't no one would ever have found his body. You hear me?"

"So you *don't* have an alibi for the night Jake was killed?" she asked.

Frankly, I was proud of Ruby. She was no bigger than a mouse, but she had guts. I'd give her that.

Markie stood. He unpeeled his banana and tossed the peel on the table. "Take care of that for me, will ya, sweetheart? And try not to drop the tray this time."

CHAPTER SIXTEEN
RUBY

"I don't think I'm cut out for this," I whispered as Markie strode away, shoving great big bites of banana into his mouth as he walked.

For the fifth time now, I cleared away the remains of lunch. I was getting to be a pro at that. I got the impression that Jake's coworkers didn't waste a single second of their break, and since I was asking them to give some of it up to chat with me, this was the least I could do.

"Five guys. Three of them thought Jake hung the moon. Other than Markie, his coworkers loved him. His supervisor? Not so much. Called Jake a slacker." I wasn't sure how much Cordelia had missed, but repeating what I'd learned help me sort things out in my own brain. If it had the added bonus of bringing my ghostly roommate up to speed, all the better.

I chewed on my bottom lip, barely conscious that I was doing it. "Markie hated him. But I get it. If someone cheated on one of my sisters, I'd be salty, too. That's part of the reason I never told them about Jerkface cheating on me. I was afraid they'd kill him and end up in jail. Well, not kill him, but at least slash his tires." I don't know why I was telling Cordelia any of this, other than the fact that she was easy to talk to. And I needed to talk to *someone* about Jeffrey. He'd broken my heart, and instead of dealing with it, I'd run away to Boston like that was going to fix everything. Instead, I was lonely, broke, homesick, cold, and attempting to hold a conversation with a ghost in the middle of a noisy cafeteria in a busy warehouse while I interrogated potential suspects in a murder investigation.

Sometimes I questioned my life choices.

Slowly, a question mark appeared in the crumbs on the table left behind from Markie's sub. "Do I think Markie's our guy?" I asked in return. "I don't know. Maybe? I wouldn't rule him out just yet." I thought about the barely disguised threat. "Seriously, why would anyone brag that they'd never find the body if he'd done it? I sure wouldn't say that if someone was questioning *me* about a murder."

But was anyone—other than Cordelia and myself—actively investigating Jake's death? The cops were convinced it was a robbery gone wrong, and were putting little effort into finding the person who pulled the trigger. Even if it was a random robbery, why was it that the only thing missing was a watch that may or may not have been worth much? Why snatch an old watch and leave the brand-new cell phone? Did Jake even have anything of value worth stealing? As far as I could tell, every penny he earned went to pizza or his sports bookie.

It was hard to imagine anyone killing Jake in cold blood. According to everyone I talked to, he was almost universally loved. His cousin, the guys at the bar, and his coworkers painted a picture of a happy-go-lucky guy who was always up for a good time. Then again, they also admitted he was a habitual womanizer. Which was gross, but was hardly worth killing someone over.

The Patty angle was interesting. He'd broken her heart. Her brother was certainly not the forgive-and-forget type. I'd like to talk to her, get her take on the whole situation. I doubted Markie would give me her phone number no matter how nicely I asked, but even if I thought there was a chance, there was no way to get to the warehouse floor to ask him a follow-up question, which was why I was chatting up people in the cafeteria in the first place.

When I showed up, I'd tried using Jake's badge to sneak in, but an eagle-eyed security guard caught me. It didn't help that I looked lost, and not at all like I belonged. I was the only person trying to enter in the middle of the shift, and I wasn't wearing a blaze orange vest. They confiscated the badge, but once I gave my—very convincing if I do say so myself—sob story that I was a friend of Jake's, they were kind enough to let me wait in the cafeteria so I could talk to his coworkers on their breaks.

Now that lunch traffic was dwindling, it was time to head home. I hadn't struck out, not exactly. I knew more than I had this morning, but that wasn't saying much. Short of anyone bragging about killing Jake and getting away with it—which Markie stopped just shy of—the best I could hope for was to gather snippets of information to patch together later.

I was the only one waiting for the bus, but I wasn't alone, not really. I could practically feel Cordelia breathing down my neck. Which was how I'd known that she hadn't been with me earlier. I didn't know when I'd first noticed her absence. At the guard station, maybe? And then, the fork started spinning and I knew she was back.

"Where do you go when you leave?" I asked the empty air around me.

I opened the notes app on my phone. I minimized the note I'd started earlier and opened a fresh one. I held my phone out on my flattened palm, with the keyboard open on the screen and facing away from me. "Seriously, I need to know. Where do you disappear to? And why'd you leave me all alone?"

The display on my phone spun, as if trying to orient itself. The notes app closed. An error appeared on the screen, then another, and another, rolling though my notifications like a group chat blowing up. Even through my gloves, I could feel the phone overheating. I jabbed at the power button and held it until the phone shut down, letting out a single discordant chime before it died.

"What was that? Sheesh. If you don't want to tell me, don't. You don't have to destroy my phone." I shoved the still-too-warm phone back in my pocket.

I was grateful that the bus stop nearest to the warehouse provided some shelter from the frigid temperatures. The bus stop itself was maybe twelve feet long, with glass—or maybe some kind of polymer—on three sides of it and a roof on top. There was an advertisement on one of the walls, a bus route map mounted to one of the back panels, and several flyers advertising everything from get-rich-quick schemes to lost dog notices taped at irregular intervals along the sides.

The walls started about a foot or so off the sidewalk, providing no protection for my freezing ankles. Dirty slush clumped around the metal posts holding up the bus stop and under the bench, and a thick layer of frost clung to the walls. I would be able to see a city bus approaching through the haze, but it would be distorted like looking through a funhouse mirror.

Then letters began to materialize on the frosted glass.

SORRY

I stared at the word for a second. Sometimes I forgot that Cordelia was older than me, then she spelled out whole words like "sorry" when "sry" would do just as well. At least this time it was printed, instead of in her illegible cursive handwriting. "No need to apologize," I told her. "I just don't get it. One minute you're here and then you're just . . . not."

RECHARGE

"What do you mean recharge? Like a battery?" Then I thought about it. "Wait a second. You disappeared after that display at the library. Then after you showed me the money in the envelopes under the silverware drawer. And today, after the incident on the bus. That must have cost you a lot of energy, didn't it?"

A crudely drawn smiley face appeared on the frosted glass.

"I'm right? That makes sense, I guess. But how is it you can toss a full-grown man through the air, but just opening a silverware drawer knocks you out?" I shook my head. "I don't understand."

PAWN SHOP

"Pawn shop?" I asked. I shook my head, unable to figure out how the pawn shop fit into the conversation. "Don't worry, I haven't forgotten about Jake's watch. I'll make some calls. We'll find it."

Before Cordelia could write anything else, the bus pulled up. I got on and chose one of the seats at the very front of the bus, right behind the driver. I wasn't looking for a repeat of the earlier encounter anytime soon. The bus was about half full. There were just enough people around that I knew I couldn't hold a conversation with Cordelia without anyone noticing. Too bad she apparently didn't like communicating through the phone app.

Although, come to think of it, my phone going wonky was similar to what had happened to the reporter's phone earlier, and the computer at the library. Maybe it wasn't that Cordelia had anything against technology. Maybe technology had something against Cordelia.

It made a certain kind of sense. I thought back to how many light bulbs I'd gone through since moving to Boston. I'd lost count. There was the door buzzer constantly short-circuiting, and the pawn shop's neon sign exploding. And what had she said earlier? She needed to recharge?

Cordelia didn't have a physical body anymore, but still, she existed. As what? A spirit? A manifestation? Pure energy? It stood to reason that her ghostly energy messed with modern electricity.

Her presence didn't seem to interfere with the big diesel bus engine, but what if one of the newer electric buses had shown up instead? Once they finished upgrading the fleet, would she have to walk everywhere? Did ghosts even walk? Did they float? "This is giving me a headache," I muttered out loud, not caring who overheard me. No one in their right mind would assume I was talking to my dead roommate.

Despite my paranoia that the guy from earlier would make good on his threat to bump into me again, I swapped buses, got off at my familiar stop, and walked the rest of the way home without incident. I stopped briefly at the corner market to buy an overpriced sandwich from the deli. I could have gone home and ordered a pizza with one of my many coupons for the same amount—and had food left over—but I was hungry now and didn't want to wait for delivery.

I wondered if back home Mom was already prepping for dinner tonight. It was Sunday, which meant the whole family would be there. She'd be making something that could feed a small army. Chili, maybe, with warm cornbread. Or shepherd's pie with her famous gravy. Just thinking about her cooking made the expensive sandwich I was holding look sad and unappetizing.

The prices here were astronomical, which struck me as unfair. Why were groceries so much more expensive in poor neighborhoods than in wealthy, suburban ones? If I could afford a car and a huge apartment with a pantry and a big refrigerator, I could get a membership to one of those cheap bulk foods stores, but without those things, I was paying more to get a lot less.

The answer, of course, was simple. Don't be poor. But digging myself out of that hole once I was in it wasn't as easy as just cutting back on avocado toast. Joke's on them. I couldn't afford avocados. I could barely afford toast.

But what was Cordelia's excuse for living here? She had a decent job, but rented a tiny apartment in a sketchy neighborhood. She didn't have a car, at least not as far as I knew. She was old enough to have decent credit and a legit bank account, maybe even one that paid interest, but kept cash stashed in the silverware drawer. She had stacks on stacks on stacks of books on her shelves, which weren't cheap, but didn't exactly have a Van Gogh hanging in her bedroom. So where did she spend all of her money?

It wasn't like I could ask her. I mean, I *could* ask. As long as we were in front of an extensive magnetic poetry collection or a frosted pane of glass, I might even get some answers. But I couldn't ask about money. That was just weird. I didn't know why it was such a taboo subject, but it was.

I was still thinking about that—and how hungry I was after watching five men shotgun their lunches in front of me—when I arrived back at our apartment. As I approached the end of the hall, Jake's door clicked shut. I stopped in my tracks. "Cordelia, was that you?" I asked, but I already knew the answer.

Cordelia hadn't needed to open the door to walk through it the other day when Bobby had shown up, demanding to have a look around his cousin's apartment. If she'd been trying to tell me something, she would have opened the door, not closed it. "Here goes nothing," I muttered to myself as I approached 4H. I turned the doorknob. Nothing happened.

I knocked, quietly enough that I (hopefully) didn't draw Milly's attention but loudly enough that whoever was inside would hear me. When there was no answer, I knocked again. Still, nothing. "A little help?" I asked. The doorknob turned and I pushed it open.

The woman standing on the other side of the door shrieked.

"Hey, sorry," I said, holding my hands up and backing into the hall. "I knocked."

"So?" she asked, hugging herself. With long, dark hair, big, dark eyes, and a slight build, she could have been my sister or, at the very least, my cousin. She didn't look happy.

"The door was unlocked."

She shook her head. When she did, her hair shifted, and I could see a bruise blossoming across her cheek. "It was locked. I checked."

She was jumpy. I didn't blame her. If I had a nasty bruise on my face and was caught red-handed in a dead man's apartment, I'd be jumpy, too.

"I don't know what to tell you. Maybe it didn't latch. The building's old, and everything's falling apart. My door never locks unless I remember to pull it real hard." I was rambling. I did that even when I wasn't nervous. "I'm Ruby. I live across the hall?" It came out sounding like a question. I jerked a thumb over my shoulder toward my apartment. "I don't think you should be here."

She pulled something out of her pocket, and held up a key attached to a heart-shaped keychain. "It's okay. Jake gave me a key."

"Jake's—"

She cut me off before I could tell her he was dead. "I know." Her face fell.

We stared at each other for a moment. My elbow suddenly felt like it was on fire.

Two summers ago, I'd gone to Ocean City—Maryland, not Jersey—with my then-boyfriend, Jerkface. We'd been playing in the surf when a jellyfish brushed past me. It hurt like nothing I'd ever felt before. My elbow felt like I'd just gotten stung by a jellyfish again, only worse.

I rubbed at it, and the sensation faded as quickly as it had come. Good thing, too. The jellyfish welts had taken days to go away.

"Ask what her name is," a voice next to my ear said.

"What's your name?" I asked. I glanced around, expecting to see Milly standing beside me. Between my knocking and this woman's shriek, surely we'd attracted the attention of my neighbor. But we were alone.

"What's it to you?" the woman asked. When she tilted her head, her hair hid the bruise on her cheek.

She obviously wasn't in the mood to cooperate, and I wasn't sure I had the right to compel her to. Was she trespassing? I didn't know. She had a key to the apartment, so she probably had as much right as anyone to be here. More right than I did, that much was certain. And if she wasn't going to back down voluntarily, what could I do?

I held up my sandwich, the one that had cost way too much. They were stingy at the market deli. I'd skipped breakfast and I could have eaten the whole thing by myself and still been hungry, but in the moment, it felt right. "I just picked up lunch. Wanna split it?"

She looked at me with suspicion. "Why would you do that?"

I couldn't tell her the truth, that I'd spent the day interrogating

Jake's friends and coworkers and none of them looked as guilty as she did right now. She shouldn't be here, which put her at the top of my list of suspects. I had no intention of going away until she answered my questions, even if it cost me half of my lunch. "Because I hate to eat alone?" Again, it came out like a question. I didn't mean it to happen, it just did.

She nodded. "I hate to eat alone, too." She shuffled toward the kitchen. I took a few steps into the apartment and closed the door before Milly could join us. Then again, if Milly wasn't here, whose voice had I heard? There was one obvious answer, but if it was Cordelia, why hadn't she ever spoken to me before? It would have made communication so much easier.

Jake's kitchen was significantly cleaner than the last time I'd been in here. Someone had hauled off the pile of pizza boxes and put away the dishes that were in the sink. The woman pulled out plates from the first cabinet she tried, and got a knife out of the drawer closest to the refrigerator. She knew her way around Jake's apartment and looked comfortable here, but she kept glancing in my direction to keep an eye on me.

She stood on her tiptoes to grab a bag of chips off the top of the fridge. I would have offered to help, but we were both the same height. Women our size didn't store a lot up high for this very reason. Just when I thought she wasn't going to be able to reach it, the chips slid toward her grasping fingers. That was all the proof I needed that Cordelia was nearby.

"Beer?" she offered. Her voice, like everything else about her, was mousy and her manners were immaculate. My mom would have loved her.

"I'm good," I told her.

"Suit yourself." She got a beer out of the refrigerator, popped the top, and took a swig. "Shannon," she said. "My name's Shannon. And you're Ruby?"

I nodded. "Yup." I was half-surprised she wasn't Patty, but I knew I wasn't that lucky.

She held out her hand. I handed her the sandwich. She unwrapped it, cut it in half, and placed a piece on each plate. She shook a serving of chips onto her plate, then looked at me. "Chips?"

"Please."

We took our plates over to the enormous sectional that took up most of the living room. She put her beer on the low coffee table in front of us. It was already covered with overlapping rings. "I know, I know. I've been on Jake to get some coasters, but he wouldn't hear anything of it. Stubborn, that man." She gave me a sad smile.

"You've known him long?" I asked. She was obviously hurting. Part of me wanted to hug her, but the other part, the more sensible part, was suspicious.

"Long enough," she replied.

Well, that was no help whatsoever.

Why was she so at home in Jake's apartment? Was Shannon the new girlfriend, one of the exes, or someone else entirely? Another cousin, maybe? Was she also after the family heirloom watch? I glanced around the apartment. Everything had been straightened, and the stale scent of beer was replaced with the cloyingly sweet smell of air freshener.

I took a bite of my sandwich and chewed, trying to figure out what to ask next. My elbow tingled and I jerked it toward me out of reflex. The last thing I wanted was another jellyfish-level shock. I swallowed and started to ask my next question, but Shannon beat me to it.

"I suppose you're wondering what I'm doing here."

"The thought had crossed my mind, yes," I admitted. "I haven't seen you around before, that's all."

"Why? Are you in the business of spying on your neighbors? Ruby, you said?"

I nodded. Again.

"Not Milly then?"

I was taken by surprise. Jake had told her about Milly? "No, that's the other neighbor. The nosy one."

"*She's* the nosy one?" Shannon asked. She crinkled up her nose. "I don't see Milly barging in here without an invitation."

"Fine. You've got a point. Maybe I am nosy," I said. I moved my plate from my lap to the coffee table. "How do you know Jake?"

"Don't you mean *did*?" she asked ruefully, looking down at her hands. Then she answered the question. Kind of. "We were... close."

"I thought Jake wasn't dating anyone," I said, remembering what his cousin and his friends at the bar had said. Then again, according to Markie, Jake had dated, and subsequently broken up with, Patty. Or rather, she'd broken up with him because she caught him cheating on her. Was Shannon the one he was cheating with? Or, considering Jake's apparent lack of attention span when it came to women, was Shannon old news already?

"Where'd you hear that?" she asked.

I shrugged. "Around."

"Around, eh?" She took a bite of chips and chewed thoughtfully, staring me down the entire time. "Go ahead. Ask me."

"Ask you what?" I asked, confused.

"Ask me if I killed Jake."

CHAPTER SEVENTEEN
RUBY

"Did you?" I asked. "Did you kill Jake?" Not that I thought she'd tell me the truth if she had, but it sure felt good to finally ask a straightforward question.

Shannon shook her head. "No. No, I did not. Did you?"

"No way," I said quickly, taken aback. Why would anyone think that I would kill Jake? I barely knew him.

"Good. Now that that's out of the way, why don't you tell me what you're really doing here?"

"I, uh . . ." My voice trailed off. Short of telling her that the ghost of the woman who'd killed herself in my apartment had told me that Jake's death wasn't random and that she had recruited me to help prove it for reasons I didn't fully understand, I didn't know what to say.

"Were you and Jake close?" she asked.

My cheeks flushed. "No, no," I insisted. "Nothing like that. He's not my type."

"Really? Because you're certainly *his* type."

"Really," I insisted. Shannon wasn't the first person to tell me that. I wondered if what I'd interpreted as Jake's niceness wasn't something more. Which, yuck, no. Even if I was anywhere close to being ready to date again—which I wasn't—Jake was old enough to be my dad.

"But you were friends?" Shannon pressed.

"Not really."

"But you think that there's more to Jake's death than the police, the professionals, do?"

I thought about it for a minute. Shannon said she didn't have anything to do with Jake's death. Did I believe her? Maybe. Maybe not. If I told her that I thought Jake had been murdered, and she was the killer, what was the worst that could happen? Cordelia was by my side, and I'd already seen her in attack mode on the bus. I nodded. "Yeah, I do."

Shannon took a swig of her beer. She put it down, then said, "Me, too."

We stared at each other. Could I trust Shannon? She was being frank with me. I could return the favor. "I've got this feeling that Jake's death wasn't some random event. And if it wasn't random, then it was premeditated. Murder. But the cops wrote it off like it's nothing," I said.

"Yeah, but why do you care?" Shannon asked. "You weren't dating him. You weren't friends. Why does it matter to you?"

I blinked at her. Why did it matter to me? Other than Cordelia asking me to look into it, I didn't really have a reason. I could have said no. What was the worst she could do? But I wasn't doing this because I was afraid to upset my ghostly roomie. I *wanted* to help her. And I wanted to help Jake. "Um, because?"

"Because?" Shannon let out a dry laugh. "And it has nothing to do with being worried that whoever did this to Jake is still running around your neighborhood, free as a bird. Free to kill again?"

"Now that you mention it . . ." Her logic was a lot better than mine.

"Jake was chivalrous, you know," Shannon said.

Only, I didn't know that. I barely knew him at all.

"He was a good guy, and he wouldn't want you to put yourself in danger for him."

"He was a cheater," I blurted out. As soon as the words were out of my mouth, I wished I could take them back. Why had I said that? I could have nodded along and agreed that Jake was this wonderful, kind-hearted, fun-loving, chivalrous dude that everyone else saw him as.

Instead of arguing with me, Shannon nodded her head. "We all have flaws."

"But he cheated," I insisted again. Maybe having been so recently cheated on myself, I had less leniency for cheaters than everyone else apparently had. I leaned forward as if maybe she didn't understand the gravity of the accusation. "It wasn't like he stole Netflix. He cheated. On women. Women like you."

Shannon let out a bitter laugh. "Trust me. Jake was an enormous step up from my ex."

"That doesn't make it okay," I sputtered, shaking my head. "I dated a cheater. I never want to go through that again."

Why had I said that? I glanced at my sandwich. Had the guy at the deli slipped truth serum into it? The only person I'd confided in about that was Cordelia, and now this virtual stranger sitting next to me in a dead man's apartment. I didn't know why the memory filled *me* with shame. I was the one who was cheated on. I was the victim. It wasn't my fault. The only thing I was guilty of was trusting the wrong man.

"I'm sorry to hear that," she said. "Men suck."

"They really do," I agreed.

She took another bite of her sandwich. Chewed. Swallowed. Then she asked, "Did you see anything, or hear anything, that night? The night Jake was killed?"

I guess I wasn't the only person in the apartment who had questions. "Nothing out of the ordinary," I confessed. Was she, like me—and Cordelia—gathering information, or was she gauging whether or not I was a witness that needed to be dealt with?

But her question did spark a thought. I wouldn't have heard the shot that killed him. The building had thin interior walls, but the exterior walls muffled most of the street sounds. Besides, my apartment was on the fourth floor, at the back of the building. I wouldn't have heard anything that happened outside. I knew this for a fact, because according to Milly next door, one of the women on the second floor regularly got into arguments with her significant other by the front door, and I'd never heard them until they got into it in the narrow strip of land behind the building, directly under my window.

However, if he'd gotten into a fight with someone in the hallway, I would have heard it. Heck, if Jake had his television up too loud or had friends over, I heard it.

I thought hard. Like me, he always slammed his door to make sure it shut and locked behind him. Had I heard him leave his apartment that night? I didn't think so, at least not that I remembered.

Living in an apartment building in the middle of the city wasn't much different than growing up in a large household. Having two boisterous sisters, and the occasional additional relative or two staying with us, prepared me for communal living. There was always someone coming and going, someone talking too loud, someone burning something in the kitchen. It got so that I could tune it all out. Jake's killer could have walked upstairs and knocked on his door and I never would have noticed.

"Sorry. I didn't see or hear anything useful," I said, more to myself than to Shannon.

She stood. "I'm going to get a refill. Are you sure I can't get you anything?" she asked, like the perfect hostess.

"No thank you. I don't drink." As soon as she had her back to me, I whispered, "What are we even doing here, Cordelia? What do you think we can learn from her?" No answer was forthcoming.

"Excuse me?" Shannon asked, returning with another beer.

"Um, nothing. Just talking to myself." I let out a nervous chuckle. "Old habit."

She sat. "Uh-huh." She pointed at my mostly untouched plate. "Are you going to eat that?"

I snatched up the sandwich and took a big bite out of it. Half a sandwich was a small price to pay for a chance to interrogate a potential suspect, but a whole sandwich was too much to ask for anything less than a full confession. In writing. Signed. And notarized. As soon as I finished chewing, I said, "Well, we ought to get going."

"We?" Shannon asked. "I'm gonna stick around." She paused. "Jake is paid up until the end of the month, and it's not like he's going to kick me out." She looked around. "Who knows? Maybe I'll take over the lease."

"Okay then," I said. I stood, still clutching the rest of my sandwich. That last bit didn't sit right with me—what Shannon had said, not the sandwich. Maybe I was looking at this all wrong. How desperately did Shannon need a place to stay? I've heard people say they would kill for an apartment, but certainly they couldn't mean one in this neighborhood. "I guess I'll see you around, then."

"I guess you will."

I scurried out of the apartment, crossed the hall, and unlocked my own front door. "Cordelia?" I whispered, as soon as the door was closed behind me. I didn't know why I was whispering, to be honest. I guess with these thin walls, I was afraid that sooner or later, one of my neighbors was going to overhear me having a conversation with the previous tenant and call the men in the little white coats to come check on me.

There was no answer, but it wasn't like in Jake's apartment, where I could sense Cordelia's presence but there was no way she could communicate with me without drawing attention to herself. It was like she was gone.

Did she have to recharge again so soon? How many times a day did she need a boost? Was she like a cat, napping all day, only coming out to eat or be entertained?

The thought made me giggle. "Hey, if you're here, do something," I said. When nothing happened, I realized that I was well and truly alone for maybe the first time since moving into this apartment, and I was going to take full advantage of it.

I dumped a few globs of bodywash into the tub as I ran water as hot as the ancient boiler in the basement could provide. The tub wasn't big, but that was okay. Neither was I. And as far as bathtubs that were older than I was in an apartment building that had stood as a sentinel through the majority of American history, it wasn't half-bad. It was certainly clean. Maybe the only thing in this apartment that had been really, professionally clean when I moved in.

Not that Cordelia was a slob. The carpets were worn but recently vacuumed. The stove was well used and stained by a generation of cooks, but it was as clean as could be expected without replacing half of the hardware.

But the bathtub was spotless. There were no hints of a ring. No hard water streaks. If it weren't for the discolored cracks around the drain, I would have thought it was brand-new, out of the box. Assuming, of course that tubs came in a box. What did I know? I'd never bought a new bathtub. Maybe they shipped them directly from the bathtub factory stacked together like bowls.

I stuck my toe in to test the water. It was perfect. I climbed all the way in and let the bubbles settle around me. I knew it wouldn't last, but I was warm, really warm, for the first time since moving to Boston.

As petite as I was, even I couldn't quite stretch out the full length of the small tub. My knees poked out of the water as I leaned my head back. I doubted Cordelia had ever experienced the luxury of a good soak in this tub. She couldn't have been comfortable. From what I knew about her, mostly from the picture in the article I'd found online and sorting through her clothes to donate, she was a big woman, tall and broad-shouldered.

It was odd how little I actually knew about Cordelia. What was her family like? Who were her friends? She didn't have any sign of them in her apartment. No framed pictures on the walls. No photographs stuck to the fridge. She didn't even have a digital photo frame.

Maybe everything was online. Just because I hadn't found her Facebook page didn't mean she didn't have one. I made a mental note to dig around harder, trying to find her social media accounts. I'd need to make a trip to the library for that, or wait until I'd upgraded my phone plan. And I'd want to go sometime when Cordelia wasn't around. I didn't want her wreaking havoc on the library's computer lab again.

Gosh, how would that conversation go? What was the protocol for telling a ghost that you were going to the library to snoop on her life and you'd rather be left alone while you invaded her privacy? There was just no way to do it without coming off as rude.

I'd asked for her to stay out of the bathroom when I was in there. So far, she'd mostly respected that, but then again, I'd always felt alone when I was in the bathroom. It was the only place in the apartment where I didn't feel like someone was watching me. I gripped the sides of the tub as I sat up quickly enough that water splashed over to the bathmat. Of course Cordelia didn't want to go into the bathroom. She'd died in this bathroom. She'd died in the very tub I was now soaking in, in a tub where I barely fit.

Which didn't make any sense. Sure, if I was going to slit my wrists, I'd probably do it in a bathtub. But Cordelia didn't bleed out. She'd washed a bottle of painkillers down with a fifth of Jack Daniel's. That's the kind of thing most people would do in a bed or on a couch. Someplace soft. Someplace comfortable. Not in a tiny bathtub they couldn't even stretch out in.

I jumped out of the tub and yanked the stopper free. Water gurgled down the drain, taking the pretty bubbles along with it, but it couldn't wash away the image of Cordelia wedged in here, uncomfortable up until the very end.

Considering the copious amount of liquor bottles I'd taken to the recycle bin when I was moving in, Cordelia had been killing herself slowly for a while before she finally finished the job. I couldn't imagine what it must be like to reach that point where suicide seemed like the only option, but if I ever did, I'd rent a luxury hotel before I'd kill myself in this dump.

"That's enough, Ruby," I scolded myself. Nothing good ever came of negative thinking. I shivered as I dried off and wrapped myself in my fluffy robe. I got dressed in a footed unicorn onesie. Why not? It was warm, and I had no plans to venture back out tonight. I pulled the unicorn hood up over my head and headed into the living room where I could curl up on the loveseat near the radiator.

"You back yet?" I asked. Nothing moved. There were no flickers or scurrying darkness where there was nothing to cast a shadow. "Guess not."

I queued up my phone to a podcast I'd downloaded earlier, but when the sweet, comforting tones of the host started describing a grisly murder scene in great detail, I turned it off. I'd had just about enough murder for one week.

Cordelia's bookshelves held an extensive collection of well-read paperbacks. I picked a book off the shelf more or less at random and carried it over to the loveseat. Then I curled up under a blanket and started to read.

CHAPTER EIGHTEEN
CORDELIA

Despite the late hour, all the lights were on in the apartment when I got home. I soon found the cause of it. Ruby was asleep on the loveseat with one of my favorite books in her hand. She was wearing a ridiculous outfit with a unicorn head and a rainbow mane and tail. Seriously? I wouldn't have gotten caught dead in that, even when I was a kid. But Ruby's fashion choices were her own and I had to respect that.

My old afghan was pooled on the floor beside her. It must have come off when she'd rolled over. I picked up the blanket and spread it over her, tucking it around the absurd attached feet of her pajamas. What would she do if there was a fire in the building? Would she run out of the apartment dressed like this? Knowing Ruby, she probably would. And she wouldn't feel even an ounce of embarrassment.

I would be embarrassed for her, for what it was worth. I might be dead, but I still had my dignity. I looked down at myself, with my chipped, chewed fingernails, an old ribbed tank top that was fraying at the seams, and a pair of purloined gray fleece pants I'd stolen from my married boyfriend. "Face it, Cordy," I said out loud to myself. "If you ever had an ounce of dignity, it's long gone."

Wrapping Ruby in the blanket was easy. The lights posed a bigger challenge. If I got close enough to turn them off, the bulbs would blow. I could turn them off at the wall switch, but I'd risk frying all the wiring in the building. In the end, I left them on. Ruby could deal with the electric bill later.

At least she was gainfully employed now. I'd been afraid she was one week, maybe two, away from selling her plasma for cash. And a little thing like her, who ate like a bird even when she could afford food? She didn't have any plasma to spare.

I sank cross-legged onto the floor. I couldn't remember the last time I'd done that comfortably in life. Ten years ago? Twenty? It's true what they said. I woke up on my fortieth birthday feeling every ache and pain that my body had ignored for the first four decades of my life, and it was downhill from there. Not that I had to worry about that anymore.

The building was silent this time of night. It was that magical hour between when the night owls had finally gone to sleep and before the early birds got up, when televisions sat dormant and phones charged quietly in do-not-disturb mode. The streets were empty. Doors were locked. It was as if the earth itself was at peace for just a tiny sliver of time each day.

Before I met Ruby, this was my favorite time of night, when I was completely and utterly alone, but never lonely. Lonely was sitting on a stool in the middle of a packed bar, nursing a cocktail, and hoping to catch a smile, a wink, or a glance in my direction, but instead having no one notice me, not even the bartender. Alone was balancing on the top of the tallest building in Boston long after even the pigeons had gone to sleep, screaming my heart out over the empty streets of the city without disturbing another soul.

In life, I'd never been comfortable with heights. I wasn't afraid of them, exactly. I was just never the person who stood on the edge and looked down. I'd rather stand a few feet away from the rail and take in the horizon.

In death, things had changed. *I* had changed. The worst had already happened. It wasn't like I could die a second time. I could climb to the top of the highest radio tower on the biggest skyscraper without worrying that I might lose my grip. Nothing could hurt me now.

I studied Ruby while she slept. She had no idea how fragile she was. She was young, and felt invincible. People like her never realized that they were one bad day away from losing everything. What if I hadn't been with her on that bus? That creep could have hurt her. Not to mention that there was a killer stalking our street, and she was actively looking for him. It wasn't safe.

I wondered if I could solve Jake's murder without dragging Ruby any deeper into it. I didn't need her help, not really. Sure, she could interrogate people. That was great, but I could do so much more without her. Spending the evening with Shannon had proven that.

Not that Shannon had done anything suspicious, but the fact that she hadn't was something. Of course she was on her best behavior when she knew that she had company. After Ruby left, she relaxed, assuming she was alone. She didn't make any freaked-out phone calls. She didn't rush out of the apartment to meet someone in a shadowy alley. She didn't spontaneously confess anything in the empty apartment.

Instead, she curled up on the enormous sectional and drank another beer while watching *Housewives* reruns. Then she took a shower. She fiddled around on her phone for a while. I couldn't get too close, but as far as I could tell, she was scrolling her social media feed without ever clicking on any of the stories. Finally, she cried herself to sleep.

I wondered about her bruises. There was the one on her cheek that she tried to hide under her hair. That one was a couple of days old, at most. She had older bruises on her legs and around her upper arm that I saw when she was getting dressed for bed. There was a wicked scar on the back of her shoulder that could have been fixed by any halfway decent doctor, which made me think she hadn't sought medical attention for it. There was a cigarette burn on the inside of her elbow. I recognized it because I had a few of them myself.

But what she didn't have was track marks. There was a bottle of melatonin in her purse, but she hadn't taken any before she went to sleep. I didn't see any cigarettes. No vape pens. No crack pipe. Shannon had obviously had a rocky past, but from what I could see, she was remarkably well adjusted. I'd bet the same could not be said for whoever had given her those nasty bruises.

Sure, it would be nice to ask her. "Who punched you in the face, Shannon? What's his name? What's his address? I just want to have a little talk with him."

Nothing serious. I just wanted to push him out a window. Third floor would be best. Anything lower, and he might walk away with nothing to show for it. Anything higher, and I ran the risk of killing him. Not that it would be a great tragedy. Accidents happened.

On the plus side? If he became a ghost, I'd have a second chance to make him see the error of his ways. As painfully as possible.

Not that Shannon would tell Ruby anything, even if she asked. I knew what Shannon was going through. I'd gone through it myself. I didn't always have the best taste in partners. It said something about me that my healthiest relationship to date was with a married man who was never going to leave his wife.

Then again, that was always part of Adam's appeal. I knew from the beginning that he was unavailable. Neither of us could get hurt. Yeah, right. Look how good that turned out.

I got up and crossed to the window, pulling back the heavy curtains. It was too bright inside and too dark outside to see much, but it was better than letting my mind wander down that road again.

"Cordelia?"

I turned to see Ruby still asleep on the loveseat. She'd rolled toward me. Her grip on the romance novel she'd been reading loosened and the book slid to the floor. I picked it up. Detective Mann had given Ruby his business card. It was on the end table. I slid it into the book to mark where she'd left off, then sat the book down.

"I'm right here," I told her. I wished I could do more. Comfort her, maybe. Help her feel less alone in the world. Make her feel safe.

"Okay," she murmured. "'Night."

She didn't actually hear me. She was just talking in her sleep. Her unconscious mind was filling in my side of the conversation.

Just like it was probably a fluke earlier. I'd been paying attention to Shannon, studying her, when I should have been watching out for Ruby instead. I didn't realize that we were on a collision course until it was too late, and her elbow passed right through my arm.

That one hurt. Not as bad as the other day in front of the pawn shop, when she'd walked completely through me. She didn't even realize that was me. Next to that, the encounter this evening was little more than pins and needles. The jerk on the bus was different still. I'd managed to grab him by his coat and fling him away without ever touching him. It had been exhausting, but not painful.

The way Ruby had grabbed her elbow surprised me. I could feel her, but I hadn't expected the feeling to be reciprocal. I'd touched other humans before I met Ruby, usually by accident. If they reacted at all, it was with a twitch or a startled exclamation that quickly turned to them explaining to their friends, "It was nothing. A charley horse. Nothing to worry about."

I'd heard the expression "a goose walked over your grave" before. I'd used it myself, to explain away an uncontrollable shiver that came out of nowhere. Now, looking back on it, I wondered if I'd walked through a ghost and never even knew it. Then again, ghosts weren't all that common, at least not that I'd found.

As Ruby was rubbing her elbow, I was trying to distract myself from the jolt of lightning in my arm, knowing it would go away if I let it. It made sense. I didn't have any physical capacity for pain, therefore I only felt pain if I believed it hurt. Mind over matter. I'd repeat that to myself as often as I had to until it finally became part of my base code.

Yes, that was a nerdy way to think of it. Working at TrendCelerate, and other similar tech companies before that, must have rubbed off on me. Everything we were, everything we thought, even *how* we thought, was programmed into us. People were nothing but walking, talking machines. Our brains were quantum processors and our bodies were hardware. Even our diets followed the most basic rule of computer programming: Garbage in, garbage out.

And I should know. I'd put a lot of garbage into my body over the years. In the end, that was my undoing. I drowned enough pills in booze to fry the old motherboard, and pulled the plug on myself.

"Seriously, Cordy, do you have to be so morose all the damn time?" I asked out loud.

"Morose," Ruby muttered in her sleep. "All the damn time."

I froze. It was dead quiet in the apartment. The only sounds were Ruby's metered breaths and the high-pitched buzz of electricity traveling through the ancient wiring in the walls. The radiator rattled as a warm burst of steam traveled through the pipes. In the distance, I could make out the faint rumble of traffic.

"Just now, you heard me, didn't you?" I asked, turning to study Ruby.

"Nuh-uh," she murmured.

"Yes, you did." I squatted down in front of her. "You heard me just now. And you heard me in Jake's apartment earlier."

I'd been trying to distract myself from the burning sensation in my arm from brushing her elbow. Trying to change the channel in my head, as it were. "Ask her what her name is," I'd muttered. I remember thinking that if Ruby could just stay on track for one second without wandering all over the place, maybe we'd actually learn something. She should be interrogating this stranger who'd made herself at home in Jake's place, but instead, she was standing there gaping at her.

And then Ruby asked, "What's your name?"

That was a coincidence. It had to be. Asking the stranger's name was the next logical step. Anyone would have done it. The timing felt suspicious, happening right after we accidentally collided, but it was a coincidence. Wasn't it?

Anything could, and did, happen, at any time. I'd once read an article about a woman named Lisa who got hit by a car at 3:03 p.m. on March 3. Ten years later, to the day, another woman named Lisa got hit by a car in that same intersection at 3:03 p.m. Spooky, right? Wrong. Could be it was a dangerous intersection. Over the years, maybe lots of people had gotten into accidents in that same exact location. Probably more than two of them were named Lisa. It was a very common name.

Even the time didn't mean much, the more I thought about

it. Who could be certain that both accidents happened exactly at 3:03 p.m.? Maybe one had been at 3:01 and one at 3:04. For that matter, maybe a nearby school let out at 3:00, and parents were always rushing to pick up their kids on time. One way or another, coincidences happened.

I told Ruby to ask Shannon what her name was.

Ruby asked Shannon what her name was.

Big freaking deal.

But try as hard as I could, I couldn't explain away "Morose all the damn time." Unless, maybe, she *could* see or hear me under some circumstances? I was still trying to figure out the rules. At the pawn shop, I'd walked through her, and then she could see *and* hear me for a second. In Jake's apartment, our arms had barely brushed before she apparently heard me. But we hadn't come into contact just now, not even when I moved her blanket. All I could do was add it to the growing list of questions I didn't have answers for yet.

CHAPTER NINETEEN

RUBY

"I had the absolute weirdest dream last night," I told Cordelia as my coffee brewed. At least, I thought I was talking to Cordelia. I could have been talking to myself, but I sensed that she was in the room.

It was Monday morning, and I was looking forward to my first day on the new job. I'd fallen asleep on the loveseat. Sometime in the middle of the night, probably trying to escape my surprisingly vivid dreams, I'd gotten up and crawled into my own bed. Now, I was up bright and early so I wouldn't be late to work.

As I reached for the silverware drawer, it slid open. "Aha. You *are* in here. I knew it. How do I always know when you're in the room?" I asked. There was no response. "Yeah, me neither. We need a real way to communicate better. Preferably, something more portable than a refrigerator."

The coffee maker gurgled to a stop. I poured my coffee and topped it off with some brown sugar. It was the only sweetener in the apartment. I planned on taking the cash Cordelia had liberated for me the other day and going grocery shopping later. Sorry, not sorry, Mrs. Agnes Astor, or whatever that rude rich lady's name was. I glanced over at the refrigerator.

HOW

I assumed she was talking about the communication problems. "I don't know yet. Any suggestions? The magnets work well enough at home, but it's impractical when we're out and about. Pen and paper might work, as long as we were alone and you printed neatly. I don't know how I would explain it if someone saw the pen floating in the air on its own."

***LAST* night**
you *DREAMED*

"Oh, sorry. I misunderstood. I thought you were asking how we were going to come up with a system to communicate. Come to think of it, I guess the magnets aren't perfect, either, are they?" The words moved, only for the same words to reform again in the blank space in the center of the refrigerator door.

***LAST* night**
you *DREAMED*

"Yeah. The dream. It was weird. Spooky, but not really, you know?" I knew how I sounded. People always sounded wacky when they were trying to describe their dreams. Well, either wacky or boring.

"I have a theory about dreams. They're a distraction. Even when it feels like we're working something out, it's just our brain tricking us into staying asleep a little longer. One time, I dreamt I was on a gorgeous tropical island, and I was exploring the caves behind a waterfall. When I woke up, I realized that our upstairs neighbor had let his sink overflow and the ceiling was dripping on me. Drip. Drip. Drip. My mind had concocted the dream about the waterfall so I wouldn't wake up. Trippy, right?"

The silence in the apartment was palatable. I could almost imagine Cordelia glaring at me. "You know, sometimes I get the feeling that you don't like it when I go off on a tangent. But anyway, in my dream last night, you and I were having a conversation. A *real* conversation. Like back and forth." I gestured between me and where I assumed Cordelia was standing near the fridge.

"We were in the apartment. But it wasn't our apartment. I mean, it kinda looked like this apartment but it was in the middle of the jungle. It was hot. Really hot. And there were insects. They were so loud I could hardly hear you."

I took a tentative sip of my coffee. It had cooled enough to drink. "So anyway, you and me were just chatting away. I don't remember what we were talking about. It was inconsequential. It just felt so normal."

Cordelia had nothing to say to that.

"It was just a dumb dream," I said hastily. I should have known my dreams would be of little interest to her. It was just so vivid. The two of us were having a face-to-face conversation for once. She hadn't been wearing makeup. It was weird, the little details that stood out in my dream, like her freckles and her bright auburn hair. "I'd forgotten you were a redhead."

HOW

"I mean, I knew you were a redhead. I saw your picture on LinkedIn. And the article I read about your death had a real nice picture. You looked happy. But in my head, I guess I picture you as a brunette, like me. In my dream, you had the most gorgeous red hair. You don't dye it, do you?"

CHRIST

I snorted. "What box of magnetic poetry did you find that one in? Is there a cursing edition? I bet that one's real popular with kids." Something on the ground in front of the refrigerator caught my attention. I set my coffee down so I could investigate. It was a tiny magnet with three letters printed on it.

MAS

"Seriously?" I laughed. "You broke the Christmas magnet?" I popped the broken half back on the fridge with the rest. Who knew when we would need it again? Maybe Cordelia would have a hankering for mashed potatoes. Or she would encourage me to join Toastmasters. Lots of words had "mas" in them.

"Fine. You're a natural redhead," I said. Under my breath, I added, "Methinks the lady doth protest too much." I picked up my coffee and took another sip. "But enough about dreams and Shakespeare. We still need a system. Any bright ideas?"

There was no answer forthcoming, which was just as well because I had more important things on my mind. Well, maybe not more important. Equally important. I had a new job to crush.

Even though the sun hadn't come up yet, the morning bus was crowded with commuters. I got to the TrendCelerate office early.

I'd been so excited about getting this job that I'd forgotten to ask what time the office opened, and I figured it would be better to have to wait a little than be late and make a bad impression.

What I hadn't counted on was no one else showing up until almost nine thirty. At least that gave me plenty of time to think about all the possible reasons why Jake had been killed. I was convinced it had to do with love, or more accurately, sex, but that didn't narrow down the pool of suspects much. Between all of the women he'd wronged—and I had a feeling we'd only uncovered the tip of that iceberg—and any friends or family who might feel the need to avenge them, there were any number of people who might have wanted Jake dead. By the time someone showed up to let me into the building, I was nearly frozen to death myself.

Finally, Adam, one of the owners I'd met when I came in to interview, arrived. "Hey, Ruby," he said as he recognized me standing in front of the building. He glanced at his Rolex. "Getting a late start, I see."

He was every bit as handsome as I'd remembered. I knew he was one of the bigwigs, but he seemed approachable and down-to-earth, or so I told myself as an excuse to blurt out, "I've been here since seven forty-five." My teeth were chattering.

"Why on earth are you waiting outside?" he asked. He swiped his badge over a reader mounted next to the front door, then looked down at the badge in his hand and cursed under his breath as he ushered me into the lobby. "I'm sorry, Ruby. I assumed that Sally would be here this morning to let you in and get you settled. I forgot it was her day off."

My feet felt like bricks of ice as I followed him to the elevator. "No worries," I assured him.

The morning was a blur of information. First, I was issued my own access badge. Adam taught me how to use the phones and intercom system so I could buzz visitors into the lobby. More importantly, he showed me where the coffee supplies were stored and started the first pot. Once Melissa, one of the coders at TrendCelerate, showed up, he turned me over to her.

"Dude, I don't know the first thing about running the front desk," she complained.

He turned to me. "Lesson number one. Never call the company owners 'dude,'" he told me. Then he retreated to his office and closed the door behind him.

"Sorry," I told Melissa. I wasn't entirely sure what I was apologizing for.

"Don't be," she said. "It's not your fault that we haven't been able to keep a decent office assistant since Cordelia . . ." Her voice trailed off. She cleared her throat. "Don't worry. I'm sure you'll be fine." Melissa hurried off to her desk, leaving me alone.

I didn't have a login for my computer, so I sat behind a blank screen. Over the course of the next two hours, I took a grand total of three phone calls. I was all but asleep at my desk when Adam poked his head out of his office.

"What's for lunch?" he asked.

My stomach grumbled. I'd eaten my last granola bar for breakfast while waiting for the bus and was hoping that would tide me over until I got to the grocery store this evening. "I didn't bring one today," I told him.

"Bring one?" he asked, looking confused. "No, I mean, what did you order?"

I shrugged.

"Melissa!" he shouted.

Melissa's head popped up over the cubicles. She wore enormous headphones and a sour expression. Several other developers had straggled in after her. Supposedly there was a team calendar that showed what hours everyone worked, and when they worked from home versus working from the office, but since I couldn't log in to my computer, I didn't have access to it yet.

"Did you order lunch?" he asked her.

"Why are you asking *me*?" she replied. "Ask what's-her-name. Ruby."

"She's new," he said.

"It's not my job to train her. Why don't you ask someone else to order lunch?" She gestured at the other desks. They were all filled by men who pretended to not notice the conversation going on over their heads. "Or is having boobs somehow a qualification for answering phones and placing lunch orders?"

"Never mind," Adam snapped. I hid my grin. I guess he didn't like being called out on his sexism. "I'll take care of it."

As he retreated back into his office, my cell phone buzzed. A text from Jake's cousin Bobby came through with photos of the front and back of the watch, where the inscription was legible. "Finally!" I exclaimed. I had something to work with now.

There was a phone book in one of my desk drawers that was a few years old. I didn't know anyone printed those anymore. I thumbed through it until I got to the pawn shops. With Adam still in his office and everyone else hard at work in their cubicles, I picked up the phone and called the first pawn shop on the list.

CHAPTER TWENTY
CORDELIA

I struck out at the first pawn shop. And the second. And the one after that.

After getting bored watching Ruby calling her way through the phone book at the TrendCelerate office, I decided to start working my way out in a spiral pattern with our apartment at the center. If Jake's killer had taken his watch, it made sense that he would have pawned it close to the scene. It might take me months to search every pawn shop in Boston, but time was the one thing I had plenty of.

As I wandered toward the next shop on my list, I took a minute to enjoy the day. It was sunny. Pleasant. Perfect for walking, if you didn't mind a bit of a chill in the air, which I didn't. Not anymore. It was one of those days that wasn't quite spring, but spring was right around the corner. If I'd been alive, I would have opened all the windows in my apartment to let in some fresh air, if only for a few minutes.

The night Jake died hadn't been nearly so nice. It had been at the end of the last cold snap of the season. Knowing that a wicked storm was coming, Boston had plenty of warning to batten down the figurative—and, in the case of fishermen out in the harbor, literal—hatches. Bars and restaurants closed early. Buses and Ubers stopped running. Even 24/7 pawn shops locked their doors and sent employees home to their families when the weather turned really nasty.

But I no longer had to worry about the food in my fridge spoiling if the power went out or getting frostbite if the heat in my apartment died. I hadn't cared that night that taxis weren't running. Since I could literally transport myself anyplace in the entire world just by thinking about it hard enough, I couldn't get snowed in.

However, I also couldn't enjoy hot cocoa made on the gas stove because the microwave didn't work when the power went out, or appreciate the smell of woodsmoke coming out of fireplaces when the steam heaters went kaput. I couldn't bundle up in a comfy sweater and spend the whole day rereading my favorite book. I couldn't join a snowball fight in the street with strangers or doodle in the frost on the window. Well, I could. In fact, it might be fun, being invisible while I pelted people with snowballs. It wasn't like anyone would catch me. Too bad. Since that storm was probably the last big snow of the season, I'd have to wait until next winter to try it.

The night when Jake had died? That would have been prime frost-drawing time, but instead, I was out roaming the streets of Boston, as the snow came down in sheets. I'd been enjoying watching the storm blanket my city while Jake had bled out in a snowdrift just steps away from the warm lobby.

Who had killed him? Why? Where had they come from, and more importantly, where had they gone afterward?

If my theory was correct, and the person who killed Jake had taken his watch, he would have wanted to pawn it as soon as possible, before anyone could report it stolen. But with the storm, everything was closed or closing. He might have had to hold onto the watch for another day, which meant he wouldn't necessarily have pawned it anywhere near my apartment and my search pattern was for nothing.

That thought was *almost* enough to make me give up the ghost. No pun intended. Sure, the watch could be in a pawn shop in the suburbs or even New Hampshire, but even in good weather, criminals didn't drive down to a bad neighborhood to rob someone if they lived in the 'burbs. Muggers, pickpockets, and petty thieves didn't generally wander far from home to commit larceny, which meant that this wasn't just my neighborhood. It was likely the mugger's, too.

It was all good in theory, but if the mugger had pawned the watch locally, I should have found it by now. I didn't have access to Google Maps anymore—damn my pesky new allergy to electronics—but I grew up here. I knew this city like the back of my hand back when I was alive. And since my untimely departure from this earth, I'd spent most of my time wandering around exploring every nook and cranny of Boston. As a result, I didn't need Google Maps anymore. I *was* Google Maps.

The next nearest pawn shop was over a mile away. It wasn't far, not on a day like today, but on the night of the storm and even the day after, it had been bitter cold and the side roads had been impassible between plow truck passes. A few blocks would have felt like a million miles to a living human that night.

It was time to admit defeat. The mugger kept the watch. Or Jake hadn't worn it that night. Maybe it fell off in the snow. Or the clasp broke and it was sitting at the repair shop, waiting to be picked up. Maybe an EMT with sticky fingers took it off Jake's body. There were a dozen things that could have happened to the watch, assuming Bobby was telling the truth about the watch being missing in the first place.

I took the most direct route back to the apartment. The shortcut meant literally walking through stranger's living rooms, but they wouldn't notice, not unless I walked through their television or something. Plus, if I saw something interesting, I could always stick around and watch. Entertainment was at a premium these days and I never knew what I was going to walk in on. Or, if nothing was going on and I hurried, I might get back before Ruby got off work. Sounded like a win-win to me.

The first building I cut through was a snooze fest. At the second, an apartment filled with way too many cats caught my attention. As soon as I stepped through the wall, five cats turned toward me. They watched me with laser-like focus, even though they didn't approach or move out of my way if I got too close. I kinda wished someone had been home to witness the cats watch my every step until I passed through the far wall.

I cut a wide path around a building that should have been empty. It was condemned, but that didn't mean unoccupied. The kinds of people that called it home—junkies, crazies, and the otherwise altered—were unpredictable. I steered clear of them.

By skirting the flophouse, I ended up passing the nearest bus stop to the apartment, the one where Ruby caught the bus to work from every day. It was still early, but I kept my eyes open in case she'd gotten off work and was walking home. I didn't see her.

"Psst!" someone hissed, and I stopped in my tracks.

I turned in a slow circle, taking stock of the neighborhood around me. Two kids with backpacks sat on a stoop, hunched over a tablet screen. A pair of older white women chatted over a chessboard set up outside a corner store. A young man around Ruby's age waited for the bus in the covered bus stop. A man in a shirt right out of the eighties, bright pink with the collar popped, stood in the doorway to Lizard Pawn. A woman walking four dogs—one huge Irish wolfhound and three tiny Yorkies—was letting them sniff a discarded food wrapper while she was distracted by her phone.

"Psst," the noise repeated. "Over here."

The man in the doorway of Lizard Pawn gestured at me.

I pointed at myself. "Me?"

"Do you see anyone else?" he asked.

I spread my arms out to indicate everyone else on the block. "I mean, yeah?"

"They don't count," he said dismissively. "They're breathers."

"Breathers?" I asked, stepping closer. As I approached, I noticed things I had missed before. The man had on pristine vintage Chucks, only they probably weren't vintage when he last laced up his shoes. He was wearing short sleeves. It was a warm day compared to the winter we'd just had, but it wasn't short sleeves warm. Plus, he had big bloody stains on his bullet-hole riddled pink polo shirt. I knew from experience that the outfit you died in was the one you were stuck in for the duration, and his screamed 1980s preppy having the worst day of his life.

Then again, I wasn't one to judge anyone's fashion. I was stuck in the clothes I'd died in, too. I'd be wearing sweatpants that didn't fit right and a tank top that was falling apart for eternity. My long red hair was twisted up in a messy bun and held in place with a plastic clip that was missing several of its teeth. I didn't think I had any outward signs of my death. I certainly didn't have any bullet holes or bloody stains, but I had to assume I wasn't exactly the picture of health, either.

"If not breathers," he asked me, "what do *you* call them?"

"I hadn't much thought about it." We were now eye to eye. He was taller than me, and tan. He had hazel eyes and frosted tips in his hair. "I'm Cordelia. I live—"

He cut me off. "I've seen you around. And you've got to knock it off with that breather talk. Ain't none of us living no more."

"Us?" I asked, allowing myself to feel hope. I'd finally found another person like me! That could mean that there were more of us than I realized. "I've been searching for so long. I thought I was the only one. I mean, there was Jake, but he only lasted for a few minutes. Are there a lot of us ghosts?"

"Sure. Tons. We meet to play bridge every Wednesday," he said sarcastically. "Not."

I felt my buoyant mood plummet. "But there's you. And me. That's a start."

"I don't need much company," he said.

"But surely you—"

He cut me off again. "I seen your friend in here the other day."

"Ruby?" I asked.

"Short little breather chick? Real talkative?"

"Yeah, that sounds like Ruby." The last time she was here, I'd just bumped into her on the street. Literally. The encounter had left me dazed, and she'd gone into the pawn shop alone. I hadn't noticed the man in the bloody polo on our last visit, but I might not have noticed the President of the United States playing hopscotch with Dwayne "The Rock" Johnson in my state at the time. "Who are you?"

"Call me Harp," he said. He headed inside.

I followed. "Hello, Harp."

"What can I do you for?" he asked.

"I'm looking for a watch." I thought back to how Bobby

described the watch while he was searching Jake's apartment for it. "Leather band. Silver face. There's an engraving from Pops on the back. Ring any bells?"

He nodded. "Yeah, I seen it. It's in the back."

"In the back?" I asked.

"It came in recently. Lizard wouldn't give more than twenty bucks for it, but the guy who sold it seemed desperate, so he took the deal. Then Lizard buried it in the stockroom."

"Why would he bury it?"

"Because it was hot. Duh."

I continued to follow him through the shop, past the counter, and into the crowded room in the back. Wire shelves stood in rows. Hand-labeled bins lined the shelves. "Rings." "Cameras." "Action figures." "Knives."

We stopped in front of a bin labeled "Watches." Harp gestured toward it. "It's in there. Near the bottom."

I dug through the bin, and sure enough, Jake's watch was buried near the bottom. "Bingo!" But now that I had it, what should I do with it? I couldn't just walk out with it.

"What's wrong?" Harp asked. "You're thinking so hard I can practically see your gears turning. Just take the watch and go."

"Go where?" I asked him. "To the cops? I can see it now. A watch floats into the station and drops onto the lead detective's desk."

He snorted. "That would definitely get their attention. But if you want to be more subtle, why not just palm it?"

"Palm it?"

Harp rolled his eyes skyward. "Don't you know nothing?" He took the watch. The face of it was in the palm of his hands, with the bands laying out on either side. "Now you see it." He closed his fist. The watch disappeared, even the bands. "Now you don't."

"How'd you do that?" I asked.

Instead of answering, he opened his palm and dumped the watch into my hand. "You try it."

I closed my palm. The watch face disappeared, but the band ends were still there. If any livings, or breathers, as Harp called them, were watching, it would look like the band was floating in midair. "I can't do it," I said.

"Of course you can't, not with that attitude."

Then it hit me. I believed it was impossible, so it was impossible. If I could just believe that it was possible... Poof. The watch disappeared.

"That's my girl," Harp said with pride evident in his voice.

I opened my fingers. The watch reappeared. "Cool." I could scarcely believe my luck. Not only had I found a capital-C Clue, but I'd met another ghost. Ruby and I managed to communicate, somewhat, but I could hold an honest-to-goodness conversation with Harp without me being in pain from touching him, or him being sound asleep.

"Can we, uh, hang out sometime?" I asked. I wanted to spend more time with Harp. Unlike Jake, he'd been around the spirit block a few times already and probably knew lots he could teach me. Plus, he wasn't about to go making a rookie move like thinking himself out of existence, or he would have done it already. "Maybe you can show me more tricks."

He grinned lasciviously. "Anytime, dollface. I've got lots of tricks and nothing but time on my hands."

"I didn't mean it like *that*," I said. Sure, it had been months and I was lonely as hell, but if brushing past Jake was any indication, touching another ghost wasn't any more pleasant than touching a living human. That and—no offense to Harp—he wasn't my type.

"Your loss. There's this thing I can do with my—"

This conversation was going downhill. I needed to change the subject, fast. I cut him off in mid-sentence. "What can you tell me about the guy who brought this in? What did he look like?" I asked.

"Big dude. Rough around the edges. Had a thick Southie accent," Harp said.

"Gee, thanks for narrowing it down." Our mugger was local. Go figure.

"He wore one of those saint necklaces," he added.

"Oh, come on. Now you're just describing everyone in Boston. You've got to give me something to work with. A scar. A limp. A tattoo with his name on it. Something."

"White guy. Average height. Average build," he said. "I don't pay much nevermind to the breathers, unless they're wearing short skirts. The only reason I even noticed your friend the other day was because you were with her."

"Another dead end," I muttered to myself. "Figures."

"Would his ID help?" Harp suggested.

"Would his ID—" I started to repeat sarcastically, but then I stopped myself. It wasn't Harp's fault that he was the most annoying ghost on the planet. For all I knew, this was his first interaction with a non-breather in years. Decades, maybe. I couldn't fault him for having rusty social skills. Come to think of it, mine weren't all that great even when I was alive. I nodded my head. "Yes, Harp. His ID would help immensely."

"Rad," he said. Then just stood there, not blinking. Not breathing. Not moving a muscle.

"Well?" I prompted. "His ID? I don't suppose you have a copy?"

"Sure do. It's the law. If you wanna sell anything to a pawn shop, you gotta provide ID on account of if it turns out to be stolen, the cops can trace it back to the guy that sold it."

"How do you know all this?" I asked.

Harp gestured at his blood-stained polo. "Used to work here, until some junkie decided to rob the place. The retirement package is to die for. Literally."

"Sorry," I said.

He waved his hand in dismissal. "It was ages ago. So anyway, anything that comes in, the ID gets scanned and is attached to the file, which is linked to the number on the tag." Harp gestured at the watch.

There was a printed tag hanging off the clasp of the watch with a long series of numbers and letters on it below a barcode. "Scanned?" I asked. "As in into a computer?" Fat lot of good that was going to do me. I couldn't get near enough to a computer to pull out the information I needed.

"And now you see why I didn't think the ID was relevant," Harp said. "Information's useless if we can't access it. At least in my day we kept everything in file cabinets. Now it's in the cloud, whatever that means. We're out of luck."

An idea hit me, and I let go of the watch. It fell back into the bin with the other watches. "Good thing we have an ace up our sleeves."

CHAPTER TWENTY-ONE
RUBY

When I got home from my first day of work, I was exhausted. I'd lugged my grocery bags up four flights of stairs and was busy unpacking them when I got the now-familiar sensation that I was no longer alone in the apartment. "Cordelia?"

The refrigerator door, which I had left open while putting the groceries away, swung shut.

"Hey, there you are," I said. "I hope your day went smoother than mine. I guess no one remembered I was supposed to start today, so no one was there to give me the orientation. And I'm starting to think that Adam is kinda a jerk."

A box of cereal I hadn't put in the cabinet yet wobbled and fell to the ground.

"Sheesh," I said, picking it up and shelving it next to the other boxed meals. "I thought you'd want to hear about my first day on the job, a job that you got me in case you've already forgotten."

In response, the top of a family-size bag of Skittles ripped open.

The bag tipped over, and Skittles scattered all over my kitchen floor.

"Okay, this isn't funny anymore," I said, bending over to scoop up a handful of the colorful candies. "These aren't cheap, you know." As much as I was craving them, I tossed them in the trash. No matter how clean I tried to keep my apartment, I wasn't going to eat floor food. At least, not with Cordelia watching and silently judging me.

A few of the Skittles started rolling in a line toward the door.

"Come on, Cordelia. Not the orange ones. Those are my favorite," I complained. Every time I picked up one of the candies, another one appeared in front of it. "Fine. You want me to follow you?" The front door opened. "I'll follow you," I promised. "Just let me get my coat first."

By the time I had my coat, purse, and keys, there was a line of green Skittles leading down the hall and toward the stairs. "Now you're just being wasteful." I hurried down the hall, picking up candy as I walked. If I wasn't going to eat the ones on my own floor, I certainly had no intention of eating food from the common hallway, but I couldn't leave them, either. They would attract ants. Or mice. Or worse, the attention of neighbors.

I took the stairs down. Cordelia was dropping the Skittles farther apart now. I was grateful for that. "You're reimbursing me for these out of the silverware drawer," I warned her. Granted, my budget was better now than it had been last week, when I was trying to stretch a single pack of ramen noodles into multiple meals, but I didn't have money to throw around. My first paycheck couldn't come soon enough.

There was a single yellow Skittle in the lobby. I scooped it up and went through the doors leading outside. Night had fallen. I waited a second for my eyes to adjust. There were no Skittles on the steps, but there were three red ones in a line pointing down the street toward my bus stop.

A block later, my pockets were filled with Skittles. "I hope we don't have too much farther to go, or you're going to run out," I told Cordelia. This was weird. Weirder than usual, I mean. It's not like there was a bag of Skittles floating in front of me. That, I could have followed easy enough. Instead, individual candy pieces appeared on the sidewalk to let me know I was still on the right path.

Then, an entire handful of yellow Skittles showed up. They formed a right-hand turn into an alley entrance. I hesitated. "You sure?" I asked aloud. As much as I tried to see the bright side of things, there wasn't much brightness to be seen down the dark, sketchy alley. There was a delivery truck parked with its hazards on, and beyond that, overflowing dumpsters. A few of the businesses that had back doors opening into the alley had lights over their entrances, but either the bulbs were broken or burnt out.

In response, an entire handful of Skittles scattered at the alley entrance and began rolling into the dark. "Whatever. I get the picture," I grumbled. I trusted Cordelia wouldn't intentionally lead me into a dangerous situation. Then again, if she was so smart, she wouldn't be dead, now would she?

I reluctantly followed the candies down the dark, narrow alleyway between two buildings. The ground was covered in muddy slush leftover from the last snowfall. On the plus side, it was too cold for the dumpsters to stink. Either that, or my nose was too frozen to smell.

The Skittles abruptly stopped in front of a door that slowly swung opened as I approached. Say what you will about sharing an apartment with a pushy ghost, she certainly came in handy at times. I glanced at the label on the door. "Lizard Pawn," I read aloud. I stepped inside. "Should we be worried about the security system?" I asked. Pawn shops usually had something to protect their inventory.

I heard a beeping behind me and turned to see a flashing alarm panel. "I hate it when I'm right," I muttered. "You wouldn't happen to know the code, would you?"

As I watched, one of the buttons was depressed. The beeping sound turned into a whine. Another button twitched. The whine turned into an electronic squeal, almost like feedback. A puff of smoke appeared above the keypad and then the entire panel sparked and went dark. The alarm let out one final blip, then fell silent.

"Well, that's one way to do it," I said.

The room I was in was only lit by two glowing "Emergency Exit" signs, so I pulled out my phone and turned on the flashlight. Finally, I had a good use for my phone that didn't cost me any minutes. I ran the beam over row after row of shelving units packed tightly together. "A little help?" I asked. "At least tell me what I'm looking for."

I heard a scrape in the darkness and followed the sound to see a plastic bin sliding out of its spot on the shelf. It tumbled to the floor, scattering its contents. I focused the light from my phone on the resulting mess, illuminating a tangle of watches. "Oh! Jake's watch!"

There were several dozen watches to sort through. I probably would have been there all night if not for the fact that one watch lay slightly apart from the others, ringed with multicolored Skittles. "What do we have here?" I grinned as I picked it up.

I pulled up the picture that Bobby had texted me. "We have a match." Just to confirm, I turned it over and checked the inscription. "'Love, Pops,'" I read aloud. "Score."

Then my face fell. "Uh, Cordelia, I don't know how to break it to you, but this doesn't actually help us figure out who killed Jake unless we can trace it back to whoever pawned it. And I don't think Lizard, the pawn shop owner, is going to be very helpful, considering when I asked him the other day, he lied and said no watches had come in recently."

I slipped the watch over my wrist, rationalizing that it was more secure on my arm than in my pocket or purse. I fumbled with the clasp in the dark, but something prevented it from closing. There was a tag stuck to the clasp. The tag had a barcode and a jumble of letters and numbers on it. "What's this?" I shone my light on it. "Of course! There has to be a way to keep track of all this junk. All we need is access to their books."

There was a creaking sound. I jumped and whirled, expecting to find myself at the wrong end of an angry Lizard's shotgun. Instead, the door between the storage room and the main floor of the pawn shop was now open.

I glanced down as I walked through the open door, expecting to see Skittles on the floor, but there were none. "I hope that doesn't mean the bag is empty," I said. "The least you could do is leave me a serving."

It was brighter on the showroom floor of Lizard Pawn because the street light shone through the barred windows, leaking in between the sales signs. I turned off my phone's flashlight.

Stopping by the grocery store after work had taken longer than I'd expected. It was getting late, but the door advertised that Lizard Pawn was open 24/7. Then I noticed the hand-lettered sign below it: "**BACK IN 5**."

"Uh-oh. We better hurry," I said. I had no idea when the night shift clerk was returning. They had to have left before I showed up, or they would have noticed the alarm wasn't working. How long had I been in the back room? A minute? Ten? Longer?

I scurried around to the computer on the counter. It was on, but it was on the login screen. "I don't even have a login at TrendCelerate. How am I supposed to get in here?"

The keyboard skittered sideways, revealing a layer of sticky notes. And by "sticky," I mean it looked like someone had poured cola on them, not that they were intentionally manufactured to cling to surfaces. One of the notes nearest the top was notably less grimy than the others. I hoped that meant it was more recent, so I typed it in.

The password didn't work. I grabbed another sticky note and typed it in. Still nothing. But the third note was the charm, and the screen sprang to life.

I waved the barcode attached to the watch's clasp under a handheld reader attached to the computer, and a record popped up on the screen. "Bingo," I said. I dropped the watch into my purse as I hit the print button on the computer. The printer behind the desk whirred and spit out a piece of paper into the waiting tray.

A noise caught my attention, and I looked up to see someone at the front door. They were hunched over, concentrating on the doorknob. I ducked down behind the counter before they could look up and see me. I fumbled behind me, trying to grab the printout, but it was just beyond the reach of my fingers. Then, like magic, the paper wafted out of the tray and into my waiting hand. "Thanks, Cordelia," I whispered.

There was a sharp metallic click as the door unlocked. Someone stepped inside, triggering an electronic squeal from the door sensor. In another minute, they would come around the counter and see me. "Goddamn cheap piece of shit alarm," a man said. He let out an exasperated sigh. "When is this thing *not* broken?"

I risked poking my head over the counter to get a peek at him. He was standing with his back to me as he jabbed at the dead alarm panel. While he was distracted, I took the opportunity to crawl toward the door separating the main store from the stockroom. There were several feet between the end of the counter and the open door. In order to make it through the door, I'd be exposed.

There was a loud crash near the front of the store as a display of bicycles tumbled to the floor. "Who's there?" the man asked. He reached out and flipped the switch, flooding the pawn shop with light. "I'm calling the cops," he said, reaching for his phone.

The lights flickered and went dark.

Taking advantage of the distraction, I bolted for the door and it slammed behind me. "Close call," I said, slightly out of breath as I weaved my way through the shelving units to reach the back door. Before I reached it, there was another crash behind me in the main store room. Satisfied that the night clerk was sufficiently busy, I dashed to the door.

It sprang open and I ran through it. "Good thing you can be in two places at once, Cordelia," I told her. Keeping the clerk busy in the front while still handling the doors in the back was an impressive trick.

Without waiting for any encouragement from my ghost, I scrambled through the alleyway. Luckily, I didn't slip on any black ice or refrozen slush. I reached the sidewalk and slowed down, partially so I didn't look like I was fleeing the scene of a crime and partially because I had a stich in my side from my mad sprint down the alley.

As I speed-walked back to the apartment, I noticed a Skittle that I'd missed before and slowed to scoop it up. "You're a litterbug," I chastised Cordelia. When I passed a trash can, I emptied my pockets into it, leaving a rainbow of candy on top of previously discarded trash.

I let myself into the building lobby and paused to catch my breath before the long climb up to the fourth floor. Once I was safely in the apartment with the door locked behind me, I headed straight for the kitchen and poured a glass of water from the tap. I downed it. "That was close," I said.

I pulled Jake's watch out of my purse and, not having a better place for it, shoved it into the back of the silverware drawer. I had stuffed the printout in my bag. I pulled it out now and smoothed it out.

"Well, well, who do we have here?" I asked, staring down at a photocopy of Markie Brown's driver's license.

CHAPTER TWENTY-TWO

RUBY

The rest of the week went by mind-numbingly slowly. From eight to five, I tried to keep my mind on work as I settled into my role at TrendCelerate. I finally got a login to my computer. I found where the bathroom key was kept. I located a stash of menus. I even figured out how to clear a printer jam, thanks to a video I found on YouTube.

I'd left two messages at the warehouse for Markie Brown, but he hadn't called me back. Big surprise. If I'd just killed a guy and some stranger was calling me at work after interrogating me on my lunch break, I wouldn't have called them back, either.

Maybe I should go to the police with what I knew, but even if I could convince them to re-examine Jake's death as a homicide, how was I supposed to point the finger at Markie without admitting I'd broken into a pawn shop with a ghost and then stolen evidence? If I'd been thinking straight, I would have left the watch right where I found it and called in a tip to the cops later, but when the shopkeeper came back from his break, I was more worried about getting out without being seen than preserving the chain of custody. Rookie mistake.

The watch was a critical clue, but until I could confront Markie with it, I had no way of proving he was connected to Jake's death. I had Markie's address from his driver's license, but going to his place alone seemed like a bad idea. Every night, I stopped by O'Grady's after work, hoping to bump into Markie. Or Bobby, who also wasn't returning my texts. Or any of Jake's friends or exes. Every night, I came up empty. Several times, I stopped by Jake's apartment and knocked, but Shannon didn't answer the door. My investigation was officially at a standstill.

I tried to throw myself into my day job, but it wasn't mentally taxing work once I got the hang of it. I was starting to understand why Cordelia had so many paperbacks at her apartment. As long as the phones were answered, no one seemed to care what I did in my downtime, and I found myself working my way through her collection of novels. Unfortunately, I couldn't concentrate because my mind was preoccupied with Jake's death, and I often ended up rereading the same page multiple times.

Sometimes, Cordelia came to TrendCelerate with me. I could tell when she was in the office because the guys—and Melissa—in the cubicles would complain about weird computer glitches, and various toys and squeeze balls would fall off people's desks. If I was this bored at work, I couldn't begin to imagine how dull her days must be to have her choose to spend them with me at the front desk.

On Thursday, I got to work to find a red Etch A Sketch sitting next to my keyboard. "I wonder who left this here," I said, slipping it into the bottom desk drawer that served as the office lost and found. I got up to brew a pot of coffee, and when I got back to my desk, the Etch A Sketch was on my chair.

"Okay, okay," I muttered, even though I was one of the few people in the office this early. Marc was here, too, but he was in his cubicle with his headphones on. I doubted he could hear me. "I can take a hint." I played with the dials. I vaguely knew what an Etch A Sketch was, but I'd never had one as a kid, and it took me a minute to get the hang of it. One knob drew a vertical line. The other drew a horizontal one. Used together, I could make shaky loops and swirls.

I shook the toy, clearing my doodles. "I lied. I can't take a hint. What's this for?" I asked.

The dials began to turn on their own accord. In blocky letters connected by a thin underline, the word "**SYSTEM**" appeared on the screen.

"Cordelia Graves, you sly dog," I said with a grin. I'd mentioned several times that we needed a better system of communication, and she'd come through.

"Excuse me? What did you just say?"

I looked up to see Adam standing over my desk looking at me with a dark expression on his face.

"Oh! Mr. Rees! I didn't hear you come in!" I opened the lost and found drawer, dropped the Etch A Sketch into it, and pushed the drawer closed.

"You were in the break room making coffee when I got here," he said, with a frown. "What's that?"

"What's what?" I asked, trying to sound innocent.

"What were you doing just now?"

I shook my head. "Nothing. Just straightening up my desk."

"Who were you talking to?" he asked.

"No one," I lied. My mind raced. What had I said? I was in the habit of talking to Cordelia. What had he overheard?

"Let me see that," he said, holding out his hand.

"Yeah. Sure. Of course." I retrieved the Etch A Sketch from the drawer. I glanced at the screen before handing it to him. It was blank.

"Is this yours?"

"I, uh, found it."

He turned it over in his hands. "I used to have one just like it when I was a kid. I didn't know they made these anymore." He handed it back to me. "If you need anything, I'll be in my office."

"Okay," I told him, setting the Etch A Sketch to the side.

Adam walked away, but paused at his open door. He turned back to me. "Did you say . . ." His voice trailed off.

"Did I say what?" I asked, trying to sound innocent.

"Never mind," he said. "Imagination's playing tricks on me." He retreated into his office and closed the door behind him.

"That was a close call," I said to Cordelia.

Without the dials on the Etch A Sketch moving, neatly printed words appeared on the screen. Each word was connected by a thin line. I guess there was no way to create spaces. But the mechanics of the Etch A Sketch were less interesting than the message itself:

Jake_had_GUN_in_apt

"What? Really?" From what little I knew about Jake, he didn't seem like the gun type. "Why?"

The words disappeared off the screen, replaced by a giant question mark. I guess Cordelia didn't know either.

"Where is it now?"

cops

I nodded. "Makes sense. I wonder why he had one in the first place." Having a gun added another layer of intrigue to Jake's death. Up until now, I'd been assuming that the worst thing he'd done was sleep around, but maybe that was just the tip of the Jake iceberg.

. . .

Saturday morning, I'd just dragged myself out of bed—why was it so hard to get up on the weekends?—when there was a knock at the door. "Are we expecting anyone?" I asked Cordelia. Of course, I was answered with silence. For all I knew, Cordelia was already at the door, checking out our visitor. Or she was standing right in front of me.

There was, however, an easy way to find out who was knocking. "Coming, coming," I called out.

I checked the peephole. There was a woman on the other side of the door. She was about my height. Slim build. Darkish hair. She had bangs and bright pink lipstick. I didn't recognize her.

I opened the door. "Hello?"

She was in the middle of trying to blow a tiny bubble with the kind of stick chewing gum that wasn't meant for bubbles. When I opened the door, she snapped it and sucked it back in. She tilted her head slightly as she studied me.

The woman was white. Not just white, but pale. She had dark brown eyebrows, thick but kempt, and black hair, darker even than my own. Her eyes were shockingly bright blue as her gaze shifted to stare past me into my apartment.

"You wanted to talk?" she asked, returning her attention to my face. Unlike her, I didn't have any makeup on and my own brows could stand some TLC.

"Do I know you?" I asked, even as I felt like I should have. She seemed to know me. I was good with faces. I didn't recognize her, but she felt vaguely familiar, as if we'd ridden the same bus for years but never spoken.

"We've bumped into each other," she said. She made a vague gesture with her hands. "Literally." She looked over her shoulder at Jake's door, and that's when I remembered her.

I was going down the stairs, carrying a laundry basket piled high with dirty clothes. She was coming up the stairs with a pizza box. Neither of us were looking where we were going, and it had been a near miss. I'd seen her in the hall before that, coming out of Jake's apartment.

"You're Patty," I guessed. "Markie's sister." I felt myself tense. I wonder if she knew what her brother had been up to. More importantly, had she been in on it? Her ex had been killed in a supposed mugging, his watch had been stolen, and then her angry brother had sold the watch to a sketchy pawn shop after he died. It was a slam dunk case, as far as I was concerned. It didn't look good for either of them, but I still needed to prove their guilt. "I've been trying to reach him."

"You're Jakey's nosy neighbor," she said. "I'd be happy to get a message to my brother for you."

Even as she said that, the door next to Jake's opened just a crack. I couldn't see her, but I knew that Jake's *actual* nosy neighbor, Milly, was straining to listen to our conversation.

I didn't want to invite a potential accessory to murder into my apartment, but I didn't want to have this conversation in the hall with Milly listening to every word, either. At least I had a ghostly ally in my apartment. "Come on in," I said, opening the door wider. Patty stepped inside. "Morning, Milly," I yelled into the hall in a cheery voice. Milly's door slammed. I closed my own with considerably less force.

Now what was I supposed to do? It was hard to act normal, knowing Patty, or her brother, might have been instrumental in Jake's death. "Uh, can I get you some coffee?" I asked, making sure to keep a wide distance between us.

"Beer?" she asked.

"It's barely nine o'clock in the morning," I blurted out.

"I know. And I'm gonna be late for work. My shift starts in thirty minutes." She made the move-it-along gesture with her hands. "How's about that beer?"

"I'm not legal," I said. I was starting to second-guess myself. Patty didn't seem much like a killer. She wasn't acting nervous or guilty. Then again, she didn't seem to be too worried about being late to work, either. Maybe she was good at masking.

"So what?"

"So, no beer."

"Okay. Whatever." She glanced around my living room. "It looks like an old lady lives here."

The temperature in the apartment dropped ten degrees. Even Patty shivered and drew her coat tighter around here.

I could have explained that I'd rented the apartment fully furnished and hadn't had the money to put any personal touches on it yet. I could have explained that the furniture was picked out by a dead woman, a dead woman who happened to be in the room with us right now, and that she didn't appreciate being called old. I could have even told her that she should have seen it when every surface was covered in leafy green plants, each in a unique planter.

Patty flopped down on the loveseat in what my mom would

have called a decidedly unladylike manner, and dropped her oversized handbag to the floor with an audible thud. Sorry, downstairs neighbors. "It's drafty in here," she said.

"It's an old building," I said. The printout from the pawn shop was on the coffee table in front of us. I slid one of Cordelia's magazines on top of it before she could notice it, then sat next to her. I turned sideways on the cushion so I could face her. "I understand you and Jake were close. I'm sorry about your loss."

She snapped her gum again. "Not so close, not these days." She looked around, twisting in her seat to glance at the bathroom. "That's where she did it, right?" I must have looked confused, because she explained, "The redhead. She killed herself in the bathroom, right? Oh, I guess that was before your time. Duh."

"Yeah, before my time," I agreed.

"She was okay." Patty snapped her gum again.

"Wait, you knew her?"

Bobby, the bartender, and everyone else I talked to had all said that Jake didn't have anyone special, not for long, but Patty had been coming around back when Cordelia was alive and was still around after I'd moved in. I didn't know how serious they'd been, but they'd had to have been seeing each other for a few months at least.

That could explain why Markie was so upset when they broke up. It would have been bad enough to find out that one of your best friends treated your baby sister like a one-night stand. But they'd dated for a longish while. Then Jake cheated on her. As far as murder motives went, it didn't suck.

Patty shook her head. "Only to nod in the hallway. And once, around Christmas, I came over to borrow a six-pack."

"This Christmas?" I asked, leaning forward. Cordelia had

killed herself around Christmas. Patty might have been one of the last people to see her alive.

"Well, yeah. I certainly wasn't dating Jakey the Christmas before last. Can you even imagine?"

"Yeah, I can," I said. I'd dated Jerkface for a little over two years before we broke up. We'd spent three Christmases, three New Years, and two Fourth of July holidays together. It was the longest and most serious relationship I'd ever been in. Sometimes, late at night, I wondered how many times he cheated on me before I caught him. Was that his first time? His fifth? His fiftieth?

I could feel my blood pressure rising just thinking about it. But even if I found out he'd cheated on me a hundred times with a hundred different women, I would never have killed him. I didn't know that I could say the same about Patty, though.

Patty was staring at me with a pitying look on her face, so I steered the conversation back on track. "You said you came over to borrow beer?" I wasn't sure exactly how one would borrow a six-pack, but more than that, I was curious why Cordelia would have beer in the first place, especially since all the empties I'd found in her apartment were square Jack Daniel's bottles. I hadn't seen any beer bottles. Not in the recycles, and not in the fridge. "Did she drink beer?"

"All she had was that frou-frou microbeer stuff," Patty explained. "Said it was her boyfriend's but I could have it. Nice lady."

"Really?" I was interested in this boyfriend Patty had mentioned. Cordelia had a boyfriend when she died? How did I not know this? And one that drank microbrews? While I wanted to learn more about my ghostly roommate, I forced myself to concentrate on Patty. Cordelia and I could chat later. "You and Jake . . . ?" I let the question hang in the air.

"Me and Jake," she agreed, without adding anything to the conversation.

"You were serious?"

"I was. He wasn't. End of story."

"But you thought he was?" I probed. I wondered about Shannon. She also thought that she and Jake had something special. Had Jake been serious about her, or was she just another one of his conquests? Would they have lasted more than a few weeks, or was Shannon fooling herself, too?

"End. Of. Story," Patty repeated.

"I understand. I've been there," I said. "Want to talk about it?"

She snapped her gum again.

"Do you know anyone who might have wanted to hurt Jake?" I asked, trying a different tactic.

"Besides me?" She let out a sharp bark of a laugh. "My brothers. Markie, Connor, and Johnnie aren't exactly chipping in on his memorial, if you know what I mean."

"Markie was mad about your relationship?" I asked, even though I already knew the answer.

"Mad? He was furious."

I wondered if he was furious enough to do something about it, like ambush Jake, shoot him, and steal his watch to make it look like a robbery. "You sure have a lot of brothers," I remarked, hoping she'd tell me more about Markie.

"Do I?" She shrugged.

"And Markie is your favorite?" I asked. I knew siblings weren't supposed to have favorites, but I'd be lying if I said I didn't have a soft spot for my baby sister, not that I'd ever admit that out loud.

She snapped her gum again. "All three of them are meatheads. I love 'em, you know? But also, if I could have traded any of them for a puppy growing up, I'd have three dogs and zero brothers."

That I couldn't relate to. My sisters were my best friends, even my less-favorite one. I missed them every day. Sure, we texted each other constantly, and when I had data on my phone, we'd Facetime, but it wasn't the same as living under the same roof.

Before I could get too homesick thinking about my sisters, I tried getting the conversation back on track. "What was Jake like?"

"Look, Jakey was Jakey, okay? What you saw was what you got. He worked hard. He played hard. Baseball. Football. Hockey. Didn't matter what sport it was, he loved it all, especially when he had money riding on the game. He was cute, but you knew that. And liked to screw around. I found that out the hard way."

"He cheated on you?" I asked. I already knew that from talking to Markie and Shannon, but it didn't hurt to get confirmation straight from the source.

She nodded. "Idiot. Men. Amiright?"

I matched her nod. "Men."

"Were you sleeping with him?" she asked.

"What? Me?" I sputtered. I shook my head vehemently. "With Jake? Not on your life."

"What, you too good for him?"

"No, it's just—"

"You're his type, you know," she said, before I could add to my defense.

"People keep saying that," I admitted. "Short? Dark haired?" I guessed.

"Bubbly," she said. "Young."

"He was too old for me," I said.

Patty laughed. "He was too old for me, too."

I thought about that for a minute. I didn't know her age, not exactly, but she was older than me.

She continued, "But, he was cute."

"You said that." Personally, I didn't see it, but just because he wasn't my type didn't mean he couldn't be hers.

"Can I be straight with you?" she asked. Then, without waiting for an answer, she plowed ahead. I held my breath, wondering if she was about to confess to murder. "Jake Macintyre broke my heart." She shrugged. "But he wasn't the first mook to do that, and he won't be the last." Patty heaved a deep sigh. "That's life, you know? Markie got his panties in a wad because they were friends. Jake and me kept it a secret that we were dating, at first. He got it in his head that Jakey was supposed to ask him permission before sleeping with his baby sister. Like it was the Middle Ages or something." She rolled her eyes. "Markie was livid when we broke up, but he was also relieved, you know? Like Jake wasn't good enough for me."

"He wasn't," I blurted out. I hadn't known Jake for long, or very well. He was a middle-aged man chasing women half his age, when he wasn't hanging out at the corner bar drinking and betting on sports. Not exactly winner material, no matter how fun he was to hang out with.

"Don't you think I know that?" Patty said. She stood and discreetly dabbed at the corner of her eyes. "I'm late and really got to get going. Am I going to see you at the wake?"

"I don't know. Is Markie going to be there?" If I was going to confront Markie, what better place to do it than at a crowded wake with plenty of witnesses?

"What's your obsession with my brother?" Patty asked. "You're not into him, are you? I mean, he's kinda a jerk, but you could probably do worse. You should go to the wake. It's tomorrow, noon, at O'Grady's." She let herself out.

I was a little surprised that she was going to be at the wake. If something happened to my lying, cheating ex—not that I wished ill on him, of course—I wouldn't go to his funeral. I wouldn't be celebrating in the streets, not publicly at least, but I wouldn't pretend to pay my respects, either.

It could be that Patty needed to say her goodbyes. Or she really was over him already and just wanted a free drink. Maybe she was just putting on a brave face. In any event, could a person kill someone in cold blood and then attend their wake? I guess I was going to have to go and find out.

CHAPTER TWENTY-THREE
CORDELIA

After our adventure at the pawn shop, I couldn't get Harp out of my head. We worked well together, almost as well as Ruby and I did. The Skittles trick was his idea, inspired by a movie that came out not long before his death. I remembered watching it in a movie theater as a kid. Ruby was probably too young to have ever seen it, at least in its original format, which was a shame, because it was a classic.

As frustrating as our communication challenge could be, I liked spending time with my roommate, but it was nice knowing that there was another ghost nearby if I needed a change of pace. I was starting to feel not so alone anymore.

I'd spent the morning following Ruby as she ran errands, which included a quick stop at the library to send a message to her mom on Facebook. I didn't know why she didn't just log in to Facebook from the comfort of her own home like everyone else in the world. Then again, if she did that, I'd have had to stay at a safe distance or risk blowing her phone up.

Not that it would be a bad thing, to be honest. Her phone was almost as old as she was. It was a prepaid one that in the end probably cost a lot more than a phone with a contract would have, but this way, she could pay whenever she could afford to instead of being tied to a monthly bill. Being poor was expensive that way. Everything ended up costing more in the long run.

There had to be more I could do to help. Yes, I'd gotten her a job. The pay wasn't great, not for the front desk position, but it was fair. Of course, by the time she got her first paycheck, she might have starved to death if I hadn't liberated a few bucks for her and led her to my secret cash stash. It wasn't much, not in the grand scheme of things, but the way she reacted, it might have been more than she'd ever seen in one place before.

I knew that feeling. Growing up, I hadn't had much. It made me appreciate every penny I earned in a way most of my friends didn't. I was frugal, always socking away as much as I could afford to in preparation for the inevitable rainy day. Besides, I had expenses, and people that were counting on me. Sometimes I wondered how they were faring, now that my contributions had literally dried up overnight.

Did my baby brother even know I was dead? I'd listed Ian as my emergency contact when I started at TrendCelerate, but at the time, he was still living in Connecticut. He'd moved a couple times since then. He'd been in New Jersey for a short while, but his current address was a state prison in upstate New York. If Ian got out early on good behavior, and he almost always did, he'd come looking for me. In the meantime, he was probably fuming that I stopped my monthly deposits to his commissary account.

There was nothing I could do to help Ian, not now, but I still had a chance to do something good for Jake. Sunday afternoon, we found ourselves at his wake. It was held at, out of all places, O'Grady's, the shady bar on the corner. Sure, Jake had spent much of his life there, but by that logic, they could have held it at TD Garden where the Boston Bruins played, or the warehouse he worked at downtown.

The bar was packed and appropriately noisy, which took my mind off Ian. It would have been convenient if it were wall-to-wall rich bitches with easily accessible wallets that I could Robin Hood into Ruby's pocket, but we weren't at that kind of party. We were at a dive bar in a working-class neighborhood of Boston filled with working-class Bostonians. I wouldn't pick their pockets any more than I would kick a puppy.

"Oh look, there's Patty," I said, spotting Jake's ex near the center of the room.

"Hey, Patty's here," Ruby said.

I took that as a sign that we were on the same wavelength.

She hurried over. I was a few steps behind. It wasn't easy keeping up with her while navigating the crowd, all of whom were milling, mingling, and otherwise making it challenging to get around without bumping into them. I didn't know why touching someone let some people but not others see or hear me, but it always hurt and I'd rather not take the chance.

"Patty," Ruby said brightly once she reached her, like she was a long-lost friend.

"Ruby, you came!" Patty gave her a one-armed hug while holding a nearly empty glass of beer in her free hand. "Thanks. I'm sure that means a lot to the family."

"Nice turnout," Ruby said, glancing around the bar.

I took a moment to look around as well. I recognized a few faces. Several carbon copies of Patty roamed around. I wondered if they were all Jake's exes, or if it was just a coincidence. I spotted a woman who looked like an older, female version of Jake. His mom, I assumed. What was it Bobby called her? Aunt Jackie?

As if by thinking about him, I'd conjured him out of thin air—which would be a neat trick. I should try it sometime—Bobby appeared at Patty's side. He looked unsteady as he took the glass out of her hand and sat it on a nearby table. The wake had just started, and already, he was well on his way to getting drunk.

"Why do men think we're completely helpless?" Patty asked Ruby as Bobby handed her a fresh beer.

"Wishful thinking?" Ruby suggested.

Adam had been that way, too. Which was ridiculous. I'd lived on my own, more or less, since I was a teenager. I'd raised my kid brother. Was still raising him, to be honest, and he was almost forty. And yet, Adam always worried about me, like I didn't know how to take care of myself.

"Sorry," Bobby said. "I was just trying to help. You looked like you could use a refill."

"Yeah, okay. Thanks," she said. "Sláinte." She raised her glass and clinked it against his beer.

"Sláinte," he echoed.

Ruby just looked confused.

Despite my red hair, as far as I knew, I didn't have a drop of Irish in me. But living in Boston my whole life, I'd picked up a thing or two. "Sláinte" was a common way of saying cheers. And despite what my best friend in third grade had tried to get me to believe, póg mo thóin was *not* an old Irish blessing.

"You two know each other?" Ruby asked, glancing between Patty and Bobby.

"Boston's a small town," Bobby said, a little too loudly. But it was loud in the bar, and soon everyone would be shouting to be heard over the noise.

"And Jakey knew absolutely everybody," Patty added.

They sure did seem chummy, standing close together, side by side. Although, as the bar continued to fill up, it might have been more from necessity than a sign of overt familiarity. I'd taken to sitting in the center of a table to keep out of everyone's way, so I probably shouldn't read much into it. And yet, right after Jake died, the day I let Bobby into his apartment, he had claimed to not be able to recall the name of Jake's latest ex-girlfriend, a woman he was apparently close friends with.

Then again, Jake had so many girlfriends and exes, I was having a hard time keeping track of them all. Was it any wonder his friends and cousins couldn't keep up, either?

"Ask them about the gun," I tried to coach her. She didn't hear me. There had to be *some* way to reach her without making a scene.

Someone jostled the table I was perched on as they tried to navigate their way to the bar, nearly tipping over Patty's almost-empty glass. That gave me an idea. Slowly, careful to not draw any more attention to myself than necessary, I eased the glass over, letting beer spill over the table to drip off the edge.

"Oh!" Ruby said, reaching for the upended glass as it began to roll toward the edge of the table. "Someone grab a napkin."

Bobby turned around and snatched the roll of coarse paper towels that served as napkins in this fine establishment from the next table. He held the roll while Patty pulled a few sheets off and crumpled them into balls. While they were distracted, I traced the word "gun" in the spilled beer. Ruby grabbed the wad of towels and dabbed at the letters before the others could notice, then wiped at the rest of the spill. She stuffed the wet paper towels into the now-empty glass, and set it in the middle of the table. I had to shift over to make room for it.

"Close call," she said. Elsewhere in the bar, there was the sound of shattering glass as someone elsewhere failed to keep a hold on their drink. "Oops."

"Oh please. That won't be the last glass to get broken tonight." Bobby said, taking another large sip of his drink.

"I'm sure you're right," Ruby agreed. "Hey, you wouldn't happen to know why Jake had a gun, would you?"

"Seriously?" I asked. "Think you can be a little more obvious?"

I guess she didn't mind the awkward question coming out of nowhere, because Patty answered, "Don't be silly. Jakey didn't have a gun."

"Sure he did," Ruby countered. "The police found one in his apartment."

"No, that's impossible," Bobby said, emphatically. "Jake hated guns. He said only dumbasses need a gun."

"Then why did the cops find a gun in his apartment?" Ruby asked.

Patty shrugged. "Maybe they planted it."

Ruby shook her head. "That doesn't make any sense."

"Sure it does. Cops plant guns on people all the time," Patty insisted.

"But Jake was the victim," Ruby said.

"Maybe that's just what they want you to think," Bobby said. "Ever think of that?"

"Huh?" Ruby asked.

"Huh" was right. What he said made absolutely no sense. Then again, at the rate he was pounding beers, his ability to form words, much less coherent thoughts, was going downhill.

"Think about it. Everything came so easy to Jake. Anything he wanted, he got," Bobby continued emphatically. By the way he slurred, I wondered if he even understood what he was saying.

"I don't think he wanted to get shot in the face," Patty said, frowning. Ruby bobbed her head in agreement.

"That's not what I mean. It's just that everyone knows Jake was a good guy, but was he? Was he really?"

"Hey, Bobby!" someone called from across the room. "Get over here!"

Bobby looked over at the speaker. "Hold that thought. I'll be right back." He stumbled away.

Once he had gone, Patty turned to Ruby. "You'll have to forgive him. He's having a hard time. Jake was his favorite cousin."

"No, I get it." Ruby leaned in and asked, "Are you two seeing each other? I thought I was picking up on a vibe there."

"Who? Bobby and me? Nah," Patty said with a dismissive gesture. "We're just friends."

"Uh-huh," Ruby agreed. "But does *he* know that?"

"I'm sure he does," Patty replied. "I see some people I need to say hi to. Catch you later?" She squeezed between two boisterous groups and melted into the crowd.

Ruby took that as her cue to circulate. She was good at this mingling business. She moved from one clump of mourning revelers to the next with a fluid ease, blending in and asking probing questions. I'd never been that comfortable in a crowd. I was more at home on the fringes. Not like I had much of a choice anymore. I tried my best to keep an eye on Ruby while staying far out of everyone's way. It wasn't easy.

I was busy sidestepping a woman carrying a pitcher of beer when I saw a man's hand grab Ruby's shoulder. "Just who I was looking for," he said.

Ruby spun to face him. "Markie!"

"You're not . . ." He looked around the room. "I'm sorry, for a second, I thought you were my sister."

I could see the resemblance, but they didn't look *that* much alike. Sure, they were both petite, with long, dark hair. That's where the similarities ended. Patty was—dare I say it?—ghostly pale, whereas Ruby had a healthy tan, even in the middle of winter. Patty's hair was set in big, bouncy curls while Ruby's was bone straight. Patty was dressed like she might be hitting a club after the wake. Ruby wore a pink T-shirt with a picture of a unicorn on it that said "I believe in you!" Personally, I wouldn't have chosen that particular shirt for a wake, but I was barefoot and wearing someone else's sweatpants, so I wasn't one to judge.

"Sorry, nope," Ruby said. "It's just me. But I *have* been wanting to talk to you."

"Sup?" he asked. I knew that Ruby had left him a few messages that he hadn't bothered to return, but he didn't seem in a hurry to dodge her now. Maybe it was the party-like atmosphere of the wake that left him in an amenable mood.

She pulled the printout from the pawn shop out of her purse and shoved it at him. "Spill it."

"Spill what?" he asked.

"That's Jake Macintyre's watch." She rattled the paper. "A family heirloom that he always wore."

"So what?" Markie didn't sound defensive, just confused.

"So, you sold it to a pawn shop."

"And?" he asked.

"And? Is that all you have to say for yourself? I'm taking this to the police," Ruby said.

I hoped she wasn't serious about that. The printout didn't prove that Markie had killed Jake, but it did implicate her in the break-in at Lizard Pawn. I was starting to think that Harp and I shouldn't have involved her in the pawn shop heist. Not my finest moment. Then again, how would we have gotten into the computer without her to learn that Markie was the one who pawned the watch?

"Why for? It's not like he needs it anymore." Markie gestured to where Jake's framed photograph was propped up on the bar, surrounded by a drunken ring of men dressed in Bruins sweaters. They lifted their glasses and roared "Sláinte!" loud enough to be heard over the din of the crowd.

"I think he's long past caring what time it is," Markie continued.

"You took it," Ruby hissed, lowering her voice so they wouldn't be overheard. I didn't know why she bothered. It was too loud at the wake for anyone to eavesdrop on their conversation.

I hoped she knew what she was doing. Cornering a potential killer was never a smart move, but if she was going to confront him, at least she was doing it in public.

"You killed him, then you stole his watch to make it look like he'd been mugged."

"The hell you say," Markie said. He snatched the printout out of her hands.

"That's not my only copy," she said.

That was a lie. We'd only had time to print out one copy at the pawn shop before the clerk caught us, and neither of us had thought to make a photocopy. We really should have thought this through better.

"Look here." He poked his finger at the printout. "See this date? I sold that watch a full week before he died."

"You *what?*" She grabbed it back and looked down. I studied the printout over her shoulder in disbelief. He was right. This was dated six days before Jake's death. How did I miss that before? "You still haven't explained what were you doing with his watch in the first place."

He scowled at her. "Jake was like a brother to me. Until he stomped all over my baby sister's heart. He was dumb enough to leave his watch at her apartment the night she found out he had a side piece. He's lucky he didn't leave his phone, or I would have sold that, too. Guy at the pawn shop thought he was pulling one over on me by offering me twenty dollars even though the watch is worth a lot more. But I would have given it to him for free."

"You would have?"

"The only thing Jake loved more than a good time was that damn watch." Markie grinned. "I hope losing it hurt him half as much as he hurt Patty. Now, if we're done here, I need a refill." He walked away.

CHAPTER TWENTY-FOUR
CORDELIA

After Markie's confession failed to materialize, I tried to keep up with Ruby without brushing up against any of the patrons. It was a losing battle. If several members of the Boston Fire Department weren't here already, I would have been tempted to try to figure out a way to summon the fire marshal to check for maximum occupancy.

Eventually, I retreated behind the bar, the only place where I could minimize contact in the growing crowd. Even so, the bartender, Sean something or other, walked through my foot, and had been so startled by the sensation that he'd dropped a pitcher of beer, which drew a round of applause from the patrons lining up at the bar for a refill.

I wondered what that felt like from Sean's point of view. Did he get a jolt like the one that ran through me? A cold spot? Was it more like a shock or a shiver?

A stool opened up in front of the bar and a man quickly claimed it. Normally, I would have judged a man for snatching up one of the few open stools at a crowded bar, but there were relatively few women around. I counted Ruby, Shannon, Patty, and a few other women who fit Jake's "pattern." Several older women mingled near Jake's portrait in the corner. His mother and aunts, maybe? Or just women from the neighborhood?

The man right here in front of me I recognized as Jake's friend, Scotty. The tall one. I'd seen him in the hall before, as he was coming or going from Jake's apartment. He was one of the usuals for pizza, beer, and sports nights. He'd also been playing pool at the bar the first time Ruby had been here.

How long ago had that been? I couldn't tell. That had been the same day that she got the job at TrendCelerate, and she'd worked there for a few days now so maybe it had been a week ago? More? It was getting harder and harder to keep track of time. Before Ruby moved in, I'd been so bored, the days melted together. Now, I wanted to be present but ended up exerting more energy and found myself drifting off more often. When I came back to the here and now, I had no way of knowing how much time had passed.

Scotty was staring into space. At first, I thought he was studying the bottles behind the bar, but then I realized he wasn't focusing on anything. In fact, I wasn't sure if he was capable of focusing on anything at this point. Like most of Jake's friends, Scotty had downed more than his fair share of the free-flowing booze.

He held up one finger to get Sean the bartender's attention. "Jameson," he slurred.

"Coming right up, buddy," the bartender said, before turning to address other patrons at the bar. He'd likely ignore Scotty a few more times before bringing him a watered-down beer or maybe a cup of coffee. By the time the raucous wake was over, Scotty wouldn't be the only one too blitzed to see straight, but that was kinda the point of having a wake in a dive bar, wasn't it?

I leaned over the bar until Scotty and I were nose to nose. Up close, he wasn't quite as attractive as he'd seemed when I passed him briefly in the dimly lit hallway of my building, but he wasn't unattractive, either. He had a chicken pox scar on his forehead and a puckered slash through his eyebrow where hair refused to grow. His ears were pierced but he wore no earrings. He'd shaved this morning and gotten a haircut recently.

It was hard to tell his exact age, but I'd put him in that sweet spot between old enough to have a respectable job and his own apartment and young enough to pay full price at the movies. Even slumped over at the bar, he was tall. I'd always liked tall men. I wondered why I'd never talked to Scotty when our paths had crossed before. "Then again, I'd been obsessed with Adam for so long that I never really gave other guys a chance," I admitted aloud.

"Who's Adam?" Scotty slurred.

I almost fell through the bar. I caught myself at the last second, chiding myself, "Cordy, don't forget yourself." It sounded like something a well-heeled woman would tell a young finishing school student, but in my case, it was literal. If I forgot where I was and what I was doing, I could fall right through the floor, or in the worst-case scenario, literally slip out of existence.

"You talk funny," he said.

"Who are you talking to?" I wondered, looking around. The bar was busy, but no one was paying any attention to him. "There's no way you could hear me."

"Of course I can hear you, Cordy," Scotty slurred. "Where's my drink?"

I chuckled. Anyone else in the bar would see a man so wasted he was talking to himself. I was the only one who knew he was so wasted he was talking to *me*. I wondered if there was something special about Scotty, or if it was just the alcohol breaking down natural inhibitions that would normally prevent him from perceiving me. Ruby had interacted with me—briefly—as she was falling asleep, but later thought it was a dream. Maybe Scotty was in a similar state of mind since he was inebriated?

I'd spent a good deal of my adult life—not to mention my formative teenage years—under the influence, and I'd never met a ghost, to the best of my knowledge. But Scotty didn't seem to notice anything was amiss about me. Maybe I'd met lots of dead people and never realized it. Or, and this possibility tickled me, my superpower was I could commune with drunks. Wouldn't that be ironic? "It's in your hand, champ," I lied.

Scotty looked down at his empty hands. "Oh. There it is." He traced one finger through the condensation on the bar. "This Adam, he your boyfriend or something?"

"Or something," I said. I thought back to the morning after the company holiday party. Karin had finally figured out that Adam was cheating on her. Or, more likely, she'd never been oblivious, and the holiday party was the last straw. In any event, we thought we were being discreet, but we got caught anyway. It probably would have been a better idea to sneak off to my room for a quickie instead of using theirs.

He called me, saying she'd kicked him out. That their marriage was over. Asked if he could stay at my place.

I was tempted to say no. My apartment might be a shabby substitute for his palatial downtown condo, but it was mine and I didn't want to share it with anyone. But this was Adam. "I never could say no to him," I admitted, remembering that day. "I put on the good sheets. I straightened up the living room. I even bought some of his favorite microbrew for the fridge. But he never showed up."

"Sounds like a jerk," Scotty muttered.

"It wasn't his fault," I said. "Not really. He reconciled with his wife. It was probably for the best. It's not like I wanted to share my apartment."

"Roommates suck," he commiserated.

"Ruby's not bad." I'd had a change of heart about her. She'd gone from the annoying intruder in my personal space to my dearest—and, not counting Eunice the philodendron and potentially, Harp the preppy pawn shop ghost, only—friend. "Sure, she talks incessantly and bops around the living room like a toddler high on Pixy Stix, but it's kinda endearing. I guess she's grown on me."

But, no offense to her, our conversations were a challenge riddled with misunderstandings. Even when we *were* on the same page, she rarely ever knew it. The magnet trick was limited, and exhausting. Brushing past her gave us a few seconds to really talk, but then I was drained for hours. Most of the time, it was like sharing a dorm room with a foreign exchange student who only spoke a few words of English. We communicated, but only just.

"Ruby sounds nice," he said.

"She really is," I agreed.

Scotty and I were having a full-blown conversation, not that he would remember it judging by the amount of liquor he'd put away in the last hour. If he wasn't blackout drunk by the end of the wake, I'd be impressed. Still, I wasn't going to let the opportunity to interrogate one of Jake's friends myself go to waste. "How long have you known Jake?" I asked.

"Jakey and me, we go way back," he said.

"You didn't kill him, did you?"

"What kind of question is that?" he slurred angrily. "He was my friend."

The woman sitting next to him looked over her shoulder at

Scotty, then scooted her barstool a little closer to her companion. I didn't blame her. If the weird drunk next to me was talking to himself, I would have moved, too.

"Do you know anyone who wanted to kill him?" I asked. Ruby might be convinced that Markie had murdered Jake because he'd cheated on Patty, but I wasn't so sure.

"Nah. Jake's a good guy, you know? Solid." He slumped over a little more, and I worried he might fall off his stool. "Salt of the earth."

"He owe anyone money?" I asked. The watch was damning evidence, yes, but what if instead of Markie stealing the watch, Jake had given it to him to cover a debt?

"Ha!" Scotty's laugh was loud and harsh. A few heads turned toward us. "More like anyone Jakey *didn't* owe money to?"

I leaned closer. Ruby seemed fixated on the love-and-exes angle, but money was also a classic motive for murder. "I thought he had a good job," I said. "A union job."

"Union don't pay your bookie," Scotty said with a chuckle.

"Bookie?" I asked. I remembered his cousin mentioning that Jake had a betting problem. Guys like Jake didn't play the odds, the bartender had said. They bet on their favorite team, no matter what kind of season they're having. That never ended well. "What's his name?"

"Dunno. Hey, Cordy?"

"Yeah?" I asked.

"Where's my drink?"

I sighed. I might as well be interrogating a toddler. This was going nowhere fast. But I wasn't ready to give up yet. "Hey, Scotty, before I get you that drink, I've got one more question for you. Why'd Jake have a gun?"

Scotty shook his head violently. "He didn't."

"Yes, he did," I insisted. "I saw it."

"Not Jake's gun," Scotty slurred.

"Then whose was it?"

Scotty made a zipping-the-lips motion with one hand. "Not telling you."

"Um, excuse me?" Ruby asked. She'd elbowed her way through the crowd at the bar to stand in the space between Scotty and the woman who'd inched away from him again. I'd been so busy talking with Scotty that I'd lost track of Ruby. Now she was trying to get the bartender's attention.

"Hey, Ruby," I said.

"Hey, Ruby," Scotty echoed.

She studied his slack features. "Do I know you? Wait a sec. We met at that pool table over there last week, didn't we? You and"—she wracked her brain and came up blank on their names—"your friends."

"Did we?" he asked. "Did you take my drink?"

"Nope," she said. "What was your name again?"

"Cordy?" Scotty said.

"I'm pretty sure that's not your name," Ruby said.

"Cordy, where's my drink?" he repeated.

Ruby leaned toward him. With her standing and him slumped over on the stool, they were almost the same height. "Is Cordelia here? Do you see her?"

"She's supposed 'a be bringing my drink," he slurred.

"I think maybe you've had enough already," Ruby said. Then she looked around. "Cordelia?" she whispered.

In front of me was a plastic organizer filled with square napkins, plastic stir sticks, cut limes, and dried-out cherries. I took one of the plastic stirrers out, laid it on the bar, and spun it. "Right here," I said.

"Right here," Scotty aped.

"I've talked to just about everybody. No one knows anything useful, at least not that they're telling. I don't know what I'm missing," she said, addressing me directly.

"Well, I know what *I'm* missing," Scotty said. "Where the hell's my drink?"

I shuddered and doubled over in pain as the bartender reached through me to plunk a tall glass of ice water down on the bar in front of Scotty. I'd been so intent on Scotty and Ruby that I'd forgotten to keep an eye on Sean. "You've had enough, buddy. Drink up. You're scaring my customers. I've already called you a cab."

"I'm not a cab," Scotty said, belligerently. "*You're* a cab."

"Whatever you say, buddy," Sean said, shaking his arm as if his hand had fallen asleep before turning to help another customer.

"That looked like it hurt," Scotty said, apparently to me.

"It did," I agreed, clutching my shoulder where it felt like the bartender had shoved a hot poker through me. At least Sean didn't seem to be able to see me, even after touching me. I guess that was a silver lining. I wondered what it was about Ruby, and Scotty, that made them special.

"What hurt?" Ruby asked.

"Dude put his arm right through her like she wasn't even there." Scotty looked down at the ice water in front of him. "You think that's what happened to Jakey? Man put a bullet in him by accident 'cause he didn't see him there?" He paled, turned his head, and vomited all over Ruby's vintage Doc Martens.

"What the actual hell?" she exclaimed. She jumped back, jostling the woman on the next stool.

"Watch it," the woman said, then wrinkled up her nose. "Oh, you didn't."

Ruby held up her hand. "It wasn't me."

The bartender appeared again, this time on the other side of the bar. He grabbed Scotty by the elbow. "You're out of here." He started dragging him toward the door. "You too," Sean said, pointing at Ruby. "I don't ever want to see you in my bar again."

"What did I do?" Ruby asked.

The bartender pushed them both outside. I followed them, careful not to touch anyone else in the crowded bar. I'd already had enough physical encounters with breathers for one day. "When you're old enough to drink, find yourself another bar. I'm not losing my license over you."

She blinked as she stepped out of the bar. It was bright outside. Ruby glanced down at her shoes and then quickly looked away. She was wearing her best pair of boots, and even with two pairs of socks on, they weren't sufficient for a Boston winter. She kicked her boots against the curb and then rubbed them against a block of slush that had frozen into ice. It got rid of most, but not all, of Scotty's parting gift.

A cab pulled up. Sean the bartender tried to load Scotty into it. Scotty resisted, and the cab drove off. "Fine. You're on your own, then," Sean told him before retreating back into the bar.

Scotty slumped against the wall, looking like he was going to be sick again.

"You gonna be okay?" Ruby asked. Dear, sweet Ruby. She ought to be yelling at him, but instead she was worried about him getting home or, at the very least, not freezing to death.

"Who are you?" Scotty asked.

Ruby sighed. "Ruby? From the bar?"

He shook his head. "Ruby from the bar, you don't look old enough to drink."

"I'm not," she said.

"Where's Cordy?" he asked.

"I'm right here," I said.

"Where's my drink?" he asked.

"Good riddance." I turned to Ruby. "Come on, roomie, let's go home."

She glanced over at her other side, opposite of where I was standing. "Come on, Cordelia," she said. "Let's go home."

CHAPTER TWENTY-FIVE
RUBY

I threw my boots in the bathtub the second I got home, and ran hot water over them before scrubbing them with shampoo and a washcloth. If I could have afforded a new pair of boots, I would have thrown them in the trash, but these would have to make do. When they were as clean as I could get them, I set them on the bathmat to dry before scrubbing out the tub.

"I hope that Scotty gets the hangover he deserves," I grumbled as I dried my hands and left the bathroom. As usual, the second I stepped into the living room I knew that Cordelia was in there with me, even if I couldn't see her. It was like having a cat.

"Did you and Scotty at least have a nice chat before he tossed his cookies?" I asked the empty air. "Frankly, it doesn't seem fair. How come he can see you but I can't?"

I'd left my purse on the floor by the door so I could yank my boots off as soon as I got inside. In the time that it had taken me to wash my boots, someone had shoved another Caparelli's Pizza flyer under the door. I was getting tired of all their junk mail, but I could see how the constant stream of advertisements might have worked on someone like Jake. I snatched up the flyer and my purse, and noticed that my bag was heavier than normal. I opened it and found a small bottle of vodka.

"What's this?" I asked. I pulled the bottle out and examined it. "You know I don't drink."

I put the bottle on the counter. A glass materialized next to it. "I'm not interested, Cordelia. Or should I call you Cordy?" Scotty had called her Cordy at the bar. "I mean, we live together. Well, not *live*, but you know what I mean. I should probably call you by your preferred name."

I grabbed the glass and put it back in the cabinet where it belonged. When I turned around, it was back on the counter. Plus, there was the jug of OJ from my fridge sitting next to the glass and the bottle of vodka. "Seriously, Cordelia, I don't drink. Don't make me pour that bottle down the drain."

The bottle hovered for a second before the cap spun off. It tipped over in the air, half filling the glass.

"Nice trick," I said. I couldn't help but be impressed. Most of the time, things moved without me actually seeing them move. Even though I had absolutely zero intention of actually drinking it, watching the bottle float through the air was entertaining.

I didn't see the OJ move, but I blinked and the next thing I knew, my glass was filled to the brim and the liquid inside was now orange.

"Thanks, but I mean it. I don't drink." I picked up the glass and poured the drink down the sink. I glanced down, and the glass was full again. "I can do this all day," I warned her.

• • •

Monday morning came way too bright and *way* too early. I was tempted to turn off my alarm and huddle under my covers until spring, but then I remembered that I had to get to work. It had taken me months to find honest employment, and I wasn't about to blow it by not showing up the second week on the job.

At least Cordelia didn't mess with the curtains or my outfit choices this morning. She seemed to realize that I needed it to be dark just a few minutes more. And no one at the office had a problem with my clothes. On the contrary, I was getting compliments on my cute, punny T-shirts.

I went to take a quick shower and tripped over my boots on the bathmat. Why were they in the bathroom? At first, I thought Cordelia was playing a trick on me, but she wouldn't have come into the bathroom without a good reason. Had I left them there? I couldn't remember.

Going to Jake's wake was the last clear memory I had from this weekend. Everything after that was fuzzy. I just couldn't remember why.

There was no time for breakfast—which was probably for the best, because my stomach was in knots and I could grab free coffee at the office. As I walked past the kitchen on my way out the door, I noticed a bottle of vodka on the counter. It gave me a nasty twist in the pit of my gut.

The small bottle was empty. Beside it was a sticky orange ring and an equally empty glass. I picked up the vodka bottle and immediately recoiled as the taste of one too many screwdrivers threatened to make a reappearance in the back of my throat. Which was not acceptable, considering I didn't drink. But my accompanying headache and queasiness told me that maybe that wasn't exactly true.

"Cordelia?" I called out, even though the room felt deserted. "What exactly did you do to me yesterday?"

I tossed the vodka bottle into the recycling bin under the sink, next to an empty bottle of orange juice I didn't remember opening, much less finishing. "That was organic," I muttered. I'd paid a premium for the good stuff, and I didn't even remember drinking it. "What a waste."

The cold air outside made me feel marginally better, but the swaying motion of the crowded city bus did not. When I finally dragged myself into the office and swiped my badge at the front door to let me in, I collapsed into the seat behind the front desk. I closed my eyes and prayed that someone would kill me and put me out of my misery.

"I know that look," a woman's voice said.

I looked up to see Melissa approaching my desk. "I didn't expect anyone else to be in the office this early," I told her. TrendCelerate had an incredibly liberal work-from-home policy. During my interview, Sally had mentioned that other than me and Marc—who I'd since learned had young twins and couldn't get any work done from home—almost no one worked out of the office on Mondays or Fridays. I'd only been here for a week, but I'd barely met half the staff because they hardly ever came in unless there were mandatory in-person meetings.

Mine was the only position that required being physically present, although technically I could do a lot of my job anywhere as long as I had a phone and a reliable internet connection. I didn't have either of those things at home. Besides, I liked working from the office. The bus ride—on days I wasn't hungover at least—was pleasant, and unlike in my apartment, the office was amply heated and the refrigerator was well-stocked.

"How was your weekend?" I asked. Melissa had mostly avoided me ever since Adam had tried to get her to show me the ropes last week. Frankly, I didn't blame her. She had her own job to do, and didn't deserve to get saddled with showing the new girl around just because she was one of the few other women in the office.

"Same old," she said. She looked at my shirt. It had a cartoon dragon flying with a minivan clutched in its claws. The caption read "Takeout again?" She smiled. "Nice shirt."

I grinned back. Maybe the shirt had broken the ice with us. "How can I help you this morning?" I didn't really know my way around yet, but I smiled, acted pleasant, and, whenever anything came up, promised I'd take care of things. Then as soon as I had a second to myself, I'd figure out how to do it. So far, it seemed to be working out.

"It's more how I can help you." She held out her hands. In one hand, she had a metal bottle. In the other hand, a package of aspirin. "Don't worry, it's just water," she said.

That's when I remembered during my interview, how Adam had flipped his lid over some water bottle he'd found that turned out to be filled with vodka. I wondered if that was hers. "Thanks." I took them. I ripped open the packet of aspirin and downed them with the cold water.

"Looks like someone had fun this weekend," she said, sitting on the corner of my desk.

"Uh-huh," I agreed, although I couldn't remember any of it. This sucked. I didn't understand why anyone would do this to themselves on purpose. What was the point of having a good time if you couldn't even remember it later? And how long was I going to walk around with a throbbing headache and a stomach that threatened to revolt at any minute?

Freaking Cordelia. This was all her fault.

Why had she done this to me? More importantly, *how* had she done this to me? It wasn't like she could force me to drink. Or could she? I wish I could remember.

"Don't worry, you'll feel better as soon as the aspirin kicks in. What were you drinking this weekend?"

"OJ?" I said, tentatively.

Melissa laughed. "Yeah, okay. Sure. Because I always look like roadkill after a glass or two of orange juice. What was the occasion?"

"A wake," I admitted.

"Yeah, that will do it." She gave me a sympathetic smile. "I'm sorry for your loss."

"No, it wasn't like that." I shook my head, and then immediately regretted it. If my head was in a vice, it would hurt less. "It was for my neighbor. We weren't close."

"In that case, where do you live? My roommate situation is"—she paused, looking for the right word—"complicated. That's why I work from the office so much. Get some peace and quiet, you know? Your neighbor, is their apartment open?"

"Maybe? His girlfriend is staying there for now, but she's not on the lease." Shannon had mentioned possibly picking up the remainder of Jake's lease, but I had no way of knowing if she would go through with it or not. I gave her my street name. "It's not too far from here."

"In that case, never mind," Melissa said, standing up.

"My neighborhood isn't that bad," I said. Frankly, I was tired of people looking down their nose at my neighborhood. It was a perfectly fine, affordable place to live.

"Oh, it's not that, but didn't some dude get killed near there walking home the other day?" She held her hands out flat like she was physically weighing her options. "A pack of feral roommates"—she let her left hand drop—"a killer on the loose." Now her right hand dropped and her left hand sprang back up. "I can deal with the roommates. For now." She squinted at me. "Unless you're looking for a roomie."

"I already have one," I said without thinking about it. I should have kept my mouth shut. If she pressed, how was I supposed to explain that the deceased former tenant was still hanging around my apartment?

"Of course you do. Well, if anything changes, you let me know, okay?"

"Sure thing," I agreed. "Oh, and Melissa? Can I ask you something?"

"Sure!"

Despite living with her, I knew virtually nothing about Cordelia save for the fact that she used to work here. Last week, I'd been so busy getting acclimated that I hadn't had much time to socialize, but with Melissa in a chatty mood and the phones not ringing. I couldn't think of a better chance to start asking about her. "Did you know a woman named Cordelia Graves that used to work here?"

Melissa glanced around the nearly empty office. "Look, you're new and I like you, so let me give you some advice. Don't ever say that name around here."

"Cordelia?" I asked, confused.

"Shh," she hissed. "You didn't hear this from me, but something hinky was going on with her."

"Hinky? How so?"

Melissa sat on the corner of the desk and fiddled with my cup of pens. "I didn't know her well. To be honest, I don't think anyone did. She was friendly enough at the office, but it was all surface, you know? Mostly, she just kept to herself. And then she, well, she killed herself. No one will talk about it, but something weird was going on."

"Weird?" I prompted. "Weird how?"

"For starters, her company laptop turned up missing. Then our biggest competitor got a jump on a project that she had access to, and brought it to market before we could. Plus, there's the rumors."

"What rumors?" I asked, leaning in, wondering what could possibly be more salacious than what she'd already revealed.

The front door opened and Adam stepped in. Melissa jumped up off the desk. "Good morning, Mr. Rees," I said.

"Morning, Adam," Melissa said brightly.

He nodded at us. "Ruby. Melissa. Everything okay here?"

"Yup!" Melissa said. "Hunky-dory."

"Well then, don't mind me." He looked at both of us one more time before heading to his private office and closing the door behind him.

"Rumors," Melissa whispered, jerking her thumb at his closed door. "With Adam, if you know what I mean." She scurried back to her cubicle.

"Oh, Cordelia," I muttered to myself as soon as Melissa was out of earshot. It didn't feel like she was in the room with me, but I'd gotten in the habit of talking to her even if I couldn't prove she was around. "What did you get yourself into?" I pulled the Etch A Sketch out of the drawer and set it beside my keyboard, inviting Cordelia to respond, but the screen stayed blank.

I'd been raised to not speak ill of the dead, which I guess applied to ghosts, too. Maybe that was why I'd struck out at the wake yesterday. No one wanted to say anything bad about Jake, even if it would have helped catch his killer.

Wait a second. The wake. The aspirin had helped clear through some of the fog in my head and I could think straight again.

I'd gone to the wake with Cordelia, or at least I'd left the apartment with Cordelia. About halfway through, she vanished. Metaphorically speaking. I figured she was off doing her own thing. Eavesdropping, maybe?

But then that guy at the bar. Bobby? Charlie? Scotty? That's it. Scotty. The tall dude. He was sitting at the bar, holding a full-on conversation with Cordelia. It was all coming back now. Then we got kicked out.

Back at the apartment, Cordelia tried to convince me to have a drink. Not wanting to have a replay of that wild house party in Baltimore when I'd gotten drunk and sick, I'd poured the first one down the sink. Then she mixed another screwdriver. I took a sip, to appease her more than anything else. To my surprise, the drink was tasty. When she offered me a refill, I took it. Halfway through the second drink, things started getting fuzzy.

I vaguely remember talking to her, actually talking and getting a response. I cringed, recalling how I'd unloaded on her. I'd told her all about Jeffrey cheating on me and breaking my heart. What had she said? Something about knowing how I felt. Had she been talking about Adam? I wish I knew, but the rest was just a blur. Apparently, with a little vodka in my system, I could hold a real conversation with Cordelia. Unfortunately, the memory of most of what we talked about was gone now.

Not only were my memories gone, but Cordelia was MIA this morning as well, and just as I wanted to get her take on these rumors about her and Adam. It figured.

The rest of my workday dragged on slowly. Melissa sequestered herself in her cubicle. At some point when I'd had to leave my desk, she must have snuck out the front door because when I went over to ask her to lunch, she had already left for the day.

I tried—and failed—to picture Adam and Cordelia together. Gross. I mean, sure, love is love and it's beautiful and all that jazz, but it was also messy and squishy and really not something I wanted to picture other people doing. Especially not people I know, not people I'd repeatedly watched online presenting TED Talks about a range of fascinating topics. And *especially* not the sharply dressed Adam Rees with his wedding ring and a picture of his smiling wife displayed prominently on his desk, next to a framed vintage comic book and a still-in-the-box action figure.

Melissa probably didn't have any idea what she was talking about. She admitted that despite being coworkers, she barely knew Cordelia. She was mistaken, that was all. She'd gotten the wrong idea from listening to nasty rumors. That was the only thing that made sense.

Adam stopped by my desk on his way out. "I'm meeting my wife for lunch, then I'll be working from home for the rest of the day." He looked around the empty office. "You okay alone for a few hours?"

"No problem," I assured him. I was most certainly *not* picturing him and Cordelia in compromising situations.

"If that changes, or you need anything, you've got my number," he said, then left.

A few calls and emails came in, breaking up the next few hours, but for the most part, I was bored out of my skull. I finished the book I was reading, and kept myself busy making doodles on the Etch A Sketch until five o'clock rolled around.

On the bus ride home, I wondered what Scotty and Cordelia had talked about at the wake. Maybe, if I asked nicely, he'd tell me. I got off the bus and started the walk home. As O'Grady's bar came into view, I headed over. I didn't have Scotty's number, but I knew where he'd be. Or if not him, his friends.

As soon as the door opened, the bartender barked. "You! Out!"

I waved at him. "Don't worry. I'm not here to buy booze." Even if I'd been tempted to, after all the vodka I'd had yesterday, I had absolutely zero desire to taste alcohol ever again.

"That's right. You're not. Get out," he said.

"I just need to—"

"Christ on a cracker. Are you daffy?" He slapped the bar rag he'd been cleaning with against the edge of the bar. "Get out of my bar, kid."

Undeterred, I kept talking as I approached the bar. "The guy you tossed out last night. Scotty? I need to talk to him."

"That's it. I'm calling the cops." The bartender pulled out his phone.

"Jeez, okay, whatever." I turned and hurried toward the door. I paused with my hand on the door handle. "If he comes by, will you let him know I'm looking for him?"

"Out!"

I scurried outside. Well, that had been a waste of time. I vaguely remembered the bartender escorting Scotty out, but couldn't for the life of me figure out why he was upset at me. I glanced down at my boots, the ones that Scotty had thrown up on yesterday. Surely the bartender didn't hold *that* against me. Maybe it was because I was underaged? Or, more likely, he suspected that I'd stolen a bottle of vodka from his bar.

One thing I did know was I didn't have a bottle of vodka in my purse before I went to the wake, and there was a full bottle in it when I got home. Obviously, Cordelia had slipped it in there when I wasn't looking so we could have a chat that I could barely remember. On the plus side, now that I was banned from the bar, Cordelia might not be tempted to pressure me to drink again.

CHAPTER TWENTY-SIX
CORDELIA

Ruby's normal chipper demeanor was notably absent when she got home from work, which was a first. Even yesterday, when she was halfway through the bottle of vodka, she was a happy drunk. But now, she looked miserable. "Everything okay?" I asked, trailing along behind her. "Something bad happen at work today?"

I was glad Ruby was working at TrendCelerate. It was a good company, with good people. For the most part. But every time Adam walked into the room, it felt like getting punched with an icepick. It shouldn't hurt this bad. I'd been hopelessly in love with Adam, even though in my heart, I knew it wasn't reciprocal. I was never more than a sidepiece to him.

I couldn't face him this morning, so I'd stayed home and cleaned the whole apartment instead, top to bottom, until it shone. I'd done everything but laundry and trash. The laundry machines in the basement might be ancient, but they were still electronics and therefore off-limits. The trash I left for Ruby, because if any of our neighbors—and I'm looking at you, Milly in 4F—saw a bag of trash or recyclables floating down the hallway on the way to the bins outside, they'd call the cops. Or ghostbusters. Or the tabloids.

Ruby marched past me and stood in front of the refrigerator. "Is it true? Were you having an affair with Adam Rees?"

Where did that come from? I doubted Adam would have confided in her. He barely knew her. I wanted to ask her where she'd heard that, but almost as soon as I reached for the magnets, I changed my mind. This was *not* a conversation I wanted to have. Not with Ruby. Not with anyone.

"I know you're here, Cordelia," Ruby said. "Is it true or not?"

I took a step back and crossed my arms over my chest. "I'm not gonna dignify that question with a response," I said, as if I had any higher ground in this one-sided conversation.

"Fine. Whatever. Be that way. Don't answer me." Ruby opened the refrigerator and studied its contents with a sigh. It was nearly empty again. That was the problem with being alive. You had to eat, which meant cooking, cleaning, and shopping was an endless cycle.

I grabbed one of the pizza delivery flyers out of the trash, smoothed it out, and let it drift gently to the ground. She bent over and picked it up. "Oh, now you're talking to me? Whatever. Why not? That delivery guy promised me twenty percent off my next order." She dialed the number on the flyer. Once she'd placed her order, she sat down on one of the barstools. "Cordelia, if you can hear me, we need to have a chat."

"A chat?" That didn't sound good. I felt like I'd just gotten called into the office. Which, come to think of it, wasn't the worst thing in the world. I missed getting called into Adam's office in the middle of the day, especially when everyone else was working from home. Looking back, it was a wonder we didn't get caught sooner. It wasn't like we were terribly discreet.

"What happened yesterday after the wake?" she asked. "Wait, hold that thought."

She got up and disappeared into the bathroom. When she returned, she had several aspirins in her hand that she chased down with a large glass of water. "Never again," she muttered.

"Lightweight," I teased, suddenly understanding Ruby's subdued demeanor. It was just one lousy bottle of vodka, and a small one at that, but she wasn't much of a drinker. I guess it had more of an effect on her than it would have had on me. "You're hungover, aren't you?"

I was very, very young when I first realized that life wasn't fair. And then again, in my forties, I found out that death wasn't very fair, either. If you died wearing uncomfortable underwear, you spent your entire afterlife wandering around with a wedgie. Thank goodness I'd been wearing the soft sweats I'd stolen from Adam when I died, but I couldn't fix my chipped fingernail polish, brush my hair, or pluck that weird stray hair that I always seemed to miss. I had a pimple on my chin that would be there for eternity.

Yet, even though I had died pumped to the brim with liquor and pills, I was doomed to spend the rest of my existence as sober as a frigging church mouse. Sure, I would never have to endure another hangover like the one that was plaguing Ruby today, but I'd never get a buzz again, either. In those weird flashbacks—or whatever it was that I was experiencing when I needed to recharge—even if I remember being half a bottle in, I relived everything with perfect clarity.

And it sucked.

Ruby had the opposite problem, apparently. Two screwdrivers—that were admittedly more vodka than orange juice—and she wasn't just tipsy, she was falling-down drunk. It was kind of adorable. She was such a fun drunk, too. Happy. Chatty. Completely free-spirited. Although, to be fair, she wasn't much different drunk than she was on a normal day.

To my delight, my theory had worked. The alcohol had the same effect on her that it'd had on Scotty. After one drink, she could hear me. A glass later, she could see me. By then, she was having so much fun she didn't want to stop. We didn't even talk about anything of substance. For a magical moment, we were just girlfriends debating the merits of *The Bachelor* and arguing Taylor Swift versus Poe. Long after the OJ was gone, Ruby killed the rest of the vodka like a pro, drinking straight from the rapidly emptying bottle, getting sillier by the minute. And now, she was paying the price.

"What exactly do you mean by what happened? You don't remember *anything*?" I asked. I had not seen that coming. Chalk another one up for the unfairness of the afterlife. The only way I could hold a substantive conversation with Ruby was if she was blackout drunk. Great.

Even more pitiful, drunk Ruby was an absolute hoot. She kept telling me that she loved me and also how much she loved rainbows and unicorns and those hard little marshmallows in breakfast cereals. She danced around the living room until I was vicariously dizzy. I couldn't remember the last time I laughed that hard.

The doorbell buzzed, bringing me back to the present.

I followed Ruby downstairs as she paid, and generously tipped, the pizza deliveryman. He winked at her. "Enjoy, Ruby," he said with a grin.

I'd ordered pizzas from Caparelli's dozens of dozens of times over the years, and always got the same delivery person. He never bothered to learn my name. In fact, every time he delivered a pizza, it was like he'd never even seen me before, even when my name was right there on the delivery slip. But here she was, ordering once or twice, and he acted like they were best friends.

Oh, but to be young, cute, and perky.

It wasn't like I was invisible. I mean, okay, I *was* invisible now. But I hadn't always been. Guys noticed me. There was Harp, but he was dead, so he didn't count. There was the random hotel guest at the TrendCelerate holiday party, but I think that was more a case of me being drunk, low-hanging fruit than an actual attraction for either of us. There was Adam, but he wasn't interested enough to leave his wife, or her money, for me.

• • •

As I was busy feeling sorry for myself, Ruby was carrying the pizza upstairs. "Does this ever get any easier?" she grumbled as she exited the stairs and headed for our apartment. When I'd been alive, I was usually too far out of breath by the time I reached the fourth floor to talk.

I missed the silly, drunk Ruby from last night, when our banter was two-sided. Even if I could convince her to try it again—and judging by her bad mood, I doubted it—there was no guarantee she'd remember any of it. And if it was possible for life—or death—to get any more unfair, now that I'd realized that if I concentrated hard enough, I could pick up odors, that pizza smelled like heaven itself and I couldn't taste a single bite of it.

Ruby reached the end of the hall. Balancing the pizza in one hand, she rummaged in her pockets with the other. "Oh shoot." She pressed her eye to the wrong end of the peephole, as if trying to see inside. "I left my keys inside, didn't I?"

Frankly, I wasn't sure that doors that locked automatically were inherently safer than doors that didn't. After the first time I'd accidentally locked myself out, whenever I had to dash out of my apartment for just a few minutes—like to go downstairs and pick up a food delivery, check the mail, or flip a load of laundry from the washer to the dryer—I found it was easier to not close the door completely than to take my bulky keyring with me.

"Good thing I'm here, then," I said. I reached through the door. When I turned the handle from the inside to open it, there was no click. I realized the door hadn't been shut well enough to lock. Unless Ruby pulled the door shut hard behind her, the door didn't actually lock.

I was about to push the door open when a voice behind Ruby asked, "Everything okay out here?"

Ruby sighed as she turned around. "Locked my keys inside. And my phone," she told Shannon, who was standing in the crack between the door frame and Jake's slightly open door.

I'd caught a quick glimpse of her at the wake yesterday. She'd only stayed a few minutes before retreating back to the solace of Jake's apartment. I didn't blame her, especially considering that Patty and Markie were there, too. Running into your dead boyfriend's ex at his wake couldn't be fun, especially if you were the other woman. And judging from the number of Ruby-Shannon-Patty look-alikes in the bar on Sunday, I'd guess that Patty wasn't the only ex in attendance.

I wasn't much for memorials, funerals, services, or wakes. Too depressing. And I could definitively say from the point of view of someone who's been on both sides of a funeral that the dead did *not* give a shit who showed up to throw dirt on their grave.

Or rather, I imagined I wouldn't have cared. If I'd had a funeral, I didn't know about it. No one had invited me. I supposed there might have been one, but I doubted many people went. Dad was dead. Mom was who knows where. My brother Ian was behind bars. The few friends I had, I'd drifted away from in recent years. And it's not like Adam would have gone, not after he reconciled with Karin and promised to stop seeing me. Given the choice, I would have opted out of a funeral anyway.

"Want me to call the super for you?" Shannon offered, opening the door a little wider.

Ruby jiggled the handle and the door opened. "Oh, hey, thanks, Cor..."

"Cor?" Shannon asked. "Who's Cor? Is someone with you?"

"Thanks, *door*," Ruby hastily corrected herself. "I said 'door.'" She patted the door, and it swung open farther. "Good door." She turned back to Shannon. "I guess I didn't close it well enough to lock. Happens all the time."

"You should get that fixed," Shannon said with a frown. "It's not safe."

"Don't worry, the deadbolt works just fine."

"Even so..."

Before Shannon could offer any more helpful advice, Ruby said, "It's all good." She looked down at the box in her hands. "Join me for pizza?"

"Seriously?" I asked Ruby, not that she could hear me. "You're the one convinced that Jake's death had something to do with his pathological inability to keep it in his pants. If you really think that one of the many, many women in his life killed him, what are you doing inviting another one of them into our home? I swear you have the survival instincts of a lemming."

"Oh, I couldn't," Shannon said, glancing at the delivery box. "I'm kinda over pizza."

I breathed a sigh of relief, and not just that a potential murder suspect didn't want to come inside. I'd learned how to share my home with Ruby, but this constant stream of visitors was getting old fast. Fortunately, considering how often Jake ordered pizza, I wouldn't be surprised if Shannon never wanted to see another pizza in her life.

"Please? I've got more than I can eat, and I'm sure you could use some company." Ruby held the door open with her foot. "Come on."

Shannon reached down and snatched Jake's keys out of the bowl by the door. "Well, if you insist." She let the door close behind her, and scurried across the hall to follow Ruby into our apartment. "It's funny how your apartment is identical to Jake's but at the same time, so different," she said, taking a look around.

"Great," I grumbled. "Make yourself at home."

"Yeah, I was thinking the same thing about Jake's apartment when we visited you the other day," Ruby said.

"We?" Shannon asked.

"We, as in you and I," Ruby corrected herself hastily.

"Oh." Shannon still looked confused.

Ruby sat the pizza down on the counter and got two plates out. "Counter or loveseat?" she asked. "I don't have a table."

"Jake doesn't either," she said. "No room for one. Loveseat is fine."

Ruby loaded up her plate with a few slices and took a spot on the loveseat.

"Beer?" Shannon asked.

At the thought of alcohol of any kind, Ruby paled. "Don't have any."

"I do. Want me to run next door and grab some?"

Ruby shook her head. "I really, really don't."

Shannon looked startled by her conviction. "Of course. No worries." She took a small slice of pizza and sat on the edge of the seat next to Ruby. "Can I ask you something? Are you happy, living here alone?"

Ruby took a bite of pizza and chewed it before answering. "I grew up as a middle sister. So, it's kinda nice to have my own space, you know?" Then she smiled. "Not that I ever really feel alone."

I laughed. Of all the apartments in the world, I was glad that Ruby had moved into this one. I couldn't imagine my afterlife without her.

"This week is the first time in my life I've been truly alone." Shannon shook her head. "It's strange. It's too quiet. I leave the TV on all the time, but it's not the same."

"Well, if you ever get too lonely, I'm right across the hall," Ruby offered.

I groaned again. "Ruby, you're too nice for your own good."

"That's awful kind of you, but I'm thinking it might be time to get out of Boston," Shannon said.

"And go where?" Ruby asked around a mouthful of food.

"Connecticut, maybe? By the water? I hear it's nice there. Or I could head south." She stopped and shook her head. "No, I don't think I should. Too many monsters down there."

"Gators?" Ruby asked.

"Politicians," Shannon replied.

Ruby snorted. She finished off her first slice before Shannon had touched hers. She started on the next one. The grease and carbs were probably doing more to cure her hangover than aspirin ever could. Pizza was one of my favorite hangover cures.

When they were finished eating, Ruby did dishes while Shannon checked out the living room. She was drawn to the bookshelves. She ran her finger along the spines, stopping on occasion to pull one out and examine the cover or read the back blurb. "Quite a collection you have here."

"The, uh, previous tenant left them here when she, uh, moved out." She flushed crimson.

I wished I'd known Ruby back when I was still alive. She couldn't bluff her way out of a wet paper sack. I would have cleaned her out at poker.

"I haven't read this one, but I hear good things," Shannon said, holding out one of my favorites. "Mind if I borrow it?"

"Knock yourself out," Ruby said. "I've been meaning to donate them but there's just so many of them, and those stairs don't get any easier."

"My kingdom for an elevator building," Shannon said.

"Right?"

"I saw you at the wake. Thanks for coming. That meant a lot to me. And I'm sure Jake's family appreciated it, too."

I couldn't help but notice that Shannon called him "Jake," not "Jakey" like Patty and some of his friends had done.

"You left early," Ruby said.

I was proud of her for catching that. Then again, up until the end, she'd been working the room pretty well. We made a good team.

"Yeah. It was all just too much," Shannon said.

"He had quite a few exes there," Ruby pointed out.

Personally, I was convinced that Jake's death had something to do with the gun he'd hidden in his toilet tank or the copious amounts of money he'd wasted on gambling, but I was happy to see that my roomie was doggedly pursuing her own theory.

"Like I said, it was all just a little too much." Shannon sighed. "Just between you and me, I know Jake had a reputation. A well-deserved one. He liked the ladies, and they liked him right back. He had a roving eye, if you know what I mean."

Ruby nodded. "Yeah. I know."

"But it was different with us."

"I'm sure it was," Ruby agreed, but I could tell by her expression that she wasn't buying it.

"You don't believe me."

"Doesn't matter what I believe," Ruby said. "You cared about him."

"I loved him," Shannon corrected him. "And he loved me back."

"And I'm sorry he's gone."

"Me, too." Shannon stared into space for a moment. "I heard you asking questions at the wake. 'Do you know anyone that wanted to hurt him?' 'Did he piss anyone off recently?' Those aren't the kind of questions people normally ask. You sure you're not a cop or something?"

Ruby shook her head. "Nope. Not a cop."

I could tell that Shannon had other questions she wanted to ask, but she let them hang in the air. When Ruby didn't volunteer any more information, she broke down and asked, "Well? Did anyone have any interesting answers?"

"Sorry, no. If it makes any difference, everyone loved Jake. He was apparently the life of the party."

"He was," Shannon agreed. "He'll be missed. Thanks for the pizza, and the book. I'll bring it back to you as soon as it's finished."

"No rush," Ruby said. "And I meant it, about you getting lonely. You can drop by anytime. To chat, or borrow a book, or whatever."

"Thanks." Shannon took the book and headed back across the hall to Jake's apartment.

"Poor Shannon," I said. I felt for her. I knew what it was like to lose the man you loved.

"Poor Shannon," Ruby said.

"It sucks, but I can't believe she could be so naïve," I added.

"I think Jake really changed for her," Ruby said.

I snorted. I guess Shannon wasn't the only one being naïve. "Not hardly. Guys like Jake don't change."

CHAPTER TWENTY-SEVEN
RUBY

Shannon's visit got me thinking. The cops hadn't come back. As far as they were concerned, Jake's death was low priority. The only lead I'd had was the watch, and that was a dead end.

But there was one thing I could do to get a better idea of what had happened that night, and that was to revisit the scene of the crime. I grabbed my coat and made sure to pocket my keys this time. As I took the stairs, I forced myself to look on the bright side. Just think about how much money I was saving on a gym membership by living on the fourth floor! Plus, as hard as it was to heat my apartment, I could only imagine how much colder it was on the lower floors. Times were tough, sure, but they could be worse, and they were certainly looking up.

The same couldn't be said for Jake, I realized as I stepped out of the relatively warm lobby to stand on the front stoop. The sun had set, but the clouds were low and the wind wasn't blowing. For the first time in months, it was almost pleasant outside. It wasn't spring, not by a long shot, but I'd left my hat and gloves upstairs and didn't immediately feel like I was going to freeze to death, so that was a dramatic improvement. Boston was growing on me.

"What time, exactly, did Jake die?" I muttered. I'm sure the cops had an idea, but I was only guessing. The afternoon before the storm, I had a job interview that I'd bombed. It had just started snowing in earnest when I got out of it. I remember watching snow blow across the street as the bus driver announced that this was his last route of the night because the city was shutting down in preparation for the nor'easter bearing down on us, right before the bus lost traction and almost skidded into a stop sign.

It was maybe six o'clock by the time I made it home. Snow was already drifting against the building. There was no Jake outside, at least not that I saw. When I was leaving the next morning for yet another job interview at eight, his body was laying on the sidewalk, under a blanket. "A lot could happen in fourteen hours. I could binge entire seasons of a show in that amount of time," I said, more or less to myself.

I glanced across the street to O'Grady's, where I would never again be welcome. Which was probably for the best. After Sunday, I was more determined than ever to never touch another drop of booze. It was bad news.

Jake spent a lot of time in O'Grady's, enough time that his family thought it was appropriate to hold his wake there. Could he have been coming home from the bar when he was mugged? I could picture it clearly. Jake, after one too many, stumbles across the road. It's slippery. Cold. The wind is whipping down the street. He would have been easy pickings.

"But Jake was in pajama pants," I reminded myself. I closed my eyes and tried to picture that morning. There were two, maybe three police cruisers parked in the street. The plows hadn't come through yet, and any car that had been parked at the curb overnight was an unrecognizable lump under a few feet of snow.

There was a blanket covering him, but a gust of wind tore down the street and picked up the blanket, giving me a glimpse of the body. The only way I knew it was Jake from that quick glance was because the officer had already told me he was dead. "He was wearing a brown hoodie with blue and green plaid flannel pj bottoms, and orange and white fuzzy socks," I said, picturing it clearly.

I'd seen Jake in the hoodie before, one that advertised his favorite hockey team. He wore that hoodie everywhere, but it was usually half-hidden under a thicker jacket if he was going out. The flannel pants were generic. I couldn't remember if I'd seen Jake in them before. Jeans? Definitely. Sweats? Most certainly. Flannel pajamas? Maybe. Then again, I came from a generation that wore pj bottoms everywhere. I wouldn't think much of seeing someone walking around in public in them.

Jake was old school. Maybe he'd wear pjs to check the mail, but I couldn't imagine him going out in them, not even to his regular bar. Jake had never seemed overly concerned with appearances, and that could just as easily have extended to his wardrobe choices. Then again, if he was half the player everyone thought he was, he might dress up when he was planning on picking up a woman.

It was the fuzzy socks that I couldn't get over. I mean, fuzzy socks were about the best thing in the world. They were warm. Comfortable. The ultimate in home comfort. But that's just it. They're great in the house and not so great out of it. Have you ever tried to jam fuzzy-socked feet into your favorite pair of boots? It didn't work. Not comfortably, at least.

Maybe Jake had gone to the neighborhood bar in his pjs. No

judgement here. But he would have put on shoes with regular socks. I could cross the street and risk getting thrown out again to ask the bartender if he'd seen Jake the night of the storm, but I was fairly certain I already knew the answer. "Jake hadn't been stumbling back from O'Grady's when he was killed," I decided.

With one theory down, I racked my brain for other possibilities. Maybe he'd gone downstairs for a delivery, like I had just a few hours ago.

I remembered from our cursory inspection of his apartment with his cousin Bobby that Jake's wallet and keys were upstairs. But who really needed a wallet these days? Almost everyone used their phone to pay for everything. Even if Jake did tip in cash instead of using an app, he could have grabbed it on the way out the door.

Assuming Jake had gone downstairs to pick up food, where did it end up? He didn't have a take-out box on him when the police found his body. Besides, with the storm barreling toward Boston, everything was shutting down early. No one would be sending drivers out in that mess.

I shook my head. "None of it makes any sense," I grumbled. "Unless..."

A thought hit me. Shannon might be all starry-eyed about finding her soul mate in Jake Macintyre, and I wanted to believe he'd changed for her. But according to Patty, he was a cheater. So, Jake's out and about doing whatever—or whomever—when he realized a storm was coming and he ought to get home, but instead bumps into trouble on his way into our building. But it still didn't explain why he didn't have shoes.

I closed my eyes and tried to picture that night. "Maybe he was driving. He didn't expect he'd be outside, so he didn't think he'd need shoes." I shook my head. "No, that's not right." His keys were upstairs with his wallet. He wasn't driving anywhere. For that matter, how did he plan to get back into the building? Maybe he'd forgotten them in his hurry to meet a special lady friend.

"Wherever he was coming from, unless someone dropped him off, in the middle of a snowstorm that was so bad even the city buses stopped running, he had to have walked," I muttered to myself. I doubt he walked far, not sock-footed. While I wouldn't personally recommend walking through a snowstorm in fuzzy socks, there were a dozen apartment buildings within easy walking distance of ours, each with twenty or more units. That was a lot of possible women for Jake's dating pool.

The possibility gave me some measure of comfort. If I was right, then Jake had died doing what he loved. Who knew? Maybe he was out with Shannon. I still knew nothing about the killer or their motivation. Was his death random or targeted? If Jake was heading home from a hot date, that didn't explain what the murderer was also doing out on such a foul night—unless the killer was lying in wait.

I felt eyes on me. I'd gotten better about such things recently. "Cordelia? Are you trying to tell me something?" I asked in a whisper even though no one was around. Other than a few passing cars, I was alone. I looked around, expecting to see a sign from Cordelia. A floating soda can. A loose brick tumbling down the sidewalk. Colorful candies forming a trail. Something. Anything.

The only thing I saw was a curtain fluttering from a fourth-floor apartment, as if someone had been looking out, only to have ducked out of sight at the last minute. I counted the windows. The movement could have come from either Milly's apartment or Jake's. I wouldn't be surprised if Milly was upstairs watching me intently as I paced in front of the building and muttered to myself. She probably had binoculars on the windowsill for just that purpose. If Milly had a habit of spying on people on the front sidewalk, what else might she have seen?

I marched upstairs with a new purpose, giving me spring in my step. After the almost pleasantly cool weather outside, the stairwell was hot and stuffy, but I didn't mind. I'd rather be too hot than too cold any day of the week.

When I reached Milly's door, I knocked on it with the side of my fist. She didn't answer. I knocked again. "Milly, I know you're home," I said loud enough that I knew she could hear me. Milly was always home. Besides, I could hear her TV playing a catchy jingle.

The door opened a crack. Milly peered out at me. She was wearing her standard fare. Today, it was a gray velour track suit. "Make it quick. *Wheel*'s on," she said. Behind her, her TV was blaring.

Growing up, the television was almost always on in my house, even when no one was watching. When I moved to Boston, I couldn't afford cable so I went without. The first few weeks were rough. Now I hardly even missed it.

"Were you home the night Jake was killed?" I asked bluntly.

"No, I was out taking Roomba lessons at the Y while a storm was rolling in," she said sarcastically. I'm fairly certain she meant *Zumba* lessons. "Of course I was home. What kind of question is that?"

"And you didn't hear anything? See anything? Nothing out of the ordinary?"

"If I had, I would have told the cops, now wouldn't I?" she asked.

"Did you?" I probed. "Did you tell them anything?"

She shook her head. "Nope."

"And you didn't see anything outside your window?"

"I just said I didn't see nothing, didn't I? It was dark, and snowing to beat the band. *Jeopardy* was a repeat so I went to bed early."

I sighed in frustration. What good did it do to have the neighborhood busybody tracking everyone all day every day if a murder happened right outside her window and she missed it? "You didn't hear the gunshot?"

Milly flung her door open. "Come in, come in."

How often had I wondered if Milly—tiny, ancient, harmless Milly—might be a secret serial killer? Going into her apartment wasn't the best idea I'd ever had. Then again, I lived with a ghost. Compared to that, how scary could Milly be?

With only a hint of hesitation, I followed her inside. "Do you mind turning that down?" I said, wincing as a commercial came on at top volume.

Milly grabbed a remote, pointed it at the TV, and turned it down to a more reasonable, but still loud, volume. I'd always assumed that the reason I could hear practically every sound coming out of the other apartments was because the walls were so thin, but after being in Milly's apartment for just a minute, I was starting to think that the walls weren't the problem. It was the neighbors.

"It's these damn batteries. Hold out your hand."

I did as instructed. She dropped something into my palm. It was a hearing aid and a tiny battery still in its packaging. I tried not to think about Milly's earwax.

"Damn things are so small, I don't understand how anyone's expected to be able to change them without a microscope, tweezers, and an electrical engineering degree from MIT."

"Let me see what I can do." I examined the hearing aid. There was a compartment on one end that came out easily. I tore open the battery package, replaced the battery, and closed the compartment cover. I handed the hearing aid, the dead battery, and the empty package to Milly.

"Well, I'll be. You've done this before." She settled the hearing aid into position. "That's better." She picked up the remote and lowered the volume on the television a little more.

"The night Jake was killed?" I asked.

"Like I said, reruns. The battery was dying, so I took it out and went to bed early. Didn't hear a thing. Which isn't always a bad thing."

"What do you mean?"

"You can't be serious." She shook her head at me and clucked her tongue. "Living next to Jake Macintyre was like living next to a frat house. When he didn't have a dozen of his rowdy friends over, he had the game blaring from his TV. When the game wasn't on, it was a stream of girls, a different one every week. Disgraceful! Just like my last husband, rest his soul."

I was tempted to ask her what happened to her husband, and the husband (or was it husbands?) before him. But before I could, she continued, "It was one long nonstop party over there."

Everyone described Jake as the life of the party. I just hadn't thought about what that must be like for his immediate next-door neighbor. "I'll bet that drove you up the wall," I said, trying to be sympathetic. I heard the noise coming from Jake's apartment, too, but I was able to tune it out. Then again, I was across the hall. Milly shared a wall with him. Their living rooms and bedrooms lined up. I could see how that would get annoying quickly.

"It did," she agreed. "Half the time I left my hearing aid off so I could get a bit of peace and quiet, but even then, I could hear him thumping around like some big dumb Neanderthal. I started a list of how many friends came over, when they arrived and when they left. I showed it to the super. He told me to mind my own business."

"I'm sorry you had to deal with that," I said. Technically, Jake wasn't doing anything wrong by having company over. Was he rude and inconsiderate? Yeah, sure. But he wasn't breaking any rules, except maybe a noise ordinance and those were rarely enforced. Reporting him wasn't going to do anything.

Milly nodded. "I just hope the next neighbor is quieter, or I'll do a whole lot worse than call the super on them."

That sounded ominous. If the next person who moved into Jake's apartment died under suspicious circumstances, I knew who would be on the top of my suspects list. "Um, okay," was the best response I could come up with.

"You're a good egg. Not like Jake. Thanks for swapping out the battery for me. Now that the party animal is gone, it would be nice to be able to hear again."

"It's no problem. Really. And Milly? Anytime you need help, just ask. I'm right across the hall," I offered. Did I want to be at her beck and call? Not particularly. But did I want to be on her good side, especially if she was in the habit of picking off neighbors that annoyed her? Absolutely.

She smiled. "Funny thing is, the woman who lived in your apartment before you used to do those sort of things for me."

"Cordelia Graves?" I asked.

She massaged her hands. "One and the same. Ever since the arthritis got bad, she'd help me on the little things. Now that she's gone, I can't even get the tamper lids off my pills."

"I'm here now," I offered. "Anything need doing?"

"Come here, child."

I followed her into the bathroom. In my apartment, the cabinet behind the mirror over the sink held the basics. Toothbrush. Toothpaste. Nail clippers. Q-tips. Milly's medicine cabinet was packed to the brim with both prescription and over-the-counter pill bottles.

"Whoever invented child-proof lids should be shot," she grumbled. "Can you open them?"

"Sure thing." I pulled out each pill bottle carefully, and it was a good thing I did because many of them already had the lid loosened. Any of them that were closed, or sealed, I opened and put back gingerly. When I was finished, I reminded Milly that if she needed anything, I was right across the hall.

As she let me out, my mind was swirling. Cordelia had died with a lethal cocktail of pills and booze in her system, but had no pill bottles in her apartment. Without a coroner's report, which I had no idea how one might go about getting hold of, I had no way of knowing the specific combination. But I wondered where she'd gotten all those pills, and if any of them had come from Milly's extensive collection of prescriptions.

I was still deep in thought when I unlocked my apartment. The door stuck. The building was old and nothing was maintained as well as it should be. I had to shove the door with my shoulder to get it to budge. It swung open to reveal that in the short time that I'd been downstairs or over at Milly's, someone had broken in and trashed my apartment.

CHAPTER TWENTY-EIGHT
CORDELIA

This was all my fault. I *knew* Ruby should never have gotten involved with Jake's murder investigation. At first, everything I did to try to scare her away backfired, drawing her in further. Then at some point, I'd stopped worrying about her safety because her intervention was helping me. That all ended now.

I should have spent the day watching over her instead of hanging out with Harp. At the very least, I could have stood guard over our apartment. I would have seen who broke in. Who knows? Maybe I could have prevented the break-in completely.

While Ruby was technically an adult, she was still my responsibility, and she was in over her head. But what was I supposed to do? I couldn't convince her to wear professional clothes to an interview, so I couldn't possibly get her to cover herself in bubble wrap, deadbolt the door, and not come out until the killer was captured and convicted. On top of that, there was little to no chance of Jake's murder getting solved without us. I'd checked in on the detective assigned to Jake's case a few times when Ruby was otherwise occupied, and he'd made no progress at all. On the contrary, as far as I could tell, none of the approximately seventeen thousand cases on his desk were getting enough attention.

Even though the police obviously didn't give a flying leap about what happened in this neighborhood, Ruby waited patiently in the hall outside for the cops to show up. As soon as she saw that someone had tossed our apartment, instead of cataloging the mess, she'd called the cops. Sweet, naïve Ruby, thinking that Boston PD was going to investigate an apartment break-in. If the across-the-hall neighbor hadn't been killed recently, they might not have responded at all other than to advise her to come in and file a report. As it was, they dispatched a single officer, and it wasn't even someone who'd been involved with Jake's case.

"Anything missing?" the officer asked, standing in the open door looking in.

Ruby was still in the hall. "I don't know," she said. "I haven't been inside yet."

"No time like the present," he said, waving her in front of him.

There was no one lurking in the apartment. I'd already checked. The reading lamp next to the loveseat had been knocked over. It had shattered, scattering bits of broken hand-made pottery on the floor. The bookcase had been searched, and my books lay in messy heaps on the floor. Ruby's closet had been tossed, too. Clothes were ripped from their hangers and shoes were thrown haphazardly in the corner.

The intruder hadn't touched the silverware drawer where my cash and Jake's watch were hidden. Ruby's eyes went there first, but she didn't check the drawer, not with the officer present. She knew she'd have a hell of a time explaining how she came into possession of all that money.

Most importantly, whoever had broken in hadn't messed with

Eunice the philodendron. Considering how much effort it had taken to keep Ruby from killing my last plant, I considered that a win, even if it was a minor one.

"I see a lot of mess, but no real damage," the officer said. "Anything missing?"

Ruby shook her head. "Not that I can tell, but there wasn't much to take in the first place."

"You want my advice?" he asked, then continued without waiting for a response. "Whoever you've pissed off lately, find them and make peace. In the meantime, call your building manager and get a better lock on the door." He handed her a business card. "If I find out anything, I'll let you know." He left.

"He's right about one thing. The lock sucks," I said. I couldn't remember if Ruby had shut the door hard enough behind her to engage the automatic lock. A good deadbolt might have stopped them. We had one, but Ruby rarely locked it when she was out of the apartment. That was going to change.

Once the officer was gone, Ruby headed straight for the silverware drawer. She yanked it open, set the watch aside, pulled out the insert, and breathed a sigh of relief that the envelopes were right where I'd left them. "Told ya," I said.

"Cordelia, did you see who did this?" she asked.

no

Our magnet system might not be perfect, but it was more than adequate in this situation.

"You didn't do this, did you?" she asked.

It took me a second to respond. She couldn't be serious. Why would I trash my own apartment? Why would I toss my own books around or break my own reading lamp?

IN your DREAMS

"I had to ask. It does kinda seem like something you might do to get my attention."

no

Ruby chuckled. "I believe you. Sorry. I should have trusted you."

Yeah, she should have. Then again, it wasn't like I was being completely open and honest with her. I could have answered her question about my relationship with Adam when she'd asked, or let her in on the real reason I was so worried about the Eunice the philodendron, other than it being my favorite plant. But even a dead woman was entitled to a few secrets, right?

"Do you think this is about Jake?" she asked.

Instead of using the magnets to answer, I pulled back the living room curtains. The sun had gone down and now it was dark outside. The windows faced the back of another apartment building instead of the street. Most people had their windows closed at night, not just for privacy, but to keep the heat inside. As a result, the big window acted like a shiny black mirror, reflecting back the contents of the living room. Or, it would have if someone hadn't used green spray paint to write **BACK OFF!** in two-foot-high letters across the glass.

Ruby stared at the warning for a moment before saying, "I wish you had shown me this while the cop was still here."

"Yeah, sure," I replied sarcastically. "While a cop was walking around our apartment, I should rearrange the furniture, too. Maybe levitate the loveseat? I'm sure that would have gone over real well." Ruby might be just about the most open-minded person on the planet when it came to ghosts, and I appreciated that. I did. But there was no telling how a random cop off the street might react.

It was one of the reasons I'd stayed quiet as a friggin' church mouse when that reporter, Penny, had invited herself in with all sorts of questions about Jake. I couldn't afford to have the wrong person find out about me. The cop might have ignored me. He might have called an exorcist. Or, worst, he might have turned me, Ruby, and our haunted apartment into a circus.

"Unless you don't trust the cops?" Ruby asked. "You think they might be in on this?"

I didn't, but not for the reasons she was thinking. The police might be rife with corruption, but they weren't competent enough to pull off a decent conspiracy. Oh, I'm sure some of them were, but on the whole, as an organization? They had bigger fish to fry. They didn't even care who killed Jake Macintyre.

But whoever killed Jake had Ruby on their radar now.

Which meant the best—and maybe only—way to protect Ruby was to figure out who killed Jake and turn them in before they came back to finish the job they'd started on our apartment. Unfortunately, I had no idea how to do that.

The only thing I could do right now was help Ruby set the apartment back to rights. The two of us, working side by side, made quick work of it. By the time that Ruby was ready to turn in for the night, the apartment was in decent shape again, minus the paint on the window. I would take care of that later. There was a full trash bag sitting in the middle of the kitchen, waiting to go to the bin downstairs. I stood over the bag. "I can do this," I said aloud, to psych myself up.

How hard could it be to take out the trash? Harp had showed me how to make something invisible just by touching it and willing it so. If it had worked on a watch, it should work on a garbage bag. All I had to do was believe it. Easy peasy.

"I believe I can do this," I said. I tied the bag closed, lifted it, and... poof. It disappeared. Go me!

I stepped through the apartment door carrying the bag, but as soon as the trash bag hit the door, it stuck fast. The same thing had happened when I tried passing Jake's keys through his door. I could walk right through doors—and walls, and floors, and other objects—because I was essentially immaterial. But the garbage bag, visible or not, was solid matter just like the door. It wasn't possible to carry the trash through a closed door.

Then again, life after death shouldn't be possible. A ghost befriending a breather shouldn't be possible. My stubborn self finding room in my apartment, and my heart, for an annoyingly perky twenty-year-old like Ruby should *definitely* not be possible. Nothing about me should be possible, and yet, here I was.

"Nothing is impossible," I said aloud, and the trash bag slid effortlessly through the door.

I'd been so wrapped up in my garbage bag dilemma, I hadn't noticed the raised voices in the hall. Bobby and the no-good building manager were standing outside Jake's apartment arguing with Shannon, who was blocking the entrance. "Bullshit. I don't have to let you in," she said stubbornly.

"It's not your apartment," Bobby argued.

"It's not yours, either," she replied.

"I have more right to it than you do," he said angrily.

"Oh yeah? Why? Because your cousin used to live here? Guess what, buddy? I moved in before Jake died, so it's my apartment, too."

"It doesn't work like that," Bobby said, sounding exasperated.

Shannon turned her attention to the building manager. "Rent's paid up until the end of the month, right?"

"Well, yes, but you're not on the lease."

"So? Half the building is sublet. 2A is an Airbnb. As long as the rent check is paid on time, why do you care who's living here?" Shannon asked.

The building manager shrugged. "You know what? I really don't."

"What do you mean you don't?" Bobby asked. "It's my cousin's apartment."

"Which means it ain't yours," the building manager said. "Come back with proof that you've got a claim to it, and we'll talk. In the meantime, possession is nine-tenths of the law."

"I don't think that means what you think it means," Bobby protested.

"And I don't think I care." The building manager nodded at Shannon. "'Night, Miss. Sorry for disturbing you."

She offered him a cautious smile. "Not at all."

"This isn't the end of this," Bobby warned her.

"I don't expect it is. Good night." She closed the door and I heard the locks engage. All of them.

Bobby turned and tripped over my bag of garbage. I'd been so caught up in the drama going on at Jake's door, I'd stopped concentrating on the trash bag. As a result, it was sitting in the middle of the hall in plain view. "Where'd this come from?" he asked.

"Who cares? You're heading downstairs, ain't ya?" the building manager asked. "Just toss it in the can out front on your way out."

"But it's not my problem."

"Not mine, either." The building manager held out his empty hands. "Call it the price of you dragging me up here for nothing." Before Bobby could argue further, he strode down the hall and headed down the stairs to his own apartment.

Bobby nudged the bag with his toe, reminding me of how his

cousin's first instinct when coming across his own dead body was to try to probe it with his foot. The genes in the Macintyre family were strong. I could all but see the wheels turning in his head as he contemplated what to do with the trash, but in the end, he heaved a sigh, picked up the bag, and carried it downstairs with him as he departed the building.

As I followed him all the way home to Southie—I had nothing better to do tonight, and I wanted to be certain he didn't change his mind and come back to harass Shannon some more—I'd made a mental note to ask Ruby to let Bobby know we'd found the missing watch and he could come get it. Maybe once he had the watch back, he'd leave Shannon alone.

CHAPTER TWENTY-NINE

RUBY

The harder a job was, the less you got paid. I'd always known that, I suppose, or at least suspected it, but there was nothing like getting to experience it firsthand from the privileged side to really drive that lesson home. I had what I considered a cushy job. I was inside, in a climate-controlled office. I had a nice desk and sat in a comfortable chair all day. And got paid twice what I used to when I was on my feet for eight to ten hours a day working retail. Plus now I had benefits, sick leave, vacation days, and two weeks paid time off when the office closed for the winter break.

The job itself was easy enough. I answered the phones. I ordered and distributed supplies as needed. I verified the schedule. When emails came in from our website, I forwarded them to the correct people. I mailed out packages. I ordered lunch.

That was one of the perks of working from the office instead of working from home. If any of the three cofounders were in the office—and at least one almost always was—they would pay for lunch for the whole office, including me. Today I ordered sandwiches and salads from the deli around the corner.

Half an hour after placing our order, the door to the office was nudged open by a foot. Before I could jump up to help, a man burst in carrying a large insulated bag. "Hey, chica! Long time, no—" he said enthusiastically, then stopped short when he saw me. "You're not Cordelia."

I cast a surreptitious glance around, as if I might catch a glimpse of her, and then realized that he'd expected to see her because she used to work here. She used to sit in this chair. She used to order lunch for the office.

"She doesn't work here anymore," I said. I'd never stopped to think about it before, but delivery people knew us—or at least our habits—better than anyone. And what were people if not creatures of habit? From the Caparelli's Pizza driver who brought Jake a constant stream of pizza to this guy who probably saw Cordelia all the time when she'd been alive, they were a huge part of our lives and most of us barely noticed them. "I'm Ruby. I'm new."

"Marty," he said, with a nod. He gestured at his insulated tote. "Want it in the break room?"

I nodded. "Yes, please." I followed him. "Marty, you knew Cordelia, right?"

"Only that she used to order from us once a week or so. Then she stopped." He started unpacking the tote onto the table. "Guess she found someplace better to work. I always told her she was too good for this job." He stopped with a handful of chip bags clutched in one fist. "I mean, it's a great job. I'm sure you'll love it."

"Yeah, thanks," I said. The fact that he'd just insulted me and my brand-new job in one casual comment did not go unnoticed, but I was sure he didn't mean anything by it.

He hastily finished unpacking our order, tossing a handful of individually wrapped plasticware on the table. I would end up adding those to the drawer already overflowing with individually wrapped forks, spoons, napkins, salt, and peppers that the office seemed to accumulate. "See ya next week?" he asked.

"Probably," I agreed.

He scurried away. I spread the assortment out on the table before stepping out of the break room to announce to the office at large, "Lunch is here."

Heads popped up over cubicle walls, and I stepped out of the way to avoid being trampled. Blair was the first to the table. He swiped the first sandwich he saw.

"Hey, that's the vegetarian one," Melissa complained. "Give it here."

"Whatever," he said, tossing it to her and selecting another at random without checking the label.

I stopped to knock on Adam's door on the way back to my desk. I heard a muffled voice from within that sounded like "Come in," so I opened the door a crack. "Lunch is in the break room," I said.

He placed a hand over the mouthpiece of his phone. "Thanks."

A few minutes later, he emerged from his office, but instead of making a beeline to the break room, he swung by my desk first. "Did you get anything to eat?"

"I'll get something in a minute," I assured him.

"There won't be anything left in a minute," he told me. Then he raised his voice so he could be easily heard throughout the office. "Those vultures had better have left a meatball sub for me, or I'll remember this when it comes time for raises." He took his voice down to a normal level. "Come on, Ruby. Let's grab a bite before it's all gone."

I followed him to the break room. I'd ordered as many sandwiches as there were people working today, but all that was left was one of the side salads and a package of jalapeno-flavored chips. He looked disappointed. "Split the salad?" he offered.

"I'm good," I said.

"Nonsense." He pushed the salad toward me and helped himself to a yogurt from the fridge for himself instead. He bypassed the stack of plastic spoons to get a metal one from the drawer. "I hope you choke on my meatballs," he said loudly, in the direction of the doorway that separated the break room from the bullpen.

I couldn't help myself. I giggled.

"That sounded bad, didn't it?" he asked.

"It's a good thing HR isn't on-site today," I agreed. I sat down and pried the lid off the salad.

I was the lowest-paid employee in the office. I knew that for a fact from helping Sally in HR fix a spreadsheet that most of the guys out there right now chowing down on free sandwiches were paid six figures, and yet a few of them had nabbed two sandwiches—they were huge subs, so either they had a voracious appetite or planned on taking the extras home to eat later—knowing not everyone had eaten yet. Either that, or Marty the deli delivery guy had shorted us. I wasn't about to complain about a free lunch salad, but I *really* wouldn't have complained about a free sub.

"Next time, take your pick before you ring the dinner bell," Adam said, shaking his yogurt vigorously.

"Good advice," I answered. I made a mental note to knock on his door the next time we got a food delivery before telling anyone else that food was here. I speared a tomato on my fork. I was still thinking about my disjointed conversation with Marty when I asked, "You knew Cordelia Graves, right?"

"Where did you hear that name?" he asked, almost fumbling his yogurt as he peeled off the lid.

"She had this job before me, right?"

He swallowed audibly, then nodded. "Yup."

I wondered what TrendCelerate had done for the three months after Cordelia died and before they hired me. Had they hired other office managers that didn't work out? Had they brought in a temp? Or had they taken turns answering the phones?

There were a dozen questions running around my head, but I asked the one that was most important to me. "What was she like?"

"Why do you want to know?" Adam asked, sitting his mostly untouched yogurt down on the table and pushing it away from himself.

"Why does no one ever want to talk about her?" I asked, remembering Melissa's warning to not say her name around the office. "Is there a curse or something? I bet there's a curse." I said it as a joke, hoping that if I lightened the mood, he might open up. Then, I remembered I was talking to one of the cofounders of the company, a man who may or may not have been messing around with my dead roommate, and wished I hadn't been so flippant.

He took his glasses off and took his time polishing the lenses on his shirt sleeve before answering. "You're a firecracker, aren't you? She worked here a long time. She was nice. Everyone liked her. And then she died. End of story." I noticed he never used her name. I wondered if that was on purpose. He started to get up.

"She killed herself, right?" I asked before he could walk away from the table. I thought the bit about everyone liking her was stretching the truth. According to Melissa, no one knew her well enough to like her or not.

Adam glanced over his shoulder, in the direction of the bullpen. Everyone was at their desks scarfing down their sandwiches while they joked with one another over the short cubicle walls. "That was unfortunate," he said, finally.

"Why did she do it?" I pressed. It was so frustrating. I spent so much time with Cordelia, but I had no clue why she'd killed herself. She spent all day, every day, for years here at TrendCelerate. Surely, someone here had to know her better than I did. And, if there was anything to the rumors Melissa alluded to and Cordelia refused to refute, Adam knew her better than almost anyone.

"Does it matter?" He toyed with his yogurt. "Why does anyone do anything?" He sighed. "She, Cordelia"—he looked sad when he said her name—"didn't open up a lot. But I got the impression she had a hard life."

"Hard how?" I asked.

"You don't give up, do you? She would have hated you. No offense. I think you're great. It's just Cordelia was incredibly reserved and you're, well, you're not." The phone rang. "You should probably get that."

I'd gotten more than I'd expected I would from him, but it still wasn't a lot to work with. "You're right." I scooped up my salad and hurried back to my desk, catching the phone before the caller hung up.

Even as I was helping them, I kept thinking about what Adam had said. Cordelia would have hated me? Oof. But also, I didn't think that was entirely true. We certainly got along fine now, considering the circumstances.

I finished up the call. While I ate the rest of my salad, I distracted myself from worrying about whether or not Cordelia liked me by concentrating on Jake's death instead. He deserved closure. Whoever broke in and trashed my apartment wanted to scare me off, but it just made me more determined. Unfortunately, I'd run out of leads. I'd talked to everyone I could think of, and I was still no closer to figuring out who killed him and why. I needed more information.

After double-checking that no one was paying attention to me, I whispered, "Are you here?" I waited a few minutes, but nothing happened to indicate that Cordelia was hovering nearby. I wasn't sure where she'd gone or what she was doing, but if she wasn't available, I had an idea of someone else who might be able to help.

By the way Cordelia had ripped up the reporter's business card, I assumed she didn't want me talking to Penny Fisher. But Cordelia wasn't around right now, was she? I dug the two halves of the business card out of my purse, laid them out on the desk, and carefully taped them together. Before I could talk myself out of going behind Cordelia's back, I dialed the reporter's number from my desk phone.

"Penny Fisher," a pleasant voice answered.

"Hi. This is Ruby Young. You came around asking about Jake Macintyre?"

"Yes, I remember you, Ruby," she assured me. "Has something come up?" She sounded optimistic. I felt bad about getting her hopes up over nothing.

"No, not really." I'm glad I hadn't called her sooner, or I would have accused Markie of killing Jake and I would have been wrong about it. Now, I was back to square one. "I was just wondering if you had any updates?" It was a long shot, but it was the only shot I had.

"How about we meet somewhere for a chat? Is now good?"

"I'm at work." I glanced at the clock on the wall. "I get off at five."

"I can do five," she said. "Let's meet at the Dunkin' on Washington."

"Sure," I agreed. "See you then." It was only after I disconnected that I wondered why she'd chosen that place specifically. I mean, yes, according to just about everyone in Massachusetts, Dunkin' was the superior choice for donuts or coffee. Frankly, I preferred Krispy Kreme, but when in Rome, right?

The curious thing wasn't that she wanted to meet at Dunkin', but that she wanted to meet at the Dunkin' just a few blocks from where I worked. There were Dunkin' Donuts closer to home. Maybe she didn't feel comfortable in my neighborhood? That didn't make much sense, considering that she'd dropped by my apartment unannounced after Jake died. I guess I'd have to add it to the list of questions I wanted to ask her.

CHAPTER THIRTY
RUBY

Penny Fisher was waiting for me at Dunkin' at five o'clock, just like she'd promised. She waved me over to her table as soon as I entered. I didn't know why a donut and coffee shop was busy this late in the afternoon, but as always, it was packed.

I took a seat across from the reporter. "Hello," I said.

"Hey. Thanks for reaching out. I'm gonna order a drink. You want something?"

"I'm good," I assured her.

When she returned, she had two cups of coffee and a box of donut holes. She passed me one of the cups. "Caramel okay?"

"My favorite," I said. It wasn't often that I treated myself to anything other than drip coffee in my kitchen or in the break room at work, and the drink she handed me looked delicious.

While our beverages cooled to a drinkable level, Penny opened the box of donut holes and pushed them to the center of the table where we could both reach them. She took a frosted one. I took a plain.

Penny sat her phone next to the donut holes, opened an app, and pressed record. "I hope you don't mind if I record this. The file of our last conversation got corrupted and I can't use it." She popped the donut hole in her mouth. Once she had eaten it, she said, "I saw you at Jake Macintyre's wake."

"I didn't notice you," I said. "Why didn't you say hi?"

"You were busy getting tossed out at the time. I've never seen someone get thrown out of a wake before."

I shrugged. "That wasn't my fault."

"I'm sure it wasn't," she agreed, affably. "I thought you told me you didn't know Jake Macintyre."

"I didn't, not really."

"But you attended his wake?"

"Who can pass up a good wake?" I asked.

"You don't look old enough to get into a bar," she pointed out.

"It was a wake," I reminded her. "And I didn't stay long."

"You work at TrendCelerate," she said.

"How'd you know that?"

"Caller ID."

That made sense. I would make a lousy spy. I hadn't thought twice about calling her from my desk to save my cell phone minutes. It also explained why she suggested meeting at a Dunkin' so close to my office. "I needed a job. They were hiring."

She raised one eyebrow. "You took Cordelia Graves's old apartment, the one she killed herself in." Penny shivered, even though it wasn't particularly cold inside the donut shop. "You took Cordelia's old job. Anything else of hers you plan on taking?"

Instead of answering her, I said, "Coincidence?"

"I'm a reporter," Penny replied. "I don't believe in coincidences."

"Speaking of being a reporter, you wrote that article about Cordelia. Are you writing one on Jake, too? I haven't seen anything online." I'd googled Jake before leaving work. There was nothing in the news about his death besides the obit the funeral home had placed a week ago. I'd also googled Penny, reading several of her recent stories. They weren't exactly breaking news, more like fluff pieces. But they were well-written and balanced fluff pieces.

"Is that why you wanted to see me?" she asked. She picked up a chocolate donut hole and rolled it around her fingers. "Or do you have something to add?"

"Did anything interesting happen after I left the wake?" I asked.

For me, everything after the wake was still a blur. The memories felt like they had been scrambled, much like the recording Penny had made of our last meeting. The irony of that was not lost on me. Both my brain and her phone had short-circuited, and it was all Cordelia's fault.

"Define interesting," she said.

"I don't know, someone getting overwhelmed with grief and guilt after knocking back a few, and confessing to Jake's murder in a roomful of witnesses?"

"So, you think Jake death was premeditated murder?" she asked.

"I think that my neighbor is dead, and no one seems to give a damn who killed him or why."

Penny reached across the table and laid her hand on top of mine. "I give a damn."

I nodded. "I know. That's why I called."

"Has Cordelia Graves's brother been in touch with you?" Penny asked.

Her question surprised me. "Cordelia has a brother?" Was it just me, or did everyone in the world know my roomie better than I did? I wondered what else she hadn't told me.

"Had. And I'm guessing that's a no."

"I haven't heard from anyone in Cordelia's family." I thought about how odd that might sound to a perceptive reporter. "Not that they have any reason to reach out." Great. Now I was babbling, which was even worse. Not that she would ever guess the truth, that I was still in contact with the deceased former occupant of my apartment. "It's not like I knew her or anything. Did she have a lot of family?" If she noticed I was prattling on, she didn't stop me. Then again, a reporter's job was to get people to talk, right?

"Her brother's the only family I know about, and he's in prison," Penny said.

Prison? That was news to me. Then again, I wouldn't exactly go around bragging about it if one of my sisters was in prison. Not that Cordelia had opened up to me about anything personal. "Her only family?" I asked. "That's sad." On occasion I've complained about growing up in a crowded household, but it sure beat growing up in an empty one.

"Mother left when she was five. Not sure where she ended up. Father died when she was a teenager, leaving her alone to raise her younger brother, Ian Graves. He seems like a real piece of work. In and out of the system his whole life."

"Why are you telling me any of this?" I asked. "I mean, don't get me wrong. This is fascinating. But I never even met Cordelia." *Not while she was alive, at least*, I added silently to myself. "And I barely knew Jake."

"And yet you're living in her apartment, surrounded by her furniture, working at her job, and going to Jake Macintyre's wake. How do I know you're not some kind of stalker or crime junkie?"

"Please. If anyone at this table is a crime junkie, it's you," I pointed out. I selected another donut hole. "You're the one obsessed with Jake and Cordelia. And now you're interested in me. Should I be worried?" I popped the donut hole in my mouth and washed it down with some of the delicious caramelly goodness that was my coffee.

"Only if one of us ends up dead," Penny said, staring at me. All sense of humor was gone from her expression. "I can't figure out how, or why, you're involved but rest assured that I will get to the bottom of it."

"Thanks for the coffee," I said, standing. I wasn't loving where this conversation was heading.

Penny was barking up the wrong tree if she thought I had anything to do with the death of Cordelia or Jake. Last I checked, there were over six hundred thousand people who lived in Boston city limits. Add in the suburbs, and commuters and tourists, and that number soared. Not that we got that many tourists this time of year. But in all those people, I was the only one I could absolutely, without a doubt, one hundred percent be sure didn't kill Jake, and I wasn't even in the state when Cordelia committed suicide. Which meant that sitting down with Penny, caramel coffee aside, was a waste of time.

"Ruby," she said.

I cut her off. "I was telling you the truth when I said I barely knew Jake. Everyone loved him and thinks he was a real fun dude. But he wasn't a saint. He cheated on his last two girlfriends, at least, and the one he supposedly didn't cheat on—yet—had a black eye when I first met her."

"Patty?" she asked. "Patty Brown had a black eye?"

"Patty's old news. His most recent girlfriend is named Shannon. I don't know her last name. I'm surprised you didn't meet her at the wake."

"I talked to a lot of women at the wake. I don't remember a Shannon, though."

"She left early." I could have told her that Shannon was staying in Jake's apartment, and that if she just knocked on his door, she could meet Shannon for herself. But from what little I'd seen, Shannon's grief was genuine. Then again, so were her bruises.

What if Jake was the one who gave Shannon those bruises? Maybe she didn't kill him in a fit of jealousy or to take over his apartment, but in self-defense. According to Cordelia, the cops found a gun in Jake's apartment, but who could say if it was put there before or after his death?

"If you see her again, tell her to call me." I was so lost in thought I'd forgotten about Penny until she handed me another business card. I tucked it into the pocket of my purse next to my phone.

"Yeah, sure." The next time I saw Shannon, I'd have more pressing matters to talk to her about than passing the reporter's message along. Like asking her where she'd gotten the shiner, and if she knew about the gun.

"Here." Penny closed the top of the box containing the rest of the donut holes. "Take these off my hands. Please."

I accepted the donut holes, knowing they would probably be my dinner tonight unless I felt like stopping by the overpriced market on the corner on the way home to buy a Cup-a-Soup or ordering a pizza. I didn't know if it was the unexpected gift that softened me up, or if it was knowing that Penny didn't have any ulterior motive other than finding out who killed Jake so she could file her story, but I had one more question I had to ask before I left. "I know you said you don't believe in coincidences, but do you believe in ghosts?"

Penny gave me the same look I'd seen a hundred times when I tried to convince my mom that I didn't have any homework, that Sasquatch was outside my bedroom window so I needed to sleep in her room, or that I'd already brushed my teeth before bed. "Ghosts don't exist, Ruby Young."

I nodded. "Good to know."

• • •

The bus ride home was uneventful. Rush hour traffic was as thick as always. I'd looked it up, and if the weather was nice, I could turn the thirty-plus-minute bus ride into a fifteen or twenty-minute bike ride. There were plenty of bikes to rent or, for all I knew, Cordelia had a bike already in her storage locker in the basement that I could borrow.

When I'd rented her apartment, I'd rented it as is. I was responsible for cleaning up the mess she'd left, but in return I got a fully furnished apartment. I could use, sell, or donate anything she left behind as I saw fit. That included anything she had downstairs in storage. I'd felt good about the arrangement before I knew she had a brother. Now I was terrified of accidentally giving away some family heirloom. I felt bad enough that I'd given away her clothes and killed her plants, all while she was watching me.

I hadn't thought much of her locker before now, mostly because I didn't want to spend a lot of time in the basement. But now that it was on my mind, I resolved to check out the basement this weekend. And while I was going through Cordelia's locker, if I just so happened to take a quick peek into Jake's storage area, who would be the wiser?

Jake had a fat key ring in a bowl by his front door when I first went over there. Assuming it was still there and Shannon, Bobby, or another family member hadn't already started clearing out his stuff, I guessed the key to Jake's locker was on that key ring. I wondered where Cordelia's key was. I didn't remember seeing any spare keys floating around her apartment, and I'd gone over every inch of it. Then again, I wouldn't have found the cash stuffed underneath the silverware drawer if she hadn't shown me. Maybe she had other hiding spots I didn't know about yet.

Still pondering this, I unlocked the front door to our apartment. "Honey, I'm home," I called out in a singsong voice. I didn't know how to explain it, but I felt Cordelia's presence. "Where have you been all day?" I asked. I dropped the box of donut holes on the kitchen counter.

The living room curtains fluttered open, and the apartment was bathed in the last rays of the setting sun. Cordelia had scrubbed off the graffiti and now the windows sparkled.

"Wow, thanks. Sorry I'm home so late," I said. I got some water out of the tap and poured it into the big potted plant's soil. It was looking much better now. I hoped that maybe it would survive. "Hey, before I forget, where do you keep the key to your storage unit in the basement?"

A key materialized on the counter, above the silverware drawer where I'd stashed Jake's watch. I still hadn't heard back from his cousin Bobby. I'd meant to mention it to him at the wake, but I'd gotten thrown out before I remembered to tell him that we'd found the watch.

I pulled my phone out of my purse to text Bobby again. When I got it out, Penny's business card came out, too. It fluttered toward the floor but stopped midair about a foot away from the dingy tile.

The business card rose to a little above my eye level, before settling down on the counter. Considering that Cordelia had ripped up the last business card that Penny had left, she had to know this was a new one. "I can explain."

CHAPTER THIRTY-ONE
CORDELIA

Penny Fisher was like a recurring pimple. She kept popping up. When I'd torn up her business card, I'd hoped that Ruby would get the hint to stay away from her, but obviously that didn't work.

To be completely fair, Penny wasn't a bad person, it was just that bad luck seemed to follow her around like a, well, like a bad penny. I remember her cornering me one day, outside of the Trend-Celerate office. She wanted to ask me some questions about a big project we were working on. Of course, I refused. I'd signed an NDA. All the TrendCelerate employees had.

That should have been the end of it, but then she showed up at my home. I still didn't know how she'd gotten my address, but her timing could *not* have been better. I was so confused. Frightened. Alone. I needed help in the worst way, and here Penny was, knocking on my front door.

"Coming!" I yelled before she could give up and go away. I didn't get a lot of visitors. No, scratch that. I never got visitors. I'd never wanted them before now. I reached for the doorknob. My hand went right through it. Shit. I tried again. My hand passed through the knob like it wasn't even there.

"Not again," I groaned. "Not now."

Nothing that had happened over the past few days made any sense. I didn't understand why something as simple as opening my front door was suddenly impossible. I couldn't touch anything. It was like I didn't even exist.

The reporter knocked again, harder. This time, the door swung open like it did sometimes when it hadn't been completely shut. "Cordelia?" Penny asked.

"Thank goodness you're here," I said.

"Cordelia?" she repeated again. She raised her voice like I wasn't right there, mere inches from her. "Cordelia Graves? Are you home?"

She took a step into my apartment. I moved out of her way before she could bump into me. "I'm right here," I said, growing more frantic by the second. I waved my hand in front of her face. It was dark in the apartment, but light spilled in from the hallway. "Can't you see me?"

She reached for the light switch and flicked it on. The bulb in the lamp next to the door, right next to me, popped as the filament exploded, plunging the apartment back into darkness.

"Great," Penny said, shuffling deeper into the apartment. I walked backward, staying close without being in her way. "Cordelia?" She flinched and put her fist against the bottom of her nose, as if trying to stifle a sneeze. "What is that smell? Gah."

I couldn't smell anything.

"It smells like death in here," she said. She fumbled along the wall until she reached the open bathroom door. Penny reached inside, found the light switch, and turned it on. "No no no no no no no," she repeated as she scrambled backward, out of my bathroom, and out of my apartment.

"What the actual hell?" I asked, barely getting out of her way in time as she rushed past me. I stuck my head into the bathroom, looked down, and saw what had caused her to run out of my apartment. My own dead body was lying in the bathtub. And by the looks of it, I'd been that way for a few days.

A loud, annoying buzzer jolted me back to the present. I shook my head to chase away that awful memory. Like most of my recollections from the first few days or weeks after my death, everything was disjointed and confusing. I felt bad that Penny had to be the one to find me, but I wished she'd just leave us alone. Trouble followed that reporter like a dark cloud, and the last thing I wanted was for Ruby to get swept up in whatever Penny was into.

The buzzer next to the door went off again.

"Are we expecting anyone?" Ruby asked. She cringed before she pushed the button. "Hello? Hello?"

When Ruby had first moved in, I selfishly wanted her gone. I wanted my space to myself. So yeah, I tried to annoy her as much as she annoyed me, hoping to run her off. I wasn't proud of it. One of the easiest things to do was to hang around downstairs in the middle of the night and lean on the doorbell. Sure, I got a tiny jolt from the button; but Ruby got the loud, obnoxious buzz in the apartment, waking her up.

At first, she'd answer in a sleepy voice, "Hello? Hello? Who's there?"

Of course, I didn't answer. I couldn't. I'd wait a while. Sometimes it would be five minutes. Sometimes it would be an hour. And then I would buzz again. And again. And again. All night long, I'd buzz and buzz, hoping to drive her batty so she would go away.

Poor Ruby. I wished I could apologize. How many sleepless nights must she have endured because of me? How many times did the building manager come up only to tell her that there was nothing wrong with the buzzer or intercom? Desperate for a solid night's sleep, she'd even tried duct-taping a pillow over the speaker to muffle the noise, but I'd pry off the tape, go downstairs, and press the buzzer again.

It was a mean trick. I saw that now. It turned out that Ruby moving into my apartment was about the best thing that could have possibly happened to me, and I was the jerk who tried to scare her into leaving.

The way she hesitated now, just a fraction of a second, before saying hello was proof that me trying to annoy her into moving out of my apartment by ringing that buzzer all night long had traumatized her, and yet, she was still willing to help me. She volunteered to help me investigate the murder of someone she barely knew, even when it meant putting herself in danger. Ruby was a better person than I would ever be. Would have ever been.

"Pizza's getting cold," the man's voice on the other side of the intercom said. It was hard to tell through the ancient speaker that had seen better days even before I tried to torture Ruby with it, but the voice sounded familiar.

"Wrong apartment," Ruby told him. "I didn't order pizza."

"Ruby Young? 4G?" he asked.

"Yeah, that's me, but I didn't order pizza." She took her finger off the intercom. "Cordelia? Did you order a pizza?"

"Nope," I said with a chuckle. While I did feel like she could stand to eat more, I also wished she would eat better. After all, I didn't want her turning into Jake, eating pizza for practically every meal.

At the same time, the delivery driver's tinny voice came out of the speaker. "Well, someone did. And it's paid for. You want your pizza or not?"

Ruby hesitated. Unlike me, she was essentially good. She knew the pizza was a mistake and that taking it was basically stealing. But also, she was hungry. And, not counting the windfall in the silverware drawer—that for some reason, she was still hesitant to dip into—she was broke until her first payday. "Yeah, gimme a sec," she said.

She fished around in her wallet and came up with a ten-dollar bill. "There's a special place in hell for folks that don't tip on free food," she muttered to herself. It sounded like she was repeating someone else's advice. Her mother's, maybe? In any event, I wholeheartedly agreed with her.

Ruby started to put her shoes on, but decided against it. She was just running downstairs. She didn't need shoes, much less clunky boots that took forever to lace and still faintly smelled of Scotty's vomit. She did grab her keys, though. She even locked the deadbolt behind her.

"Good girl," I said. I was so proud of her. She was learning.

Across the hall, Jake's door opened and Shannon stepped out. "Be careful," she said.

"It's just the pizza guy," Ruby said. "Hey, when I get back, we need to talk."

She rushed down the stairs. I practiced drifting down between floors at the same speed so I kept pace with her. I was getting better at this. Maybe it was time to try levitating again. Nothing was impossible, right? And if that didn't work on the first try, I could ask Harp if he had any pointers. He had more experience being dead than I did, and he'd been a huge help the other night. He'd let us in the back door of the pawn shop, disabled the alarm, and showed Ruby where the passwords were hidden without frying the computer. Then, when I thought we'd been caught, he knocked over the bike rack and distracted the clerk long enough for us to get away.

Sure, he was a little fresh, but could I blame him? When was the last time anyone gave him any attention? I knew what it was like to be lonely. I also knew what it was like to touch someone else—living or dead—and it wasn't fun. Whatever Harp had in mind, I couldn't see it happening anytime soon.

As I drifted down between the flights of stairs, suddenly everything made sense. It had taken Ruby rushing out of her apartment in her socks to put it all together. I knew why Jake wasn't wearing a coat or shoes when he was killed. Why he didn't have a wallet. Why the killer hadn't taken Jake's phone.

I'd been so certain his death had something to do with the gun he'd hidden in his toilet tank, or maybe money he owed to a bookie, that I dismissed Ruby's theory that Jake was killed because of his cheating. In a way, she was almost right. It had just taken me until now to realize that Jake's steady diet of junk food and women really *had* led to his demise.

"Ruby!" I shouted. "Ruby, I figured out what happened!"

I didn't know why I was shouting. It wasn't like she could hear me. But she could, if I caught up to her and touched her. It would hurt, but it would be worth it to warn her.

Before I could act, a furtive sound above me caught my attention. Someone was following Ruby down the steps. They were trying to be quiet, but my hearing was better now than it had ever been while I was alive. I paused and craned my neck up to see. I caught a glimpse of a shadow above us.

After Ruby passed me, I started back up the stairs to find out who was sneaking along behind us. Below me, Ruby hit the door that separated the stairs from the lobby, and kicked the stopper to keep the door from closing behind her. "Oh, hello. It's you," I heard her say.

"No!" I yelled. Whoever was following us would have to wait.

I zipped down the stairs after Ruby. I was just in time to see Ruby hand a ten-dollar tip to our regular pizza delivery guy in the lobby.

"Forget the pizza, Ruby," I said. "It's not worth it." How could I have been so oblivious when the answer was right in front of us the whole time?

I'd lost track of how many times I'd had pizza delivered to this apartment from Caparelli's, the little mom and pop place a few blocks away. It was almost always the same delivery person. I didn't remember his name, but if I saw him on the street, I would recognize him as that dude who brought me my pizza.

He was always around, but like most delivery people—and like myself these days—he was invisible. Just a part of the background noise that no one noticed. Of course I'd overlooked him. Everyone did. Like Ruby said, he's just the pizza guy.

"Who ordered the pizza?" Ruby asked. She didn't sound suspicious, just curious.

"Enough small talk. Take the damn pizza and go back upstairs," I told her.

"Who cares, as long as it's paid for?" he responded.

"Aren't you at least a little bit interested?" she asked.

He shook his head. "Nope. Should I be?" He held out the pizza. Even after she grabbed the box, he continued to hold onto one corner. "You *are* Ruby, right? Ruby Young?"

She nodded.

"Arlo Caparelli," the deliveryman said, reaching out his hand to shake Ruby's. He was late thirties to early forties. Not too tall, not too short. There was nothing remarkable about him at all.

Ruby had to shift the pizza to free up her hand. They shook over the pizza, while he still held one corner with his other hand. "Nice to formally meet you, Arlo."

"Can I ask you something?" Without waiting for a response,

he asked, "Have you seen a woman named Shannon around the building? Shannon Caparelli?"

"Caparelli?" I repeated. "You hear that Ruby? Caparelli, as in Arlo Caparelli. As in Caparelli's Pizza?" I knew Ruby should have asked, but when we first met Shannon, I'd been too distracted by the idea that Ruby might have heard me speaking to her to follow up and ask for her last name.

He continued, "Real pretty? Dark hair, like yours. About your height. A few years older than you?"

"Don't you get it?" I asked, knowing Ruby couldn't hear me. I was tempted to reach out and grab her arm so we could communicate, but I didn't want to distract her. "You were right all along," I said, as I circled behind Arlo. "Jake was killed because of infidelity, but it's not what you thought. This time, he wasn't the one cheating."

Ruby's shoulders stiffened as she unconsciously leaned away from Arlo. "Shannon?" She shook her head slowly. "Can't say that name rings a bell. Then again, I'm new to the building. I don't know a lot of the folks that live here."

"You sure? Because for a second there, I thought maybe you recognized her name or something."

"Sorry, don't know what to tell you." Ruby shrugged, but her shoulders were still rigid. "Hey, if you figure out who sent the pizza, thank them for me, will ya? I've got people waiting for me upstairs." She might be naïve, but she was also a young woman living on her own in the city, and she was smart enough to not tell a stranger that she was alone.

She turned to walk away. He caught her arm. Ruby yelped. Behind me, in the open stairwell, I heard a muffled gasp.

"You're lying." Arlo shoved Ruby behind him, and hurried to the open door that led to the stairs. He stepped inside and a few seconds later, emerged from the stairwell with Shannon in tow. "Well, well. Thought I might find you here." His hand squeezed her wrist, and she let out a frightened little squeak. "Come on, Shannon. Time to go home."

Ruby stepped between them and the front door. "Let go of her."

"Stay out of this, Ruby," I warned her. "He's dangerous."

"Stay out of this," he echoed. "This is between me and my wife. It doesn't concern you."

"I knew it," I said out loud. "Jake wasn't cheating on Shannon, but he *was* sleeping with a married woman, and her husband found out."

I could see the guilt written across her face. Shannon was shrinking into herself. She wasn't arguing. She didn't pull away from her husband. Her hair fell across one eye, but I remembered the bruise on her face the night she moved into Jake's apartment. I remembered all of her scars. The cuts. The burns. How long had Arlo been abusing her? Long enough for the fight to go out of her, apparently.

"No wonder you left him, Shannon," I said. All this time, I'd been trying to figure out what was so special about Jake that had women falling all over him, but next to Arlo, he must have looked like a real catch. What had Shannon called him? Chivalrous. It made sense now. He was her knight in shining armor, protecting her from her husband, the big, bad troll.

All this time, I'd thought that Jake was a slimeball for cheating on his string of girlfriends, when Shannon was cheating, too. She had been married to Arlo Caparelli, the pizza guy, all along. Not that I was one to judge. I'd been sleeping with a married man for years. As much as I hated to admit it, what Adam and I had was no better than Jake and Shannon's relationship. Only in this case, it was Jake who fell for a married woman instead of the other way around.

"I said come on," he repeated, yanking Shannon's arm. "We're going home."

"No, I don't think so," Ruby said. She shoved the pizza at Shannon. "Take this upstairs. I'm right behind you." Shannon took it with her free hand. It was shaking.

Arlo snorted. "And what do you think you're going to do?" He let go of Shannon's wrist, but she just stood there, frozen. He took a menacing step toward Ruby. "Are you gonna stop me? What gives you the right, huh? This is a private matter between a man and his wife. Step aside before I make you."

Ruby pulled her phone out of her pocket.

Arlo knocked the phone out of her hand. It skittered across the lobby floor.

"Who were you gonna call? The cops? How long do you think it's gonna take them to respond, if they respond? In this neighborhood? Be a good girl and mind your own business."

"No," Ruby said.

He slapped her across the face. Hard. The sound echoed in the small lobby.

"Dumb bitches. All of you." He grabbed a chunk of Ruby's hair and yanked as he turned his attention back to Shannon. "I told you there was no place you can go that I can't find you. You thought Jake Macintyre was gonna protect you? That simp? He didn't even put up a fight. Not even when I shoved a gun in his face. He wasn't a real man, especially not after I pulled the trigger." He jerked Ruby roughly by the hair. "And what are *you* gonna do?"

I was shaking with rage, but helpless to do anything. I couldn't call for help. I couldn't defend her. I couldn't even tell Shannon to run. Then it hit me. I was dead, but as I'd learned when Ruby was harassed by the bully on the bus, I was far from helpless.

Arlo raised his arm and pulled it back, winding up for another slap. I grabbed his elbow.

It hurt.

I remembered when I was little. We'd been . . . somewhere. A hunting cabin in New Hampshire, maybe? It belonged to a friend of Dad's, and he'd let us use it for the weekend. Dad dragged us with him because Ian and I were too young to stay by ourselves. Dad and his hunting buddy were off traipsing through the woods. I was cocooned in blankets, reading by the fire, when I realized that my kid brother wasn't annoying me as much as he usually did.

"Ian?" It was just a little one room cabin with no place to hide. It was empty. "Booger, where you at?" There were bunkbeds on one wall, and a ratty pull-out couch on another. He wasn't hiding in, behind, or under any of them.

I wrapped a blanket around my shoulders and stepped out onto the porch. It was early spring. Snow was melting off the roof, dripping almost as loud as a steady rain. "Ian?" At the bottom of the steps, there were small footprints in the mud. They weren't leading toward the outhouse behind the cabin, but rather the other way, toward the lake where Dad had warned us not to play.

I followed the meandering tracks, clutching the blanket tighter around me as I slogged through the mud. The trees around me swayed in the breeze, shedding snow from their branches onto the path. I shivered, but not from the cold. It was the time of year that the bears were starting to come out of hibernation. My brother the idiot would be just about snack-size to a hungry bear. Despite being out of season, there were hunters in these woods, too. Hunters like my dad and his friend. I couldn't remember what Ian was wearing, but I doubted it was a blaze orange safety vest.

"Ian? Ian?" I yelled.

I found him standing on the frozen lake.

"Cordy!" he hollered at me. "Look at me, Cordy!" He slid around the ice in a wide arc, swinging a long stick that he'd found. "Think maybe Dad will let me try out for hockey this year?"

"Ian, you little booger, get back here." As relieved as I was that my baby brother wasn't halfway to becoming bear poop, the sight of him on the ice wasn't much better. A frozen lake, in New Hampshire, in the dead of winter, would have been opaque white. This lake was shiny like glass, and glossy where the warm spring sun beat down on it.

"You can't make me!" he shouted. He swung his stick at a pebble. It skittered across the thin ice. "Back of the net! Goal!" He raised his arms in victory.

"Stop fooling around, Ian." I tried to sound authoritative, but my brother had plenty of practice ignoring me. Dad expected me to keep an eye on him, but what could I do? He never listened.

"You're just a *girl*," he said in the singsong voice of a kid barely old enough to tie his own shoes. "You can't catch me."

I stepped one foot on the ice and bounced a little. It held my weight. "Last warning," I told him. He danced out of my reach. "Get your scrawny butt over here."

"Oooh, I'm telling Dad you said 'butt.'"

"Yeah, and I'm telling him that you didn't listen to—" I didn't finish the sentence as the ice beneath my feet gave way and I plunged into the freezing lake.

It was cold. So cold I couldn't think. The water was like hungry knives against my skin. The blanket tangled around me, pulling me down. I gasped, and the icy water filled my lungs, burning me from the inside out.

Grabbing Arlo's elbow felt like that. Like water so cold it

burned. Only this time, my baby brother wasn't nearby to pull me out of the icy water. Ian wasn't screaming and crying as I lay curled on the bank of the lake, hacking up freezing water. He wasn't there to help me back to the cabin so I could thaw in front of a roaring fire.

It was only me and Arlo Caparelli, the pizza guy.

"What the actual—" he asked, staring at me, directly at me. One corner of his lip curled up in a sneer as Arlo focused on me. "Where'd you come from?"

"Wrong question," I gasped. I didn't know why he could see me when I touched him, when most people couldn't, and made a mental note to ask Harp about it later. But for now, I had more immediate concerns. "You should be asking what I'm gonna do with your sorry ass." I couldn't hold onto him any longer. It hurt too much. Instead, I shoved him away from me as hard as I could.

Arlo collided with the glass lobby door with a loud smack. Cracks exploded in the glass, radiating out from the point of impact, like the surface of a frozen lake fracturing as the ice began to thaw and break. I surged toward him, ramming my shoulder into his chest. He flew backward, through the shattered glass, and tumbled down the steps leading to the street, his head bouncing off the hard sidewalk.

He lay in a heap of broken glass, blood seeping out of cuts all over him and pooling under his head. I followed, brushing myself off as I advanced on him, which was ridiculous, as the glass had gone right through me. I looked down at Arlo, who groaned and clutched at his ribs. I gave him one hard kick in the side for good measure.

"Hey? Arlo? Don't fuck with my roommate," I growled.

CHAPTER THIRTY-TWO
CORDELIA

I didn't know how long I sat cross-legged on the sidewalk in front of my building, above the man crumpled on the pavement, waiting for the cops to arrive. It couldn't have been much more than five minutes, but it felt like hours.

Ruby and Shannon huddled together on the steps behind me, murmuring in low voices. Ruby was shivering. She'd gone downstairs sock-footed to pick up her pizza, just like Jake had on the night he was killed, and now she was probably freezing.

But my attention was focused on Arlo, the pizza deliveryman turned murderer, and his ragged breaths. He was alive. For now. I supposed that was for the best. In theory.

He moaned in pain. That probably had something to do with the way his body was twisted into an awkward pretzel on the sidewalk. I was no doctor, but even I could tell he'd broken something. Maybe several somethings. Some of his discomfort was probably my fault—above and beyond the fact that I'd shoved him through the door, that was.

Since discovering that as long as I was making physical contact with Arlo, he could see and hear me, I figured I might as well get my money's worth. I uncrossed my legs and wiggled one toe into the crook of his elbow. One of the benefits of dying barefoot, I guess, was that I could put my toes anywhere I wanted, totally unencumbered.

Arlo groaned. "What do you want from me?" he asked in a hoarse whisper. He wasn't afraid of being overheard, he just didn't have any strength left. He'd lost a lot of blood. "I'll tell you everything."

I'd been singing pretty much non-stop while we waited for the cops to arrive. I stopped long enough to say, "No need." His confession in the lobby had been sufficient for me. "Just don't die on me, Arlo. I need you to live long enough to stand trial for Jake's murder."

He groaned and tried to swat me away.

"Aww, come on. Don't be like that. Like you said, the cops won't get here for ages, and in the meantime, we're gonna have a little fun." Then I started singing another round of "Happy Birthday."

He rolled his head away from me, not that it would do any good. He was going to hear me, whether he wanted to or not. "It's not my birthday," he protested.

I didn't blame him. I'd never cared much for the song, either. Beyond being a reminder of my crappy childhood, it was annoying and repetitive. Which was why I'd been singing it. "Happy birthday, dear asshole, happy birthday to you!" I finished with a flourish, before starting over again from the very beginning.

It was full dark by the time the ambulance arrived. Even I was getting bored with torturing Arlo with my off-key singing, not that I let up. No, sirree. I owed it to Jake, and to Shannon, to make him pay for what he'd done.

The paramedics bent over him, the beam of their flashlights catching the broken glass like disco night at the dance club. "Sir? Can you tell me your name?" one of them asked.

"Go away," Arlo whined. "Make her leave me alone."

"Do you know what day it is?" the other paramedic asked.

I stood and moved to the side to avoid accidentally touching one of them as they examined Arlo, but kept contact with him as I sang-screamed, "Happy birthday to yoooooou."

"I can't hear you," Arlo told me. He tried to cover his ears with his hands. As if that would block me out.

"I asked if you know what day it is," the paramedic repeated.

"It's not my birthday," Arlo said. "Just make her stop."

The police finally rolled up. I recognized the first man on scene. It was the plainclothes detective, the same one who'd run the show after Jake's death. "Don't worry, I'll be back," I promised Arlo before following the detective up the steps.

"Miss Ruby Young of 4G, fancy meeting you again," he said, dryly, as he stood over my roommate.

"Detective Mann," she said, nodding back at him without making any attempt to stand. Ruby looked shaken. Cold. Tired. But also, she looked relieved, as if she knew the worst was over.

On the sidewalk below us, the EMTs were using phrases like "multiple lacerations," "tender ribs, possibly broken," "we should get an X-ray," "psych eval," "thready BP," and "probable concussion" as they examined Arlo. They fitted him in a big foam neck brace and hefted him onto a gurney. All the while, he hummed "Happy Birthday."

"And you are?" the detective asked Shannon, drawing my attention back to him.

"Shannon Caparelli," she said. She sat up straighter. I think she was in shock. She hadn't said more than a handful of words since

Arlo went flying. The pizza was still in the box, on the lobby floor, getting cold. No wonder Shannon had said she was over pizza. It wouldn't blame her if she never ate it again. "I mean Shannon Green."

"Which is it? Caparelli or Green?"

"Green," she said.

"Okay, then." Detective Mann wrote something on his notepad. "Excuse me, do you mind?" Before she could respond, he reached out and tucked Shannon's long hair behind her ear.

Her bruises had faded since I'd first met her almost two weeks ago, but traces were still there if you knew what you were looking for. The detective lifted her chin gently with his hand to get a better look at her face. "Who did this to you?"

She pointed at the man being loaded into the back of the ambulance.

"And he is?" he prompted.

"Arlo Caparelli, the pizza guy," Ruby supplied.

The detective ignored her. "Who, exactly, is he?" he asked Shannon.

"My soon-to-be ex-husband."

"And what, exactly, happened to Arlo Caparelli, your soon-to-be ex-husband?" he asked.

When Shannon didn't answer, Ruby spoke up. "He showed up at the building and said someone had bought me a pizza. Then he saw Shannon in the lobby and flipped his lid." She turned her face up to the detective, where her cheek was bright red, even in the dim light. "He hit me. He yanked me around by my hair while bragging about killing Jake Macintyre. Then he stumbled backward, fell through the door, and landed out here."

"He confessed to murder, then fell backward through a solid glass door?" the detective asked.

Ruby shrugged.

He focused on Shannon. "Care to tell me what really happened?"

She blinked up at him. "He stumbled," she said.

"And then?"

"He fell through the door," Ruby repeated. "Then we called nine-one-one. We were afraid to move him. He hit his head pretty hard." She glanced over at the departing ambulance.

"I'm sure he did," Detective Mann said. "Anything you want to add?" This was directed at Shannon.

"I left him," she said. "I don't know how he found out I was staying with Jake, but he showed up the night of the storm to bring me home."

"He being Arlo?" the detective clarified. "And Jake? Jacob Macintyre in 4H?"

Shannon nodded. "Jake said I'd be safe with him. When Arlo buzzed up saying someone had bought Jake a free pizza, I begged him not to go downstairs. But Jake wouldn't hear reason. For once in his life, he didn't even care about the pizza. He just wanted to have a word with my ex. Said he was gonna teach Arlo a lesson, make sure he left me alone for good."

"That's why Jake's keys were still in his apartment," Ruby said. I nodded along with her. That had bothered me from the beginning, too. "He knew you were upstairs, so he wasn't worried about the door locking behind him."

"And you knew his keys were upstairs, how?" the detective asked.

Instead of answering him, Ruby twisted around to look up at the building. I followed her gaze. Jake's apartment overlooked the street. "You were watching from the window," Ruby said. "You saw the whole thing, and didn't tell anyone."

Shannon closed her eyes. "I couldn't see anything, not really. It was dark." She gestured around at the street. The nearest streetlight was out. Out of two security lights mounted over the front door, only one was working, and it was pointed up the street, away from where Jake's body had been found. If it weren't for all of the emergency vehicles, they would be sitting in the dark now. "I heard shouting. I heard a gunshot. When Jake didn't come back upstairs, I knew something horrible had happened."

"You didn't call us," Detective Mann said.

"I was terrified," she admitted. "I thought Arlo was coming for me next, and I panicked. I couldn't find my phone anywhere. I didn't realize until much later that when I plugged it into the charger, it slipped between the dresser and the bed."

I remembered seeing a phone charging in Jake's apartment but hadn't thought anything of it at the time, despite knowing that he'd died with his phone in his hand. Some detective I was turning out to be. Then again, I'd found the killer, hadn't I? Well, Ruby and I had. To be fair, I didn't figure it out until it was almost too late, but what mattered was we made quite a team.

"And when we came to check out Macintyre's apartment the next morning, where were you?"

"Hiding," she said in a soft voice. "I spent all day holed up in the laundry room in the basement. I couldn't go home to Arlo, and I didn't know where else to go. I figured this was the last place he'd think to look for me once Jake was dead."

"You've been staying here ever since," he said.

She nodded.

"How'd you get back into his apartment if Macintyre's keys were locked inside his unit?"

"I have my own key." She reached into her pocket and produced a heart-shaped keyring with a single key on it. "Jake gave it to me."

The detective took a deep breath. "Don't go far. I may have more questions for you later." He took the steps back down to the sidewalk. The ambulance was gone. There was blood and broken glass on the sidewalk. "Just one more thing." He turned and focused on Shannon. "Macintyre had a gun in his apartment. Why didn't he take it with him when he went outside to confront your husband?"

"It wasn't his gun," she said, confirming what Scotty had told me at the wake.

"Then whose was it?" Detective Mann asked.

"Arlo's. He told me a dozen times what he would do if I ever tried to leave him, so I took it with me when I left. I don't know how he found me, but Jake said he wanted to settle things man-to-man."

And just look how well that had turned out. Jake's need to feel macho and take justice into his own hands had gotten him killed. I'd been so busy looking for answers that I'd missed the obvious. A jealous husband. An abused wife. And a chivalrous life of the party who had a thing for pretty brunettes. It was that simple.

"Did you know that Arlo had a second gun?" he asked.

"I begged Jake not to go," she said, instead of answering.

"I'll take that as a yes." He surveyed the street. There was a beat-up Toyota double-parked in front of the building, facing the wrong way. It had a Caparelli's Pizza logo on the driver's side door.

"You're still legally married to Arlo Caparelli?" Detective Mann asked.

Shannon nodded. "But not for long."

"Do I have your permission to search your vehicle?"

"You do," she said.

Detective Mann tried the driver's side door. It was unlocked. As he opened the door, the overhead light came on. He slid behind the wheel. I slipped into the passenger side. He looked over his shoulder at the back seat. Then he reached over me and opened the glovebox. On top of the usual paperwork and junk that accumulated in a glovebox was a gun. He took a few photos, then made a phone call.

Assuming he would be occupied for a while, I exited Arlo's car and headed back to the building. As I got there, Ruby stood and helped Shannon up. "Come on, Shannon, let's go inside and warm up. Maybe get something to eat."

"Not pizza," she said.

"No, not pizza," Ruby agreed. "I have half a box of donut holes upstairs we can split."

Shannon bobbed her head. "Yeah, okay."

I trailed behind them as they climbed the stairs. I knew Ruby was safe now, but I wasn't quite ready to let her out of my sight, so I was content—this time—to not try to take any shortcuts. I'd have plenty of time to learn how to levitate later. Once inside our apartment, Ruby started a fresh pot of coffee and divvied up the remaining donut holes onto two plates.

"I'm so sorry," Shannon said, playing with her food instead of eating it. "This was all my fault."

"No need to apologize. You're not responsible for what Arlo did," Ruby assured her.

"It's not that." She frowned. "I didn't want you getting involved. I knew Arlo had a temper. I couldn't save Jake. When I realized you were poking around, I didn't want you getting hurt. I tried to warn you off the best I knew how."

"Wait, that was *you* who broke into my apartment and graffitied the window?" Ruby asked, looking betrayed.

I growled. After all we'd done to help Shannon, that was her? Talk about ungrateful. But it did explain how someone could have gotten in and out of our apartment without Ruby ever seeing anyone in the hall or on the stairs.

"I'm sorry. I was scared that you were getting too close to the truth, and I didn't want Arlo to hurt you, too. I should probably leave you alone now."

"No. Stay. You could have told me," Ruby said. "You could have gone to the cops. We could have gone to the police together."

"I know. I should have. I was afraid of what Arlo would do." She popped a donut hole in her mouth and chewed. "I guess people who make good decisions don't end up like me."

Ruby shrugged. "Everyone has bad days." She toyed with one of the last donut holes. "That's why I moved here. To get away from a bad relationship. He didn't hit me, but he was bad news, and I was scared that if I didn't put some serious distance between us, I'd end up going back to him. You're not gonna take Arlo back, are you?"

Shannon shook her head. "No way. You had the right idea. It's time for me to start thinking seriously about getting out of town. Even if Arlo doesn't make bail, the farther I am from Boston, the better it is for everyone."

"But you'll be back for the trial, right? Someone's gotta testify against Arlo."

"I'll think about it," Shannon said.

I wondered what would happen if she didn't testify. If the gun in Arlo's glovebox was a match, then Detective Mann had the murder weapon. And, if he couldn't get Arlo to confess to him, maybe I could. A couple more rounds of "Happy Birthday," and he would do anything I wanted him to do. He was going to pay for killing Jake, with or without Shannon's testimony. I would see to it.

While they were polishing off the rest of the donut holes, someone knocked. I slid my head through the door and came face-to-face with

Penny Fisher, the reporter. When Ruby made no move to open the door, I slid back into the apartment. My roommate was standing perfectly still, one finger held up to her lips. Penny knocked again before giving up and sliding her business card under the door.

Ruby passed the card to Shannon. "I know this isn't the best time to be talking to a reporter, but for what it's worth, I trust her. Call her if you want to. Or don't. Your decision. But you have nothing to be ashamed of and no reason to protect Arlo. Not after what he did."

Shannon studied the card, then looked up at her. "What really happened tonight? I mean, you saw that, right? He just flew through the glass. And who was he talking to?"

Ruby grinned. "From where I was standing, it looked like a bad man got what he deserved." She opened the door a crack and poked her head out. The hall was empty. "The reporter left. Coast is clear, if you're ready to go home."

Shannon stepped out into the hallway before turning back and asking, "Do you think maybe I have a guardian angel or something?"

Ruby nodded. "Or something," she agreed. She waited until Shannon was inside the apartment across the hall before shutting the door. Ruby watched as she bumped it to make sure it was completely closed, then threw the deadbolt for good measure. Shannon was learning.

"Something, like a ghost," she added, with a chuckle. Ruby closed and locked our door before walking over to the loveseat. I slid the throw pillow away from her normal seat to make room for her to sit. "What a day. We did it. We found Jake's killer. I had no idea you were such a badass, Cordelia."

"Neither did I," I admitted. "Feels pretty good."

I could barely think straight anymore. The darkness was tugging at me. If I let myself relax for a second, if I even let myself blink, I was done for. I'd probably crash, or whatever it was I did when I had to recharge, for a week. Maybe longer.

Ruby was safe, but I wasn't ready to leave her alone just yet. Not after the day she'd had. I knew she'd be okay now, but I needed *her* to know it as well. I took the afghan off the back of the loveseat and draped it over her lap. It took more effort than it should have.

"You know, all this got me to thinking," she said. She sounded as drowsy as I felt. She tucked her legs up under her and curled up on the loveseat. I was too tall to have ever been able to do that comfortably, but it was just the right size for Ruby. "Something's off."

"Like what?" I asked.

As far as I was concerned, everything was wrapped up in a neat bow. We found the killer. A witness. Even found the murder weapon. Arlo was going to pay for his crimes. And, if all else failed, I could always throw him through a glass door again.

Not that I would.

Of course not.

Well, maybe a little.

Ruby closed her eyes. I tried to tug the afghan up over her shoulders, but I couldn't get it to budge. I didn't have enough juice left in me.

"It doesn't make any sense," Ruby murmured, fighting back sleep.

"It makes all the sense in the world," I assured her. "Shannon was leaving her abusive husband for Jake. Arlo couldn't accept that. He killed Jake out of a jealous rage. Case closed." My heart ached for Shannon. She still had a difficult road ahead of her.

Ruby's eyes popped open. "I don't think you killed yourself."

"What?" I asked. Goose bumps sprouted along my non-existent arms and legs. "Of course I killed myself." Sure, I had no memory of actually doing the deed, but I'd suffered from chronic depression my entire life. I'd been too stubborn to see a professional. I thought I could handle it alone, which, in hindsight, was the wrong choice. It had gotten worse the last few years. Adam dumping me right before Christmas hadn't helped.

But I was the only family Ian had left. I wouldn't have committed suicide and left my baby brother alone in the world, would I? And where had I gotten the pills?

If I was being totally honest with myself, I might have had a teensy, tiny alcohol problem. But pills? Not my scene. So where had they come from? And who was the man Jake had seen leaving my apartment? When Penny had come over, the door hadn't been shut properly, or it wouldn't have opened when she knocked. If I'd been inside, by myself, the door would have been closed. And locked. And deadbolted. I never invited anyone over, but someone had been in my apartment, and when they left, they didn't close the door behind them hard enough for the lock to catch.

As I struggled to make sense of it, I could feel the effects of today's overexertion tugging at me. Right before exhaustion snatched me away, I heard Ruby say, "I think you were murdered, Cordelia, and they tried to cover it up by making your death *look* like a suicide."

ACKNOWLEDGMENTS

The funny thing about writing a book is that while the words might come out of my head, there's an awful lot of hard-working people who helped get them down on paper. For starters, there's Dare. This poor guy's probably read the first (and often the second to seventy-seventh) draft of pretty much every book I've ever written, including this one. And still, for some reason, he hasn't blocked my number yet. Weirdo.

Then there are the zany folks who keep me entertained, motivated, grounded, and encouraged: My Pucking Around ladies who always know the score. The talented and hilarious Killer Caseload, where murder, romance, and French fries are always on the menu. The forty-year running joke that is the Little Screaming Eels. And of course, the wild, wonderful, and always supportive Berkletes.

While I'm at it, I guess I'm legally obligated to give a shout-out to Potassium, too, because if it weren't for him, I would probably forget to feed myself. He's the best partner, husband, and friend I could ever ask for, plus after a gazillion+ years together, I still enjoy his company. Gag. Here's to many more years of cheap pizza and other adventures!

A HUGE thanks goes (as always) to reviewers, bloggers, Bookstagrammers, BookTokkers, librarians, booksellers, and distributors. I'm so grateful to the early readers (including Darcie Wilde, Lyn Liao Butler, Eliza Jane Brazier, and Amanda Jayatissa) for taking time out of their busy schedules to blurb an uncorrected draft. But most of all, I want to thank YOU, the reader. Yeah, you. I see you. And I appreciate you more than you will ever know!!!

If you're in the mystery community, you probably already know Dru Ann Love. She is the book champion, blogger, author, and advocate we all rely on. When I hit a wall on the first draft of *A New Lease on Death,* it was Dru Ann who inadvertently gave me the push I needed, and she does it so often and for so many authors, I doubt she even realizes how much she contributes. For that, I want to give a very special acknowledgment to Dru Ann and dru's book musings for everything she does to keep propelling mysteries forward!

Getting words on the laptop screen is one thing, but turning all these typos and words into a book? That's where the real magic happens! Specifically, thanks to Lisa Bonvissuto, my rockstar editor, for really getting this unlikely crime-solving duo, and for always calling me out when I get lazy or twisted around—and then helping find inspired ways to fix the problems I caused. And to Maddie Houpt, much love for stepping in and getting us across the finish line! I'm looking forward to many more books together and can't wait to see what Cordelia and Ruby get up to next. Thanks to Sara Beth Haring, marketing genius, and Sara LaCotti, publicist with a heart of gold (send more baby rhino pix and say hi to Melissa for me!), for getting *A New Lease on Death* into the hands of readers, taking such great care of my stories, and for putting up

ACKNOWLEDGMENTS

with my nonsense in general. As always, a ginormous thanks to James McGowan, my amazing agent extraordinaire, for keeping me (more or less) on track.

To all the fantastic folks at Minotaur—Jen Edwards (interior designer), David Rotstein (jacket designer), Alisa Trager (managing editor), Laurie Henderson (production editor), Lena Shekhter (production manager), John Simko (copy editor), Jennifer Stem (proofreader), and many others (including some I don't know yet!). From creating amazing art (OMG, this cover!) to pointing out the difference between "affect" and "effect," this book literally would not exist without your hard work and attention to detail. Y'all (ironically?) brought *A New Lease on Death* to life.

And of course, a giant shout-out to Nettie Finn, who believed in Cordelia and Ruby before anyone else. Thanks for giving this bananapants murdery ghostly romp a chance. XOXOXO.

Finally, it's true what they say—writing the first 95,000 words of a book is the easy part. Writing the acknowledgments, that's the real challenge. I'm always afraid I'm going to leave someone out or, worse, misspell their name. To all the friends and family I canceled plans with (or showed up for, but was never fully present because I was too busy playing with the voices in my head) because I was neck-deep in drafting, editing, or promoting, thanks for sticking with me through it all. I don't say this enough, but I love y'all.

Discussion Questions

1. The novel begins with Cordelia on the sidewalk outside her apartment building, waiting for a dead man to sit up. Why do you think the author chose to start the story this way?

2. What were your first impressions of Cordelia and Ruby?

3. When readers first meet Ruby, she remarks, "Ever since I could remember, I've wanted to believe in ghosts. And not just ghosts. All sorts of paranormal creatures . . ." What about you? Do you believe in ghosts? The paranormal? Why?

4. In Chapter 13, Cordelia says, "There were some secrets that I got to take to the grave." What kind of secrets do you think she's hiding?

5. Cordelia didn't receive any instructions on how to be a ghost, and has to figure out the mechanics of being dead by herself. If you were a ghost, what is one thing you would want to do? Is there anything you'd struggle with?

6. Why do you think the author chose to alternate POVs between Cordelia and Ruby? How would it have been different if it was all told from one perspective?

7. Ruby and Cordelia—though not able to see each other—find ways to communicate and investigate the murder together. What are the different ways they communicate in *A New Lease on Death*? Are there any other ways they could talk to each other that they haven't thought of?

8. Ruby and Cordelia are both haunted by their pasts and hoping to start anew. How are their pasts similar? How do they differ?

9. Why do you think that there are so few ghosts in Boston?

10. Given the ending, what do you see next for Ruby and Cordelia?

Turn the page for a sneak peek at the new novel by **Olivia Blacke**

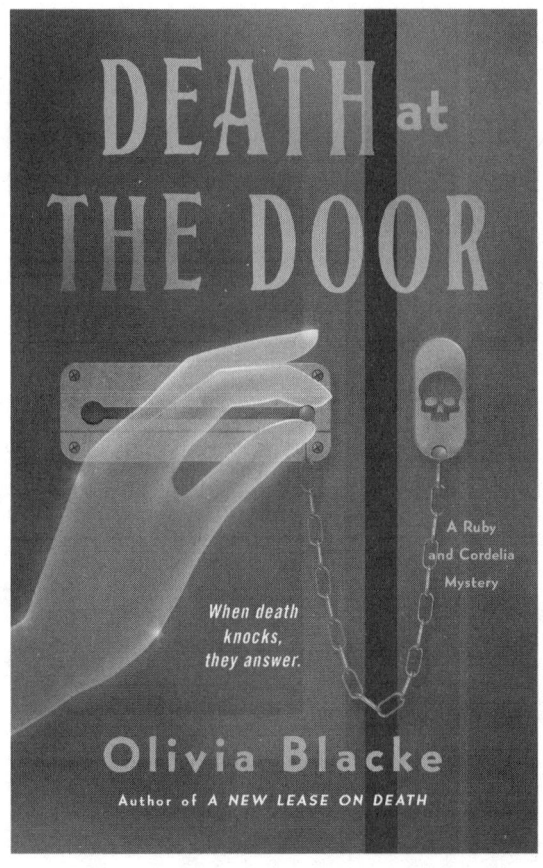

Available Fall 2025

Copyright © 2025 by Olivia Blacke

CHAPTER ONE
RUBY

It's hard to keep secrets from my roommate, especially since my roommate's a ghost.

We were at the supermarket picking up ingredients for Sunday night dinner. *My* dinner, that was. I, Ruby Young, needed to eat, preferably a couple meals a day. My aforementioned ghost roommate, being dead, didn't need food anymore, but she was teaching me to cook. Tonight's meal was eggplant parm, which was a little ambitious in my opinion, but Cordelia believed in me and was certain I could manage it.

Even though Cordelia Graves was dead, she always encouraged me. She was a little bossy at times, but I didn't mind, much, since I didn't always know what I was supposed to be doing or how to do it. I had a tenuous grasp on this adulting thing, but luckily my roomie had more life experience. And more death experience, too.

While Cordelia was checking the gazillion tomato sauce options, I snuck back into the front of the store. I passed the produce, with a giant selection of eggplants that looked absolutely *nothing* like the emoji, and wound my way back to what I always thought of as the apology aisle. Which was appropriate, considering I owed Cordelia big time.

Just inside the front doors was a colorful selection of cut flowers and balloons, but that wasn't what I needed. Tucked in behind them were potted plants ranging from a selection of small, colorful cacti—who knew that cacti came in so many shapes and colors?—to several leafy options.

"How to choose? What to choose?" I asked myself, not caring if anyone overheard me. We lived in an era where people were constantly on their phones, with barely visible AirPods in their ears. Strangers didn't pay attention to people talking aloud when seemingly alone, and that came in handy when I was chatting with a ghost.

When she was alive, Cordelia loved plants. No, that wasn't precisely true. She was *obsessed* with them. I learned this when, a short while after her unfortunate death, I moved into her fully furnished apartment in a low-rent building in Boston. Judging from her decorative choices, I'd assumed that the previous tenant was in her eighties with a penchant for Afghan blankets, paperback novels, and potted plants. It turned out that she was in her late forties, and all of her furniture came from second-hand stores, which accounted for the old lady smell I hadn't quite managed to rid the apartment of yet.

Her plants—in a variety of lovely, unique pots—turned the otherwise shabby space into a lush green jungle. Despite my best efforts to nurture them, they shriveled and died—all but one. I felt plenty guilty about killing them off *before* finding out that the previous occupant was still hanging around, in the form of a ghost. I couldn't bring Cordelia's plants—or Cordelia herself—back to life, but I could try to replace some of them.

Looking through the selection at the supermarket, there were lovely purple flowers on one of the plants. I read the label. "'Requires lots of light.' That won't do." My apartment, the one I shared with Cordelia, got little natural light.

The next plant had gorgeous white blossoms. It didn't require much light but needed to be watered several times a week. I wanted to think I was up for it, but despite my best intentions, I knew that was more responsibility than I was prepared for.

The third one had no flowers and looked similar to the only plant Cordelia had left, but the leaves had long, irregular holes in them that formed interesting patterns. "'Doesn't require direct sunlight or frequent watering,'" I read. "Nailed it!" That's the perfect amount of maintenance for me. I'd found my Goldilocks plant.

I flipped over the tag. "'Monstera.' Appropriate." I couldn't think of a better plant for someone living in a haunted apartment in Massachusetts, home of the infamous witch trials. Not that I was a witch. I was just your run-of-the-mill twenty-year-old living away from home for the first time, almost on my own. And like any other run-of-the-mill twenty-year-old, I needed to bring this pretty Monstera plant home to make the ghost who lived in my apartment happy. I picked it up and hurried back to the canned tomato aisle, hoping to slip the plant into the cart before she noticed.

I could tell by the absence of that weird skin-tingly sensation I sometimes got when Cordelia was around that she hadn't followed me to the plant aisle, because the feeling returned as I approached the cans and jars of tomatoes. I hoped that Cordelia was too busy choosing from the wide selection of low-salt, no-salt, and extra-salt options to realized I'd slipped away for a minute. Unfortunately, she'd also been too distracted to notice that we were no longer the only ones in the aisle.

When two jars of tomato sauce levitated off the shelf seemingly all by themselves, the unsuspecting shopper standing near my cart shrieked. Cordelia dropped the jars. Glass shattered. Tomato sauce splashed everywhere, transforming the aisle into a crimson crime scene that smelled of basil and garlic.

I could barely hold back my laughter as the other shopper, her face ashen and her breaths shallow, turned to me. "Did you . . . Did they . . . You saw that, right?"

"Saw what?" I asked, trying to keep a straight face. Knowing Cordelia, she'd selected the most expensive tomato sauce in the entire store, but I snatched two jars at random off the shelf and tossed them into the cart. I hurried off, the squeaky wheel of my cart chirping louder the faster I walked.

At the end of the aisle, I nearly barreled into a store employee who'd been alerted by the woman's shriek, the sound of breaking glass, or both. "Someone made a mess down there," I told him, pointing over my shoulder. My face was as red as the splattered tomato sauce as I hastily rounded the corner down the next aisle.

"Cordelia," I said under my breath, as a giggle escaped. "You should leave the shopping to me."

I couldn't see her. I couldn't hear her. But I had that someone-standing-over-my-shoulder feeling I got when she was around.

"What's next on the list?" I asked aloud, knowing Cordelia couldn't answer me.

I pulled a crumpled piece of paper out of my pocket and consulted the ingredients. I was the only person in the store with a hand-written grocery list in this, the twenty-first century, instead of keeping one on my phone. That would be Cordelia's doing.

There was something about a ghost in the vicinity that made electronics go wonky. Since she was almost always nearby, I'd adapted by relying on my phone less and less. Sure, it meant occasionally getting on the wrong bus or missing a call from home, but part of me was relieved to not be tethered to a screen like I had been before I moved to Boston.

I stopped in front of a wall of eggs, feeling a little dizzy at the selection. Organic? Heirloom? Local? Free-range? I grabbed a cardboard carton at random and put it in the basket.

The eggs levitated out of the cart and settled back on the refrigerated shelf. A different dozen floated into the front basket of my cart, next to the Monstera plant. "Showoff," I told her.

From what I could tell, Cordelia was making up the rules as she went along. Sometimes, when she picked something up, I could see it moving on its own—like some special-effects trick, but in real life. Other times, things just appeared like magic out of nowhere. Sometimes she would walk through a solid wall; other times she would open and close the door like anyone else. There were entire days when she wouldn't leave me alone, and others when she wasn't around at all. It was almost like living with a cat, random glasses getting knocked off the counter and all.

I glanced at the price sticker. "I can't afford these," I argued. "They're three times as expensive as the ones I picked!" I could comfortably afford groceries for the first time since I'd moved out of my family house in Baltimore, but even with a steady paycheck, I didn't throw money around.

In response, my cart started rolling away from the display of eggs.

"Fine," I said, knowing that arguing with a ghost was fruitless. "But you're chipping in on the grocery bills this month."

Cordelia could contribute when she wanted to. She'd left behind an envelope of cash in our apartment, could shoplift when the mood struck her, and once—when money had been particularly tight—had pilfered three hundred dollars out of a rich white lady's wallet after she'd been rude to me.

We took the bus because I didn't have a car, and the last time I'd gotten an Uber, the driver had shown up in an electric car. We didn't get two blocks before every warning light on his dash lit up like a Christmas tree. That was Cordelia's doing, I presumed.

Now that we were home, I had to carry the groceries up the stairs to the fourth floor. Technically, there was an elevator in our building, but it'd been out of service as long as I'd lived here. Then again, according to my neighbor Milly, the elevator had been broken ever since *she* moved in, way back in the nineteen hundreds, 1995, to be exact.

Our apartment building was old. The wiring was shoddy. The heat barely worked and water pressure was nonexistent. The neighborhood was questionable. It would never make any of the "Places to Visit in Boston" lists, but it was home.

Also, there had been a murder in the building earlier in the year. Or, two murders, really. When Cordelia was found dead in the bathroom of apartment 4G—now *my* apartment—her death was immediately ruled a suicide. Case closed. She had a long history of depression, substance abuse, and bad decisions. No one questioned that her death was anything other than self-inflicted— that is, no one but me.

As I climbed the stairs, I wondered about the wisdom of buying all these ingredients when a microwave meal would have been quicker, and lighter. The longer I carried the groceries, they heavier they got. Even so, I was used to deferring to Cordelia's judgment, even though some of her decisions were questionable, like her actions on the night that ended with her dead in her bathroom.

There plenty of indications that Cordelia's death wasn't what it seemed. She was found in the bathtub, but she was almost fully dressed. Her front door was ajar, even though she lived in a bad neighborhood and always locked her door. The night she died, a neighbor saw a strange man leave her apartment carrying a laptop bag, even though Cordelia rarely had visitors. And, while she'd fatally overdosed on sleeping pills and booze, there were no pill bottles anywhere in her apartment.

I'd laid all this out for her, but I guess it was a touchy subject. She refused to talk about it. And trust me, if a ghost didn't want to communicate, there wasn't a lot I could do.

I paused on the third-floor landing to catch my breath. "I swear, Cordelia, if I'd known how bad it sucked to live in a fourth-floor walk-up, I would have never signed that lease," I said. "Then again, if I hadn't, I never would have met you."

Despite all those annoying stairs, I loved my apartment, and Boston. Like any city on the East Coast, the obscenely wealthy lived in pretty high-rises overlooking the water. And then there were the rest of us. By American standards, it was an old town with a rich history.

With old relics everywhere I turned, from narrow stone streets to my ancient neighbor Milly, it was a wonder there weren't ghosts on every corner. As far as I could tell, Cordelia was the only one. She had to be lonely, which made me sad. That's why she hung around me so much. We both got a friend out of the arrangement, and as a bonus, she was teaching me how to cook. Or at least, she would, if I ever managed to drag my groceries all the way upstairs to my fourth-floor apartment.

CHAPTER TWO

CORDELIA

"Is it ready yet?" Ruby opened the oven and peeked inside. Cheese threatened to bubble over the casserole dish filled with eggplant parmesan.

From what I could gather, the most elaborate thing she'd ever made before this was Rice Krispies Treats. Her mom apparently didn't have a lot of patience for her and her sisters in the kitchen. As a result, here she was, a nearly grown woman, living on her own, unable to cook anything that didn't involve peanut butter or instant noodles. It ought to be a crime.

I yanked the oven door out of her hand and slammed it shut before the heat could escape.

My roommate meant well, but sometimes she was too eager for her own good. After a rocky start, I'd grown to like the kid. A lot. She had a good heart. Plus, unlike mine, her heart was actually beating, which came in handy sometimes. But if I wanted to keep it beating, I needed to teach her how to take better care of herself.

"Fine. You made your point." She saw that there were still five minutes left on the timer. "How am I supposed to wait when it smells so good?"

"You could start on the salad," I told her, handing her a cucumber. She didn't hear the words, but she'd get my drift.

She stared at the floating cucumber. One of the first tricks I'd learned as a ghost was how to move small objects. I couldn't pick a car up and toss it. I wasn't the Hulk. A cucumber was child's play, but the tricky part was making it invisible while I was touching it. It took a lot of concentration, and I was still hit-or-miss on that one, as evidenced by the spaghetti sauce incident at the grocery store earlier. I'd *thought* it was invisible, but apparently it hadn't been. Oops.

Ruby studied the cucumber as if expecting it to cut itself. "Come on, Cordelia. Are you pulling my leg? I read the recipe. There are no cucumbers in eggplant parm."

"You need to eat more vegetables," I told her. Yes, I knew lecturing someone who couldn't hear me was the very definition of "futile," but that never stopped me. "Preferably organic." I pulled a sharp knife out of the block and set it down on a well-worn cutting board on the counter. I flicked the end and watched it rotate in a lazy circle.

"Fine. You win. I'll cut it."

"That's my girl," I said. Even though she couldn't hear me, it felt like we were having a real conversation.

Being dead had its perks, but it wasn't all sunshine and roses. It was mostly boredom. Hours and days and weeks of soul-crushing boredom. I didn't know what I would have done without Ruby. Getting used to her living in my apartment wasn't easy. She was perkier than any human had any right to be. Even when she was broke and rationing out cheap ramen noodles half a packet at a time, she was an optimist, almost as if she believed that everything would work out in the end.

In her defense, it *did* work out, but I deserved a lot of the credit for that. I'd slipped her a little cash until I could find a job for her that covered her rent and expenses. Which was, for the record, twice as high as what I'd paid when the lease was under *my* name. Our cheating scumbag of a landlord was more than happy to take advantage of poor, naïve Ruby.

As Ruby diced up the cucumbers, I pulled the large wooden salad bowl off the high shelf I knew she couldn't reach and sat it down on the counter.

"What's next?" she asked.

"You really are helpless in the kitchen, aren't you?" I opened the refrigerator.

Ghosts and electronics didn't mix. Something about my presence fried their circuits, and caused a feedback loop that was excruciatingly unpleasant on my end. The fridge, however, was ancient and the motor was in the back. I could open the door without affecting the refrigerator much, not counting that poor light bulb. It hadn't stood a chance. If Ruby ever upgraded to one of those fancy models with a video screen in the door, it wouldn't last a day.

I carried the lettuce, carrots, and a vine with juicy red tomatoes on it to the cutting board, not caring that she could see the produce floating. It wasn't as if I was keeping any secrets from her. Well, I was, but not the secret of my presence. I was hiding from other people—they couldn't accept the truth of my existence—but not from Ruby.

"Go ahead and chop these up," I instructed. Yes, I could have done it for her, but that wouldn't have taught her anything useful. The girl needed to learn how to cook.

Her cuts were sloppy and uneven. Instead of thin slices, her tomatoes were a smushed mess. "What did those poor tomatoes ever do to you?" I asked her as seeds squirted out from beneath her knife.

Even though she took twice as long to chop the salad ingredients as it would have taken me, she was trying to grow up, and I was proud of her. Granted, sloppily diced carrots were just a start, but she'd also snuck a lovely little Monstera into the grocery cart while I wasn't looking. She had a long way to make up for all my plants she'd killed when she first moved in, but this was a step in the right direction.

The timer went off, and Ruby hastily scraped all the salad ingredients off the cutting board into the bowl. She left the knife on the counter. I moved it to the sink as she opened the oven. "Smells amazing," she said as the hot air curled around her.

I took a deep whiff. Nothing. "You can do this, Cordy," I told myself.

The sheer amount of concentration I needed to do things that used to come so naturally to me was a pain. I could see in the dark. I had hearing like a bat. So why did I have to work so hard to smell anything? And then the scent hit me. Cheesy, garlicky goodness. I could almost taste the bubbling marinara. Almost.

I'd tried eating some of my favorite foods, but it wasn't the same as when I'd been alive. I couldn't taste anything, and the food went right through me. Literally.

Ruby pulled out the eggplant and the bread and set them on top of the stove to cool.

"Aren't you forgetting something?" I asked her, but she was already walking away. "Come on Ruby, pay attention." I opened the door to the oven and let it drop with a clang.

"Huh?" Ruby asked. She closed the oven door. I opened it

again. "What am I missing? Ohh." She reached over and turned off the oven. "Thanks for the reminder."

"Good girl," I told her, closing the oven door.

Like the refrigerator, the oven was older than dirt. I could open and close the door all day, but if I got close enough to the circuits to turn it on or off or set the temperature, it could do anything from blowing a fuse to burning down the whole building. Plus, if the oven died, the landlord would probably replace it with an even older model from a vacant apartment or the basement storage, one that hadn't been cleaned in years.

"Smells great. Am I forgetting anything else?"

I grinned. This was the part I was looking forward to. Sure, I wanted Ruby to learn how to cook. Everyone needed to know how to feed themselves. But I had an ulterior motive.

"Timing's everything, Cordy," I told myself as I opened the front door. There were only a few steps between the tiny kitchen and the common hall, so there was no way Ruby would fail to notice the door opening.

"We expecting company?" she asked, going to the door even as I slipped out and rapped on the door across the hall.

ABOUT THE AUTHOR

Olivia Blacke (she/her) had her first encounter with a ghost when she was only five years old, but her first involvement with an active crime scene wasn't until much later, when she accidentally stepped into a chalk outline on a Manhattan sidewalk. Armed with a criminology and criminal justice degree, she finally found a way to channel her love of the supernatural and passion for writing into the darkly humorous Ruby and Cordelia Mysteries. She is also the author of the Record Shop Mysteries and the Brooklyn Murder Mysteries. She still wants to be a unicorn when she grows up.